THIS BOOK BELONGS TO

_____

ABOUT THE AUTHOR

Nick Levy loves traveling and writing to understand the world and our place in it. An award-winning scriptwriter and novelist, he has lived in dozens of countries, including Australia, the USA, Singapore, Mexico, Peru and Thailand. His passion for adventure has taken him from the highlands of Scotland to the coral reefs of Belize, and from the pyramids of Egypt to the tea plantations of Sri Lanka. With degrees in English, History and Education, he has taught in schools on three continents. His writing, directing and producing work in movies has crossed the genres of comedy, drama, thriller and action. Inspired by his parents' love of travel, film and books, he enjoys taking readers on a journey of discovery so they can appreciate our incredible planet and its fascinating inhabitants.

THIS BOOK BELONGS TO

Nick Levy

CECIL PRESS

First Published 2022
Paperback ISBN 9780645300208
E-book ISBN 9780645300215

Published by Cecil Press.

For the women in my life who shaped me into the person I am: my mother Marilyn, my godmother Golda, my sister Sally, my aunties Barbara, Denise and Linda. Thank you for everything.

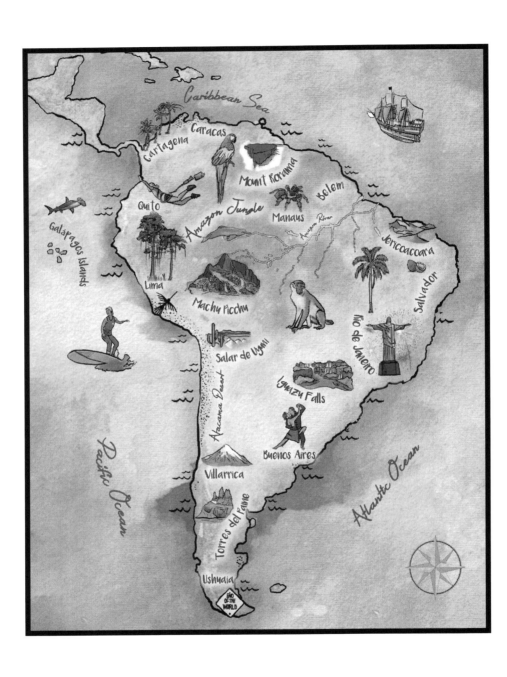

PART I

PROLOGUE

Present Day, 18th July – Mount Roraima, Venezuela

Where do you conquer fear?

Ellie hoped it was twenty yards away, on the edge of a 1200-foot cliff.

It better fricking be there.

Clouds swirled around the table mountain, which rose above the jungle like a block of unformed clay. Sprawled across its flat top was a landscape belonging to another world—twisted rock formations, quartz fields and unexplored caves. Off its sides cascaded some of the tallest waterfalls on our planet.

Ellie sat alone near the northern tip, shivering in a muddy t-shirt and feeling about as small as the tick she'd scraped off her leg this morning. Nature had a way of doing that to you. With arms wrapped around her knees to keep out the cold, she stared into the fog that first greeted her an hour ago. She still couldn't get her stupid feet to move.

It'd taken four days of grueling trekking to get to this point, in thick jungle, deep mud, and through a waterfall that tried to wash her away to an early death. Now was the last chance to face her greatest test. She needed to push herself out of the comfort zone she knew so well. That she'd lived in for too long.

If only it were that easy.

Ellie's hair whipped across her neck and her eyes welled with fear. Here she was fulfilling a dream to visit one of the most unique places on earth, but she couldn't have imagined a worse nightmare. She grabbed a stone and tossed it toward the precipice. It tumbled over the lip and was swallowed by the fog, never to be seen again.

Maybe that'll be my fate too.

Brushing away a tear, Ellie closed her eyes to visualize her goal: combatting her mortal fear of heights by standing on the very edge of Mount Roraima—1200 feet above the ground. If she made it, what would be her reward? Courage? Happiness? Donuts? Surely just a taste of one would be worth the pain.

Focus, Ellie.

A deep breath of crisp air filled her lungs with inspiration. She stood, bracing against the biting wind. Her nose flared and she took her first tentative steps away from the safety of solid land.

The clouds circled so fast that supernatural figures seemed to appear, like ghosts from a horror movie grabbing at her limbs to pull her into the abyss. They parted for a second and she glimpsed the vista beyond, a valley of emerald rainforest topped by a soaring blue sky. Her heart leaped, teasing her forward.

"C'mon Ellie. You can do it. You *have* to do it."

She felt like a child, but knew it was time to be an adult or this entire journey would be for nothing. It was time to grow up, goddammit.

Even if it killed her.

CHAPTER 1

Three Weeks Earlier – New York City, USA

The only sign Ellie had of the fiery midsummer sunset over Manhattan was a reflection in the corner of her computer screen. Trapped amongst rows of empty cubicles that stretched from wall-to-wall like a factory farm, she tapped on her keyboard with flawless posture.

"Boo!"

"Oh, gosh." Ellie tried not to let on that she'd been startled by Dennis Koslowski, a bald man in a power suit who'd crept up behind her. "Do you mind?"

"You're like a scared little kitten." He sat on her desk as if he owned it. "Why are you always so jumpy when D.K. comes around?"

"I'm not jumpy. Just busy," Ellie replied pointedly. She'd long given up trying to communicate with Dennis the Douchebag, or understand why he referred to himself in the third person.

"How's the final draft coming?" he said. "Tomorrow's the big day."

"Almost done." Ellie's eyes remained fixed on her screen. She didn't need to be reminded that the report valuing a potential takeover target was scheduled to be presented to the C.E.O.

and Partners at 9 a.m. It would be the most important moment of her five-year career as a research analyst at DeWitt Financial Consultants.

"I need it tonight so I can prepare."

"You'll have it," Ellie said. When had she not come through on a deadline? And since when did Dennis prepare for anything? In fact, what was he doing here so late?

"I was thinking we could drill down into it together," he continued, spreading his arms across her workstation. "Take a look at the charts. Discuss areas for organic growth. D.K. is a great sounding board."

"I work better alone." Ellie hit her keyboard harder. If he really wanted to help he could've offered any time in the last month. But Dennis was the guy in your high school group project who did nothing then took all the credit, without a smidgen of shame.

"I'm just saying, if you want to spitball cost synergies or pivot opportunities going forward, D.K.'s your man."

And if you drop one more buzzword, I'm going to smash this keyboard over your ugly bald egghead.

He opened the jar containing Ellie's emergency jellybean stash and stuck his fingers inside. "Don't forget there's a promotion up for grabs at the end of this week."

"I'm aware of that."

"Do you know who the frontrunner is?"

Curiosity got the better of Ellie and she stopped typing. "Who?"

"Well, if you don't know, it's not you." Dennis shoved a jellybean in his mouth and flashed a shit-eating grin.

Ellie's jaw hardened. She *needed* this promotion. Not just for the juicy pay bump, but to know spending the best years of her life working her ass off to make other people rich had been worth it for her too. 'Ellie Bartlett, Senior Analyst' had a nice ring to it. It would also put her one step above Dennis so she wouldn't have to tolerate his bullshit anymore.

"You know I can help, Ellie. Put in a good word for you with my uncle."

"I don't have time to play games."

"No games. Just an offer. I'm sure we could figure something out." He winked in proposition.

Ellie bristled, but swallowed her disgust. Working in the cold heart of the financial system was like being stuck in some weird parallel universe where what passed for acceptable behavior hadn't caught up with the #MeToo movement. Dennis got away with being a beady-eyed sleazeball because he happened to be the C.E.O.'s nephew, and male of course, which were the only two 'advantages' Ellie couldn't match.

"I've always wondered what your hair looks like down," he said.

Oh, for Pete's sake!

It took every ounce of willpower to resist murdering him. "Excuse me," Ellie forced out, reaching for one of the neatly-labelled, color-coded, folders above her workspace.

Dennis stared at her before moving. "D.K. has a hot date anyway. Email the report when you're done." He walked off without a goodbye.

Ellie shook off the uncomfortable exchange. A hot shower wouldn't be enough to remove the slime, it would take a full chemical delousing. She looked mournfully at her jar of jellybeans, then poured them into the trash.

Hopefully his hot date gives him herpes.

Gabby McMillan, a chirpy woman with pale skin and striking orange hair, skipped over to Ellie's desk. "Let me guess, Dennis is still auditioning for a place on *Love Island?*"

"Regrettably."

"So are you coming out for drinks? You've been staying late all week and God knows you could use a break. Especially tonight."

"I'd love to…" Ellie returned to her screen.

"But you have to work. It's always the same old story, Ellie. You're missing out, y'know." Gabby paused, emphasizing the point: *not just missing out on tonight, but missing out on life.*

Ellie was entirely aware of this fact. Being perennially single, there'd been a lot of time to think about how she'd become a skilled practitioner in relationship avoidance, or as she liked to call it—pain prevention. She'd never expected a fairytale Prince Charming to sweep her off her feet, but heck, at this point even the Phantom of the Opera would've been an upgrade.

We could live together in the Paris Opera House, ring the bells to start the show and scare tourists throughout the night. We'd be happy, eating croissants and watching boats sail by on the Seine. Perhaps we'd even make some rugrats.

"Ellie, if you don't come out you can't meet men." Gabby brought her back to reality. "And if you can't meet men, you can't—"

"I can meet them online."

"Do you even know what Tinder is?" Gabby raised an eyebrow. "Listen, we're going to C.J.'s for beers and wings and we'd love you to come celebrate, even for one drink."

"I might join you later if I have time." Ellie avoided eye contact, because it was obvious she wouldn't be joining them later.

She waited until her friend had gone before checking her phone. 7 p.m. and three missed calls from her sister. Alone with only the drone of air-con to keep her company, she took off her glasses and let out a pained sigh.

Why are you doing this to yourself again?
On your birthday, too.

Juggling a pizza box and bottle of wine, Ellie eventually got her key in the front door. There was a small package at her feet and she kicked it inside, dumped her bag on the sofa and everything else on the kitchen bench.

The one-bedroom brownstone was a shoebox, but meticulously kept. Ellie liked to try and control her environment and had lived this way long enough to believe it was possible. Unfortunately, she couldn't control the creaking pipes or view of the brick wall through the window.

She poured a glass of wine and took a gulp-and-a-half, relishing how it instantly relaxed her brain.

The. Best. Part. Of. My. Day.

Slipping off her heels and releasing her hair from its bun, Ellie's eyes fell to a notepad on the bench with the heading THINGS TO DO. It included a long list of items, mostly mundane tasks such as BUY MILK and PAY RENT. She'd drawn cute little boxes next to each one so they could be ticked off when completed. There was just enough space for two more items.

Ellie picked up a pen and wrote in clear block letters: DO WHAT MAKES YOU HAPPY.

She read the words again, stunned by the radical idea. Then quickly crossed them out. But that just created a new problem because now her perfect list had been ruined. Ellie wrote an item on the final line: MAKE A NEW LIST. Then drew a little box next to it.

There was a beep on her phone with a message from Gabby: 'You need to get here. Raining men!' Her friend had sent a photo with Finance Bros she'd met at the bar, all holding up beers and grinning wildly at the camera. Ellie took another hit of wine.

Dropping onto the sofa, she opened her bag with a gaping yawn and pulled out a laptop and folder of papers. If she didn't get this promotion, Ellie wasn't sure how much longer she could keep burning the candle at both ends. Lately it'd felt more like a firecracker—about to explode.

Ellie picked up the package she'd kicked across the floor and tore it open. Inside was a book and birthday card with a picture of a hammock strung between palm trees. She flipped it open and read the printed quote:

> *"When you're old and weary, sitting in your rocking chair, you'll regret the things you didn't try rather than the things you did try. So pull up the anchor, head away from land, let the wind catch your sails. Travel. Learn. Explore."*
> *– Anonymous*

On the other side was a handwritten note:

> *To my gorgeous sis, Happy 31st Birthday! Posting this because you never make time to see us. Found it in a box of dad's old stuff and had your name inside. Hope one day you let the wind catch your sails. Much love, Donna.*

Ellie turned over the book and gasped. It was a thin, faded, novella with a jungle font title—*The Lost World by Sir Arthur Conan Doyle.* Underneath was a drawing of a flat-topped mountain with a band of motley adventurers at its base.

Ellie held the book to her chest. Its woody scent transported her back to when she used to lay in her dad's lap while he read aloud to her. His deep voice emphasized each word as if the story were happening that very moment. Often excited, sometimes scared, she'd been enthralled by the adventures of Malone, Summerlee, Lord Roxton and Professor Challenger, facing danger at every turn on their trek up Mount Roraima. And she'd often imagined what heroic journeys she would take after growing up.

Oblivious to her dinner and work, Ellie felt an emptiness rise from the pit of her gut. A black hole threatening to consume her from the inside out. It was a feeling of lost dreams and missed opportunities—a life not lived to its fullest. She knew the feeling well, but over time had become adept at suppressing it. To keep distracted by focusing on her career, binge-watching trash on Netflix, the rabbit hole of the internet, anything to avoid facing it. But no matter what she did it was always in the background, haunting her like a shadow.

Now, as the sensation grew more intense than ever, Ellie understood she needed to exorcise this demon or it would completely consume her potential for happiness. She just wasn't sure how.

CHAPTER 2

Two Weeks Later – Caracas, Venezuela

Bathed in the late-afternoon sun, Ellie stood inside the ageing arrivals terminal of Simon Bolivar International Airport. She'd spotted a reflection of herself in the automatic doors leading to the road. Her petite frame was overloaded by a blue backpack strapped on her shoulders and across her chest hung a small daypack that provided just enough counterweight to stop her tipping. Besides the wearable luggage, her clean hiking boots and milky-white skin gave away Ellie's status as a newly-arrived traveler in a foreign land.

She smiled at the ridiculous image of her carrying such a massive pack like a snail lugged its shell. But the smile was a nervous one. This 'backpacker' was so alien to her life back home that she felt more than a bit apprehensive—terrified, actually—as a question raced through her head.

What the fuck am I doing?

Outside, the humid air stuck to Ellie's skin and she coughed through fumes from the cars and buses honking past the airport. More than ten men shouted in her direction, "Taxi! Miss, you need taxi!" It smacked of a demand, not a question, and Ellie felt like a squirrel about to be devoured by a pack of coyotes.

The first driver to approach took both packs off her before she could protest and threw them in the trunk of a taxi that'd seen better days. "Please, Miss. Quick, quick," he urged, opening the rear door and practically pushing her inside.

Ellie scooted across the splits in the vinyl seat. The stench of stale cigarettes filled her nostrils. She reached over her shoulder for a seatbelt but was met with nothing. Mental note: forget that American habit. The vehicle lurched forward before they'd even discussed destination or price.

"Where you go?" the driver asked in scattered English.

"Hostel Caracas Backpackers, please, *por favor*," Ellie replied in Spanglish.

"*Sí, sí.*"

"Is the meter working?" Ellie pointed hopefully at the device.

"No meter, no meter."

"How much?"

"*Veinte*, twenty, good price."

"Twenty bolivars?"

"*Dólares de Estados Unidos*. U.S.A. dollars. Good price. *Me gusta U.S.A.*"

Ellie bobbed her head reluctantly, suspicious but captive. The taxi swerved across the highway and she slid all the way to the other side of the seat. If she were never heard from again, at least C.N.N. would report she'd made it out of the airport. That was something.

Night had fallen when the deathtrap pulled up outside a stucco building in urgent need of repair. Ellie climbed out, wondering what horrors lay behind the decaying facade.

She struggled to open her moneybelt while the driver dumped her backpack and daypack on the sidewalk. "Sorry. I haven't got the hang of this thing yet." The zip sprung open, breaking in the process. "Oh, great." She fumbled for a US$20 note.

The driver snatched it and ran to his taxi, speeding off without a word.

"You're welcome," Ellie said, picking up her daypack.

Oh, no…

It felt lighter. She ripped it open and saw her iPad was gone.

"Hey, come back!" Ellie ran down the street after the taxi, but it surged away and disappeared around a corner. "You bastard." Ellie kicked the ground, but really wanted to kick herself. How could she be so careless? Her sister had warned to keep her wits about her, *at all times*. This was the worst possible start to her trip.

Ellie realized she was standing in the middle of the road. None of the streetlights were on and a sickly cough jumped out of the shadows. She hurried to her backpack and dragged it inside the hostel.

The door closed behind her with a miserable groan and Ellie's doubts were confirmed. The place was a dump. Paint peeled off the walls, an internal window had been broken, and only one light bulb worked.

"*Hola.*" A young man greeted Ellie from behind the reception desk. He grinned through his scrappy beard.

"Hi, *hola…*" She was breathless. "Um…a taxi driver just stole my iPad."

"Yes, sometime that happen." He seemed unconcerned.

"Do you have a number for the police…so I can call them and get it back?"

"Sorry, but your iPad not come back. Need to say bye-bye."

Ellie stood in a vacuum of hopelessness while reality sunk in. It wasn't so much the device, which was a few years old and password protected, but it contained meticulous planning for her journey. All gone.

"*Hablas Español?*" the man asked in a sing-song Venezuelan accent.

"No, English."

"You are American?"

"Yes."

"So you speak American."

"That's right," Ellie managed a smile.

"My name is Benicio. Don't worry about your iPad. This physical thing come and go but in Venezuela you can always be happy." He was so earnest she almost believed him. "You have a reservation?"

"Under Ellie Bartlett."

He checked his computer. "How much you pay for taxi?"

"Twenty dollars."

"*Dólares? Gringa* price!" he howled.

Ellie half-heartedly chuckled along. "Twenty dollars plus an iPad. I guess I am a *gringa* now."

"OK, I have your booking. Here is towel." Benicio reached under the desk and handed Ellie a frayed towel that wouldn't have been out of place in a rag pile. "You are in bed six, dorm two. Upstairs and go left."

"Is there a key?"

"No key. We are all friends here."

Ellie resisted the urge to turn and run, because she had nowhere else to go. "OK…um, I'll just head up now."

This is definitely a different check-in process compared to the hotels I've stayed at. I'm guessing there's not going to be a complimentary mint on the pillow.

Ellie attempted to pull her backpack up the flight of rickety stairs, but only made it a third of the way before it slipped from her hand and tumbled back down. Benicio appeared at the bottom and offered to help.

Each carrying one end like a body bag going into a morgue, they reached the second floor and headed along a hallway with missing floorboards and unexplained holes in the wall. Benicio ushered Ellie into the dorm and flicked on the light.

Holy crap.

There were four sets of bunk-beds jammed into the room, most with unmade sheets. Battered backpacks, dirty underwear and random socks littered the floor as if a hurricane had hit. The weather service must've named it Hurricane Stink. The travelers who owned the appalling mess weren't around, but Ellie was already forming an image of what they might look like. It included dreadlocks, nose rings, and hairy armpits.

"You can use these for valuable things." Benicio waved at a set of lockers by the wall, some missing doors. "And the bathroom is down the hall."

Ellie felt the colour drain from her face and took a step backward.

"*Todo bien?* Everything OK?" he asked.

"Yeah. I'm just…I think I need sleep."

"First time in *dormitorio?*"

Ellie nodded.

"You have earplugs?"

Ellie shook her head.

"Maybe you buy them. This is your bed." Benicio tapped a top bunk, which looked incredibly high. "OK, *buenas noches.*"

"*Gracias,*" Ellie squeaked out before he left.

She made space for her backpack by pushing a pair of cruddy boxer shorts out of the way with her shoe.

You can deal with this, Ellie. It will be good for you.

There was no ladder to her bed so she grabbed onto the frame and tried to swing herself up. It didn't end well. She fell back to the floor with a thud. On a second, more energetic attempt, Ellie made it up and rested on her tiny piece of rented real estate.

Surveying the chaos below, it was hard not to see it as a pool of sewage that would give her nightmares about drowning in germs. She took a bottle of anti-bacterial gel from her daypack and rubbed it over her hands. Just to be safe.

Ellie checked the bed and promptly concluded the sheets weren't Egyptian cotton. There was also a fishy yellow stain on the pillow. A heavy sweater? Something else? She flipped it over. 'Out of sight, out of mind' had never worked before, but it better work tonight. She curled into a ball and shut her eyes tight.

CHAPTER 3

New York City, USA

"OK, OK, shut up," Ellie implored, finding her phone on the floor and shutting off the alarm. It took a few seconds to blink her eyes awake. She'd fallen asleep on the sofa, and the last thing in her fuzzy memory was emailing the report to her team in anticipation of the 9 a.m. meeting.

Ellie sat up, pushing away the mop of hair that flopped over her face. Something jabbed into her hip. *The Lost World* book. A dream from last night surged back into her head. In it she'd seen Mount Roraima with her own eyes. Climbed to the summit with her own feet. Soaked her soul in the mysterious aura of the ancient mountain.

She shook the dream away. It was just that—a fantasy.

Still disoriented and desperately needing coffee, Ellie walked out of the subway and into Manhattan's bustling financial district. The sidewalk was crowded with hundreds of businesspeople dressed in black, blue or gray. Harsh shadows made it look even more monotone. Ellie shielded her eyes. The straight lines of the city struck her as severe and she had a burning desire to break away from all the planned roads and square buildings. To leave the tedious routine of city life and go somewhere with fewer hard edges.

At the start of her career, Ellie had enjoyed working in the Big Apple, with all the excitement and status that brought. And she loved how proud her mom and dad had been when she landed a job here. But now all she saw were grim faces lost in their own worlds but living the same lives: balancing in heels, adjusting ties, fudging numbers to meet quarterly targets, plotting to slit their best friend's throat to get ahead.

Nope, it'd never felt like home. To be honest, Ellie didn't know where home was anymore.

In the middle of this washed-out scene, a splash of color appeared. A man and woman, barely out of their teens, strolled by with large red backpacks. Wearing jeans and t-shirts, they moved at half the speed of everyone else. They bought a pretzel to share from a food cart and, unlike the office workers sidestepping them, smiled and laughed freely.

"Bonza? Nobody uses that word anymore," the tanned woman said in a thick Australian accent.

"I'm bringin' it back. It's bonza, mate!" the man replied with a mouthful of pretzel and equally strong Aussie twang.

"You're a dickhead," she laughed. "So whatcha wanna do today?"

"Dunno. How about we hang in Central Park? Just chill."

"Sounds bonza. You got a map?"

"Na, let's head this way tho'. She'll be 'right."

Ellie stared at the pair, backpacks happily bobbing up-and-down as they continued to their next unplanned adventure. Her eavesdropping had been brief but enlightening, because everything about them screamed one word.

Freedom.

It was impossible to concentrate, and she still hadn't found coffee. The pages spitting out of the printer put Ellie in a trance only broken by Gabby describing her latest sexual conquest in far too much detail. Oral? On a first date? What about STIs? And Ebola?

Ellie excused herself, making her way through the cubicles to the conference room. Every time she took this walk it reminded her of the morning last December when she got called into a meeting to be told she'd been passed over for yet another promotion. The guy who got it couldn't even program Excel.

Get it together, Ellie. Today's your shot.

You're going to impress the boss, make the firm a ton of money, and get that damn promotion.

Ellie pushed her shoulders back, lengthened her stride, and rounded the corner to the conference room.

She stopped in her tracks. Through the floor-to-ceiling windows she could see Dennis standing at the head of the table, presenting to the C.E.O. and a dozen Partners. On the screen behind him was the report. *Her* report.

Ellie's chest caved in. She struggled for air. Checked her phone. 8.45 a.m. Why had the meeting started early? It must be a mistake. A pre-meeting meeting. They were waiting for her to arrive and take over. Yes, that was it. After all, she knew the report better than anyone. Hell, Dennis had trouble counting. So why did he look so confident up there?

She grabbed the handle and pushed inside. A round of applause filled the room. For a second Ellie thought it might be for her entrance, then realized the Partners were applauding Dennis. He basked in the glory, grinning like a thief who'd just gotten away with the diamonds. It dawned on her that the meeting wasn't starting—it had ended.

The C.E.O., sharing his nephew's bald genes, stood and shook Dennis' hand. "Fantastic work. Very thorough. I knew you'd come through."

Ellie's jaw dropped. She caught Dennis' eye and he winked back.

The C.E.O. quietened everyone with his hands. "OK folks, I was going to announce this on Friday but don't see any reason to delay. I'm pleased to say that our new Senior Analyst will be… Dennis Koslowski."

More applause. And handshaking. And backslapping.

Ellie felt like she was going to black out. She steadied herself on a chair as the conference room emptied. "What's going on?"

"D.K. killed it, that's what's going on," Dennis replied, gathering his papers.

"We were supposed to start at nine."

"It got changed."

"Why didn't you message me?"

He didn't answer.

"Why didn't you message me?!" Ellie demanded to know.

Dennis shrugged. "My phone died."

There was a wash of silence as Ellie processed his lie.

"We make a great team. Well done, shorty." He moved to punch her shoulder.

She batted his hand away. "Don't touch me."

"Hey, calm down. You're acting crazy."

"You stole my fucking job!" She was surprised by her outburst.

Dennis leaned in close and his eyes narrowed. "Don't be so naive, Ellie. It was always mine."

Ellie stiffened. Opened her mouth. Closed her mouth. Her heart beat so fast her cheeks flushed. She felt sweat running down her back.

"C'mon, don't look so pissed, we'll still be working together. I'm your new boss," Dennis said, his grin dripping with grease.

Ellie ran out. Down the hall to the bathroom. Pushed inside a stall—and puked.

She flushed and slammed the toilet seat closed and sat in disbelief. Her eyes grew hot with tears. It made her blood boil that not only was she more competent than him, but five years of forced smiles at all the filthy jokes told by the boy's club at DeWitt Financial Consultants counted for nothing. Ellie had been raised to believe hard work would always be rewarded, but now everything she'd sacrificed suddenly seemed worthless.

What have I been doing with my life?!

She slammed a fist into the wall.

Head held high, Ellie marched down the hallway. Washing her face and fixing her clothes had restored some confidence, and helped her figure out what came next.

Dennis was the center of attention at his cubicle, getting fist-bumps and bro-hugs from colleagues, and doing some idiotic handshake that belonged in middle school. "Hey, Ellie. Come out with us tonight to celebrate," he said.

She walked straight past him while giving him the mental middle finger.

"Y'know, you could at least smile." Dennis high-fived and whooped some more.

Ellie took a long breath, slowly turned around, and gave him the actual middle finger. "I quit."

The cocky grin slid off Dennis' face. His colleagues fell quiet behind him. "You…can't leave."

"I can do whatever I want," Ellie said. Her mind miraculously cleared, the way it always does when you choose a path that restores your own power. She straightened her spine, turned on her heel, and left without waiting for a response. The sound of Dennis' silence played like glorious background music.

Holy shit.

I did it.

I really did it!

Adrenaline surged through Ellie's body and her steps morphed into energetic strides. A genuine smile spread from ear-to-ear for the first time in years. Reaching her cubicle, she took her purse then went to grab her laptop bag. Wait. She wouldn't need it anymore. In fact, there was nothing here she wanted. She looked around at all the order in her world, then left, without regret.

Ellie could only imagine all the incredible ways this decision would change her life.

CHAPTER 4

Caracas, Venezuela

Ellie sat bolt upright. Sunlight crept through the curtains, but the roar of a traveler snoring like a grizzly bear was the clue she'd just spent her first night in a hostel. And lived to tell the tale!

She swung her legs over the bunk. Her feet didn't reach the floor and she accidentally stepped on someone's nose. Luckily, the man rolled over into his feral dreadlocks to keep snoozing. Ellie had to jump the last foot.

Towel and toiletries kit in hand, she tiptoed down the hallway to the bathroom. The door had both male and female figures painted on it.

Unisex bathroom. Awesome. That always ends well.

Ellie cautiously pushed inside and her skin crawled. There was no natural light, making the beige tiles look even further past their use-by date and breeding a blackish mold. Then the smell hit her like a porta-potty had dropped on her head. A ghastly mix of fungus and poop. Ellie gagged into the basin before noticing it was littered with pubic hair.

What the hell...?

She steeled herself and pulled back the shower curtain. The

recess was a concrete shell with only one tap—cold. And instead of a drain cover there was a cavernous hole that threatened to suck its victims into a grubby void.

Just when Ellie thought things couldn't get any worse, a cockroach scurried out of the hole. It lingered for a moment as if to tell her she didn't belong here, then dove back into the drain. Ellie let out a horrified sob.

Desperate to pee, she turned to the toilet. The seat was cracked in half and someone had left an epic deposit. That explained the smell. A notice on the wall instructed: 'Do not flush paper. Throw in trash.' The overflowing bin hadn't been emptied in a week. That also explained the smell. Ellie grabbed the last sheet of paper and flushed the handle. At least something worked.

Surrounded by grime and bugs and other people's butt wipes, Ellie shut her eyes. "It's all part of the adventure," she reassured herself.

And it's why I brought enough hand sanitizer to disinfect a hospital ward.

Ellie bounded down the stairs to reception, daypack slung over her shoulder. She was thrilled about surviving the bathroom, but even more so about her first day in a new country. Well, thrilled *and freaking out.*

"*Buenos días*, Benicio."

"*Cómo estás*, Ellie? How are you?" He took a sip of coffee and turned down the folksy music.

"I need some help. Do you have a map of Caracas?"

"*Sí*. We have *un mapa*." Benicio searched behind his desk. He flipped over piles of paper but was clearly having trouble finding one. "Do you know where you want to go?"

"That's my problem. All my notes were on my iPad." Ellie was still angry at herself for not being more careful with it. "I think the historic district would be a good place to start but, yeah, I'm not sure how to get there."

"We don't have a map." Benicio's shoulders slumped.

"How about a WiFi password? I could download a map onto my phone."

"Internet not working. This is problem in Venezuela."

"OK…then maybe you could just point me in the right direction?"

"No, no," he warned with a raised finger. "It is not safe to walk if you don't know where to go. I will call you a taxi—"

"No taxi," Ellie insisted. Not after last night's disaster. "I'm not usually like this," she continued, twisting her lip in embarrassment. "I would usually have a backup plan but I was so stressed out by leaving that I didn't think to print a hardcopy of all my notes and highlight everything in different colours and—well I figured my iPad would be my guidebook." She finally took a breath.

Benicio's face lit up. "We have a guidebook!"

He took a few steps past Ellie to a bookcase. A sign above it read BOOK EXCHANGE. All the books were used, some had been passed along many times given the condition of their spines, and they were in a variety of languages: English, Spanish, German, French. There were even a couple in Hebrew and Japanese. Benicio searched until he found the one he wanted, a slightly worn *Unique Planet: South America On A Budget* with a photo of Machu Picchu on its cover. He passed it to Ellie with a satisfied grin.

"Wow, thank you," Ellie said, rubbing a light coating of dust off it. "Oh, I have one to exchange." Ellie opened her daypack and pulled out a book titled *How To Avoid Getting Killed in South America*. "My sister gave me this, but I don't plan on needing it."

The phone rang and Benicio excused himself.

Ellie opened the *Unique Planet* and turned to the chapter on Venezuela. She found a map of Caracas, which had various landmarks circled in blue pen. There was also handwriting in the margins.

Her curiosity sparked, Ellie flicked through the other chapters and saw there were detailed notes for nearly all the countries in South America. There was barely a page that hadn't been written on—advice about adventure activities, places to visit off the tourist trail, and places to avoid. Some comments were warnings ('Be careful, pickpockets here'), others were recommendations ('Watch a sunset in Huacachina, you won't be disappointed'), or funny one-liners ('Bed bugs biting. Check in at own peril!'). There were also cryptic messages such as 'You made the right choice. Only she who walks knows her way.'

Hmm, interesting...

The notes had been written in a variety of colors but all the same neat cursive script, which Ellie figured belonged to a female. It was obvious a lot of work had gone into annotating the guidebook and Ellie felt fortunate for stumbling across it.

She did wonder though, who had gone to all this effort?

CHAPTER 5

San Francisco, USA

"Breakfast!" Jerry shouted in the general direction of the second story. No response. "Pancakes!" he tried again, and immediately heard feet scrambling down the stairs and along the hallway.

Always works like a charm.

Jerry's six-foot four-inch frame, smartly dressed in a pressed white shirt tucked into tan chino pants, towered over the benchtop while he sliced bananas into bowls of cereal. At thirty-eight years-old, he had dark eyes and wavy black hair that showed no signs of retreat—though his family were trying their best.

"Pancakes!" seven year-old Mia screamed as she ran into the kitchen. Her sister, twelve year-old Andrea, followed closely behind, putting Mia's hair into pigtails. "Wait, where are the pancakes?"

"Dad was joking," Andrea explained. "Again."

"Sorry honey, but I had to get you girls down here somehow or you'd never be ready for school. We're trying to arrive on time this week, remember?"

Mia scrunched up her face. "I'm not hungry." Unlike their Caucasian father, the two girls had olive skin with round faces and brown eyes.

"You were hungry for pancakes."

"I lost my appetite when my dad lied to me." She crossed her arms for maximum effect.

Oh boy, it was going to be one of those days.

"Don't be so dramatic," Jerry said, carrying the bowls to the table. "You know you can't concentrate at school without food in your tummy." Summer had well and truly arrived by the second week of July and the renovated Victorian in the Haight Ashbury neighborhood glowed with natural light.

"OK, you're done." Andrea gave Mia's hair a tug and sat to start breakfast. After glaring at Jerry while he read the newspaper, Mia grudgingly took a seat but still refused to eat.

"Did I hear someone say 'pancakes?'" Another girl joined her family in the kitchen. It was seventeen year-old, going on twenty-one, Yasmina. She was as beautiful as she was tall, with large eyes and dark hair that fell to her waist.

"Dad lied," Mia explained.

"He lied to us about Santa Claus for years so it's no surprise really."

"I'm still angry about the Santa Claus thing."

"Can we not make this another pick-on-dad day, please?" Jerry said. For the love of God, please. "Besides, it's time for our weekly global affairs challenge."

The children groaned. "Must we do this every Monday? It's too early."

"The planet doesn't stop turning just because you're tired, Yas. Best answer gets to choose takeout on Saturday. Let's see what is happening..." Jerry flicked through the paper. "Here we go. 'Devastating rains have lashed Guatemala, causing flash flooding around the historic city of Antigua. Thousands of people have been dislocated and roads, schools, and hospitals washed away. Guatemala has appealed for international assistance to deal with the crisis.' OK girls, what should we do?"

"What does 'dis-lo-cat-ed' mean?" Mia said it syllable-by-syllable to make sure she got it right.

"It means people's houses have been destroyed and they have nowhere to live."

"Then we should build them new ones!" she suggested enthusiastically.

"A very good idea."

"The most important thing is to make sure people have safe drinking water and medicine because there might be an outbreak of disease," Andrea said, always keen to contribute. "So we should immediately send bottled water, drugs, and also tents so they have a place to sleep. In the future we could help by sending engineers to stop the flooding from happening again."

"Excellent suggestions. Do you have anything to say?" Jerry looked over the paper at Yasmina.

"I'm not playing."

"Dad?"

"Yes, honey."

"They won't be able to go to school, will they?" Mia asked.

"Not for a while."

"That's sad."

"Is it?" Yasmina slurped her juice.

"I like school," Mia declared with all the eagerness of a second grader. "I think we should build them new schools so they can learn to be engineers and then we won't have to send any next time."

"It looks like we have a winner." Jerry and Mia high-fived. She beamed and finally tucked into her breakfast.

"Oh, Dad." Andrea rolled her eyes.

"What? She made a good point." Navigating the power-dynamics of three daughters meant that he lost, in some way, every day.

Jerry's eyes darted between the road and mirrors as he drove his SUV through peak-hour traffic. "What about your homework? Did you finish reading *The Odyssey*?"

"Yeah," Yasmina replied, tapping on her phone like her life depended on it. She sat up front next to her dad, while Mia was in a booster seat in the back with Andrea.

"What did you think about the ending?"

"Dad, can't you see I'm busy here?"

"Did you actually finish it?"

She kept playing with her phone.

"Jesus, Yasmina. *The Odyssey* is an important piece of literature. You have an essay on it this afternoon."

"How do you know that?"

"I signed up to Mrs. Pearson's website."

"I hate that bitch."

"Hey!" Jerry shot her a glance. "Don't be disrespectful."

"Odysseus was disrespectful. He shouldn't have left Penelope at home all those years."

"Well, I'm glad you got that far into it. But the language you use around your sisters is important. We've talked about this before." Too many times.

Andrea and Mia leaned forward to listen to the argument unfolding up front.

"Whatever. I didn't see the point of reading the whole thing. It's a stupid story anyway."

Jerry sighed. "Besides it being one of the oldest stories in human history, and a classic tale about a man on a journey against all odds back to the woman he loves, the point is you have an assessment on it. And if you haven't read it, how will you be able to write anything meaningful?"

"I read the online summary. I just can't remember the ending right now."

"Oh, that's great." Jerry's voice rose ominously. "It's not just about writing an essay, you know. It's about critical thinking. Developing the skills to analyze a question and come up with a solution. And you practice that in school because when you get out into the real world that's what you have to do every day."

Yasmina mocked her dad's advice by mouthing her lips as he spoke.

"Your mother would be so disappointed in you."

She stopped playing with her phone, and the girls in the back stopped giggling.

There was a long silence until Jerry pulled the car to the curb outside their school. "A kiss for Dad, please girls."

Andrea and Mia kissed Jerry on the cheek. Yasmina jumped straight out to greet a group of friends standing nearby.

Jerry opened the window and called out, "A kiss for Dad, please Yas!"

She stopped dead and turned around. "Dad," she gasped through clenched teeth.

"Do you want me to say it again? A kiss—"

"OK!" Yasmina ran back to the car and reluctantly pecked him on the cheek. "I'm going to kill you."

"Yas, I know things are tough. But your mom and I didn't raise you to be lazy."

"I know, OK. It's just... I know." She nodded faintly before joining her friends.

"Love you, Stardust!" Jerry shouted as he drove off. In his rear-view mirror, Yasmina fumed while her friends collapsed in hysterics.

If he couldn't win, at least he was going to have fun losing.

CHAPTER 6

Caracas, Venezuela

You'll be OK.

Ellie stepped warily into the cable car as it glided through the station. The door closed behind her and she lunged for a seat, shutting her eyes as it launched into the air.

It's not going to fall.

Ellie heard the only other passenger calmly continue knitting as the gondola bounced over the first tower on the line.

It's probably not going to fall.

Heights had never been Ellie's strong suit, especially after she fell from a tree as a five year-old and landed on her face and in hospital. But as her newfound *Unique Planet* suggested, what better way to get to know a city than flying through it?

Ellie opened one eye to check it was safe, then the other, taking in the sprawling metropolis. In the distance she could see office buildings glimmering in the morning sun, and below her were the poorest *favelas* of Caracas.

Gripping the handrail, Ellie looked down at the haphazardly constructed homes. They were all made from the same orange brick and corrugated iron, but with splashes of bright paint in the yellow, blue and red of the Venezuelan flag. There appeared to be millions of them, like someone had emptied a giant Lego set on the ground. Inside this maze, moms hung washing on balconies, kids played soccer in the streets, and fresh fruit was sold off the back of trucks. Motorbikes zipped between them all at hair-raising speeds.

Ellie's eyes couldn't stop searching, engrossed with this totally unfamiliar scene. She took out her phone and snapped the first photo of her trip.

The gondola shuddered over another tower. Ellie grabbed the handrail and didn't let go until they reached the end of the line. She followed the map in her guidebook to navigate by foot through the *centro historico*. The streets erupted with activity. Shopkeepers opened bodegas under crumbling buildings. Street hawkers set up carts selling *papelón* (sugar cane juice with lime), *tostados* (salted corn kernels), and *tajadas* (fried plantain slices). Ellie inhaled the mouth-watering aromas as she passed each sizzling hotplate, quickly forgetting her anxiety about being alone in a foreign city.

Outside a hole-in-the-wall cafe, craggy-faced old men sat on crates, smoking cigarillos and sharing laughs with life-long friends. The sound of Spanish all around was a bird's sweet song to Ellie's ears and she walked in a daze, like a child experiencing the wonder of the world for the first time.

So this is what it feels like to travel, to backpack, to experience new things. Everything is amazing. I haven't been this exhilarated about life in...forever.

Ellie impulsively decided to ignore her sister's warning about steering clear of street food. If she was going to be here, she was going to eat it all, goddammit.

"*Bom día*," a hawker said while flipping golden-brown patties.

"What's that?" Ellie pointed. The man just stared back. "Wait a sec, please." Ellie opened the Google Translate app on her phone. She typed in a phrase and read the translation. "*Qué es?*"

"*Arepa.*"

"*Arepa,*" Ellie repeated. She typed again. "*Cuánto cuesta?*" Her pronunciation must've been terrible because the man laughed.

"*Dos.*" He held up two fingers.

"Ah, two thousand?" She handed over the cash and received a hot *arepa* in a napkin. "*Gracias.*" Ellie took a bite and instantly succumbed to the crispy corn bread filled with creamy cheese. Food love was so much easier than human love.

She'd almost finished gobbling breakfast when she reached Plaza Bolivar, the main square of Caracas and an oasis of jacaranda trees and fountains. The sun gleamed off a twelve-foot high bronze statue of a man triumphantly riding a horse. A flock of pigeons flapped above, landing on his cape.

Ellie wiped her mouth with the back of her hand and read a passage from her guidebook: 'The capital was founded at this location in 1567. This monument to national hero Simon Bolivar is a tribute to the man who liberated Venezuela, Colombia, Ecuador, Peru and Bolivia from Spanish rule in the early 1800s.'

There was also a handwritten note next to the text: 'Bit dashing, isn't he?'

Ellie looked up at the statue. With his noble posture and oh-so-serious expression, Bolivar was handsome in that old-fashioned kind of way, a bit like Mr. Darcy from Jane Austen's *Pride and Prejudice*.

"Hello, Mr. Bolivar. Nice to meet you. Are you busy later? Dinner? Drink?" She took a photo of him. "Well, maybe next time. I'll wait for your telegram."

The sound of drums filled the air and Ellie turned to see a brass band marching around the corner. Dressed in dazzling silver uniforms, they played trumpets, saxophones and traditional instruments she didn't recognize. Hundreds of cheering people streamed down the street alongside them. The lively *samba* tune had everyone in the crowd grabbing a partner and dancing to the rhythm. How did they move their hips like that? Even children danced adorably together on the sidewalk. It was like being in *Footloose*, except everyone but Ellie was Kevin Bacon. All she could do was clap and bop awkwardly from side-to-side.

I don't care, because everything is amazing!

New York City, USA

Ellie switched off the Shakira track. The knocking got louder. She finished wrapping a plate in newspaper and dodged around cardboard boxes on her way to the door. Checked the peephole. Oh shit, moment of truth.

"Hi—"

"Drink this." Donna, Ellie's older sister, shoved a cup of coffee in her direction, kissed her on the cheek, and stormed inside the apartment. "And while you're drinking it tell me what the fuck you've done."

"Lovely to see you."

"Blah, blah, you too. Now what's got into your head?" Donna took up residence on a stool in the kitchen. With curly auburn hair and full shoulders, she was more solidly-built than Ellie.

"I told you on the phone. I can't afford to stay here without a job—"

"So get a new one."

"It's not going to be that easy in this economy. Besides…" Ellie tucked her hair behind her ears and crossed her arms. "I need a change."

Donna looked at her blankly, an expression Ellie understood from years of silent interrogation. Yep, this was going to be painful.

"So a few nights ago I was working on a report, all night, again, and I reached a point where I said, 'I'm not enjoying myself. I'm not living life as I want it to be.'"

"None of us are living life as we want it to be. You try raising two boys under ten with a husband as useless as Roger. I'd love to escape, but we all have responsibilities. You can't just throw away a career you've spent a decade building."

"I've put it on hold, for a little while. I want to spend some time figuring out what I'm doing here. On the planet. I mean, there has to be more to life than selling it to a company that doesn't appreciate you. And, y'know, I haven't felt this good—this excited about the future—in a long time. It was you that inspired me."

Another blank look.

Ellie grabbed her birthday card from the coffee table and passed it to her sister. "Your message got me thinking, or rather it summed up what I've been feeling. I'm thirty-one. And I haven't explored the world, really explored it beyond a short tour to Europe and a Hawaiian beach resort. I haven't had that grand adventure we all dream about when we're kids. The other night I read your message and realized—it's now or never."

"I wrote that message because it's what you're meant to say to someone on their birthday. It doesn't mean you should go and do it. Jesus, no-one actually goes and does it, because it's stupid!"

"You know, some understanding would be nice."

"I'm trying to understand! So you read some clichéd Hallmark card and decided to screw up your life?"

"I'm not screwing up my life, I'm taking control of it. Can't you see that?"

"What do you want from me, Ellie? To come over here and pat you on the head and tell you everything's going to be all right? That you made a great decision even though you don't have an income or insurance or future."

Ellie retreated to a stool on the other side of the bench. "I've been through years of school, college, and work with nothing to show for it except a job that occupied me twelve hours a day and demanded even more. What else do I have? I'm single.

Lonely. Unhappy. I want to try something different. I *need* to try something different. Before it's too late."

"Did you even think about me? Or your nephews?"

"Don't throw a guilt trip on me, Donna. Of course I'll be sad to leave you all, but it's only for a few weeks. This is something I need to do for my own sanity. And I get that it may be the dumbest decision I've ever made, but I have to interrupt this pattern I've been stuck in. To change from a life I grew to hate to a life that I love." Tears streamed down Ellie's face and she wiped them away with a snort.

Donna exhaled loudly. She got off the stool and took her sister's hands. "I'd say Johnny Pardello was the dumbest decision you ever made."

"OK, this is the second dumbest decision then," Ellie smiled.

"I will always love you, no matter what you do. I just want you to be happy." Donna pulled Ellie into a hug.

"Thank you. I want to be happy."

They held each other a while before Donna spoke again. "Now, where are you going?"

"Venezuela."

"Oh holy fuck!" Donna flung her arms in the air. "Out of all the countries you chose Venezuela? Are you crazy?"

"It's really cheap."

"Because it's a banana republic."

"So I'll eat lots of bananas. I've done heaps of research already." Ellie flipped open her iPad and showed Donna detailed plans for flights and accommodation. "There's a ton of travel blogs with great advice but, y'know, I've never backpacked before."

"Backpacking?!"

"That's the idea."

"This just keeps getting better. You'll be lucky to last one night in a hostel surrounded by filthy hippies before running to the nearest Marriott."

"I can't afford to stay in the Marriott. I don't have that much saved."

"Eleanor Rose Bartlett, what's got into you?" Donna fell onto the sofa, head in her hands. "Do you know how dangerous it is in South America? You're going to get killed."

"I could get killed in New York."

"They prey on short blonde tourists who don't speak a word of Spanish."

"I've been learning from Shakira. *Hola,*" Ellie said, trying to lighten the mood. She sat beside her sister on the sofa. "Y'know, a minute ago you were supporting me."

"Reluctantly. And that was before you told me you were going to the murder capital of the world. You know they hate Americans."

"Everyone hates Americans."

"But why not...Canada?"

"I want to climb Mount Roraima."

"Mount what?"

"The book you sent." Ellie picked up *The Lost World* and handed it to Donna with loving care. "Dad had it when he was a boy and passed it down to me. I must've read it a hundred times as a kid. It's about a team of explorers who go into the Amazon to find a mountain where, according to legend, amazing creatures still live."

"Amazing creatures, huh?" Donna said with a roll of her eyes.

"Yes! The cliffs of Mount Roraima are so steep that the surface has been isolated for millions of years and there are still dinosaurs living up there." Ellie sounded as giddy as when she was a girl listening to her dad read the story.

Donna threw her a look that said: *are you fucking nuts?*

"Of course there's not really dinosaurs up there." Ellie was suddenly embarrassed at her child-like enthusiasm. "But it's still meant to be interesting..."

Donna put the novella down. "My little sister has lost her mind and is going in search of dinosaurs."

"I haven't lost my mind. I've found it. I used to love the idea of travel, of discovering new places and people. I want to live that dream. But this is hard for me, y'know." Ellie's voice cracked. "Remember Dad always told us stories about the places he'd gone before we came along? How he hitchhiked all the way to Alaska? I know he would've loved to climb Mount Roraima, but he never got the chance. So I'm going to do it. And some support from my sister wouldn't go astray. In fact, I really need it."

Donna took a breath. "If this is what will make you happy, then go for it. Just come back quick."

"Thank you. That means a lot. And don't worry, I'll be staying in your spare room before you know it." They hugged again, longer this time. "So now you've stopped being a complete bitch, can you help me pack?"

CHAPTER 7

San Francisco, USA

The elevator doors opened and Jerry strode onto the fourteenth floor, his long legs propelling him forward with what his wife had once described was less grace than a giraffe. He had a satchel across his torso and carried a long tube of drawings. His assistant, Kyra Khuman, stood with arms impatiently crossed next to a sign, 'Townsend, Vasquez & Associates, Architects.'

"You're late," she said.

"Good morning and I have three kids to deal with. How many do you have?" Jerry kept moving into the open-plan office space, where his employees worked on drafting tables and oversized CAD monitors.

"If you mock my single status again I'll sue for discrimination. And don't think that your natural height advantage scares me, Jerry. I could have your ass in a second."

"I don't doubt it."

She handed him a manila folder. "These are the amendments for the Pata Project."

"It seems thick."

"Because they are thick. And I know how you like to compromise your vision to satisfy a fickle client."

Jerry recognized Kyra's sarcasm well enough to avoid taking the bait. Instead he said hello to his staff as he walked past.

"Also, your mother called. You need to call her back because I'm getting tired of making excuses."

"What did you say?"

"That you were in the salon downstairs getting a butt wax."

"Remind me again why I hired you, Kyra?"

"Because I'm awesome."

They arrived at a large office, walled in glass. Jerry dropped the tube on his desk and it rolled onto the carpet, while unravelling the satchel proved more difficult than anticipated. Something had to go right, and soon.

"You have the Dobson pitch at nine-thirty, Ari at eleven, Fiona what's-her-name at twelve, and—"

"OK. Let's just get through the morning before you tell me how you've planned out the rest of my life."

"It's always a good strategy to avoid facing responsibility, Jerry."

"Morning all," a cheery voice at the door interrupted their banter. Kevin Connelly, the firm's plump civil engineer, had ginger hair and a meaty beard that made him look like a dwarf from *The Hobbit*. "How were your weekends?"

"I got drunk," Kyra said.

"Not nearly as relaxing as it should have been." Jerry turned on his laptop. "How's Rhiannon doing?"

"On the mend, thanks. I'm back on deck full time this week."

"That's good to hear. Just make sure you're there if she needs it."

"Thanks Jerry. I'm here about the latest Pata amendments. Have you got time to go over them before our site visit this afternoon?"

"I don't know. Have I got time?"

Kyra grunted. "Fine. I'll fit you in."

"Excellent. See you later then." Kevin left Jerry and Kyra alone in the office.

"Would you like some advice about how to relax more on weekends?" she said.

"From you? Absolutely not. I'll see you later too no doubt."

"No doubt." Kyra left as abruptly as she'd greeted him.

Jerry sat at his desk and puffed out a sigh at the thought of his day ahead.

Is there some way to invent more hours? Or slow time?

He looked through the glass to a scale model that held pride-of-place outside. It was a five-story building, but not typical in design. Instead of straight sides it had a series of stepped terraces down to the ground and, like a pyramid, the terrace levels increased in size as they got closer to the bottom. They were curved along their edges to give a fluid, natural, appearance, and each terrace was covered with grass, flowers and sculptures. The walls were made from elaborate stonework that fitted together like a jigsaw, while along the boundaries ran channels of water, an exposed drainage system funneling rain down from one level to the next to create a series of waterfalls. A plaque on the front of the model read, 'The Pata Museum.'

Jerry's focus moved to a framed photo on his desk. He was with his daughters and wife, Bella. She had dark olive skin, long black hair, and welcoming eyes that drew a person in. That still drew him in. Her beaming smile, mirrored in their children, still made his heart leap. His family was sitting on the grass of a curved terrace constructed by the master stonemasons of the ancient Incan civilization of Peru, just like those in the model. Nearby, a llama lounged in the sunlight. They'd been so happy that day exploring the ruins of Machu Picchu, and it influenced this latest project. If only he could finish it.

I could use your help on this one, Bella. God knows I could use your help right now. Why on earth did you have to leave, baby?

Jerry climbed a mound of dirt on a construction site in the SoMa district of San Francisco, flanked by Kevin and two other men. All wore hardhats, orange safety vests, and steel-capped boots. Above them a crane lifted materials off a flatbed truck, below them a massive hole had been dug for the basement of the museum.

A platoon of workers synchronized to move a pipe pouring wet concrete across layers of steel rebar for the first floor. It'd been seven months just to get to this point. With seven more to go before the deadline of opening day. That was on an accelerated, potentially impossible, schedule.

"The reinforced support we had to build on the west side put us behind." Harry Falcone, the hard-nosed construction manager, had a gravelly voice mirroring the rough and tumble of the industry. Even his face resembled a stiff block of concrete.

"How far behind?" Jerry shouted over the racket of machinery.

"At least a week. We also had to clear the site for a day while those redundant gas pipes that weren't on the city's plans were capped."

"What's the new E.T.A. on finishing the floor?"

"It'll be done by Friday."

"We also need to talk about the placement of the water recycling system," Kevin said. "The angle of the intake chutes is going to cause problems we didn't expect before that reinforced support went in."

"Anybody got good news?"

An earthquake? The Big One?

"I received an email from the client's lawyers this morning," replied Brandon Wong, the youngest of the group, who as quantity surveyor was responsible for controlling costs.

Jerry couldn't decide if liked lawyers or earthquakes less.

"They're seeing delays less than half-way into the build and are getting nervous about the budget. They'd like to see if you can strip back some of the, uh…unnecessary features, like those water channels on the terraces."

"The channels are necessary," Jerry shot back. "They're essential to the aesthetic of the building. Just keep them calm for now. We're going to make this work, gentlemen."

Bella needs me to make this work.

As with all significant things in our lives, the alternative was too awful to consider.

CHAPTER 8

Caracas, Venezuela

The four-seater taxied nervously out of the hangar. Squashed next to the pilot, Ellie peered through the gloom. Rain bucketed so heavily she could barely see its wingtips.

Would wings even be useful in this weather? Wouldn't a keel be more helpful?

They swung around and lined up for takeoff. A crack of lightning illuminated the tarmac ahead, but it looked more like a river than a runway. Ellie's anxiety at being in a prop plane for the first time could've filled an A380.

She'd taken the handwritten advice in her *Unique Planet*: 'Call Francesca at Gran Sabana Air. They speak English and will organize a direct flight.' Except this tiny tin can wasn't the type of flight Ellie had pictured. In hindsight, the 'Relax and sit tight!' part of the message had been a joke.

The pilot gave her a stern thumbs-up. Was it too late to jump out? He roared the engine to full throttle and unleashed the brake. Yep, too late. Ellie white-knuckled her seat as they bounced down the runway and lifted into the storm.

Gran Sabana, Venezuela

The sun beat mercilessly on barren terrain that sucked energy from all life forms, including Ellie. Sitting alone outside a mud-brick guesthouse, she sheltered in a pocket of shade and played tic-tac-toe against herself in the sand.

It was over an hour past the scheduled pick-up time, which tested her desire to kill someone, but had provided an opportunity to update her TO DO list. She ticked off START MY ADVENTURE and EXPLORE CARACAS. The next item: CLIMB MOUNT RORAIMA.

Ellie lifted her sunglasses and squinted at the horizon. A 4WD appeared out of a mirage, dust billowing in its wake. It bounded over a rise before coming to rest by the guesthouse. She turned her face away to avoid eating dirt.

"Miss Bartlett?" A muscular man in his early-thirties jumped out. His black hair was cropped military short and he wore a camo t-shirt.

"That's right." Ellie shook his huge hand.

"I'm Javier. Let's put your bag up top." He wasted no time picking up Ellie's backpack. "Do you have rocks in here?"

She gave a sheepish shrug. "No, just clothes and stuff."

The back door of the 4WD flung open and a bubbly young woman got out. "Hey, I'm Hannah." She was joined by a man who had a long-lensed camera hanging around his neck. "This is my boyfriend Eric." They were both tall, with striking white-blonde hair and well-worn traveling clothes.

"I'm Ellie. Nice to meet you."

"I can help with packing if you like," Hannah offered.

The 4WD again charged along an unsealed road. Ellie's backpack, significantly lighter now her excess crap had been left at the guesthouse, was strapped to the roof with the others. On reflection, she really didn't need to bring shampoo. Or the hot water bottle, portable coffee grinder, inflatable bed, and solar-powered camp shower. Where they were going, none of that would be useful, and every ounce of weight made a difference.

"I've never met anyone from Finland before. If you don't mind me saying, you both look really young." Ellie sat in the back with Hannah and Eric, holding onto the door as they were thrown about with every crash of the tires on rocks.

"I'm nineteen and Eric is twenty."

"And you're backpacking around South America?"

"Four months already."

"That's amazing." Ellie was impressed, but also jealous. She wished she hadn't waited so long to begin her own trip. And that she was traveling for more than two weeks.

"How about you?" Hannah said.

"I've only been on the road for a few days so, y'know, I have no idea what I'm doing."

"Don't worry, we've done a lot of trekking. You're from the U.S.A?"

"New York. I mean, I live in New York but I'm from Lewisburg. It's a small town in Pennsylvania but not many people go there."

"Nobody comes to our hometown either. That's why we decided to go to the world."

"OK, listen up!" Javier shouted above the engine. "We're five minutes away." He held up a crumpled map and traced the route they would take with his finger. "We start at this checkpoint. Today we walk three hours before lunch, then another three hours to our campsite at the base of Mount Roraima. Tomorrow we must wake early to avoid the heat and begin our ascent to the summit. Understand?"

Ellie and the Finns nodded, then stiffened when the tires hit another rock.

"Now a warning. Mount Roraima is a *tepui*, a flat mountain. It's on this plain with three others, and because they are the only tall things they create their own weather systems, which are *completely unpredictable*. One minute sunshine, the next rain or snow, and sometimes clouds make it impossible to see more than a few meters. You need to follow my every step. Understand? I don't want to lose any more people."

Ellie replayed Javier's words to make sure she'd heard them correctly. Lose any more people? Was that *lose* as in they got lost and went home? Or *lose* as in they fell down a ravine and their crumpled bodies could only be identified by what was left of their teeth?

"Only joking!" Javier slapped his thigh. "I never lose a person yet. OK, are we ready to climb Roraima?"

"Yes!" Hannah and Eric shouted.

"Yeah," Ellie said. "Definitely."

Later that afternoon, Ellie sweated heavily under her cap as the group hiked through a field of sunburnt grass. In the past few hours they'd walked up-and-down ridges, crossed rivers on felled tree trunks, and passed through villages where children ran out of huts to wave hello. Now they ascended the crest of a lumpy hill.

"We rest here," Javier announced after they'd made it up. He sprayed bottled water on his face.

Hannah and Eric unclipped their packs and collapsed to the ground.

Ellie didn't join them. Instead, she stepped forward to take in her first glimpse of Mount Roraima.

The sides of the *tepui* jutted up vertically from the jungle like castle walls, while the top looked as if it'd been sliced clean off with a sword. There weren't any clouds so it sat naked and majestic, threatening yet inviting. Ellie couldn't pull her eyes away.

"Beautiful, isn't it?" Javier said.

"More beautiful than all the photos. I've wanted to come here my whole life and now…it's a special moment."

"It's a special place. The Pemón people believe a spirit lives inside Roraima and protects them from evil. You need to ask permission of the spirit to climb it, but only those worthy will be allowed to discover its secrets."

Ellie gripped the straps of her backpack. "I hope I prove worthy."

New York City, USA

One whole wall of the outdoor goods warehouse was lined with backpacks of various sizes and colors. Ellie took a couple off the shelf to check against her height.

"What are you looking for exactly?" Gabby said.

"I'm not sure. Something not too big but not too small."

"I wasn't asking about the backpacks."

"I was talking about the backpacks," Ellie deflected, like she always did when questioned about sex or, heaven forbid, emotions.

"Have you thought about finding a husband while you're down there? Or maybe…*a lover?*" Gabby blew her friend a kiss over a row of thermal underwear.

"I like this one." Ellie pulled a medium-sized blue backpack off the shelf. "Adjustable harness, lockable zips, matching daypack. Can you give me a hand?"

Gabby helped Ellie put the straps across her shoulders and secure the waist belt. "You do realize you're going from an apartment full of stuff to your whole life being in just one bag?"

"That's kind of the point."

"I couldn't get everything I need into this thing. My dildo collection would take up half of it. It looks good on you though, like it fits."

"Will it still look good on me when I'm covered in mud and haven't shaved my legs in ten days?"

"Unlikely."

Ellie walked up-and-down the aisle to test the pack. "I'm actually looking forward to not worrying about my appearance. Tonight might be the last time in a while that I have to get dressed up."

"I hope you're ready for it. Shonda has booked us into Florentinis."

"Excellent. This is the one."

"OK. What else do you need?"

"Let me check my list. Ah, hand sanitizer—"

"Surprise, surprise."

"Fun stuff like tampons, and really fun stuff like hiking boots and a waterproof jacket."

"Let's go shopping."

A few hours later, Ellie and Gabby joined a long line at the cashier. It took both of them to carry all of Ellie's gear, which in addition to the items on her list now included sun-protective cargo pants, moisture wicking t-shirts, a headtorch and first-aid kit. Gabby had also talked her into buying something called Snake-Off, which marketed itself as shark repellant for anacondas. It seemed unlikely, but then again...

"Just promise me you'll try to be patient with people on your trip, OK?"

"What do you mean?"

"I mean that you can be impatient. You get frustrated and then you end up hating people."

"I don't hate people."

"You sometimes hate people."

"OK, fine, sometimes I hate people. But only when they're dimwits. Like the cashier here." Ellie gestured in the direction of a pimple-faced teenager behind the register. "Look at him pushing buttons slower than a baby sloth. Seriously, how difficult is it to scan a barcode and tap a credit card?"

"You're gonna try to be less judgmental too?"

"Starting tomorrow."

Ellie did wonder how her journey would change her, and if she would return a different person. She'd read that backpacking had a way of throwing up surprises as nothing else could. To be on the road, away from the comfort and safety of home, away from everyone and everything she knew, would be the most challenging thing she'd ever undertaken. But to not attempt it—that would be the only failure, right?

CHAPTER 9

New York City, USA

"Ouch." Ellie trod on one of the toys strewn along the hallway of her sister's home in suburban Queens. It didn't help that she was drying her hair with a towel and feeling like a few more hours sleep would've been useful.

She made it to the kitchen, where Donna put the finishing touches on a salad. In the backyard, Benji, ten, and Alex, six, chased each other around a plastic swing set. The boys were the spitting image of their mom with the same curly hair.

"Good afternoon," Donna said without looking up. "How was the last hurrah with your girlfriends?"

"Too many martinis," Ellie groaned. "I think Gabby threw up in the Uber, but I can't remember much else. Can I help with something?"

"Setting the table. But we need to talk first."

"Can it wait? My head is still kind of…pulsing."

"Not really, if you're leaving tomorrow."

Ellie didn't have the energy to argue. She leaned against the bench for physical and emotional support. "OK. What is it?"

"I've been reading up on this Mount Roy thing."

"Mount Roraima."

"It's really dangerous. People have died."

Ellie sighed. "Well...it's already paid for."

"But how are you going to climb the fucking thing?!" Donna put a bowl of carrots in the microwave and slammed the door. Ellie's skull almost exploded. "You've never been up a mountain. You haven't done any training. You're completely unprepared."

"I figure I need to do things I've never done before, or else why am I going?"

"A very good question."

The bell on the oven put a merciful period on their conversation. Sometimes it was hard to believe they'd come from the same parents.

Donna took out a spinach lasagna and shouted through the window. "Benji, Alex, come wash your grubby paws. Now!"

Ellie pulled on a sweater before joining her family in the dining room. Donna's ashen-faced husband, Roger, wearing his weekend outfit of track pants and Cheetos-stained polo shirt, grunted his approval with the lasagna. Benji pushed it to the side of his plate as if it were radioactive.

"Aunty Ellie?"

"Yes, Alex."

"Benji said you're going away because you don't love us anymore." His innocent eyes looked across the table at her like his whole world was about to disappear.

"Oh, sweetheart, that's not true. I will always love you, wherever I am. Nothing will change that."

"But I don't want you to go."

Ellie walked around the table and bobbed down next to her nephew. "I know you don't, but in our lives we need to go on adventures because it helps us grow. Do you remember an adventure you went on?"

"Um... I went to the water park with Mommy."

"And what happened?"

"I was scared of the slide because it was big. Like, really big. And I didn't want to go down it because I was so scared. But then I just went down it and I was happy and now I can go down it whenever I want because I'm a big boy now."

"I'm very proud of you." She squeezed Alex and planted a kiss on his cheek. "A real adventure. That's what I'm going to do."

"You're going down a big slide?"

"Maybe…and some other things too. I hope to be as brave as you."

"I want Aunty Ellie to be brave."

"Thank you, sweetheart." She appreciated his encouragement because the last thing she felt was brave.

"OK, now eat your lunch," Donna told her son while Ellie returned to her chair.

"Dad says you're leaving to become a lesbian," Benji said. The little brat's smirk gave away that he was old enough to know better.

Ellie turned to Roger. Face down to his plate, he continued to shovel food into his mouth.

"Benji, that's not a nice thing to say," Donna scolded.

"Dad said she should be married by now but no-one wants to marry her so—"

"Benjamin Wallace!"

"There are lots of people my age who aren't married," Ellie explained with more patience than she thought she possessed. If not so hungover, she would've dumped the lasagna on his head. "That doesn't mean they're lesbian or gay, and it wouldn't matter if they were. These days some people aren't getting married at all."

"Because they're fugly," Benji sniggered.

"Shut your mouth or you'll get a spanking!" Donna's threat finally silenced Benji, and he went back to playing with his food.

"But Aunty Ellie, aren't you lonely?" Alex said. "Momma has Daddy and Daddy has Momma. Who do you have?"

Sigh. It was hard to argue with a child's logic.

⌒

"Can you slow down? I'd like to make it out of my own country alive." Ellie consulted her TO DO list while Donna drove the station wagon down the highway at warp speed. She'd ticked off CHANGE MONEY and PACK BACKPACK, which left just two items: DRIVE TO AIRPORT and START MY ADVENTURE.

"The only other time I drove like this was to drop Benji at summer camp because if I had to deal with him a minute longer I would've murdered my own child."

"That's an advertisement to breed if ever I heard one. Please slow down."

"Sorry." Donna ignored her and weaved into the fast lane. "I'm stressed out about you leaving."

"You're stressed?! I'm the one flying to Venezuela." Ellie did a fifth check of her daypack to make sure she had everything for her flight.

"Got your phone?" Donna said.

"Check. But remember I'll only be on WiFi."

"Ticket?"

"Check."

"Cash?"

"Check."

"Passport?"

Silence.

"Passport?!" Donna screamed.

"Just kidding. Check," Ellie laughed.

"Ha-ha, very funny. OK smart-ass, there's something in the glove compartment for you."

"Did you get me a going-away present?"

"It's a care package. I thought you'd need some help."

"You didn't have to do that."

"I did. You need it."

Ellie opened the compartment and found a paper bag. Inside was a book titled *How To Avoid Getting Killed in South America*. "That's very…thoughtful."

"Keep going."

She pulled out a small cylindrical object. "What's this?"

"Pepper spray. Don't argue with me, Ellie. You have no idea what situations you'll find yourself in. I'm not letting you on the plane unless you promise to take it."

"How exactly are you going to stop me getting on the plane?"

"I haven't thought that far ahead. Just promise me you'll carry it with you. For your sister."

Ellie registered the concern in Donna's strained eyes. "I promise."

"Good. Now there's one more thing."

Ellie reached into the bag and took out a packet of condoms. "Seriously…? Seriously?!"

"You never know who you're going to meet."

"You think I can't buy condoms for myself?"

"Are they on your O.C.D. list?"

"No."

"So you proved my point. You do need help."

"And it's not an O.C.D. list."

"Then throw it away."

Impossible. Ellie wasn't anywhere near ready to give up the TO DO list that structured so much of her life.

After all, what would happen if I didn't have my list? I might forget to drive to the airport and start my adventure. That'd really ruin my trip.

"Ellie, listen to me. You're going to meet a lot of men. Latin men."

"Oh God, here we go."

"And everyone is more liberal in those countries, sexually. It's the humidity."

"Please don't start, Donna."

"When was the last time you had sex?"

Ellie silently toyed with the condoms.

"Exactly."

"But ribbed condoms? Why ribbed?"

Ellie and Donna walked slowly toward the sliding doors that led to immigration control at J.F.K. International Airport. They came to a stop surrounded by the hubbub of passengers, security personnel and p.a. announcements.

"This is it," Donna cried, unable to hold in her tears any longer. "Take care out there little sister. I love you." She embraced Ellie and held her.

"Love you too."

"Mom and Dad would've been so proud of you."

Ellie fought a lump in her throat. "Why'd you have to say that?"

"Because they're not around to say it anymore, and they would want you to know it. Besides, you need to be more open with your emotions. I think this trip will be good for you that way."

"OK, you're making me wet." She pulled away. "I'll be in touch."

"Message me."

"I will." Ellie headed to the sliding doors. Panic punched her in the gut, but she forced herself to ignore it. There was something bigger at stake.

Beyond these doors, everything changes.

She turned and waved at Donna one last time, flashing a smile as wide as the Brooklyn Bridge—the irrepressible smile of someone about to fly to an exotic land and embark on the adventure of a lifetime.

Then Ellie stepped into the unknown.

CHAPTER 10

Mount Roraima, Venezuela

After a sleepless night on a mat thinner than a stick of gum, Ellie got up at the crack of dawn. In the folds of her sleeping bag she found *The Lost World*, which she'd been reading last night by the light of her headtorch. She flicked to a book-marked page:

> *I was still drinking in this wonderful panorama when the heavy hand of the Professor fell upon my shoulder. "This way, my young friend," said he; "Vestigia nulla retrorsum. Never look rearwards, but always to our glorious goal."*

When Ellie was a girl, she'd always felt protected within the shelter of her dad's strong farmer's arms. But who would protect her now?

Oh, Dad. What would you think about me being here? At the place we used to read about, that I used to dream about. How I wish you were with me. Today is the day I climb Mount Roraima. Vestigia nulla retrorsum.

Ellie tied her hair in a ponytail, pulled on her boots and fumbled out of the tent. Up close, the *tepui* towered over her miniscule human form, reaching all the way into the cloudy heavens. Out of those heavens, as if they'd sprung leaks, gushed spine-tingling waterfalls.

A solitary ray of sun filtered through. Ellie closed her eyes and let it bathe her face, giving her strength for the challenge ahead.

"*Buenas dias.*"

"Good morning, Javier."

He tossed her an orange. "Are you ready to climb it?"

"Absolutely," Ellie said with more conviction than yesterday. "But I'm not sure *how* we are going to climb it. Those cliffs look vertical."

"That's why nobody made it up until 1884, when two British explorers found a way around the back that avoided most of the cliffs. We'll take the same route. There is one thing though. You see that waterfall on the left?"

"Yep."

"You have to go *through* it."

"I do?"

"Don't worry, I'll help." Javier looked nervously to the sky. "I just hope it doesn't rain because it can get very dangerous up there."

By noon, rain pounded Ellie's group as they trekked in the dense jungle on the side of Mount Roraima. A cruel joke from whoever controlled the sprinkler system around here. Everyone wore waterproof jackets and had rain protectors on their packs, but the deluge was so heavy they were still soaked to the skin. The steep path had become mud, creating a slippery-slide and covering them in orange clay. Ellie looked like she was wearing war paint, but sure-as-hell wasn't winning any battles.

She caught up to Javier and the long-legged Finns in a small clearing. He dug into his pack and passed around a bag of sweets while they took a break. "This is the end of the jungle level. From here, we go through the waterfall."

So. Fricking. High.

Ellie gazed up at the colossal river tumbling down from 350 feet above. Beyond the point where they stood, it hit a slanted area of rocks and spread out to about forty feet in width. Though Ellie didn't think she could possibly get any wetter, being here seemed to fill up her insides too.

"We need to climb up and across!" Javier shouted to be heard above the roaring cascade. "Understand? Up and across. Follow my steps. Be careful. Very slippery." He turned and charged into the waterfall. There was so much spray, he disappeared like a magic trick.

Ellie sucked in a deep breath and dashed after him. The pressure shoved her head down like a wrestler had it pinned to a mat. She could barely see her own hands, let alone Javier, and soon became disoriented, unsure where to step next.

She caught a flash of the red laces on his boots and moved quickly to track them, finding her rhythm—two steps forward, one step back as her feet slipped on the rocks. In the center of the waterfall the pressure was so powerful Ellie had to shut her eyes and just hope her feet were landing in the right pla—

Oh fuck.

The loose rocks underneath her fell away.

Ellie felt herself sliding.

Her heart jumped into her mouth and she grabbed for something, anything, to hold onto.

Nothing stuck.

Below, Ellie saw water tumble off the cliff and into oblivion. She kept sliding. In a second it would be to her death.

Please no.

Ellie grasped at a rock jutting out of the ground.

It held firm.

She gripped the lifebuoy with both hands. The water kept pummeling her like a jackhammer. But she was determined not to die here.

Not yet.

Using every fiber of grit, and some she never knew existed, Ellie pulled herself up. Away from the edge. One painstaking inch at a time.

Through the spray, she spotted a blurry figure—Javier. He climbed down and shouted something, but she could only see his lips move.

Ellie grappled her way higher.

He stretched out his hand.

They touched fingers.

Broke apart.

Touched again.

C'mon!

With a final lunge he pulled her to safety, and together they scrambled out the other side of the waterfall.

"Thank you," Ellie coughed, collapsing on the ground and gasping for air. Her heart thumped so hard her whole body shook.

Hannah and Eric emerged next, holding each other close, and joined Ellie in the mud.

"I'm surprised we made it," Javier said. "That's as tough as it's ever been. The good news is it's only thirty minutes to the top. Ready?"

It abruptly stopped raining as Javier led the battle-tested group along the final section of the trail. First they squeezed through a narrow gully, then climbed over a boulder that sat as the ultimate obstacle to their glorious goal.

Javier jumped up with ease, pulling Ellie, Hannah and Eric onto the top of Mount Roraima. "This is it!" he shouted.

The hikers shared high-fives and relieved hugs.

Ellie looked out over the vast stretch of sandstone, astonished she'd got this far and bubbling with enthusiasm at what lay ahead. "So...where are the dinosaurs?"

They all cracked up.

For the next three days, Ellie and the Finns stayed on the heels of Javier from the southern end of Mount Roraima to the northern tip. The views into the valleys from 9000 feet above sea-level were spectacular, and Eric took hundreds of photos with his high-powered camera.

They navigated rocky, ankle-twisting, terrain, climbed through caves lined with quartz crystals and blind spiders, and swam in sink holes to cool off from the midday heat. Ellie felt like she was in a surreal dream. One she didn't want to wake up from.

They slept in tents and caves, huddling around a fire each night to defend against the icy air. Over pasta or beans or Ellie's chocolate stash, she got to know her companions well, sharing laughs and making memories to last a lifetime. Along the way, Javier sought out plants and animals to show them, such as the purple bellflowers and black frogs which were found nowhere else on earth.

Ellie also had a lot of time to spend inside her own head. Back home there were a myriad of distractions, but here she could think, really think. About her late parents, how much she missed their guidance, and how she'd ended up here on her life's journey. She still blamed herself for being so obsessed with work that she didn't visit her dad before he passed three years ago. Hopefully this trek would ease the heaviness of that guilt.

At one point her mind drifted back to her ex-boyfriend, the investment banker whose name she refused to say out loud and whose idea of date night was discussing bond yields. Ellie smiled at how crazy he'd have thought she was for taking this risk. It'd been devastating to learn he was breaking up with her because his 'other girlfriend' was pregnant, but it meant she was able to embark on this epic quest, which she wouldn't have traded for anything. Life was funny like that.

There wasn't much sound up here, away from civilization, except for the voice of the wind and the occasional flutter of a bird's wings. It was as if someone had turned down the volume on the planet.

Peaceful. I've never known the world to be this peaceful.

On the fourth afternoon they reached their destination—the sharp northern point of Mount Roraima, jutting out from the mainland like a ship's bow.

Ellie instinctively took a few steps back toward the shrub line, while Hannah let out a shriek of joy and ran toward the cliff. She raised her hands in victory. Then did a handstand just one yard from the edge as Eric snapped pics for their Facebook.

"Please, no!" Ellie cried.

Everyone found her reaction hilarious.

"What could go wrong?" Eric said, pretending to trip over near the edge.

Ellie's stomach tied itself in a knot and she buried her face in her hands.

"Come on." Hannah waved her over. "You'll be OK."

"No, no, I can't. It's not possible."

"I'll hold your hand," Javier offered.

"I'm fine right here. Thanks guys." Ellie calmed her nerves by rubbing her temples. She peeked through her fingers and saw Hannah and Eric looking over the cliff.

"That's incredible. It has to be half-a-kilometer straight down." Eric maneuvered his camera into position.

Ellie watched Javier sneak up on the Finns and slap them on the back. They flinched and laughed hysterically. "Be careful," she pleaded.

Where the hell did they get their courage?

CHAPTER 11

San Francisco, USA

Jerry tasted the stir-fry. For a meal at the end of a long week, it wasn't too bad. No-one could cook like Bella, but under the circumstances he was doing his best. He just hoped the kids wouldn't notice he'd burnt the rice again, or if they did they'd cut him some slack this time. He gave the wok a final toss and carried the plates into the dining room where Andrea and Mia had spread their homework on the table.

"Dad, what's this point in the triangle called?" Andrea said.

"That's the vertex, honey. Now can you both pack up and go tell Yas dinner is ready?"

"I'm here." Yasmina drifted in and looked at her dad's effort with disdain. "What is it?"

"I made Thai."

"You burnt the rice again."

"At least taste it," Jerry sighed. "And turn off your phone, please. This is family time."

Yasmina flipped her phone upside down, but didn't turn it off. "This doesn't look appetizing. We eat with our eyes first, y'know."

He wondered how he was going to survive Yasmina's adolescent phase. Some days boarding school seemed like a good option. Or boot camp. "Do you remember in Ecuador when you didn't want to try the guinea pig?"

"*Cuy cuy cuy!*"

"That's right Mia, the *cuy*. But then you loved it."

"That was different." Yasmina pushed her plate away. "And I'm a vegetarian so I can't eat this."

"Since when are you a vegetarian?"

"Yesterday."

"Well, you can eat the vegetables then. Who'd like to share what happened at school today?"

"We learnt about sex," Andrea said matter-of-factly.

Jerry dropped a chopstick and it clattered across the table.

"What's sex?" Mia asked.

"It's when—"

"Andrea, please," Jerry cut her off. "Mia is too young to learn about that. Are you trying to be as difficult as your older sister? Come on girls, I know you're still hurting but the only way we are going to get through this is as a family. We need to support each other."

"Sorry," Andrea mumbled.

"In fact, given you two are apparently so grown up now, I'll leave it to you to decide how you can help out more around here. It's time you both took on more responsibility."

"We could take turns cooking dinner or cleaning up," Andrea suggested. "Maybe take out the trash?"

Yasmina gave her sister a side-eye that suggested she was going to punch her.

"Excellent. Why don't you draw up a roster? Yas, do you want to add something?"

Her phone buzzed and she hurried away from the table.

"Yasmina!"

It was 11 p.m. when Jerry pressed send on his last email of the night. He shut his laptop but stayed at his desk in the cozy upstairs study. The walls were dotted with college degrees and sketches of architectural projects, and a window looked over the backyard.

I have no idea if I'm doing any of this right, Bella. The girls… they need their mom.

He was about to switch off the desk lamp when a shadow in the doorway startled him. "Geez, Mia. You scared the heck out of me."

"I can't sleep." She hugged a much-loved teddy bear and blanket.

"What's wrong, honey?" Jerry wrapped the blanket around her shoulders.

"I was thinking about Mommy."

"Well, she would be very happy you were thinking about her. And you know I think about Mommy a lot as well."

"It makes me sad."

"It's OK to be sad. But we had some wonderful times together, right? Do you remember for your birthday last year when she dressed up as Princess Jasmine?"

"And fell in Grandma and Grandpa's pool!" Mia laughed.

"You know even though she's not here with us, your mom still loves you very much. And she would want you to go to sleep so you can wake up tomorrow and not be tired. Do you think that's a good idea?"

Mia nodded.

"OK honey, then let's get you to bed." Jerry picked up his daughter and tossed her in the air. She squealed with delight and he carried her down the hallway to her bedroom. "Let's make sure you're nice and warm." He tucked her into the sheets.

"Don't forget teddy."

"Oh, I won't forget teddy. We need to make sure he's comfortable too."

"Daddy?"

"Yes, honey?"

"Can you pat me like Mommy did when I was a baby?"

"Of course. How many pats do you want tonight?"

"Ten. No, twenty."

"OK, twenty pats it is. Close your eyes now. *Buenas noches.*" Jerry kissed Mia goodnight.

"*Buenas noches, papi.*"

He kneeled next to the bed and patted her hair, softly counting each stroke. "One, two, three, four…" By sixteen, Mia had fallen asleep. Jerry looked at the contented smile on her precious face.

I'm not sure I can do this, Bella. This is not how we thought our lives would turn out, baby. Not even close.

CHAPTER 12

Present Day, 18th July – Mount Roraima, Venezuela

"C'mon," Ellie said. "You're almost there." She took another step toward the edge.

Clouds still churned around her like a ghostly soup, but she was now only ten yards from the edge of Mount Roraima. The previous ten yards had taken just a few minutes, but it seemed like an hour as fear and courage fought a pitched battle in her head. It didn't help that her legs felt like concrete, resisting every move.

Focus, Ellie.

Another step forward.

The sun broke through and the clouds began to lift. In the distance, she could make out a panorama of jungle with no end.

"Just a bit farther."

Ellie's steps became quicker, longer, more confident.

Five yards from the edge.

She spread out her arms for balance, trying not to look down.

"Only three more. One. Two. Three…"

And with a final step, Ellie stood on the sharp precipice of Mount Roraima.

She threw her hands in the air and shouted at the top of her lungs. "Woohoohoo! I'm the queen of the world!"

Her voice bellowed across the valley, echoing back at her five-fold. She marveled at her own strength, the power of her mind to overcome her greatest fear. To conquer it. To smash it. "Woohoohoo!"

Dad, I made it.

I made it for us.

I love you.

"That's a great photo," a voice from behind said.

Ellie spun around, almost losing her balance.

At the shrub line, Eric clicked rapid-fire photos while Hannah and Javier cheered her success.

"Thanks guys. I did it." Ellie beamed with pride. She felt superhuman. A real-life Wonder Woman.

"Sit on the edge," Hannah said. "We'll get a pic of you looking at the horizon."

Ellie snuck a peek at the sheer 1200-foot drop.

Holy. Cow.

But she knew now she could master it. She crouched and swung her legs over the edge, feeling the stiff pull of gravity as they dangled in the air. The uninterrupted view across the valley made her think she was flying.

I've never felt this alive.

It dawned on her that challenging—and defeating—her mortal fear of heights was not just a great personal accomplishment, but a point of reference in her life. Everything suddenly seemed possible.

I want to feel like this every day. For the rest of my life.

Alive!

CHAPTER 13

Four Days Later – Gran Sabana, Venezuela

Back at the guesthouse, Hannah and Eric had passed out cradled in each other's arms. Ellie lay on her stomach on a nearby bunk, blistered feet covered with band-aids. Her hair, wet from showering away a week's worth of dirt and sweat, dripped onto the screen of her phone while she messaged Donna.

Toughest thing I've ever done
Whole body is hurting
Serious pain 😨 😨 😨

See, I told you not to go
and now you're suffering

It was worth it
And I've never been so tanned!

I'm glad you're safe
What's next?

One more stop
Tomorrow taking a bus then
plane then boat to Angel Falls

> *None of those sound good*
> *The State Department website warned*
> *about buses crashing down there*

There's no other way around
so I'll have to take my chances
If I survived Roraima, I can survive a bus

> *Please take care*
> *And drink lots of water*
> *See you next week*
> *We love you* ♥

Love you too
See you soon ☺

Ellie put down her phone and wrote three additions to her TO DO list: BUY WATER, PURGE BACKPACK OF UNNECESSARY STUFF and KEEP DOING THINGS I'VE NEVER DONE BEFORE.

Satisfied with her plan, she rolled onto her back and stared at the ceiling fan. It was hard to believe her adventure would be over in a few days. It was even harder to get excited about returning to New York and applying for jobs. The thought of being stuck in an office again made her shudder.

Ellie picked up her *Unique Planet* and admired the glossy cover photo of Machu Picchu, 'Lost City of the Incas,' high in the Peruvian Andes.

Wow, is there a more spectacular sight? It would be amazing to visit. Imagine hiking the Inca Trail to Machu Picchu! If only I didn't need to go home.

Ellie flipped open the guidebook and noticed something peculiar. On the first page, under the heading THIS BOOK BELONGS TO, the previous owner had written their name:

Bella Vasquez Townsend

And there was a note:

Fellow explorer, I hope you find this book useful on your own intrepid adventures. Go far and go wild! bellavasqueztownsend@gmail.com

Go far and go wild... Ellie ran her fingers over the writing, feeling its indent on the page. It was nice to know the name of the person who'd given her all this travel advice. She opened her phone, typed in the email address, and began to compose a message.

Dear Bella,
You don't know me but I am the lucky recipient of your Unique Planet guidebook for South America. I found it on a book exchange shelf in a hostel in Caracas, Venezuela, and your suggestions have been incredibly helpful. I loved visiting the Chacao market, where I stuffed myself on local chocolate. Bonus point to me for not getting lost. So I just wanted to write and say a huge THANK YOU! Your book has become my travel bible and I'm taking good care of it. All the best,
Ellie.
PS Do you have any more adventures planned?

Ellie's finger hesitated for a second while contemplating whether contacting a stranger this way was OK. She decided no harm could come of it and tapped send. The email flew away into cyberspace.

San Francisco, USA

Wiping the leftover shaving cream off his face, Jerry stepped out of the bathroom. He needed to look fresh even if he didn't feel it. He'd decorated the master bedroom in cherry wood and built a king-sized bed opposite a bay window that drew in the dawn light. A print of *Roots* by Bella's favorite artist, Frida Kahlo, hung on the wall above the bed.

Jerry opened the closet and frowned. Great, no clean shirts. He looked at the laundry basket, overflowing with clothes, and picked up the shirt on top. It just passed the smell test. He pulled it on and headed down the hallway to his study, thinking he better get his act together soon or he'd be leaving the house naked.

He scrolled through a long stream of emails, but only one grabbed his interest. The subject line was 'To Bella From Ellie' and it came from a sender he didn't recognize, someone named Ellie Bartlett.

Jerry cautiously clicked on the email. Tears welled in his eyes as he read it. Memories of Bella came flooding back. Of the love they had. Of the loss he still felt.

"Dad, I'm hungry!" Mia yelled from downstairs.

"OK," his voice broke. He cleared his throat and tried again. "OK, honey, I'm coming."

Jerry closed Ellie's email. The background image on his laptop stared back at him. It was a photo of Bella and him holding hands as Mount Roraima rose majestically behind them, as sure of its place in the world as they were of their love for each other.

Morning had faded into afternoon, but Jerry still couldn't concentrate. He turned away from the activity outside his office. The email from this Ellie woman seemed so random. Or was it? It didn't read like spam, or some elaborate internet plot to defraud him of his kids' college fund. So what did he have to lose? He'd already lost so much. He swiveled his chair around and started to type a reply:

Dear Ellie,
Thank you for your message. It's nice to hear someone is making use of the guidebook. You emailed my wife, Bella.

Jerry paused to compose himself.

She passed away 6 months ago.

The finality of the words hit him like it was yesterday.

I'm not sure how the book ended up back in Caracas as she left it in a hotel in Buenos Aires, Argentina, our last stop. It has taken a quite a journey. Bella would be so happy to know that someone is finding her advice useful. She always wanted to help people and made all those notes so other travelers could get the most out of their experience. I kept telling her it was a waste of time but she stubbornly—and correctly, as usual—disagreed. We loved South America and I hope you have a wonderful time too. Kind regards,
Jerry.
PS Where are you headed next?

He hesitated, then clicked send and the email flew back into cyberspace. For better or for worse.

PART II

CHAPTER 14

26th July – Salto Ángel, Venezuela

Ellie sat at the head of a thin boat, putt-putting up a river. Morning mist still hung in the air. The farther she traveled against the current the more suffocating the jungle became, closing in around her like the jaws of the crocodiles lurking in these waters.

The captain, an unsmiling man, cut the engine and glided the boat to a bamboo jetty. Now all Ellie could hear was a rock opera of insects, birds, and animals that probably wanted to eat her.

"*Adelante*," he growled.

"Through there?" Ellie pointed to a track disappearing into the vegetation.

"*Sí.*"

Ellie grabbed her daypack and clambered onto the jetty. "Aren't you coming?" she asked.

The captain lay down in the boat and pulled his cap over his face.

Um…well, crap.

When Ellie had booked this expedition to Angel Falls—the tallest waterfall in the world—she assumed other people would be tagging along *and* there would be a guide. Now it looked like there was only one way forward. On her own.

But I can't go by myself.

I mean...can I?

Well, yeah, if you just put one foot in front of the other, as always.

OK Ellie...let's go far and go wild!

Exhaling her anxiety, she headed into the jungle alone.

Ellie heard it first. The thundering sound of water captured by gravity's relentless grip. Each step closer increased the volume, and the anticipation quickened her pace. After an hour, she emerged from the stifling heat of the jungle and looked up.

And up.

And up.

Angel Falls towered above her from a cliff so high, over half-a-mile above, that its source was barely visible. A single column of water pouring off the mountain as if Mother Nature had turned on a gigantic tap. A rainbow arced over the falls and Ellie's jaw dropped.

As a kid on a school excursion she'd visited Niagara Falls, but that natural wonder was just 160 feet tall. Angel Falls was 3,200 feet tall—twenty times as high.

Ellie walked forward and let the spray cool her skin. Opened her lips to drink it in. Totally alone in nature for the first time, she was surprised she hadn't lost her shit. Instead it brought unexpected clarity.

I can't go back to my previous life. It wasn't healthy, and it definitely wasn't happy.

I need freedom. Freedom from the stress that crippled me, from other people's expectations, and freedom to choose my own path in life.

A lagoon pooled at the base of the falls. It had a pinkish bubblegum color from the minerals the water had collected on its journey through plants and soil on top of the mountain. And it looked too refreshing to pass up.

Ellie removed her pack, boots and clothes until she was completely naked. She waded into the water and dove under the surface, letting it invigorate every inch of her body.

I'm not flying home tomorrow. Not yet. I'll find a way to tell Donna I'm staying longer, and then, somehow—Machu Picchu. Yep, I'm free.

"Ouch!" Ellie landed on her ass. Not the greatest start to freedom. She'd attempted to sit in one of the hammocks on the veranda of her hostel, but misjudged, well, everything, and flipped over backward onto the deck.

She rubbed her backside and slid into the netting again, though with less elegance than she'd have liked. Connecting her phone to WiFi, a bunch of messages came through from Gabby and other friends back home.

There was also an email with the subject 'Re: To Bella from Ellie.' She opened it first, and as Ellie read Jerry's words her face crumpled at discovering Bella was dead.

Dear Jerry,

I am so sorry to hear about the recent passing of your wife. I'm in shock because I've been reading Bella's messages and laughing at her jokes and imagining the person who wrote them. So to find out she's no longer here is incredibly sad. I can't imagine how you are feeling.

She was clearly a smart and generous woman, with a great sense of humor to boot. I wish I could thank her for all the work she put into the guidebook. In fact, I've taken her words to heart and decided to extend my trip!

If you feel up to it can you tell me more about Bella? I'd like to know her better and also hear why you were in South America.

I hope you are doing OK at this difficult time, Jerry. Please don't hesitate to email me anytime ☺ My heartfelt condolences on your loss,
Ellie.

CHAPTER 15

San Francisco, USA

Jerry sat in the shade of a large umbrella at one end of his parents' backyard. From behind sunglasses, he watched his daughters skid down a slide and splash into the pool. Yasmina and Andrea then took turns pushing Mia around on an inflatable flamingo. After everything they'd been through, it sure was heartening to see them having fun again.

"Who'd like a brownie?" Carol, Jerry's mom, came out of the house with a tray of freshly-baked treats and glasses of milk. She had a relaxed face and ponytail of sandy hair that made her look younger than her sixty-five years.

"Me, me, me!" the kids screamed.

"You'd better come out and dry off then. We don't want food dropping in the pool or your grandpa will get grumpy." Yasmina, Andrea and Mia scrambled out of the water and grabbed at the brownies. "Jerry?"

"No thanks, Mom."

"You look thin."

"I'm not—"

"I'll just leave this here." She wrapped a brownie in a napkin and placed it on the table. "You used to eat ten of these a day when you were a teenager."

"Thanks," Jerry sighed. Unfortunately his metabolism had slowed drastically since then. He took a bite and went back to his laptop.

Dear Ellie,

Thank you for your condolences. Bella was an extraordinary woman with a tremendous passion for living, and people always wanted to be around her to soak in that energy. She was also an outstanding mother to our three daughters. Everything she did in life, she did for them. There's not a minute goes by when we don't miss her.

We traveled to South America last July, so about a year ago now. At first it was just Bella and me in Venezuela, finally celebrating the honeymoon we never had because she was pregnant when we got married—scandal! Then our girls joined us in Colombia to start a 3 month family vacation. Unfortunately, we had to come home a few weeks early because Bella fell ill in Argentina, suffering from terrible migraines. It was only after we got back that the doctors found the tumors. Too late, it turned out.

We were blindsided by the diagnosis. How do you cram a whole lifetime into a few months? There wasn't enough time to say all the things we wanted to say to each other. Bella was so frail in the end, I couldn't even hold her. She passed on the 11th of January.

Oh geez, I've rambled. Sorry about that. I could talk about Bella for days and then some. So now you know about my family, what about you and yours? Who are you traveling with? How long are you traveling for?

And, most importantly, why are you traveling?
Keep safe and thanks again for your kind words,
Jerry.

"When are you going to get off that thing?" Don squeezed his son's shoulders from behind. He was almost as tall as Jerry, with gray hair flowing in lush swells over his head. "You can't work all weekend."

"It's not work."

"What is it then?"

"Nothing." Jerry closed his laptop.

"You look tired."

"I am tired. What's up?"

"I'm trying to avoid your mother's cooking. Her latest health trick is to grate carrots into the brownies. Not sure if the kids noticed, but it ruins a perfectly good brownie if you ask me."

They watched the girls gulp down their milk. Yasmina pushed Andrea and Mia back into the pool, then jumped in after them.

"How are they going?" Don said.

"Doing it tough. Not exactly saying so, but it's coming out in other ways."

"You know we want to help out. Take some pressure off."

"I can do it, Dad. I'm not hopeless."

"No-one's saying you are hopeless, Jerry. You're doing a fantastic job. But a little help never went astray. Let us make some meals for you at least. Or we could take them to see a movie. Your mother would love it if you asked her to do that. You don't have to raise these kids alone, you know."

"I know," Jerry nodded. So who was he trying to prove it to?

"Dad, come play with us!" Mia shouted.

Jerry pulled off his shirt and ran toward the pool, jumping high in the air and landing with a massive bomb.

CHAPTER 16

Somewhere in Venezuela

What on earth have I done?
That was the question cycling through Ellie's head as she sat squashed in the last row of a bus hurtling down a pockmarked highway. They'd left Caracas eleven hours ago and Ellie stayed awake since then, arms wrapped around her daypack to protect her most valuable possessions. The seat was as hard as the bleachers at Yankee Stadium and the woman sleeping beside her had invaded—then occupied—her personal space. It didn't help that her period had arrived this morning and Ellie felt like her ovaries were going to explode.

If Donna could see me now, she'd have a fricking field day.

Ellie's sister had been unimpressed, to put it politely, about her decision to stay in South America. But she held firm, even when Donna threatened to send a team of mercenaries to drag her ass home. In the heat of the fight Ellie had yelled, "Sometimes you need to throw a grenade into your life and see what happens!" She wasn't sure she believed it, but it sounded good at the time.

The bus jumped over a pothole and the woman's head slid further down Ellie's arm. She tried to keep sane by reading up on her destination in the *Unique Planet*. At the top of a page with information about visiting a coffee plantation in Colombia, Bella had drawn a sketch of Ringo Starr and scribbled a note: 'Get high with help from your friends! Start your morning with a mind-blowing, heart-pounding, love-making coffee direct from the source.'

Ellie smiled, because she worshipped the brown bean too. It was the one vice she never planned on rehabbing. She opened her TO DO list and added GET HIGH ON COFFEE PLANTATION to the bottom.

Ellie sensed the bus slowing. She pulled back the curtain. The night was murky, but she could make out an empty warehouse with a tattered flag. Was this the border? A band of soldiers swaggered out of the warehouse, machine guns slung across their necks like baseball bats and restraining a pair of barking dogs. Ellie checked her phone—3 a.m.

Awesome.

The bus driver shut off the engine and shouted something inaudible, not that Ellie would've been able to understand it. The half-hour each day learning *Español* on Duolingo hadn't got her very far. Passengers began moving out of their seats and she joined the exodus with little clue what would happen next.

Stepping off the bus, Ellie felt even more vulnerable. The soldiers leered at her like she was the only female at a sausage party. She *was* the only white person. Ellie kept her head down to avoid their penetrating gaze.

The compartments under the bus were thrown open and passengers somehow retrieved their luggage despite the chaos. It boggled her mind that lining up wasn't a thing in Latin America. How did society function? After being jostled on all sides, Ellie eventually got a hand on her backpack and dumped it in the warehouse with the others.

Everyone took a silent step in retreat as the dogs scrambled over their bags, furiously sniffing for God-knows-what.

Emergency supplies of candy weren't illegal, right? Ellie waved air at her sweltering face, swatted away a few unidentified bugs, and concluded that middle-of-the night border crossings sucked.

"*Pasaporte*," an officer said. His scowl seemed painted on.

Ellie wondered why no-one else was being targeted, but this probably wasn't the time or place for an argument. She opened her daypack and dug out her passport.

"*Norteamericana?*" He flicked to the photo page.

"*Sí*," Ellie replied, trying not to sound too patriotic. Out of the corner of her eye, she could see other passengers watching, nervous about befalling the same fate. Sweat ran down the front of her neck, tickling like a feather duster. She waited as long as possible before wiping it off. The officer noticed, and she noticed that he noticed, making her sweat even more.

Damn. It's hard to look innocent when you are actually innocent.

"*Cuál es tu maleta?*" he said.

Ellie shrugged her shoulders, unsure what he meant.

"*Cuál es tu maleta?!*"

Ellie flinched as he raised his voice and gestured to the luggage on the floor.

"That one." She pointed to her backpack. "The blue one."

The officer handed her passport to a second uniformed man, who walked away with it.

"Hey, that's my passport," Ellie said, but no-one cared.

The officer carried her backpack to a trestle table. She followed close behind, growing more concerned with each shallow breath.

"*Ábrela.*"

She opened the combination lock and stood motionless while he pulled items from her pack. He started with pants and t-shirts, then moved onto her underwear, which he took sick pleasure in holding up to the light and examining as if it were evidence in a murder case.

Ellie fumed blazing red. She had to bite her tongue to stop from verbalizing that he was an asshole.

He unzipped Ellie's toiletries bag next, and her heart sank. He took out packets of tampons and pads—then the condoms Donna had given her as a going-away present. He inspected them like the safety of the Colombian state depended on it.

Ellie was sure she heard someone stifle a laugh, but didn't turn around. Her rage was focused on only one man. And she let him know it through a glare that bore into his skull like Supergirl's laser vision.

Giant. Asshole.

After removing everything but finding no contraband, the officer waved dismissively for Ellie to put it all back in.

"What about my passport?" she asked as he walked off. "*Pasaporte?*"

Meanwhile, the other passengers had been given the all-clear to collect their bags and return to the bus.

Ellie shoved her belongings into her backpack. But without time for the methodical Ellie Bartlett Packing Process™, they wouldn't fit. She frantically punched the top to squash it all down.

Most of the passengers had already made it onto the bus. Surely it wouldn't leave? The engine roared to life.

"Wait!" Ellie yelled. She pulled out her jacket so the backpack would close. Fumbled with the lock. Dropped it on the concrete. "Shit. Where's my passport?"

The second officer returned and handed it back without comment.

She threw on her backpack—and ran.

CHAPTER 17

Santa Marta, Colombia

After twenty-four grueling hours, the insect-splattered bus finally limped into a terminal. Ellie shook out her legs before dodging through a mob of hawkers selling snacks, phone accessories and pirated DVDs. Cheerleader porn appeared to be popular.

She found a currency exchange shop, where a chubby man straddled a stool with his pot-belly flopping out. Ellie had checked the U.S. dollar to Colombian peso rate online before leaving Venezuela so rejected his first offer. She did a quick calculation on her phone and they compromised somewhere in the middle. Truth be told, she just wanted to get to her hostel and pee. Really, *really*, pee.

The bathroom attached to the four-bed dorm provided much-needed relief. There was also sublime air-con and privacy curtains around each bed. Outside the window, guests lazed on deck chairs by a pool, soaking up the sun and drinking beers, just like at a hotel. There was even a cafe serving hot food. Ellie's stomach rumbled but sleep took priority. She rolled over and closed her eyes. It felt so good to be horizontal.

"Hey, what's ya name?" A young woman with a cockney accent pulled back the curtain.

Ellie sat up and rubbed her face, unsure how long she'd been in shut-eye mode. Weren't the curtains supposed to keep people out?

"I'm Nora. Nora the Explora." Slim as a rake, with a baby-face and bob of black hair, Nora had so much energy she bounced from foot-to-foot.

"Nora the Explorer? That's funny."

"It's Explor-a, with an 'a.' You on Insta? You should follo' me."

"Where are you from?"

"East London. And proud of it, bitch." She made a sign with her hand that Ellie didn't recognize but took to mean *proud of it, bitch*. "How long you been travelin'?"

"Two weeks."

"You're a 'noob. Sweet. You wanna come out late-a? We're gonna hit Taganga."

"I'm not sure. I'm super tired."

"C'mon, it'll be fun."

"What's there? In Taganga." And if you hit it, does it hit back?

"Clubs. Drinks. Boys. Should be lit A.F."

"Lit A.F? I'll think about it."

"Perfect! It'll be, like, cool to have someone new to chat with."

Ellie wasn't sure she'd agreed to anything, but smiled at how quickly you became friends with strangers while traveling.

"Where'd you fly in from?" Nora grabbed hold of the bed frame and swung on it like a monkey.

"I took the bus from Venezuela."

"Fuck me! I heard that's dangerous. Much respect. Hey Suse, this chick just arrived from Ven–iz–wayla."

"Holy shit, bitch!" a girl who must be Suse said, coming through the door and offering Ellie a fist bump. "Baller move.

Nothin' like a bit of danger to get the juices, y'know, flowin'."

She was practically the spitting image of Nora, except with brown hair, and it occurred to Ellie that they both knew how attractive they were.

"Where have you guys been?" Ellie asked.

"We start'd in Asia, like, two months ago, Thailand and Vietnam and shit. Then Peru, Brazil and now we're here for a week of sun and beach—"

"And boys," Suse added.

"Yeah, and boys. Then headin' back to the U.K. 'cos my beauty course is startin' soon."

"It sounds like you've had a great time."

"Totes amazeballs. T.B.H. we've been fucked-up for most of it tho', so it's good to have some chillax time here, innit?"

"This hostel does seem really nice compared to the others I've stayed at," Ellie said.

"One of the best. Hot water, too. Suse, you 'member that twenty bed poohole in Hanoi? Mofo was horrific. I'll give ya some advice, if the hostel has a *chicas*-only dorm, jump in it. You won't meet as many *hombres*, which might be a problem if you're horny as a fucken' rabbit like Suse here, but there's less chance of some random tosser snorin' all night."

Between the accent and slang, Ellie took a while to comprehend what Nora was saying.

"I'm goin' with this t'night. What do ya girls think?" Suse cocked her hips and held up a red dress bright enough to attract a bull.

Oh uh.

By nightfall, the quaint fishing village of Taganga had morphed into a nightclub. Ellie and her British friends zigzagged along the beach between groups of locals spilling out of sandy bars. She wiped her palms on the one skirt she'd brought for her trip, feeling overdressed but glad she wasn't wearing a butt-flashing mini like Nora and Suse. Ellie believed in leaving something to the imagination because, y'know, standards.

The men ogling as they paraded past were also half-dressed as shirts were optional in Taganga. For good reason too, because most of them had bronzed torsos and ripped abs like they'd just walked off an infomercial for the latest home gym gizmo. Ellie tried not to stare. It was hard.

Nora and Suse were right at home in this setting, making a beeline for a bar and ordering a row of shots. The bartender splashed liquor over three bigger-than-usual glasses.

"What is it?" Ellie shouted above the reggaetón music.

"Rum!" Nora passed her a glass.

Ellie sniffed the alcohol. Cheap. Probably nasty. Nora and Suse slugged theirs without hesitation. Ellie shrugged, then did the same. Her throat burned like gasoline poured down it. "Shit."

"You know it, bitch." Nora ordered a second round.

Ellie surveyed the dancefloor. The club was becoming more crowded by the minute—and hotter, as local men taught foreign women how to dance *salsa*. Their bodies moved in tandem, twirling away from each other, then coming together, getting closer until they were skin-to-skin. The way they moved was intoxicating. No wonder Latinos were considered the most sensual dancers.

Sensual.

Ellie liked the sound of that word. Maybe it was the rum.

They downed a third round, then Nora and Suse dragged Ellie onto the dancefloor. She noticed a young Colombian man checking her out from across the room. His smoky eyes tracked her like a spotlight, and his jet-black hair was combed perfectly across his head as if he'd stepped out of a classic Hollywood movie.

"You should dance with him." Nora elbowed her in the ribs.

"It's been a while since I've danced," Ellie replied. It'd been a while since she'd done anything.

"Time's up."

Clark Gable left his friends and made his way through the crowd, never breaking Ellie's gaze. Without a word, he took her hand, drew her hips close so their crotches nestled, and taught her how to *salsa*. Back and forth. Smooth. *Sensual.*

Ellie wrapped her arms around his neck and felt his warmth spread over her like really fucking hot butter. His brown skin was smooth and his sweat smelled sweet. She thought about licking it but caught herself just in time. After all, she was a bit drunk and probably shouldn't go licking people.

At least not yet.

CHAPTER 18

Santa Marta, Colombia

"Why didn't ya ride his ding-a-ling?" Nora asked mid-bite, egg slopping out of her mouth.

Ellie coughed up her coffee. Ravenous after their big night, she and Nora sat by the pool gorging on omelets, hash browns, papaya and whatever else fit on their plates. "I'm…I guess I'm not ready for that yet," Ellie said.

"Y'know, I have this theory that no-one is ever really ready for anythin'. So now is just as good a time as any. Best to be, like, spontaneous. Gets me in the shit from time-to-time but mostly works out OK. Juice?"

"Thanks. I'm glad that philosophy has been working for you." Ellie was more than a little envious of Nora's carefree attitude to life.

"Don't worry, you just start'd backpackin' so you'll loosen up. So to speak." Nora laughed noisily at her own joke and Ellie couldn't help but join in. "Hey look, our Suse is back. With a limp."

Making her way gingerly around the pool, Suse joined Ellie and Nora at the table. Clothes crumpled and hair a total mess, she hid from the day behind Jackie-O sunglasses.

"Morning, bitch! You have fun last night?" Nora stuck her tongue between her middle and index fingers and wiggled it around. That sign Ellie did understand.

"Wow," Suse said in a state of happy shock.

"So you went B-A-N-A-N-A-S with sexy Latin boy?"

"Wow," Suse repeated.

"Is there anythin' you'd like to add?"

"Wow. And tea."

"OK babe, just enjoy the moment." Nora poured her friend a cup.

"I've never cum like that. I think he broke my pussy."

The trio collapsed with laughter that rang through the hostel. Ellie hadn't laughed out loud like that in a long time. A real belly laugh releasing her body of all tension.

Maybe one day I'll let myself get that lucky.

"Hey Ellie, what ya doin' tomorrow?" Nora said after they'd caught their breath.

"I've been reading about the Lost City—"

"O.M.G. that's what we're doing! You gotta come with. It's meant to be, like, bangin'. I mean, we're not really into hikin' and shit—"

"Or bugs," Suse added.

"Yeah, or bugs, but the photos will be ace for my Insta ranking."

"Maybe I will."

"Well, remember not to think about things too much."

Ellie snorted a disappointed laugh at how easily she'd reverted to her old pattern of thinking. Except it wasn't a pattern, it was a cage.

Why aren't I more spontaneous? Am I scared of making the wrong choice? Afraid of missing out on something else? Terrified of being trapped? All of the above…

It was paralyzing. Sometimes she didn't make her mind up

until she reached breaking point, other times she waited too long and the opportunity was lost. It was no way to live. Time to change, for good.

> *Dear Jerry,*
> *Thank you for telling me about Bella. Her passion jumps off the page and I feel truly blessed to have found her guidebook. And don't apologize for rambling about your family. I'm happy to read it* 😊
> *It's great to hear that you have THREE daughters, though I imagine they can be quite a handful, especially during those tricky teenage years… How are they coping without their mom? I lost both my parents in the last few years so know how difficult it is to figure out life without them, even as an adult.*
> *To answer your questions, I'm 31 (as hard as that is to admit) and just started a solo backpacking trip in South America. I left my finance job in NYC to come down here and find a new direction in life—or something. To be honest, I'm not exactly sure what I'm doing… I hope it will reveal itself soon. It better!*
> *I've met a couple of girls at my hostel and decided to join them on a hike to the Lost City of Tayrona, so if you don't hear from me again I've either been captured by an undiscovered tribe, swallowed by an anaconda, or eaten alive by killer mosquitos. I'm not sure which would be worse* 😲
> *Ellie.*

San Francisco, USA

Jerry chuckled as he read her email. After another combative dinner with his daughters, he'd retreated to his study where this digital conversation with Ellie was turning out to be a welcome break from the twin stresses of family and work.

> *Dear Ellie,*
> *It's quite an adventure you're having and it's only just begun. I'm excited for you!*
> *Our girls were never bored down there so that says something. After we came home it was very difficult for them though. The rapid decline in Bella's health was such a shock. As the doctors kept telling us, it's hard to know with cancer—a patient could have a few months or a few years. Bella put up a huge fight, a brave one, but in the end the tumors had spread too quickly to be operated on. Of course she never let the girls know how scared she was. And as much as they drive me crazy sometimes, they are my greatest joy. There's Yasmina, 17, intense like her mom.*

Jerry flung open the door to Yasmina's room. She lay in bed, texting on her phone. The desk in the corner was stacked with unopened textbooks and dirty mugs.

"Dad, you can't just barge into my room! You have to knock."

"It's my house. I can do what I—"

"You can't! I have a right to privacy, y'know."

"Well, it's great you've been listening in civics class. I wouldn't be here if I didn't need to be, but I just received an email from Principal Mercer."

Yasmina groaned. "Why can't they leave me alone?"

"Because apparently you've been cutting class. Is it true?"

She went back to playing with her phone.

"Jesus, you can't just turn up to school whenever you feel like it. Do you want to graduate?"

"I hate science."

"You used to love it."

"When I was seven, Dad. I'm seventeen now."

"A very immature seventeen year-old who's currently acting like a seven year-old."

"I'm not. And the class is stupid!" Yasmina yelled, kicking her sheets in frustration. "Every lesson we revise the periodic table, which I memorized in week one."

Jerry almost smiled. She didn't just have her mom's stubborn streak, but her brains too. "Yas, I know you're almost an adult. And I want to treat you like one. But if you continue to act like you don't have responsibilities, I can't. And we're just going to have more conflict."

"Whatever."

"Not 'whatever.' Principal Mercer has sent extra work for you to complete so I expect it to be finished by tomorrow morning."

"I'm tired," Yasmina grumbled.

"Tired from what? Messaging on your phone all night?"

"I can message whenever I want."

"No, you can't. In fact, I pay for the damn phone and I think it's best you give it up for a while."

"No." Yasmina held her phone to her chest like it was the most important thing in her life.

"A break will do you good because you clearly can't focus on anything else. Give it to me, please."

"No." She clutched it tighter. Jerry tried to take it away. Their hands wrestled. Yasmina's fingernails dug into his skin.

"Ouch, Yasmina. Give it to me, now!"

"Fuck off!"

Jerry glared at his daughter.

Yasmina lowered her head.

They stayed that way for a while before he spoke. "Yasmina

Vasquez Townsend, you will never talk to me like that again. Ever. Do you understand?" He held out his hand and she handed over her phone.

OK, let me rephrase that last part because I just had an argument with my eldest. Yas has been pushing back so hard these past few months. She never used to be like this, and I know she isn't handling her mom's passing well, but I'm at a loss what to do about it. She's angry at the world and we've reached a new low in our relationship. Sorry to drop all this on you Ellie, I'm venting on the keyboard here.

Besides the child who hates me, there's Andrea, 12, who is quiet and well-behaved, and Mia, 7, who surprises and inspires me every day. She's so enthusiastic about discovering the world. Wouldn't it be great to be a kid again?

I am definitely outnumbered by these girls, and they know it. It's only a matter of time before my defenses are overrun—Custer's Last Stand or something like that. Bella always knew what to say to them, or at the very least we could play good-cop bad-cop. Damn, I've gone on again, haven't I?

Thanks for listening, Ellie, and good luck on your trek. If you survive the killer mosquitos be sure to spend some time exploring Cartagena. It's an enchanting place, Jerry.

CHAPTER 19

Five Days Later – Cartagena, Colombia

A gusty sea breeze blew through Ellie's clothes as she walked out of her hostel and into the beating heart of Cartagena's old town. A horse-and-cart rattled down the cobblestone street, lined with blue and pink colonial homes that had sweet-smelling flowers growing on their balconies. The solemn bell of the cathedral rang over the rooftops to complete the feeling that Ellie had been transported back to the 17th century.

Enchanting is definitely the word.

She'd taken the previous day off to wash clothes and call Donna to let her know she wasn't dead. Ellie also sent a photo of her standing on top the 1,000 year-old ruins of the Lost City, eyes stinging with sweat from bashing through the jungle and fighting off insects like a ninja. Below her, a series of circular stone plazas descended to a sacred boulder, its significance long lost to human knowledge. She'd imagined them sacrificing monkeys on it, or virgins, or her so she wouldn't have to walk back down.

Ellie stretched the muscles in her stiff legs. Her body still hadn't fully recovered, and she understood now that backpacking wasn't a vacation like her family and friends thought. It was absolutely exhausting, a non-stop test of every element of her being.

She inspected the legion of bites on her arms. They looked like red freckles and itched like poison ivy. Not such a great ninja after all. But this was the price you paid for adventure—and the decision was *forever* worth it.

Ellie meandered through narrow laneways until she reached the town square. Buzzing with activity, it was as loud as it was colorful. Food carts sold grilled *maiz* (corn on the cob), baked *almojábanas* (bread buns filled with cheese), and eye-popping tropical fruit. She bought a freshly-sliced mango from a brawny old man wielding his machete like a samurai. Its tangy nectar murdered her taste buds. In a good way.

Choosing a bench between the trees, Ellie spotted what was beginning to seem like the mandatory statue of Simon Bolivar.

"We have to stop meeting like this, Mr. Bolivar. People will start to talk. Although I wouldn't mind if they did. How about you?" Yes, it felt weird talking to an inanimate object, but he'd been the only constant companion on her trip. "Still at a loss for words? Perhaps we can chat later then. I'm sure we'll see each other again."

Ellie snapped out of her Mr. Darcy fantasy and navigated to the Castillo San Felipe de Barajas fortress that loomed over Cartagena. She rented an audio guide and explored the imposing stone battlements with their labyrinth of tunnels and hundreds of cannons still pointed out to sea.

Construction of the Spanish castle had begun in 1536 to repel British and French naval attacks, and to guard against raids from the notorious pirate Sir Francis Drake. The military strategy of the invading forces was to blockade the city and starve its inhabitants, while the strategy of the Spanish was to wait out the attackers in the hope they got bitten by mosquitos and died a horrible death from malaria or yellow fever. Brilliant.

Ellie stood on the highest turret and looked over Cartagena, hearing about the millions of people killed in the Spanish conquest of Latin America. Not just due to the actions of the Spanish kingdom, but also the Catholic Church, and not just from wars against the indigenous populations, but also the evil of slavery.

Unbelievably, *over twelve million* Africans had been brought against their will across the Atlantic by the Spanish and Portuguese from the 16th to 19th centuries. That dwarfed the approximately 400,000 taken by the British to North America. The number of people displaced and killed was staggering. The tragedy, that humanity could do all this to itself, difficult to comprehend.

Ellie's heart weighed heavy. But her contemplative mood was shattered by a loud tour group overrunning the fort. Another arrived. Then another. Soon Ellie was hemmed in by hordes of obese tourists. She tried not to be judgmental—

But. Seriously. These people are gonna pass out before they reach the top. And what's with the fanny packs? Did 1980s cruise ship fashion come back and I didn't get the memo?

The tourists moaned with each step. Some held battery-powered fans in front of their ruddy faces. Others looked like they were melting. Frustrated guides waved signs and shouted instructions, corralling them like sheep. Ellie noticed how everyone was viewing the other groups with suspicion, as if to ensure they were having more fun. But none of them were having fun!

Why do people on tours always look so fricking miserable? They're hating the humidity and just want to get back to their hotel for a nap. Why. Did. You. Even. Come.

A woman who'd eaten too many maple bacon waffles at the breakfast buffet suddenly fainted, falling backward and causing a domino effect down the line.

The whole scene reminded Ellie of the last time she'd taken a tour. Rome, four years ago, with the boring investment banker. They'd been whisked from one attraction to the next, from the Colosseum to the Trevi Fountain to the Pantheon, with barely enough time to appreciate any of them. Ellie hated most of the people on her tour, especially the bug-eyed woman who kept wanting to take group selfies.

In summary—tours stink.

Ellie dodged the crowd, escaping through an exit. Under the scorching midday sun, she stopped to take a drink of water and watched an open-topped double-decker bus rumble around the corner. Her face froze as the tourists on the top deck stood to take photos of the fortress as they drove past.

"What's going on?" Ellie said to anyone listening.

They don't even stop?

They just hang off the side of a bus taking blurry pictures they're not even in?!

Surely this was the ultimate travel offense. A goddamn felony. People could say they'd been half-way around the world but never stepped foot outside their own bubble. It was true what Paul Theroux wrote; tourists have no idea where they are, travelers don't know where they're headed. Now that she was a traveler, Ellie wouldn't have had it any other way.

Where will I go next?

CHAPTER 20

Cartagena, Colombia

'Be Alice. Go down the rabbit hole…' was Bella's cryptic message. She'd written it at the start of a wriggly green line on the city map in her *Unique Planet*.

Ellie followed the line, stumbling across vibrant murals sprinkled throughout the fisherman's district. Every corner revealed a surprise painting of traditional life by the Caribbean Sea. She also found some not marked. Ellie reveled in the freedom of being able to explore without any boundaries. She could do *whatever* she wanted, *whenever* she wanted.

Bella had also drawn a love heart to highlight the house of celebrated Colombian author Gabriel García Márquez. Ellie took a photo of his famous words painted on the front wall. Thankfully, Bella had paraphrased them in English: 'The unhappiest place in the world is an empty bed.'

The words bounced around Ellie's head like a pinball while she strolled along the massive 400 year-old stone wall shielding Cartagena from the ocean. She chose a place to sit at its most western point where waves crashed onto shore and seagulls glided on updrafts.

The sun was only a few minutes from dipping beneath the horizon—or more accurately, as her dad had liked to explain, the earth was in fact the one moving, spinning counter-clockwise around the sun. "It should really be called earthturn not sunset," he'd always said.

Dotted along the wall were local couples, holding hands or embracing, enjoying the optical illusion of sun meeting sea. Some rested in fortified nooks where musketmen once stood guard, others straddled huge cannons that remained as a symbol of a more dangerous time in the city's history.

Ellie forgot the colors of the sunset for a minute and studied the closest couple. How the boy's hand gently touched the girl's hip, how she sank into his chest, how he whispered in her ear and made her laugh, how her hair danced in the wind and draped over his neck, how they wrapped their fingers together. Their bodies melded into one beautiful, erotic, sculpture. Like they were made for each other. And when they kissed there was a surge of energy that couldn't be explained—so powerful, almost visible—yet elusive to Ellie.

As happy as she was for the young lovers, watching them with a voyeur's eye only made her feel more alone. And not just alone, because she'd been alone and happy before, but alone *and lonely*.

Ellie had usually managed to fill these gaps in her life. Eating a tub of Häagen-Dazs Salted Caramel ice-cream was her preferred activity to avoid the ordeal of finding and maintaining intimacy with another human. But now she felt naked sitting here, as if her feelings were laid bare and she couldn't hide from them any longer. She couldn't hide from herself.

Ellie knew she needed to accept the truth. She was lonely. In one of the most romantic places on the planet, she had no-one to share her life with.

Fuck, it hurts.

Dear Jerry,

Please write me about your daughters anytime. I'm sure you're doing a wonderful job raising them in very difficult circumstances.

I know it's none of my business to advise you on Yasmina…but I was a teenage girl once so know something about it 😌 You're right, she's acting out because she's in pain, but the only way to heal it is to give her an avenue to express herself. Otherwise she's just going to push you again and again and again (like I did to my dad!) So I suggest not pushing back. Talk with her like an adult, even if she isn't quite there yet. She'll appreciate it and I bet she'll step up to the plate. Oh, and be patient if you can—although that's pretty rich coming from me 😂

As you predicted, I love Cartagena. I'm sitting on one of the cute little balconies right now, watching fireworks and imagining Romeo & Juliet courting each other with poetic verses. It's so dreamy, and there's so many couples sharing time together here, but…I don't have that with anyone.

To be candid, it makes me really sad. My love life has always felt a bit like musical chairs, where I'm the kid at the party who misses out and goes home empty handed. But I really want to have a connection with someone. I guess I was unprepared for the loneliness that comes with being a solo traveler.

Anyway, I just needed to get that off my chest, even if we hardly know each other. I know you've experienced much greater pain than me, Jerry, so I hope you don't mind me ranting. Thanks for listening 😊

Ellie.

The emptiness inside her rib cage didn't subside by the time she drifted off to sleep. But Ellie did think how nice it was to have someone she could write to about her emotions without any fear of judgement. Strange, but nice.

San Francisco, USA

It'd been a helluva day. Most of the lights in the office were off and all his employees had left hours ago, but Jerry was still sketching at a drafting table. Coffee and Springsteen's *Born to Run* kept him awake, until the ding of a new email broke his concentration.

> *Dear Ellie,*
> *Thanks for your advice about Yas. I'll organize some time for just the two of us this weekend and hopefully we can talk like adults. We used to be so close, but everything's been turned upside down.*

"When are you going home?"

"Jesus!" Jerry jumped. "Are you trying to give me a heart attack, Kyra."

"You're skittish tonight."

"What are you doing here so late?"

She adjusted the hem of her evening dress. "I'm meeting a friend for dinner and didn't want to go home first."

"Meeting a friend for dinner…like a date?"

"Not that it's any of your business, but yes."

"That's nice."

"I'll let you know in the morning."

"Please don't."

"You'll be able to tell how nice it was from the smile on my face. Big smile means—"

"Why don't you take the day off?" Jerry said. "Call in sick. I don't want you even hinting at what you get up to tonight."

"You should come."

"What for? To watch you fawn over some guy in a cheap suit."

"I could set you up with my flatmate and we could double date…" Kyra trailed off into a shocked gasp.

Jerry snapped his eyes back to his laptop. His face burned as much as his heart.

"Oh God, Jerry. I'm sorry, I didn't mean to say that. That was really insensitive of me."

"It's OK."

"No, I'm really sorry. I got carried away. I should have thought my words through."

"It's OK, Kyra. Don't worry about it."

"Are you sure?"

"Yes. Go have fun tonight. You look great."

She hesitated. "See you later."

"See you." Jerry took off his glasses and rubbed his eyes. Oh, shoot. Kyra's suggestion had unsettled him. The only person he wanted was Bella, and since her death it hadn't occurred to him that he would ever go out on another date. He reckoned his race was run in that respect. Besides, he had three girls to bring up and a museum to finish.

I understand the feeling of loneliness you described, Ellie. I know it all too well. It can be unbearable. But you're still young and, as far as I can tell, grounded and intelligent. There is someone out there for you. I never thought I'd meet the love of my life when I walked into Design 101 on my first day of college, so you'll probably meet someone when you least expect it too. Isn't that always the way?

And here's a story—Bella only agreed to go on a date

with me if I won a bet to score higher than her on the midterms. I never studied so hard in my life and bested her by just 1%, but that was all I needed and within 18 months we had a very unexpected baby on the way. The same baby who is now a teenager giving me all this grief!

My point is that life has many swings and roundabouts, so just relax, be open, and enjoy the journey. Not only will there be new places, but also new people.

Take care and please keep me updated on your adventures,

Jerry.

He had to admit it was peculiar, two strangers sharing intimate details about each other's lives. But he liked this back-and-forth with Ellie. After all, nobody else was going to listen to him reminisce about Bella at eight o'clock on a Thursday night.

CHAPTER 21

Medellín, Colombia

Midnight ticked by when Ellie checked into a hostel in what had once been the world's most violent city. She was deep in the traveling groove now, moving every day or three, and the nomadic life had become second nature.

Not that it was all smooth sailing. The app she'd booked through made no mention of the 3-for-1 drinks at the hostel bar tonight. Aussies and Brits crowded inside, getting shitfaced and arguing about cricket.

She sidestepped the madness and got ready for bed. The cramped bathroom had what was referred to as a 'suicide shower'—an electric head with live wires running out of it. Smart invention. Every time Ellie endured one of these near-death experiences, she was surprised by her tenacity. It helped if you closed your eyes.

She slipped into her PJs and put in newly-purchased earplugs. With everyone else in the bar, Ellie switched off the lights in the dorm and faded to blissful sleep…

At first she couldn't identify the sound. It was vaguely familiar and loud enough to wake her up, but remained a mystery. Ellie raised her head and rested on her elbows, eyes adjusting to the darkness.

The sound got louder. And faster. She pulled out her earplugs. It sounded like a wet rag being hit repeatedly against a wall. Ellie pinpointed the direction it was coming from and turned to the bed opposite.

Oh, shit.

Her eyeballs got sucker-punched by a young man and woman having wild sex. She was lying on her back with legs high in the air while he pounded her crotch—the sound of a wet rag being hit against a wall.

Ellie stared for a moment, not quite believing what she was seeing. No-one had warned her about dorm sex. It wasn't something she'd ever contemplated. Yet here it was. Up close. And gross. And getting louder. And faster.

The man thrusted so hard the woman's head banged against the bunk like a metronome. It kept time on a chorus of beastly moans.

Hang on, I didn't pay to watch this sex show.

But what's the etiquette?

I mean, once it's started can it be interrupted? Can I say, "Excuse me, could you please stop screwing each other's brains out? I'm trying to sleep over here. Thank you very much and good night."

"Oh, yes, there."

"I love your pussy."

"I love your cock."

"I love your pussy more Amanda."

"It's Miranda. And I love your cock more. There, there!"

"Fuck yes, baby."

"What's your name?"

"Jack."

"Fuck, Jack. Fuck! Faster!"

As the physical and verbal intercourse became more extreme,

Ellie turned away and jammed her earplugs back in, for the little good they would do. She shut her eyes and tried to block out the visual, but her head flooded with emotions.

First, there was shock that people would want to have sex in public. Second, she was angry because they didn't care about waking her up. Third, Ellie was jealous. She wanted to have sex. She wanted to feel that pleasure. She wanted to be wanted. Their ecstasy reminded Ellie her bed was empty. The symphony suddenly stopped.

Oh, thank God. That didn't last long.

"It broke," Ellie heard the man say.

"Don't worry, I won't get pregnant," the woman said.

"You sure?"

"Just fuck me!"

So it started again. The sound of a wet rag being hit against a wall.

Ellie pulled her pillow over her ears and tried not to scream.

Jardín, Colombia

The sensation of soft grass tickling her skin put Ellie on cloud nine. Wandering barefoot among the coffee trees growing in the cool highlands a mile above sea-level was a pleasant respite from horny backpackers. Lush plantations coated every mountain in this caffeine lover's utopia.

Ellie had just finished a tour of a coffee factory, learning that the small fruit, or 'cherry,' became a deep red when ripe, and after harvesting was dried in the sun. The outer husk was then removed in a rolling machine to reveal a green bean, which when roasted *magically* transformed into the aromatic brown bean everyone loved. Next came grinding, and the final step of brewing to create the perfect cup of joe. Bella was right, the smell of the factory had left Ellie flying!

Up ahead, she spotted a half-dozen women sitting in the shade between the trees. They had handwoven baskets and wore traditional clothes for this region: flowing black skirts, white blouses, and red kerchiefs.

As she got closer, Ellie noticed their shoes were held together by string and they were mostly older women—or they looked older, prematurely weathered by long hours of back-breaking work under the unforgiving sun.

"*Hola.*" Ellie greeted them with a smile.

"*Hola chica. Por favor, siéntate aquí,*" one of the women replied, gesturing for her to join them.

Ellie sat cross-legged on the grass and exchanged friendly nods as the woman poured her a cup of thick black coffee from a bamboo flask. "*Muchas gracias.*" Ellie sniffed the vapors curling off the cup and fell head-over-heels for the rich aroma. She took a sip, savoring the earthy flavor flowing over her tongue like liquid gold. The caffeine hit zoomed through her brain. "Wow!"

The women broke into laughter. "*Fuerte, fuerte.*"

"That's strong."

Another woman lifted the cloth on her basket and offered Ellie a piece of *torta de guayaba*, a pound cake made with guava paste. She gobbled it up and drank her coffee while the women chatted and laughed, loud goofy laughs exposing mouths of missing teeth. With wrinkled faces, gnarled hands and hunched spines, Ellie imagined them toiling from sunrise till sunset, then heading home to take care of their families.

Though she couldn't understand them, she could sense the bond they shared. You had to be inspired by their resilience, their ability to find joy in the face of dreadful poverty.

The youngest of the group couldn't have been more than eighteen. She had a model's face, with angles revealing her indigenous heritage, outlined by pitch-black hair plaited down to her hips. Her dark brown eyes were inviting, her full-lipped smile infectious. Ellie wondered how this girl could be so happy when her life had already been laid out before her in the faces and bodies of the older women.

How spoilt we are in America. We have all the choices in the world compared to these women, yet still bitch and moan about our lives.

They work for a pittance and will never be able to afford a holiday or an $8 Starbucks pumpkin spice latte. They have nothing, yet still share their coffee and food with me, who has everything.

Ellie felt a tsunami of shame wash over her. Sitting here with these women had opened her eyes to how truly privileged she was.

> *Hi Jerry,*
>
> *I wanted to get down some thoughts about the poverty I've seen in South America. It's really shocked me. So many of the towns I passed through are just mud-brick, with no electricity or running water to speak of. It could be medieval times if not for all the pollution. One village was built on stilts over a rubbish dump and the kids were playing in clouds of flies. It's got me so sad and angry and confused.*
>
> *Today I visited a coffee plantation near Medellín and couldn't stop thinking about the lottery of birth and life. I mean, I haven't worked any harder than the women I met there. My financial position is largely because I got lucky being born in a developed country at a certain point in history, which gave me the opportunity to pursue an education and professional career. All that advantage in turn allowed me to quit my job and travel the world. But these women didn't have the opportunity to make that decision. And they never will.*

I'd like to help in some way but not sure what to do. Any thoughts? I hope you and Yasmina are getting along better,
Ellie.

CHAPTER 22

San Francisco, USA

The doorbell rang.

"Can you keep stirring, honey?" Jerry licked cake batter off the back of a spoon.

"Hey, I want some!" Mia said, standing on a plastic box to reach the bench.

Jerry gave her the spoon and she held it with open-mouthed glee. "Make sure it's all mixed in." The doorbell rang again. "I'm coming." He made it to the end of the hallway and opened the door. "Hi Mom, Dad."

"How are you?" Carol said, kissing Jerry on the cheek. Don hugged his son.

"Thanks for doing this."

"It's what we're here for, after all," she replied.

They returned to the kitchen to find Mia's face covered with cake batter and a guilty grin.

"You were meant to stir it, not eat it," Jerry scolded.

"Sorry Dad, but it said 'eat me.'"

"I bet it did."

Carol wiped Mia's face with paper towel. "We might need to start this again. What do you think?" Her granddaughter nodded eagerly.

"I expect we'll be gone a couple of hours," Jerry said.

"No rush." Don put a bag of groceries on the bench. "We'll have dinner ready for when you return."

"Can you tell me where we're going?" Yasmina had slumped despondently in the passenger seat while Jerry drove along the highway.

"You'll see," he winked.

"I hate surprises. And can you not smile? It's disturbing me."

Jerry laughed. "One of us has to smile. And given you never smile these days, I thought I'd be happy for both of us."

It won't be another one of those days. Not if I can help it.

They passed a sign welcoming visitors to The San Francisco Zoo and Jerry turned inside.

"No," Yasmina said. "I'm too old to go to the zoo."

"You think?"

"I'm staying in the car."

"Yas, can you humor your old man for an hour? Please."

A short while later, dad and daughter walked past the Big Cats enclosure. Lions and tigers dozed in the sun and a pair of cubs rolled on the grass, pawing at each other.

"See, this is fun," Jerry said between bites of an ice-cream.

Yasmina was absorbed with trying to stop hers from dripping.

"You know, when you were a little girl you didn't care about ice-cream running down your fingers. Or getting in your hair, for that matter."

"Well, I'm not a little girl anymore, in case you hadn't noticed. You need to accept that."

It's not that easy, honey.

They continued in silence.

"Do you remember what else you loved doing?"

"What?"

Jerry nodded in the direction of the Penguin Island exhibit.

"Penguins!" Yasmina's face lit up and she ran toward it.

"Wait for me," Jerry called, giving chase.

Yasmina leaned over the railing to get as close as possible to the only birds on the planet that couldn't fly. She watched the Magellanic penguins with the wide-eyed delight of a child. The females preened their black and white feathers, while the males stuck out their chests and strutted around like contestants in *The Bachelorette*.

"Look at that one, Dad."

"I see him."

A baby penguin waddled clumsily to the water's edge, then flopped in head-first.

"They are *so funny*," Yasmina giggled.

As she watched the penguins, Jerry watched his daughter experiencing the joy that'd eluded her for months.

"They're playing!" Yasmina pointed at two penguins chasing each other through the water, twisting and turning at impossible angles in their game of tag. "I want to jump in with them."

Jerry caught Yasmina wiping a tear from her cheek.

"Mom used to bring me here. When I was a kid, Mom used to bring me here."

Jerry put a hand on her back. "I know, honey."

"See them playing. They're so happy," she cried. "They're so happy…"

"You can be happy too, Yas."

She didn't respond and Jerry didn't pursue it. He let her release her emotions in peace for a few minutes before talking again. "C'mon, I want to show you something."

Out the other side of the exhibit, Jerry approached a woman in a ranger's uniform waiting by a door marked 'Staff Only.' They exchanged greetings and he introduced his daughter to

Danielle, the penguin keeper.

"Are you ready?" she said.

"Um…ready for what?" Yasmina asked.

Danielle led Jerry and Yasmina through the door and into a room behind the penguin pool. It was a clinical space, equipped with an examination table and medical instruments. She opened a temperature-controlled cage on the far wall and took something from it. "Yasmina, meet Sasha." Danielle opened her palms to reveal a tiny penguin. "She's only six weeks old so we need to be quiet."

"Oh my God," Yasmina whispered.

"A few days ago Sasha fell and cut her flipper, so we had to take her out of population and stitch it up."

"Can I touch her?"

"Yes, but be gentle."

Yasmina stroked Sasha's back, careful not to touch her bandaged wing.

"Would you like to hold her?"

"Are you serious?"

"Cup your hands close to your stomach, like I'm doing. That's good. Keep them together." Danielle placed Sasha in Yasmina's hands.

From the corner of the room, Jerry could see his daughter's face beaming.

Perfect.

Sasha fluttered her flippers and looked up at Yasmina with inquisitive black eyes. "Dad, she's looking right at me."

"I see that, honey," Jerry grinned.

More than perfect.

Sasha curled into a ball and closed her eyes. "Oh, are you tired? That's OK. Go to sleep, little one. Go to sleep." Yasmina cradled the baby penguin like a protective mom.

"That was amazing! How did you organize that?" Yasmina screamed once she and Jerry had left the treatment room.

"We did some *pro bono* work for the zoo last year so I called in a favor."

"Just for me?"

"Just for you."

Yasmina took a moment to catch her breath. "Thank you."

"You're welcome, honey. I think you needed it. I haven't seen you this happy since before your mom passed."

They walked toward the exit. "That's why you brought me here?"

"I want you to be happy, Yas. And I want us to have a functioning relationship because we haven't had one in too long. Heck, I just want to spend time together without arguing. Do you want that too?"

"Yeah."

"Then I'm willing to try harder if you are."

"I am."

Jerry put an arm around his daughter, kissed her on the head and squeezed her. "Now about this party next month."

"I can go?"

"Well, let's discuss it and see if we can reach a compromise. Why do you think you should be allowed to go?"

"I…" Yasmina toyed with her hair. "OK, so I guess I haven't exactly been on my best behavior lately."

"Instead of looking backward, let's look forward to what you can do from now on."

"I could get all my schoolwork up to date."

"That's going to take a lot of hard work. And discipline."

"I can do it."

"I'll need to see results, not just promises."

"I'll do it, Dad, you'll see. I won't let you down."

"OK. What else?"

"I could help more around the house. Stick to Andrea's roster thing."

"That'd be good. Anything else?"

"I don't know…"

"How about you wear an 'I Love Dad' t-shirt to school?"

"Don't push it."

They laughed together, for the first time in a long time.

Hi Ellie,

I took your advice and things have improved between Yas and me. It went surprisingly smoothly, and I think our relationship is headed in the right direction for now. A father always has to keep his fingers crossed when communicating with his teenage offspring!

Our girls were really affected by the poverty you wrote about, particularly Mia. She couldn't stop staring and asking why people lived like that. It's hard to explain something so complex to a 6 year-old, as she was then, but we tried to help her understand how lucky she was compared to other children.

Actually, that was one of the main reasons for our trip. We wanted to instill in our girls a sense of wonder about the world, but also show them how privileged they are—how 90% of people in the world are less fortunate. Many far less fortunate. If you're looking for ways to help, there's lots of volunteering opportunities. You could lend a hand at a health clinic or in wildlife conservation. Have you ever thought about teaching English? Once we got back, Andrea organized a fundraising drive for a charity that provides water purification systems to villages in Peru, and she gave a speech at school titled 'Clean Water is a Human Right.' Bella and I were so proud!

If you're still in Medellín, I recommend visiting the

Botero gallery. Our kids thought the fat (or is 'plus-sized' more politically correct these days?) statues were hilarious, and Yas took countless selfies with them of course. Let me know what you think,
Jerry.

CHAPTER 23

Medellín, Colombia

In an elevated train racing above the hectic streets, Ellie gripped a pole and struggled to stay awake. The bags under her eyes that'd scared her in the mirror this morning felt like they were getting heavier.

Squashed beside her was Donté, a fresh-out-of-college hipster from Atlanta she'd met at the hostel over a breakfast of stale bread and mushy fruit. He was pencil thin and wore jeans so tight they looked sewn on.

"What did it sound like?" he asked.

"Must we?" Ellie replied.

"I'm just wondering if it was dry or sloppy?"

"I'm gonna throw up."

"I had to deal with dorm sex in Berlin."

"What'd you do?"

"I turned on the lights," Donté said.

Ellie raised her eyebrows. "And?"

"They kept going! Seriously, people have no shame these days." The train arrived downtown and they got off. "And I'm gay so the last thing I want to do is watch you hetros bumping uglies. Believe me, I have zero interest in that."

Ellie and Donté spent an hour wandering through the Fernando Botero gallery, laughing at the eccentric paintings of plus-sized people that were a feature of the Colombian artist's work. They chatted about where they were from and where they were going, the usual pattern of conversation Ellie had come to recognize—a type of speed dating for travelers. And it was nice to have someone to take photos of her with the massive Botero statues outside the gallery. Ellie's favorite was the fat naked lady sitting on a fat naked horse, which didn't look too impressed about it.

In the midday heat, Ellie and Donté lay on the grass and ate *obleas* (round wafers sandwiched around sweet caramel sauce) because they figured that's what the statues would do if they came to life. A group of women walked past in the Colombian national dress. One wore leopard-print heels, another leopard-print leggings, and a third squeezed into a leopard-print boob tube.

"Welcome to the jungle," Donté dead-panned.

Ellie buckled in a fit of laughter. It was nice to connect with someone who thought in the same twisted way.

"Hey, you want to do something crazy?" he said.

Coke, blow, pearl, marching powder, the devil's dandruff… Ellie never knew there were so many names for cocaine. Donté was fascinated by the late kingpin Pablo Escobar and told her all about it on a chicken bus to a picturesque lake, popular for swimming and fishing. But Ellie and Donté hadn't come for the watersports.

They wanted to visit the mysterious private island once owned by the feared drug lord and named after his beloved daughter, Manuela. It couldn't be found in any guidebook, but Donté had heard on the backpackers' grapevine that it might be possible to explore Escobar's *finca* if they had some "pluck."

Ellie didn't know what level of pluck would be required, but her trip showed she had at least some, so agreed to join the 'Top Secret' mission.

Spontaneity is exhilarating when you embrace it.

Donté spoke enough Spanish to ask around at the pier for a boat to ferry them to La Manuela. It took a few attempts before finding a willing captain.

They crossed the lake without incident, but on arrival met the biggest obstacle to their goal: the Colombian National Police. An officer guarding the island strutted out of his sentry box like John Wayne. He yelled furiously and waved them away. Then stuck one hand on his hip and the other on his pistol.

"I think we should go," Ellie said, her heart thumping.

"Give me a minute." Donté talked with the officer and succeeded in calming him down. "He's going to let us on if we make a *donación*."

"*Donación?*" Ellie repeated. "What's that, a donation? Like…a bribe?"

Donté shrugged. "That's one way to look at it."

Ellie bit her lip. She'd never bribed a police officer before. Living in the developed world, that sort of thing had never occurred to her. "Do you think it's safe?"

"I think he's just fleecing us for beer money by the look of his gut. And he's gay."

"You can tell?"

"Yeah. And gays are always more trustworthy."

They handed over the peso equivalent of US$20 and the officer grudgingly let them onto the island.

It looked like a war zone. The approach to Escobar's crumbling mansion was a grand circular driveway, now framed by dead palm trees. The concrete facade had been attacked by creeper vines, twisting around columns and infiltrating smashed windows. Ellie felt like she was in an episode of *Narcos*, approaching the lair of the villainous mastermind. She kept her eyes alert for bad guys.

They squeezed through the steel front door and into the burnt-out entrance hall, a shell of its former glory. The staircase had been stripped of marble, and there was a gaping hole where a chandelier used to hang as if the heart of the place had been ripped out. A shiver ran down Ellie's spine imagining the ghastly acts these walls had witnessed.

The secret agents continued down a shadowy hallway. Most tiles were broken and moss spread in the damp corners. To access the rear wing of the villa, they had to climb over concrete blocks that'd tumbled from the roof when the rival Cali Cartel detonated a 300-pound bomb in a botched assassination attempt.

"Needless to say," Donté explained, "Escobar wasn't happy about it."

Feeling the adrenaline rush of illegal adventure, Ellie explored the entertainment complex by a pool filled with brown sludge and home to a lone duck, the only sign of life in this godforsaken place.

She got a boost from Donté up to the second level where they searched Escobar's bedroom and walk-in safe. Billions of dollars in cash had once been stored inside. That's Billions, with a B. Looters had punched hundreds of holes in the walls to find the money rumored to still be hidden here.

Standing amongst the rubble, Ellie contemplated what life would've been like for the 'King of Cocaine,' who amassed a $30 billion fortune from smuggling fifteen tons of white gold into the U.S.A. every day during the 1980s. Escobar had been a brutal killer, ordering the murder of thousands of civilians, police officers, judges, the assassination of a presidential candidate, and the bombing of a passenger jet. Even today El Patron remained a fascinating figure, reviled by some, loved by others. And Ellie never thought she'd be hanging out in his bedroom.

Indeed, if she hadn't decided to go backpacking, not been

in Medellín on this very day, not randomly met Donté at the hostel and bonded over stories of dorm sex, she would never have known this place existed.

Getting your butt off the couch has wonderful, unknowable, consequences.

They returned to the city with just enough time for Donté to make his red-eye back to the U.S.A. After adding each other on social media, Ellie bid him farewell with a grateful hug. By now she'd come to understand the transient nature of friendships on the backpacking trail. She would meet people for a few days, or even just a few hours, talk as if they'd known each other forever, then they'd be gone and she moved onto the next hostel where a new round of friendships would begin.

She liked that age, gender, race, nationality, social status and sexual orientation weren't a factor in any of them. It was just strangers sharing an experience in a foreign land, and it helped Ellie appreciate that everybody was on their own trip—not just in traveling, but in life.

"Caan-yoo-thee-iit?" Alex said.

Later that night, Ellie sat in the common room of her hostel video chatting with Donna and her nephews. Alex's mouth filled the screen to show the hole where his tooth used to be. "I see it, sweetheart. Does it hurt?"

"Naaaaaaah." He took his finger out of his mouth. "And I got a dollar from the Tooth Fairy."

"Lucky boy. What are you going to do with your money?"

"Buy candy."

"Of course. And Benji, how's soccer?"

He dug a nugget out of his nose. "It sucks. Coach put me at fullback so I can't kick goals. I hate him."

"I'm sure it's not that bad. Someone needs to stop the other team scoring, right?" Ellie sunk further into the beanbag. "I almost forgot, did you get the postcard I sent you?"

"I love postcards," Alex said.

"Why didn't you message it?"

"It's nice to receive a postcard, Benji," Donna explained. "It's much more fun than a phone message, so when it arrives we'll let Aunty Ellie know and say thank you."

Ellie sensed an argument brewing and changed the subject. "Hey, guess what I ate yesterday?"

"A gorilla," Benji said.

Ellie shook her head. "There aren't any gorillas here, and I wouldn't want to eat one even if you could."

"A mango?" Alex said.

"I did have some mango, but I'm thinking of something else."

Benji grabbed Donna's phone. "Tell us. What did you eat?"

"I ate…guinea pig."

The color drained from Alex's face.

"Guinea pig?!" Benji screamed.

"That's right—"

"You can't eat a guinea pig!" Alex burst into tears.

"It's a delicacy in Colombia, sweetheart. For special occasions and—"

"NOOOOOOOOOOO…" He ran from the living room.

Benji laughed so hard he fell to the floor and rolled across the carpet.

Donna picked up her phone and stepped over him on her way to the kitchen. "Fuck, Ellie, did you have to tell Alex you ate a guinea pig?"

"I'm sorry, I didn't mean to upset him."

"We bought one for his first pet. He wanted to show you tonight."

"Oh Jesus," Ellie sighed. "I've traumatized the poor child."

Donna poured herself a vodka. "It's OK, I'll explain they do things differently down there. I'm just worried Benji is gonna want to eat the silly thing now."

"On that note I guess I should go. Tell Alex I love him."

"Have you thought about when you'll be home?"

"I'm having a great time, Donna."

"I know, but I'm concerned. We all are."

"Thanks, but I'll be fine," Ellie said. "Nothing will go wrong."

CHAPTER 24

San Francisco, USA

A drooping banner welcomed visitors to 'Harry Truman High School.' Jerry marched underneath it and down a hallway with bars on the windows.

If they didn't design schools to look like prisons, maybe students wouldn't feel they were in one.

"I have a three o'clock appointment," he said to the receptionist.

She received him with the grim expression of someone who'd been doing their job too long. Jerry trailed after her through the administration block and waited while she knocked on a door stenciled with 'PRINCIPAL.'

A compact lady in her seventies opened it, forcing a smile through thick make-up. "Mr. Townsend, I'm Principal Mercer." She put an emphasis on the 'Principal' and compensated for her lack of height with a beehive hairdo and brown pants suit.

Jerry scanned the office. In the corner he spotted Andrea sitting on a couch, her jaw trembling. He rushed over and pulled her into a hug. "Honey, it's all right. It'll be all right."

"Would you like coffee or tea?"

"I just want to know what's going on."

"Let's get to it then." Principal Mercer had a foreboding tone, designed to instill terror into her pupils. She sat in an armchair and chose her words carefully. "Mr. Townsend, I asked you to come in because your daughter had an altercation with another student during the lunch break."

"Are you OK? Did someone hurt you?" Jerry asked Andrea.

"She hurt someone else."

"What? Impossible."

Andrea looked away, fighting back tears.

"Can you tell me what happened, honey? I need to understand."

"She hasn't uttered a word since the incident," Principal Mercer continued. "But from what I can gather she hit another student—"

"That piece of shit was badmouthing Mom," Andrea blurted out.

Jerry took a moment to process her use of a swearword for the first time he could recall. "What did he say to you?"

"He said Mom was a meth addict. That she overdosed on meth and that's how she died." Tears streamed down Andrea's face. "I'm not going to let anyone say that about my mom."

Jerry drew his daughter close. "Principal Mercer, no-one should be allowed to speak to my daughter that way. To degrade the memory of her mother."

"I agree, Mr. Townsend. By the same token, we cannot allow physical responses to—"

"What sort of school are you running if students can insult each other like they're in some reality-TV show?"

Principal Mercer's mouth tightened like she was sucking on a sour plum.

"Who is this student?" Jerry said.

"His name is Bailey Myers."

"I need to speak with his parents."

"I will organize a meeting with all of us. Then both children can apologize—"

"You mean this Myers boy can apologize," Jerry interrupted. "Andrea is a quiet girl, a model student. She gets straight As. You know that, right? She's never acted this way before and I know she wouldn't lash out unless provoked."

"Regardless of who provoked who, we have rules and policies—"

Jerry ignored her and turned to Andrea. "I want you to tell me exactly what happened. Step-by-step."

She wiped her face and cleared her throat. "I was in the cafeteria at break and…he was in my face, teasing me… So I pushed him away. And then he pushed me back. So I pushed him again and we fell on the floor. Then Mr. Phillips came and pulled us apart."

"What class do you have with this boy?"

Andrea shook her head. "He's in the year above."

Jerry's face hardened. "You want my daughter to apologize to an older student who was picking on her and should know better? For God's sake, her mom died seven months ago. How do you expect her to react?"

"The death of your wife was a tragedy that the whole school community had to process," Principal Mercer said. "But we must acknowledge that any physical violence, even if it is triggered by inappropriate language, is unacceptable. It's my red line."

"Your red line should be saying offensive things in the first place." And he wanted to say something *very* offensive right now.

Jerry kept his arm around Andrea as they walked out of school and into the parking lot. He opened the passenger door for her, then they sat in silence for a while.

"Honey, I know you're upset. But you need to understand this other student baited you. He wanted a reaction and got it. You can't let people push your buttons like that." Not that he was ever any good at ignoring it. "That being said, I'm so proud of you for defending your mom—and for beating up a stupid boy."

She managed a short smile. "I've never been suspended before."

"Well, it's not the end of the world. And it's only for the rest of the week." Jerry tapped the steering wheel with his thumbs, trying to find the rights words to soothe his daughter. "You know you can always talk to me about how you're feeling?"

Andrea sniffled and started to bawl again. "I can't believe she's gone, Dad. It's my mom. And she's dead. And I can't believe it. Why is she dead? Why is she dead?!"

Jerry held Andrea close. He understood exactly how she felt, because he asked exactly the same question every day.

CHAPTER 25

Somewhere in Ecuador

Ellie's eyes flashed open.

A jolt. A shattering sound.

She grabbed the seat in front as the bus swerved violently to the left. She blinked to wake up and figure out what the hell was going on.

The bus swerved back to the right. Tires screeched. A toddler screamed. Another jolt. Luggage fell from the overhead shelves, crashing into the aisle. It took a few more seconds before Ellie realized what was happening.

We're out of control.

The bus swerved to the left again, hitting something hard. Her heart froze as they tipped into emptiness.

Oh shit, this is it.

Everything turned upside down. Glass. Bags. People.

Ellie closed her eyes but felt herself tumbling.

Another crash.

Her head slammed into a window then—black.

Ellie woke up on the floor of the bus, wedged between seats. Children cried. Some adults were upright, checking on people. Someone asked if she was OK. She wasn't sure but nodded anyway. Her forehead throbbed. She touched it and felt blood.

Pulling herself onto a seat, Ellie looked around. The bus was upright, but a mess. They must've rolled two or three times. The driver was slumped over his wheel. A man held his daughter's injured arm. An elderly lady groaned in pain. The windows that weren't broken had blood on them.

They'd crossed the border into Ecuador three hours ago, in the middle of the night. Ellie was glad to make it through immigration without any of the hassle of last time. No questions, no bag searches, no intimidating stares, just a stamp in her passport and she was on her way. Things had been looking up. Now…damn, her head hurt.

In the hazy aftermath of the crash, Ellie sat in the dirt a short distance from the wreck. The smell of gas filled the air. Other passengers were nearby, hugging their children and receiving basic medical attention in the pre-dawn fog. Thankfully, no-one had been seriously injured. One family huddled together in prayer at the miracle.

Ellie held a wet cloth to her scalp to stop the bleeding and clung to her daypack. It contained her passport, phone and credit cards—everything she would need to get out of this mess.

More than the physical pain, it was the shock of the crash that troubled her most. She had zero control. And she hated that. Her life to date had been all about control, or at least the illusion of it, but tonight she was entirely at the mercy of…fate, or just dumb luck. She could have died. The words rang through Ellie's head like a warning siren.

I could have died.

San Francisco, USA

Jerry trod through the mud-clogged museum site with Kevin, Harry and Brandon—or as he'd started calling them, his Triad of Doom. There'd been some progress on the build over the past month with the first story complete and work commencing on the second, but rain was falling again so the crane and heavy machinery lay frustratingly idle.

"Jesus, it's not just another cookie-cutter office building," Jerry said. "You can't apply the same rules."

"I get it," Brandon replied, not hiding his irritation. "But we're two weeks behind now. I need some flexibility from you on the design so we can get back on schedule."

"The Flores family hired my firm, my wife in particular, to create an iconic space. Not just a building, a *space*," Jerry countered. "One that would house their collection and also provide a new park for the people of San Francisco."

"I understand that, but—"

"Everything on the plans—that they signed off on, that you signed off on—has been designed to fit together. One piece complementing the other. So if you start pulling feathers off the bird, how the hell is it meant to fly?"

"It's a nice metaphor, Jerry."

They ducked under a section of scaffolding. Jerry banged his hardhat. "Shit. My point is, which part of the project would you like me to press delete on? The entrance hall? The exhibits? Maybe we should just scrap all the toilets? People can take a leak before they come."

Kevin, his right-hand man, struggled to keep up. "Perhaps we could—"

"You can't just cut one element and not expect it to impact everything else," Jerry continued. "There are flow-on effects.

Structural. Artistic—"

"And financial," Brandon said.

Jerry stopped in the mud and planted his hands on his hips. If only construction was as simple as when he was a boy playing in his sandpit. If only *everything* was that simple.

Kevin caught up and tried again. "Jerry, we all respected Bella. And her design for the museum is exceptional. But...it might not be achievable."

Jerry dunked his boot in a puddle and watched the waves ripple away, then disappear to nothing. Now that was a metaphor. He took a breath. "Harry, we've got six months until opening. Can your crew bring it in?"

"We'll try our best. But I recommend you prepare a contingency plan."

Jerry gazed over the unfinished museum, not wanting to believe what he was being told.

Why can't anyone see what I'm trying to do here? It has to be as Bella intended, or what's the point?

His phone beeped with an email. He was glad for the interruption.

Hi Jerry,
So...I was in a crash.

"You still with us?" Kevin said.

"Yeah, it's...a friend of mine is in trouble. I'm going to need a minute here."

I'm thankful to be alive and lucky no bones were broken. It's no surprise to my sister who warned me this would happen, but I'm bummed because I've loved South America and this has put a dampener on things. It looks like I'll be returning home sooner than I thought. Anyway, we've been emailing a lot so I thought you

*should know. I'll write more when I can. Loved the
Botero gallery and have a story about breaking into
Pablo Escobar's mansion to tell you,
Ellie.*

CHAPTER 26

17th August – Somewhere over the Pacific

Ellie looked out the window at the deep blue and knew this was the right decision. The 737 wobbled from turbulence. She grabbed her cup to stop it sliding off the tray and opened the *Unique Planet*. Making her first addition to the guidebook also seemed right: 'WARNING. My bus crashed on this route—avoid!'

Admittedly, she didn't have Bella's way with words, but adding to her notes felt gratifying. Like continuing a tradition that'd been passed down, so she better do a good job.

After the crash, Ellie had licked her wounds in Quito, the cosmopolitan capital of Ecuador. Nursing a killer migraine back to a headache, she received several sweet emails from Jerry to check she wasn't in any pain. It felt nice to be cared for, like receiving a warm hug when she needed it most.

She'd also made the dreaded phone call to Donna. It went about as badly as expected. Her sister offered little sympathy, instead demanding Ellie return home *on the very next flight*. She gave it serious thought. After all, she'd come to South America seeking adventure, not life-threatening danger. But didn't bus crashes happen everywhere? Even in the U.S.A? And hadn't all the good she'd experienced far outweighed the bad?

NICK LEVY · 141

A long sleep had reset the dopamine levels in Ellie's brain, and as the cut on her head healed, she realized she would mend on the inside too.

Figuring a change of pace was the best idea before resuming her adventure, she booked a flight to the Galápagos Islands off the coast of Ecuador. It would take more than a bus crash to stop her getting to Machu Picchu.

Running away was the old Ellie. That's not me anymore.

Galápagos Islands

As the ferry approached the pier, Ellie understood why Bella fell in love with Isla Isabela, the largest island in the archipelago but also the least inhabited—at least by humans. The volcanic landscape looked as surreal as Mars, except it teemed with wildlife. Families of sea-lions lounged on the beach, black and red frigate birds swooped off cliffs, and hundreds of iguanas assembled on prehistoric lava flows with heads tilted toward the sun as if worshipping in a cult.

Being surrounded by wildlife reminded Ellie of something Bella had written: 'More than 50% of our planet lives underwater. Don't you want to meet them?' A list of pros and cons about SCUBA diving, mixed with an unhealthy dose of self-doubt, spiraled through her head like a typhoon. But Ellie pushed them aside because the only reasonable answer to Bella's question was: 'Challenge accepted!' After confronting her fear of heights on Mount Roraima, it was time to tackle another one.

After all, if I'm not going to try new things, then why the hell am I here?

CHAPTER 27

Galápagos Islands

Ellie sank beneath the surface, her blonde hair swirling in the ocean like a mermaid's mane.

I can do this.

She wriggled her facemask and looked around. To her right was the hull of the dive boat, to her left was her SCUBA instructor, Eduardo. He gave the official 'OK' hand signal and she repeated it back, just like they'd practiced. Was there a sign for 'Barely OK'?

I can do this.

Ellie took one last look at the sun's rays shooting through the water, then followed him down to the seabed. On the sandy bottom, Eduardo came to a stop and kneeled. He waved for Ellie to join him. She swam closer until she could see into his hazel eyes. A reflection on his facemask made her glance up at the ten yards of water above them. She couldn't see sky. Or land. Or air.

Oh shit.

Ellie's brain entered self-preservation mode. Death was imminent. Escape essential. She panicked, drawing too much air through her regulator. Even though she was breathing oxygen, it felt like breathing water. She coughed. Her body convulsed. Heart thumped. She pushed her legs off the bottom—

Eduardo shot out a hand and grabbed her. Pulled her down. He looked her sharply in the eyes. Took out his regulator so she could read his lips. "It's OK. Be calm."

Ellie shook her head and struggled against him.

He gripped her mask and motioned for her to inhale slowly. "Breathe in. Breathe out. Breathe in. Breathe out."

Ellie suppressed her instincts just long enough to try it. Over the next minute she slowed her breathing until it became methodical again. A calm settled over her.

I can do this.

Eduardo gave her the 'OK' signal again. She repeated it back. He pointed in the direction of a nearby reef and she forced herself to nod.

As they passed over the stretch of luminous coral, Ellie became so captivated by its medley of colors she forgot about her breathing problems. Her eyes darted all around to capture the sea-life on display: orange starfish, blue baby stingrays, and thousands of tropical fish of the brightest yellow. They moved in perfect harmony, like the world's largest ballet performance.

Beyond the reef, an eel traced a path through the sand and a giant sea turtle glided through the water as if on a leisurely Sunday stroll. And more fish. Red fish. Purple fish. Green fish. This dynamic gallery of natural art was unlike anything Ellie had experienced.

Eduardo clutched the straps on Ellie's vest and pulled her out of the water. She wrung out her hair while he took off her tank.

"Did you like it?"

"Like it? I loved it!" Ellie said, her legs shaking from the thrill. "I never thought it would be…oh, I'm so beat I can't even think straight."

"Sit down a minute. Diving can make you very tired." Eduardo unzipped her wetsuit and handed her a towel. "You did great down there."

"No, I didn't. I panicked. I almost lost it."

"It happens to everyone on their first dive. Sometimes it happens to people who have dived a hundred times."

"I used up my oxygen too fast."

"That's normal too. You'll get better at regulating your breathing. Are you always this hard on yourself?"

"I'm just annoyed I didn't get it right."

"Ellie, you got it ninety percent right today, on your first attempt. You need to relax and give yourself more credit."

If only I had a dollar for every time someone said that.

Eduardo finished stowing the gear, his shoulder-length hair dripping across the golden skin of his back. He looked like maple syrup. Maple syrup drizzled over perfectly sculpted muscles.

The thing that first attracted Ellie's attention was his accent. A hybrid of Spanish, American and British, different countries revealing themselves depending on the words he used. It made everything sound more profound, maybe even more romantic.

"Ellie? Earth to Ellie."

"Yeah, I'm here. Sorry."

"What are you doing tonight?" Eduardo raised the anchor.

"I'm on a tiny island in the middle of the ocean so I don't have any plans or many options."

"A group of us from the shop are going out for drinks if you want to come."

"This isn't one of those 'hit on the dumb tourist' things, is it?"

"No," Eduardo laughed. "I'm just being social. It's what us Latin Americans do. You North Americans are so suspicious."

Ellie thought it over as she threw on a t-shirt. Why not go? She hadn't drowned. A celebration was in order. "OK, I'll come for one drink."

"*Muy bien, una cerveza.* One drink it is." He fired the engine and they roared back to shore.

Ellie scrubbed the salt off her skin. The outdoor shower was cool yet refreshing. In a tropical wonderland, there wasn't need for anything more. She wrapped a towel around herself and headed inside the female-only dorm. The windows had a view of the ocean and a pleasant breeze played with dream-catchers hanging from the ceiling. While waiting to air-dry, Ellie opened her phone.

Hi Jerry,

SCUBA SUCCESS! Thanks for believing I could pull it off 😊 *I'm extremely claustrophobic, the result of my sister locking me in a cupboard when I was 4 years-old, so the thought of being deep underwater, breathing through a machine, kept me up most of last night. But I survived. And you were right, it was absolutely worth it. How are you? Is Andrea feeling better? I'm still angry about what happened, and hope she taught that boy a lesson he'll never forget.*

Oh, I've been learning occupations in Spanish and realized I have no idea what you do for a living. Tell me it's something exciting…like you're an astronaut or movie director or tech billionaire? And how did you go with the language down here?

I was also thinking we have no idea what each other looks like so I've attached a pic for you to put a face to my name. It was taken yesterday and is a life highlight for sure. To be so close to nature in a place as wild as Galápagos—again, words aren't enough so I'll send it without further comment!

Thanks and tell Andrea to keep standing tall 🧍

Adiós amigo,

Ellie.

San Francisco, USA

Jerry smiled as he read her email on his phone. It was great Ellie was having so much fun again. He flipped an omelet for Saturday breakfast and waited a second for her photo to download—

He froze.

Ellie was sitting cross-legged on a white beach while a sea-lion pup splashed out of the ocean and waddled toward her bare feet.

Jerry dropped the spatula and rushed to the hallway. His eyes frantically scanned the photos on the wall until he found the one he was looking for—Bella sitting cross-legged on a white beach as a sea-lion pup waddled out of the ocean toward her bare feet. He held Ellie's photo up next to Bella's. They were virtually identical.

How can that be…?

"What's up, Dad?" Andrea came down the stairs in her PJs.

"Nothing, honey." Jerry slipped his phone into his pocket.

"Is something burning?"

"Oh shoot." He ran back to the kitchen and pulled the omelet off the heat. "Dammit."

"Dad, are you OK?"

"Yeah," Jerry replied unconvincingly. "I just got distracted, that's all."

Hola Ellie,

Congratulations on the dive! You'll be the next Jacques Cousteau in no time 😊 *Are you thinking about getting certified? It wasn't the season for hammerhead sharks when we were there, but I'm sure that would really get your adrenaline going.*

Andrea is doing much better, thanks for asking. I think she'd bottled up so much anger and grief about her mom's passing that it all burst out at once. All my kids have been keeping too much inside. I do wonder how it will affect them in the long run, but can only pray it makes them stronger. There is one good thing to come out of this episode though—Yas is happy because she isn't the one in trouble for once!

We didn't have any language issues in South America because Bella spoke Spanish. Lucky me, right? She was born and raised in Chicago, but both her parents were Peruvian. Our two eldest are pretty much fluent, and I want to make sure Mia continues to learn because it's a large part of their heritage.

As for me, I'm regrettably not a tech billionaire... I'm an architect. I know, not quite as exciting. My firm is currently building a museum here in San Francisco for Latin American art. We're about 8 months down with another 6 to go, but unfortunately running way behind which is causing me major headaches.

Jerry considered telling Ellie about the similarity between the photos of her and Bella, but ultimately decided not to. He reassured himself that it was just a coincidence, and tried to push it out of his mind.

Thanks for sending the photo. It's nice to see who I've been emailing with these past 4 weeks. I've attached a picture of my family on a catamaran trip we took in the Galápagos. The kids saw dolphins so it was a very special day.

Keep studying hard and I'm sure future emails will be entirely in Español. Buenas tardes,
Jerry.

CHAPTER 28

Galápagos Islands

A pink sky hovered over the ocean. Strolling across the sand, Ellie carried her sandals and wore a light summer dress. She saw Eduardo leave his friends and jog down a dune to greet her with a peck on the cheek. Was he moving in slow motion? It was like being in one of those karaoke music videos.

"Ellie, you made it! Come meet my *amigos*."

The beach bar wasn't much more than tables and chairs made from driftwood, but it fit the location. Eduardo's group was a mix of locals and foreigners who drank beers as laid-back tunes played on the sound system.

"This is Ricardo, Flor, Alice, Sebastián and Marco."

"Nice to meet you all," Ellie said, taking an empty seat.

"Juancho, *uno más*," Eduardo called out to the bartender for another beer. "How are you feeling about the dive?"

"I want to do the full course. Try and get my PADI certification."

"I hoped you would say that." The bartender brought Ellie a drink and she toasted with Eduardo. "*Salud!*"

Damn, his smile is cute.

With good company, evening arrived in a hurry and soon the table was covered with empty bottles and chip packets.

"Tell us about the time you wrestled a tiger shark," Alice said.

"It's not a problem for me to tell that story because it's true." Eduardo shifted in his seat. "I just don't want to."

Ellie and the others pleaded with him. "C'mon, I want to hear how brave you were," she said.

"If you can tell it with a straight face the next round is on me," Ricardo offered.

"OK, OK. I'll tell it, but only because you all asked so nicely." Eduardo took a gulp of beer and lowered his voice. "It was one year ago. I'm free-diving at Cape Douglas, out past Isla Fernandina. I'm all alone. Down twenty-four, twenty-five, meters. Did I mention I was alone?"

"Yes!" his friends shouted.

"OK, I've been under for five or six minutes, looking for a pod of blue whales a fisherman had spotted the day before. But they're nowhere to be seen. I get a bad feeling. Like something is watching me. Something…big. I'm about to come up for air when out of nowhere this giant—"

"Giant!" his friends shouted.

Eduardo broke character and joined the laughter. "It's true I tell you. This tiger shark came out of nowhere. Bigger than this table."

"As big as your dick?" Marco threw a bottle cap at him.

"No, smaller."

They all cracked up.

"If it makes you feel better to believe that…" Ellie teased.

The night had become a long one. Ellie and Eduardo sat on a dune outside the bar, sharing a beer and watching moonlight shimmer across the water like a mirage. This whole place seemed like a mirage. Bob Marley's *Shelter of My Single Bed*, the all-time backpacker anthem, lingered in the background. Was it a sign?

"Do you speak Spanish?" Eduardo asked.

"I've been learning," Ellie replied. "So...*un poco?*"

"Hey, very good."

"Now you're teasing me."

"I understood what you meant, I think."

"Shut up." She laughed and gave him a shove. "Where did you learn English?"

"A bit at school, but mostly from watching TV. *SpongeBob* was my favorite. My mom insisted Saturday was English day so we would speak only English from breakfast to dinner time. That's how we both learned."

"And your dad?"

Eduardo shook his head. "I never knew him. My mom raised me on her own. You have to love that about a woman."

Ellie's heart melted. "She's very special."

"The best. She taught me everything I know, and she would tell you to keep practicing Spanish."

"*Claro.*"

"I can help. Until then we can talk Spanglish."

"*Buena idea.* Spanglish it is."

There was a lull as Ellie breathed in the anticipation bubbling between them.

"So, do you want to visit *mi casa?*" Eduardo said.

Ellie looked at him. He grinned like a cheeky kid. She knew it was coming to this, and she already knew her answer.

CHAPTER 29

Galápagos Islands

They kissed passionately while climbing the stairs to Eduardo's house. Raised on stilts, it sat on an isolated beachfront. The sound of crashing waves mirrored the necking and grabbing so intense Ellie and Eduardo slipped halfway up the stairs and took a break to giggle about it.

The petting continued inside, followed by rapid removal of clothing. Eduardo lifted off Ellie's dress. She pulled off his t-shirt. He pushed her onto the bed. She unbuckled his belt. He took off her panties. She pulled down his boxers.

"Do you have a condom?" Ellie said.

"Yes. Wait."

Ellie stared at the ceiling for that awkward-but-necessary thirty seconds while he found one in the bedside drawer and put it on.

"OK, I'm good." Eduardo rolled on top and pushed inside her.

She bit her lip and moaned in pain. "It's fine. Keep going." It'd been a long time, but nothing could stop her having this moment. *Nothing.*

Eduardo moved slowly at first as they both savored the otherworldly pleasure. Soon his animal instincts took over and the sex became fast. Their bodies moved in tandem. The sensation so amazing Ellie thought her head was going to explode. She'd forgotten how good it could feel. Pure ecstasy. Nothing else came close. Her hands dug into his back as she climaxed in the moonlight.

Hallelujah.

⁓

The sun peeked above the horizon as the two lovers lay in bed, studying each other's faces. Ellie's finger traced a line down Eduardo's forehead, between his eyes that seemed to look into her heart, and across the bridge of his wide nose. She continued over his pink lips and down to the scratchy stubble on his chin. Handsome, even if his ears did stick out a little.

"You're *guapa*," Ellie said.

"*Guapa* is for girls. You're *guapa*. I'm *guapo*."

"Spanish is weird."

"Do you want coffee?"

"I *need* coffee."

"OK, you make it. I have to swim."

"Where to?"

"Nowhere. Just swim." Eduardo jumped out of bed and pulled on a pair of shorts.

Ellie looked through the window to the raging sea. "Out there?"

"It's nothing to be afraid of. I grew up in it, remember? I have to say good morning to all my friends. Want to come?"

"I'll make coffee."

"*Perfecto*." Eduardo bounced outside and down the stairs.

Ellie watched him run across the sand and dive into the waves.

He's like a child. Without any worries. What a lifestyle!

But it's not a style, is it? It's his way of being, like there's no other way he could possibly be. I wish one day I could be that happy-go-lucky.

I am getting better though, right…? Or I wouldn't be here.

Ellie cast her eyes around Eduardo's home. It looked like a crusty old ship captain lived here, with an anchor in the corner and conch shells dotting the windowsill. A painting of a lonely boat hung on an angle on the wall.

She picked up a book from the crate serving as a table. It was a compilation of poems titled *Sea of Love* and a page by the British romantic Percy Bysshe Shelley had been dog-eared.

> *The fountains mingle with the river*
> *And the rivers with the ocean,*
> *The winds of heaven mix forever*
> *With a sweet emotion;*
> *Nothing in the world is single;*
> *All things by a law divine*
> *In one spirit meet and mingle.*
> *Why not I with thine?*

Ellie looked out the window again. Eduardo had swum far from shore and a sea-lion had joined him to say good morning. She smiled. Utterly content.

CHAPTER 30

Galápagos Islands

Time moved slowly in the Galápagos. Or, rather, there was no concept of time. The hours just weren't counted. This infuriated Ellie, who was used to allocating every minute to an activity, including scheduling time to relax, but she did her best to adapt.

Mornings were spent learning Spanish with Eduardo. She developed a knack for remembering vocab and pronouncing the *ñ* letter ('nye') and *ll* letter ('ya'), but the idea of nouns being feminine or masculine was hooey. How could shoes be male? Why the hell was a kitchen female?

The rest of the day was taken up with study for her PADI Advanced Open Water diving certificate. If successful, it would allow her to dive independent of an instructor—and three times as deep. It scared the shit out of her.

As part of the course, Ellie had to complete five more dives with Eduardo. He took her over coral reefs teeming with King Angelfish, through gardens of swaying sea grass that brought back memories of Pennsylvanian wheat fields, and into underwater caves where they needed torches to light the way. They encountered barracuda, pufferfish, and spotted-eagle rays with wingspans of more than six feet, gliding past in squadron formation. Which one was Maverick and which was Iceman?

After endless badgering about the reason for her bubbly mood, Ellie confessed to Donna about Eduardo. Her sister, naturally overjoyed, wouldn't stop taunting her about "taking a Latin lover." And of course Donna asked if she'd used the ribbed condoms. Ellie gave a firm: "No comment."

Neither of them could quite believe she'd let her guard down so easily and allowed Eduardo past the Great Wall she'd built to protect herself. It wasn't just high, but topped with barbed wire, machine guns, and explosives. For now, Ellie had switched the alarm system off.

Most afternoons they lazed in a hammock, watching the ocean change color, and making love at every opportunity. They moved from bed to sofa to floor to beach in pursuit of the Big O. Then lay in each other's arms and talked about all the important things, like life and love.

"What is it you want to do?" Ellie asked, toying with the hair on Eduardo's chest.

"Sleep."

"Not now. I mean in the future."

"*Qué pesada*," he scolded. "That is such an American question. You always want to do something different than what you are doing at the moment. To get something more than you already have."

"There's nothing wrong with achievement."

"It isn't everything."

They lay in the thick silence of their disagreement.

"There is judgment in your question, Ellie. As if I'm not doing enough by your standard. Tell me, what is wrong with living each day by the sea and enjoying everything it offers? It may sound simple to you, but it makes me happier than anything else I could do."

"*Lo siento*. I'm sorry. I wasn't trying to upset you."

"I know. You were brought up different to me. I can do what you call 'nothing' and be happy. But you always need to do 'something.'"

"I'm trying to be more *tranquilo*, but I'm not good at doing nothing."

"But it only makes you more stressed! Less happy. You need to train yourself to relax. With time you will stop thinking about your old life. What would be so wrong with that?"

Ellie thought for a moment. "Nothing."

"Good. So *tranquilo, por favor.* Maybe you need to stay longer in Galápagos. Soak up more of the island life."

Ellie watched a lone crab walk across the sand, then disappear into the wash. "It's just that as a young girl I wanted to grow up and have an impact on the world in some way, y'know? So I've always kept busy, either trying to achieve that or avoiding thinking about how I haven't achieved that yet. Now I'm starting to doubt I will ever have an impact."

Eduardo propped up on his elbow. "We impact the world by touching other people. If we touch them in a positive way, maybe just one person a day, by saying hello or smiling, then we have changed the world. Don't put too much pressure on yourself, Ellie. You're already touching people and you don't even know it."

She kissed him on the cheek. "*Gracias*."

"And now we practice relaxing!" He kissed her back and they laughed before closing their eyes to nap in the shade of the palm tree.

CHAPTER 31

San Francisco, USA

Jerry lay awake. He tried adjusting his pillow again. No luck. He rolled over onto his stomach again. Still no luck. He sat up, flicked on the lamp and checked his watch—2:45 a.m. Great.

He took his laptop from the bedside table and checked his email. Nothing. Clicked refresh to be sure. Absolutely nothing. A whole week had passed since he'd heard from Ellie and it bothered him, though he wasn't sure why. Did he look forward to her messages as an escape from work? To talk about his kids? Or because…he liked her in some way?

No. Not possible.

I barely know this woman. I've never met her. We've exchanged a few emails, that's it.

So why the heck can't I sleep?!

Jerry continued to fight his thoughts while he climbed out of bed and grabbed a glass of water from the bathroom. He downed it in one hit. The ding of a new email made his heart skip a beat.

Hey Jerry,
How's things? Sorry I haven't replied to your last message till now. The internet has been out for a few days.

Downside of being on a tropical island, I guess!
Thanks for sending through the photo of your family.
It's great to put faces to all the names. And Bella—what
a radiant smile! I'll think of it every time I open her
guidebook. Your daughters are super cute and look
just like their mom 😊 *I've been busy studying for my*
certification and the final exam is tomorrow. Fingers
crossed! I am soooooooooo happy here in Galápagos. Also,
I want to tell you that…I met someone.

Jerry blinked. He read the last line again to make sure he understood it correctly. Ellie had 'met someone'? He suddenly felt ill, like his stomach was empty but about to burst. He shook his head to throw off the jealousy gurgling up inside him, but it wouldn't budge.

That's right, after my loneliness in Cartagena I took your
advice and tried to be more open. His name is Eduardo
and he's my dive instructor. I know how that sounds, but
I'm trying not to see it as the clichéd tourist-meets-local
love affair 😬 *I'm happy, and not lonely for once, so*
that's what I'm focusing on. It's been a nice break from
all the dark thoughts in my head. I'll keep you updated!

"Keep me updated?" Jerry muttered. "What if I don't want to be kept updated about…Eduardo?"

Please tell me what's happening in your life. I hope all
is well and you're happy too. Adiós,
Ellie.

"Happy too?" Jerry slammed his laptop shut.

CHAPTER 32

Galápagos Islands

A dozen tables were roughly spaced on the beach like a bloom of jellyfish. Between them, tiki torches gave light to the diners and kept insects at bay.

"You look beautiful tonight."

"Just tonight?" Ellie frowned. She was wearing a white cotton dress with a yellow flower in her hair, while Eduardo had found a collared shirt.

"Every night. But tonight more so." His accent made every compliment sound sincere.

"I bought this dress at a market on Santa Cruz but didn't think I'd have the opportunity to wear it so soon."

"I have something to go with it. Give me your arm." Eduardo took a shell bracelet from his pocket and fastened it around her wrist.

"Oh, wow!" Ellie's eyes lit up.

"It's not expensive. I made it myself."

"That's even better." Ellie turned her wrist to look at the bracelet. "Thank you. I love it."

The waiter brought a bottle of wine and poured them both a glass. Eduardo waited until he left, then proposed a toast. "To you."

"To me," Ellie laughed as they clinked glasses.

She'd studied hard to prepare for her final exam, so when Eduardo told her this morning that she received a perfect score Ellie jumped on him and they crashed to the ground in a lustful embrace. He suggested they dine at the best restaurant on the island to celebrate.

"Don't drink too much," Eduardo warned.

"Why not?"

"Because tomorrow I'm taking you on a special dive."

Ellie leaned forward. "Where?"

"You've heard about it."

Her eyes widened. "I'm not sure I'm ready for it."

"You are. And don't worry, they don't usually eat people."

"Don't *usually* eat people? How do you know?"

"They haven't eaten me yet." Eduardo flashed his boyish grin.

⌒

"Is it crazy that I have the *Jaws* theme playing in my head?"

Eduardo chuckled and lifted a tank onto her back. They were on a boat bobbing in the middle of the ocean, with no land in sight. "There's no need to be nervous."

"Nervous may be understating it a little."

"You're qualified to dive alone if you want—"

"No. I want to dive with you. And your spear." She motioned to the sharp weapon leaning against the helm.

"OK, but remember you have the lead." They performed a final check of their regulators and gauges. "All good?"

"Now or never. Let's do it."

Eduardo looked up to the sky and performed the Catholic Sign of the Cross.

"Why did you do that?" Ellie said. "I've never seen you do that before."

"I was raised Catholic. And when I'm going to swim with

sharks it's better to be safe than sorry."

"But you said they wouldn't eat—"

Eduardo flipped backward off the boat.

"Better to be safe than sorry." Ellie crossed her chest and fell into the water.

It took six minutes to descend thirty meters. Ellie took charge and stopped them every ten meters to equalize pressure. The light had completely dissipated at this depth, as if a curtain had been drawn on the sun, and the only illumination of the dark blue, almost black, came from their flashlights.

Ellie caught a glimpse of something. She turned her head to look. Only darkness.

She saw something else and swung her head in the opposite direction. More darkness.

Is my mind playing tricks on—

A massive creature glided past and Ellie stiffened on reflex. The unmistakable form of a hammerhead shark. Twelve feet long, its front dorsal fin passed right by her face. One of its pectoral fins bumped her arm. Then it flicked its tail and disappeared.

Eduardo took Ellie's hand. She gave him the 'OK' signal. Her heart thumped like a bass drum and she imagined it creating ripples through the water. But she felt euphoric. If it wasn't for the regulator in her mouth, she would've had the biggest smile in the world.

Another hammerhead swam past. Within a matter of seconds they were surrounded by two, three, four, then five, then fifteen of the enormous beasts, swirling through the sea like a synchronized swimming troupe. The World's Deadliest Olympics.

Ellie watched in awe as they moved with precise, violent, efficiency. There were more than twenty of them now, on all sides, above and below. She was stuck in a lethal washing machine. With no cage.

One of the biggest sharks twisted and came directly at her.

She tried to remain calm by studying its freakish head with a long, flat, face and eyes perched on either edge for panoramic vision. It resembled a vacuum cleaner more than a hammer. Hopefully it wouldn't hoover her into its belly.

As the shark got closer, Ellie locked eyes with it. Black, lifeless, eyes she'd first heard described in Robert Shaw's classic speech in *Jaws*. There was no emotion in them. The beast had just one mission in life—to kill.

Its cavernous mouth, with rows of razor-sharp teeth, threatened to shred everything in its way. Ellie knew it could destroy her in an instant, bite her in half with one *chomp*. The image raced through her head. How could it not, down here in their domain where they held all the cards.

The hammerhead stared back at Ellie as if evaluating her portion size, then whipped its tail and vanished like a bolt of lightning.

Relax. Stop chugging air. Slow heart rate.

They're just curious. As curious about me as I am about them.

Ellie allowed herself to be mesmerized by the beauty of nature's creation. In what was the most dangerous place she'd ever visited, Ellie felt a wave of peace. Here she was swimming with sharks, when a few months ago she'd been sitting in an office. She was living life as it was meant to be lived. And resolved to enjoy this experience—even if it was her last.

CHAPTER 33

San Francisco, USA

The glass table reflected the iconic shard of the Transamerica building. Jerry was admiring it because he'd tuned out of the design meeting meant to choose wood for the doors of the museum while Kevin and Kyra argued, as usual.

C'mon Jerry, get a grip.

You're being ridiculous.

You can't be infatuated with someone you hardly know. Jesus, what are you back in high school?!

He worked into the evening, trying to finalize some of the thousands of decisions that needed to be made on a project of this scale. This time it was using a Virtual Reality headset to test color combinations for the entrance hall. Focus didn't come easy.

"Jerry!"

"Shit, Kyra." He pulled off the headset. "Again? Where do you hide?"

"I'm everywhere," she said in a spooky voice.

"What are you doing here at this hour? Am I paying you?"

"Obviously. And I have another date."

"With the insurance salesman?"

"He's an accountant. There's no need to be snooty." Kyra

handed him a folder. "I've been updating the projections for the Pata fit-out."

"I'm not going to like these, am I?"

"Probably not. If there's nothing else, I'll get going." She turned to leave.

"Actually, there is something. I've been thinking about what you said. A few weeks back. About going out to dinner with someone. What was the name of your flatmate?" Jerry said it all so fast that it felt even more awkward than he'd imagined.

Kyra's face grew a smile. "Her name is Carla."

Jerry pretended to look for something elusive on his desk.

"She's a lawyer," Kyra offered, trying to help things along.

"How old is she?"

"About your age. Forty, I think."

"I'm thirty-eight."

"I'm rounding up. Would you like me to talk to her?"

"No," Jerry snapped. "Well…maybe you could see if she wants to have a drink. Nothing romantic, you understand? Just adult conversation."

"I'll set it up. Friday night OK?"

"Just a drink. Nothing else. It's not a…date thing."

"It'll be good for you to get out of the house."

Jerry felt sweat pour from his armpits and wondered if what he'd put in motion would end in a train wreck. This couldn't possibly be a good idea, could it?

"My boyfriend likes her," Kyra said.

"The insurance salesman is your boyfriend now?"

"Of course. He just doesn't know it yet." She skipped out of his office.

"That's creepy," Jerry said.

"I heard that!"

CHAPTER 34

Galápagos Islands

Ellie and Eduardo shared a fiery kiss on the end of the pier. A yacht was moored nearby, and fishing boats were returning with their morning catch.

"Four days and I'll be back," she said.

"I miss you already," Eduardo whispered in her ear.

"*Listo?*" The captain of the yacht shouted, throwing off the last rope.

"*Sí.*" Ellie climbed onboard. She blew Eduardo a kiss as the sleek vessel pulled away from the pier and motored out of the harbor.

In the open ocean, the mainsail caught the wind and they powered through waves as if slicing them with a knife. Ellie dangled her legs over the edge and let water splash them.

She'd secured the last berth with a group sailing clockwise through the Galápagos archipelago before returning to Isla Isabela. Most of the passengers were retired Germans who didn't speak a whole lot of English. That was fine with Ellie. She needed time alone to think about her relationship with Eduardo, and where it was going.

She also wanted to see the evidence of evolution Charles

Darwin had described after his expedition here aboard the H.M.S. Beagle in 1835. The diverse nature rendered Ellie speechless. The amount of land, sea, and air life was incalculable. And it wasn't just the number of animals, but how close you could get to them all. As the captain explained, the wildlife had been protected for generations and therefore didn't see humans as a threat. It made Galápagos one of the most special places on our planet.

During hikes on the islands, Ellie stood within a yard of sea-lions while they dozed on the sand, pups snuggling with their mothers and feeding on milk. Between them, marine iguanas shuffled their leathery gray and red bodies into the ocean. They looked like dinosaurs that'd been left in a dryer too long and shrunk to a comical size.

So that's how ugly you have to be to survive millions of years? What hope do humans have with our fragile bodies?

Down on the rocks by the water's edge, Sally Lightfoot crabs enjoyed the spray. Their bright red shells stood out against the black volcanic rock, producing a high-def image better than any TV. If it wasn't for the lack of narration, Ellie would've sworn she was in a David Attenborough documentary.

On one of the trails, blue-footed boobies pranced about during mating season. The clumsy birds got their name from early Spanish sailors who called them *bobos* ('fools'). Ellie preferred 'boobies,' obviously. Their feet were a rich shade of blue and the males took great pride in showing them off. She was lucky to witness a pair of boobies nursing their fluffy new-born, sitting on the chick to keep it warm.

There were also hawks preening their royal-brown feathers, flocks of flamingos flying together as if a painter had stroked the sky with a pink brush, albatrosses with bodies so big they couldn't fly without jumping off cliffs and soaring on the updrafts, and Darwin's famous finches. He was right, duh.

During daily swims in shallow bays, seahorses and starfish

emerged from the sand and thousands of tropical fish filled Ellie's field-of-vision like a rainbow. There was such an incredible array of life, it was difficult to take it all in.

For the first time I feel I'm not just an observer of nature, but part of it. I have a stake in its future. We all do.

It was a realization that brought tears to her eyes. If any place on earth could make you feel this way, it was Galápagos.

Never in her wildest imagination did Ellie think she would swim with a family of sea-lions. She'd been watching them from a distance through her mask. A bull six feet long and over 400 pounds teaching his children to hunt. Suddenly, the pups swam in Ellie's direction. Coming right up to her mask to check out the human, their huge glassy eyes looked at her curiously and mischievous whiskers teased her to follow. The cuteness quota was off the charts. Resistance was futile.

She swam beside them as they glided through the water with silky ease, and noticed they mimicked her moves. If she dove, they dove. If she twisted, they twisted. If she jumped out of the water, they jumped out too. They wanted to play.

We're not so different, these animals and us humans.

In fact, we're very much the same.

Ellie spent most nights above deck, the sea breeze caressing her skin. Under the stars, she had time to think about Eduardo. She missed him, for sure. She wanted him here to share these adventures, kiss her goodnight, and hold her till she fell asleep.

But was it love? Lust? A combination of the two? It did feel nice to be desired. She hadn't felt that in years. And there wasn't any hurry, right? After all, this place was paradise. Maybe she would stay forever.

CHAPTER 35

San Francisco, USA

Fog descended over the bayside Telegraph Hill district. Jerry shoved his hands in the pockets of his jacket and pulled it close, keeping a brisk pace along the footpath. He rounded a corner and stopped on a dime.

Across the road, a middle-aged woman stood outside the lounge bar where they'd agreed to meet. She too was rugged up against the cold with a coat, gloves and scarf. Jerry turned away and let out a heavy sigh.

What the heck are you doing? You shouldn't have come.

He glanced back and saw the woman check her phone.

Dammit, Jerry. OK, it's just a drink.

Green banker's lamps on the tables provided the only light and created a cozy atmosphere inside the bar. Jerry sat across from Carla, a confident lawyer with a striking smile that she shared frequently.

They'd spent the last hour drinking *mojitos* and chatting about their families, careers, and what they wanted for the future. Jerry surprised himself by managing to hold it together when explaining what happened to Bella, and Carla gave him a sympathetic ear. But as their drinks dwindled, the conversation also wound down.

"It's funny," Jerry said. "When we're young we think life is so complicated, but it's not until we get older that we realize we have to deal with our past as well."

"It's not easy," Carla agreed. "But we wouldn't want to forget all those things that've happened to us or we wouldn't be us anymore."

"Do you ever feel some days your brain has become too full? And as hard as you try to shove more stuff in, it's just not working?"

"All the time! The location of my keys on any given morning being Exhibit A."

"I worry about that. Having created so many memories, can I fit in new ones without erasing the old?"

"It might be time to upgrade your hard drive."

Jerry laughed. "A few extra gigabytes would be useful."

"Can I be completely truthful with you?" Carla said.

"Sure," he replied warily.

"It's been real nice talking with you tonight. You are an educated, interesting, funny, very tall man. But you're not ready for me."

Jerry studied Carla's kindhearted smile, then returned to playing with the mint in his glass.

"You know you're not ready," she added.

"I do." Jerry took a breath as if a weight had lifted off his shoulders. "I'm sorry. I've had a great time talking with you too. You're a lovely woman. But my head, and my heart, are elsewhere."

"There's no need to apologize. As they say, timing is everything. And life is complicated, especially as we get older. Don't we both know that!"

"Yes, we sure do. Can I at least pick up the bill?"

"Are we still in the twentieth century?"

They both laughed about his old-fashioned offer. "It's been almost twenty years since I've done this…" he said.

Jerry closed his door and rested sluggishly on the end of his bed. He undid a few buttons on his shirt, but his hands began trembling. He looked at the side where Bella used to sleep, and tears poured from his eyes.

"I'm sorry baby. I miss you. I miss talking to you. I miss holding you. I miss…all of you."

Jerry's grief flowed heavily, like it had the night of Bella's funeral after keeping his emotions in check all day for the sake of the girls. He buried his face in his hands and let it all come out again.

When, and how, would it ever end?

CHAPTER 36

Galápagos Islands

The group had planned to spend their final night on the yacht, but the captain received a weather report indicating a storm approaching and decided to make for land. They motored back to Isla Isabela and Ellie said her goodbyes in darkness on the pier they'd departed from four days ago. Eduardo was meant to meet her here tomorrow morning, but now she'd be able to surprise him!

The gathering wind whipped Ellie's hair as she walked along the beach to Eduardo's house. She'd put on the white dress he liked and bought a bottle of wine. Their reunion was going to be perfect. The sex would be *ah-maz-ing*.

But drawing near, she saw no light in his window. She climbed the stairs to the front door and was about to knock when she heard a noise inside. Someone laughing. Now talking. Two voices? Eduardo and…a woman?

Ellie peered through the glass—then pulled back.

What the fuck?

Unwilling to believe it, she found the courage to look again. Eduardo and a woman were having sex. In the bed he'd shared with Ellie. The bed where they'd lay together and talked about all the important things, like life and love.

The bottle slipped from Ellie's hands. Bounced off the landing. She ran down the stairs, sprinted through the sand and into the night, tears streaming down her face. The storm had arrived, and heavy rain pounded around her like stones.

Out of sight of Eduardo's house, she collapsed onto her knees. Cried her heart out and screamed. The primal scream of a wounded animal. Thoughts whirled through her head like the gray clouds above. Confusion. Hatred. Self-blame. She grabbed at the wet sand and flung it into the night.

Damn you for being so naive. Damn you, Ellie.

CHAPTER 37

Galápagos Islands

Shoulders back, head high, Ellie strode into the dive shop early next morning. Coffee had rejuvenated her puffy eyes and given her a jolt of strength to get through the next few minutes. Some staff helped customers and others prepped equipment, but she quickly spotted her target. Eduardo was behind the counter doing paperwork.

"Hello," Ellie said with cool detachment.

Eduardo looked up and flashed the grin that first set her heart on fire. "Ellie! You're back. I was going to come meet you." He moved to hug her, but she put up a hand.

"I'm not staying. I only came to return this." She threw his bracelet on the counter.

"What's going on?"

"I don't accept gifts from liars."

The staff and customers turned to see what was happening.

"What are you talking about?"

"My boat got in last night. So I came to your house."

The blood drained from Eduardo's face.

"Do you recite poetry to her as well? Take her diving? Give her presents?"

"Ellie, you're mistaken. Please…I like you. All those times we—"

"Save it, Eduardo. Nothing you say can make this right. You are a lying, cheating, pig of a man."

One of the customers laughed and Eduardo realized everyone in the shop was watching him get owned. He looked back at Ellie and his eyes hollowed. "She's my local girlfriend. You're just a *gringa* fling."

Ellie bit her bottom lip to stop it trembling.

Don't cry. Don't you dare cry in front of him.

"Next you're going to tell me you can't help it," she said. "That your hot Latin blood makes you screw everything that moves."

"It's what we do here."

"And all that stuff you told me about your mom teaching you to respect women? What would your mom think of how you treated me?"

Eduardo opened his mouth to reply, but no words came out.

"You disgust me," Ellie said. "*Y tú tienes una pequeña polla de banana.*"

Eduardo's face seared at her insult about his dick being a small banana. Ellie spun on her heel and left him speechless. It took all her strength not to burst into tears until she'd walked out of the door and his life.

CHAPTER 38

San Francisco, USA

Jerry walked down a short flight of concrete steps and into his dad's garage. A single overhead light fought against the dusty corners.

"What are the girls up to?" Don asked from underneath the hood of a red 1964 Pontiac GTO.

"Mom's beating them at Monopoly. Hopefully they'll learn something about money and stop asking me to increase their allowance." Jerry offered a beer in his dad's direction.

"Thanks." Don took a swig before returning to his beloved automobile.

Jerry propped against the workbench. He picked up a few tools for no reason other than to delay what he'd come to talk about. "I'm confused," he finally said.

"Why's that?" Don kept working under the hood.

"The other night I went out for a drink with a woman."

"How was it?"

"She said I wasn't ready."

"You think she was right?"

"Yeah."

"Well, it's good to know. You wouldn't have known if you didn't go."

"I guess."

"Can you pass me the five-sixteenth?"

Jerry found the wrench and passed it into his dad's outstretched hand. There was quiet again. "There's this other woman I've been…I was, communicating with. Well, just emailing. Quite a lot. But I haven't heard from her in a while. She's seeing someone now and I think that upsets me. Even though I don't really know her… That's unusual, isn't it?"

Don stood up and faced him. "It's not unusual, Jerry. Humans are, whether we want to be or not, emotional creatures. And sometimes we can't understand our emotions because we are stuck in them. Feeling them."

"But I still love Bella."

"Of course you do."

"I always will."

"Of course you will."

"I'm just lonely, Dad. I'm really lonely."

There. I said it.

Don wiped the last of the grease off his hands and pulled Jerry into a hug. "It's natural to feel lonely after the loss you suffered."

"But I can't just go out for drinks or email this woman. I have three daughters to raise."

"You are raising them, but you also need human contact."

Tears spilled down Jerry's cheeks and he wiped them away disapprovingly. "Oh God, look at me…"

"Just take every day as it comes. If you enjoy emailing this woman, keep doing it, don't feel guilty. You know Bella wanted you to be happy."

Jerry nodded. "Thanks for listening, Dad." They both took long drinks. "Now when are you going to take this thing out for a spin?"

"It's a classic. It's not meant to be driven."

"Is a car that's never driven actually a car?"

"Is a museum that's never finished actually a museum?"

"Is a joke that no-one laughs at actually a joke?"

Jerry and Don laughed and toasted their beers.

CHAPTER 39

Baños, Ecuador

Ellie melted into the pool. The water, heated by volcanic activity beneath the surrounding mountains, felt like bathing in hot milk. Not the low fat stuff. This was full cream. She visualized it extracting all her pain.

Though she'd played it tough with Eduardo, once Ellie's plane had taken off for the mainland she imploded into a blubbering mess. He'd broken her heart, yet it still yearned for him. The stewardess had handed her a bunch of tissues and she blew her anger into them. Anger at Eduardo for being an asshole. Anger at herself for getting attached too quickly, and believing anyone could love her.

Ellie had put on her sunglasses and pulled out her trusty companion in difficult times—Bella's guidebook. She had no idea where to go after the plane landed. Where was the best place to soothe a shattered soul?

On a page describing a town near the capital, Bella wrote: 'The straightest path to self-love is through forgiveness. And a spa. Treat yourself for the grand price of 50 cents. Let Baños heal you.' How did she always know exactly what to say, at exactly the right moment?

So on a whim Ellie exchanged the heartache of Galápagos for the cloud forest of Baños. Here she could recharge her emotional batteries. And have massages. Lots and lots of massages, to grind out the despair left behind by a cheating lover. For someone who hated creepy men, she sure did a great job attracting them.

Stop it, Ellie. It's time to be kind to yourself.

The volcanic springs had three pools: medium, hot, and crazy-fricking-hot. Ellie climbed out of the hot one. In the cool air, steam wisped off her skin as if she were on fire. Locals stared at the only white body in the middle of fifty brown ones, but she didn't care one bit.

I'm here for me.

She dipped her toe into the crazy-fricking-hot pool. "Jesus!" The few people brave enough to be in it laughed. Undaunted, Ellie eased herself in, inch-by-inch, and sank beneath the surface. Like a turtle pulling into its shell, she shut out the world.

> *Hi Jerry,*
> *I haven't emailed in a couple of weeks and I want to apologize for that. You've been a huge support to me on my trip and I don't want you to think I take that for granted. I've appreciated all of it.*
> *The truth is I got carried away with that guy in the Galápagos. But it's over now, and for the best too. Apart from that disaster, I had the most unforgettable time and keep replaying it in my head like a movie. To be the star of our own movie, now that's what life should be like!*
> *Right now I'm sitting in a cafe in Baños, watching the clouds crawl down the mountains and eating this 'melcocha' taffy stuff they sell on every corner. Totally addicted ☺ Today I took Bella's suggestion and visited the hot springs. It was bliss and I'm slowly getting back*

to a healthy state of mind. I also had a bizarre massage where a lady climbed on top of me and pounded my flesh like a schnitzel 😵 Tomorrow I'm tossing up whether to go 'puenting' OMG...
Are you well? Is the museum coming along? How are the girls? I'm sorry I disappeared for a while, Jerry. I've missed our chats,
Ellie.

San Francisco, USA

How could he not smile? Her email was a wonderful surprise. Jerry sat inside a portable office on the boundary of the construction site, hemmed in by rows of pipes awaiting installation. Plans were pinned to the walls and a window by the desk let him watch the museum's progress. Jerry decided to take his dad's advice.

Hi Ellie,
I was worried you'd been swallowed by Moby Dick 😊
It's great to know you're safe and relaxing in Baños. I'm well, as are the girls. Mia has decided she wants to be a coder and programmed a game on the iPad where a princess has to defeat a dragon to rescue a prince. Talk about role reversal! I think these kids are becoming smarter than me, which is a worry...
As for the museum, we're still running behind so finding ways to catch up is taking most of my time. It's a bit like steering a big ship with a small rudder. I'm praying it doesn't turn into the Titanic.
On the topic of ships going under, we went rafting in Baños and the kids loved it when the raft flipped and threw us all into the river. And you must go puenting!

Especially now that you're a certified daredevil. I'll attach an embarrassing photo of my puenting experience. My excuse is…well, I have no excuse. It was a rush though. As I told my kids—all you need is one second of courage. Just one second. The rest will take care of itself. I have faith in you, Ellie 😊 Let me know how it goes, Jerry.

CHAPTER 40

Baños, Ecuador

Ellie rolled over to dodge the sunlight streaming through the thin curtains. She'd been in this semi-awake state for a while, thinking about Bella's message. It would be so simple to forgive herself completely. It would only take one decision. One little brain cell sparking a revolution in her head.

Forgive your desires.

Forgive your mistakes.

Fall in love with yourself, every day.

When she put it like that, it sounded so…easy. Ellie searched for her phone under the bunk bed and saw Jerry had replied. A smile spread across her cheeks, and she wondered why it was so spontaneous.

Opening his email, Ellie snorted at the photo of Jerry puenting and stifled a laugh by burying her head in her pillow. Puenting was the Ecuadorian version of bungee jumping, where you leaped off a bridge, flipped 180-degrees in the air, then swung in a massive arc before reaching solid ground. That's if everything went right. In his photo, Jerry had just vaulted off the bridge and all four of his long limbs were suspended in mid-air like a cat leaping off a hot tin roof. His expression was priceless, a wide-eyed mix of sheer terror and boyish delight.

If Jerry can do it and look so ridiculous, I can too.

All you need is one second of courage. Just one second. The rest will take care of itself.

Jerry's words echoed in Ellie's ears while she watched bold souls get harnessed, then climb the rickety wooden platform on the side of the bridge. They all looked down at what their mind surely told them would be death. Instant, brain-smashing, death. Three hundred feet below, a river raged like a blizzard. So if the fall didn't kill you, you'd probably drown.

Some people shook uncontrollably. Others broke down in tears. Many gave up and stepped off.

Ellie understood that flight response well because she'd been doing it her whole life. But this new Ellie had stood on the precipice of Mount Roraima and conquered her fear of heights, goddammit. It would be just like that—but then jumping off. Not so hard, right?

Hahahahaha—SHIT.

Next in line was a boy, no more than ten years-old. He scrambled onto the platform, waved to his mom, then dove off without hesitation, screaming excitedly all the way down.

Ellie exhaled to push out the negative thoughts about how there wouldn't be an open casket at her funeral if this went wrong.

All you need is one second of courage. Just one second. The rest will take care of itself.

The instructor fitted Ellie with a harness. It seemed loose. She walked toward the platform. Climbed up deliberately. Locked back her wobbling knees. Shuffled to the edge. The whole thing shook.

"Don't look down," the instructor said.

Ellie looked down. "Jesus, that's high!" She snapped her head up and looked straight out over the river instead.

"Jump after three. Go first time or you never go. Ready?"

"No."

"OK one, two, three—"

All you need is one second of courage. Just one second. The rest will take care of itself.

"Jump!"

Ellie closed her eyes and launched forward into the void.

ohmygodimgonnadie

She tried to grab at something. Anything. But there was only air. She felt as if time slowed but her heart raced at full speed. There was nothing to hold her, just gravity pulling as she fell.

And fell.

And fell.

"Ahhhhhhhhhhhhhhhhhhh!"

Tension suddenly jerked into the line and Ellie flipped upside down. Her hair tumbled over her head and she lost orientation.

Then she was upright again. She stabilized, opening her eyes.

Holy shit, I did it.

"Woohoohoo!" Ellie yelled as she swung over the river like a yo-yo. "Woo-fucking-hoo!"

San Francisco, USA

Jerry pulled his SUV to the curb outside his daughters' school. The afternoon bell had gone and students ran out of class to find their rides home. For once he wasn't late, but his girls knew by now not to hurry. His phone beeped while he waited. The subject of Ellie's email was 'SUPERWOMAN.'

> *OMG I puented! Thanks for your encouragement, Jerry. From here on out I've decided to call you my Supporter-in-Chief and you'll definitely get my vote at the next election* 😉 *Even though you're thousands*

*of miles away, I couldn't have done it without you!
Oh, and I peed my pants. Like actual pee came out.
It's weird I feel comfortable telling you that given we've
never met. What a strange friendship we have. Can
I call it that? I do feel I can tell you anything, even if
you don't want to hear it* 😂
Proof of jump attached, Ellie.

Jerry's laugh grew louder when he downloaded Ellie's photo and saw the absolute horror on her face as she leaped off the bridge. Big rewards often required looking silly. And peeing your pants, evidently.

The car doors opened and his daughters bundled in, along with their noise. Jerry tried to hide his buoyant grin.

"What's wrong?" Yasmina said, running a self-conscious hand through her hair.

"Nothing, honey."

It's all good.

CHAPTER 41

Mancora, Peru

Ellie pushed through the crowd and out of the club. The techno was still deafening on the beach. Taking off her flip-flops, she struck a quick pace to get away from the strip known as Cocktail Alley, where clubs had subtle names like Cocksuckin' Cowgirl. Not exactly her scene. She found a quiet spot and dropped her backside into the sand.

This place was a mistake.

After finding peace in Baños, she'd visited southern Ecuador to see the charming Ingapirca ruins, northern capital of the once-mighty Incan empire. It was Ellie's first stop on an archaeological journey she hoped would culminate in the most famous Incan site of all—Machu Picchu.

But she was unprepared for what lay across the border here in Mancora, on the coast of Peru. It was South America's most popular surfing destination and gringo central. Drunk, high, idiotic, gringo central.

This morning, Ellie got woken by a Frenchman strutting naked around the hostel like a rooster in a hen pen. His flaccid penis was a long way off Dirk Diggler's.

To make matters worse, the one toilet in the twenty-bed dorm was blocked and her only option was to hold her bladder until a surfing lesson when she could pee in the sea. Sorry, fishes. At least she managed to stand up on the board. Twice.

For the past few hours, Ellie had attempted to be social—doing everything possible to forget about Eduardo. She partied with some friendly Swiss women, but as the night dragged on she grew more distant. It was a combination of everyone funneling bargain-basement vodka down their throats till they couldn't stand straight, the inevitable fights breaking out between college bros in stickered baseball caps (seriously, what was that about?), the pair having pants-still-on sex in the corner, the other pair snorting coke out of each other's bellybuttons, and the douchebag who slapped Ellie's ass before she pushed him away to cheers from his buddies. How was this anyone's idea of a good time?!

A himbo from California had approached her to chat, but he didn't look a day over twenty-one and said 'dude' without any irony. "Where you headed next, dude?"

"I'm thinking of going to Kuelap," Ellie replied.

"Que-what?"

"Kue-lap," she shouted over the music.

"Is that like a club?"

"No. It's the ruins of a pre-Incan fortress."

"Never 'erd of it, dude. We don't do ruins." He thumbed at his identical blonde posse, bopping ineptly to the music like background actors. "We surf."

Ellie couldn't think of a polite response so just looked away.

"Hey," he said. "How old are you?"

The sound of smashing glass brought Ellie back to the present. She turned and saw two drunk Irish women tumble out of the nearest club and land in the sand. They crawled on top of each other, pulling hair and slapping faces, all while yelling "Scrag!" They didn't seem to care their boobs had fallen out of their tops. A crowd of morons gathered around, egging them on.

That's some cultural immersion right there. What do the locals think of us gringos acting this way?

Ellie told herself she really did try to have fun. That she wasn't just some old grouch. But what she'd experienced tonight was a depressing indictment of the human race.

A chant of "Bitch fight!" went up.

Ellie looked away and saw a couple sitting a bit farther along the beach, the woman snuggling between the man's legs. She was pixie-like with short hair and sharp eyes. He had spikey hair and a Gallic nose that reminded Ellie of the comic book character Asterix. "Excuse me, do you have the time?" she asked.

The man looked at his phone. "It's just after ten."

"Really? I thought it was about one."

"You're not enjoying the party?"

Ellie rolled her eyes. "I came here to relax for a few days, but it's kind of a hell-hole."

"We thought exactly the same thing!" the woman laughed.

"I'm Ellie, by the way." She scooted closer and shook their hands. It was so easy to connect with people when you had a mutual hatred.

"I'm Eva and this is Dom."

"I can't place your accents. They sound a bit like Dutch."

"We're from Flanders. Belgium."

Ellie noticed Dom's hand return to rest on Eva's stomach. "I don't mean to pry, but...are you pregnant?"

Eva and Dom looked at each other. "How did you know?"

"The way your hand...there's just something protective about it."

"Oh wow, I can't believe you could tell from that," Eva said.

Ellie shrugged. "How far along are you?"

"Twelve weeks, I think."

"And you came to South America?" Ellie's eyebrows flared. *What about the Zika virus or Swine flu or whatever else was killing babies these days?*

"We only found out this week. We have been the last few months in India and…actually we haven't told anyone yet, not even our parents."

"I think you're really brave to get pregnant while traveling. Congratulations."

Eva glowed. "Thanks. It wasn't exactly planned though… tantric sex and all that."

"Ah…" Ellie nodded, only having a vague idea about tantric sex. Was that the one where you had sex while meditating in an upside-down yoga pose? It didn't sound too comfortable. "So are you guys headed home?"

"Our flight to Brussels is in seven days, right babe?" Eva said. "But we heard about this place called Kuelap. Do you know it?"

"That's where I'm going! Do you want to come? It's a twenty-four hour bus ride so I could use some company."

"When are you leaving?"

"Tomorrow morning, if possible."

Eva and Dom shared a few words in their own language. "We'd love to come. All three of us." She gently patted her tummy.

San Francisco, USA

An NFL game played on the TV in the living room, but Jerry kept the sound low. He leaned over the coffee table where a series of plans were laid out, made an amendment to one, then checked his watch. 11:45 p.m.

Why hasn't Yasmina called yet? She's meant to be—

His phone rang. "Is everything OK, honey?" Jerry strained to hear the response. "Who am I speaking with?" Concern streaked across his face. "Alison, keep her away from any more alcohol. I'll be there as soon as I can."

Jerry brought his SUV to an abrupt halt outside a double-story house in a plush neighborhood. He ran up the steps and rang the doorbell. Judging by the loud pop music, there was quite a party going on inside. He rang the bell again.

The door swung open and a heavily made-up seventeen year-old, wearing a dress too revealing for her age, greeted him. "Hi, Mr. Townsend."

"Where is she, Alison?"

"Dad!" Yasmina shouted, stumbling along the hallway. "What are you doing here? I'm getting a lift home with…Bryan." She slurred her words and started to slide down the wall.

Jerry rushed forward and caught her before she hit the floor. "You're coming home with me."

"But the party…"

"Is over for you." In one lift, Jerry scooped Yasmina up and took her outside. Her head flopped backward like a rag doll.

"Sorry, Mr. Townsend," Alison said.

"Is anyone else in trouble in there?"

She shook her head. "Yas just wouldn't stop challenging everyone to shots."

"How many did she have?"

"I don't know. At least ten."

"Call me again if you need help. Don't hesitate. And think about turning that music down soon."

"Sure thing. Thanks, Mr. Townsend."

Jerry carried Yasmina down the steps and placed her in the passenger seat, careful not to hit her head on the door frame. He drove slowly. Yasmina graduated from mumbling to moaning and then groaning. Jerry put his palm on her forehead to check her temperature.

"Dad," she whispered.

"Yes, honey?"

"Am I dead?"

"No, you're not dead," he said. "Just very, very drunk. Let me know if you're going to be sick so I can pull over, OK?"

"OK… Hey dad?"

"Yes, hon—"

Yasmina projectile vomited on the windscreen. Then she vomited again, covering the dashboard. It dripped onto the carpet.

Jerry pulled the car to the curb. He reached over and flicked open her door. She puked again, mostly making it into the gutter.

"Keep going. Get out as much as you can."

Yasmina threw up a fourth time and final time.

"There you go." Jerry grabbed a box of tissues from the backseat. He wiped her hands and face as chunks of sick dripped off her chin and onto her dress. "Feeling better?"

Yasmina nodded sluggishly.

"We're almost home. Just hold onto these." He put the box of tissues in her lap and she hugged it like a baby. "And let me know if I need to pull over again."

Yasmina buried her head in the seat, hiding from her pain and shame.

Jerry helped her upstairs and into bed. She was awake, but groggy, and had trouble keeping her eyes open. He found a bottle of water on her desk.

"Have a drink please, Yas."

"I don't want any."

"I know you don't want it, but you need it. You'll thank me tomorrow."

She reluctantly took a sip. "Everything's spinning."

"It'll do that for a while." Jerry pulled the bedcover over her.

"I'm never drinking again."

I wish that were true. I really do.

He looked lovingly at his daughter, then kissed her goodnight.

"Dad…thanks for looking after me." Her head rolled to the side and she fell asleep.

"Anytime, honey."

> *Hi Ellie,*
>
> *So it's 2 a.m. and I've just finished cleaning Yasmina's vomit out my car. The joy of being a parent! You want to be angry, but then you look at them and melt. And it's not like I was much better behaved in my teenage years… Hopefully her hangover isn't too bad or I'll have to deal with one very grumpy girl in the morning 😮*
> *I'm glad you're heading to Kuelap. It was on our list of places to visit, but the road had washed out in the wet season. We did get up to the Túcume pyramids and Royal Sipán Museum though. I won't spoil anything except to say, prepare to be amazed!*
> *I've also been thinking about what you wrote, about how it's funny that we feel OK to tell anything to each other even though we haven't met. I like it. And I would call it a friendship. An unusual one, for sure, but still a friendship. Who else am I going to email in the middle of the night to tell them my daughter puked all over my dash? Lucky you 😉*
> *Jerry.*

CHAPTER 42

Chachapoyas, Peru

After hightailing it from the nightmare of Mancora, Ellie found her groove off the gringo trail with Eva and Dom. From the balcony of a family-run guesthouse deep in the Andes Mountains, she watched morning fog melt up the maize terraces, some on absurd sixty degree angles.

The indigenous people who called this place home scratched out a subsistence living, sheltering in mud-brick huts and tending to crops like their ancestors had done for a thousand years. They'd evolved short bodies with thick legs to deal with the punishing work, and their faces were rough, as if someone had drawn lines on their skin tracing the rivers running through their land. In the cool climate, they wrapped themselves in ponchos woven from alpaca wool and dyed in rainbow colors, dotting the mountains around the guesthouse like lollipops.

Ellie asked around town and found a guide to take her and the Belgians to Kuelap. The ancient fortress stood tall, projecting its power from almost two miles above sea-level. Its walls soared over fifty feet high and ran for 600 yards along a sharp ridge. Even at first glance she could see why it'd earned the nickname, 'Machu Picchu of the North.' As they walked through the imposing entrance, her brain ignited with questions.

Where did all these stones come from? How did they move them? How long did it take? Will they fall on me?

Their guide was a hippie with stringy gray hair who smelled of rolled tobacco and introduced himself as Alfonse, but preferred to be called Starman. Hey, why not? Ellie barely batted an eyelid anymore. He was passionate about the site and its forgotten place in history.

"Kuelap was constructed by the Chachapoyan people from the sixth century AD. That's almost one-thousand years *before* Machu Picchu had even been planned. Do you understand? Yes? How old it is? Yes?"

Starman stroked his beaded rat's tail while waiting for them to nod.

"The Chachapoyans built Kuelap to defend themselves, but were eventually conquered by the Incas, just before the Spanish arrived in the early-1500s to conquer them. History always repeats. Yes? How interesting it does that. Yes?"

Ellie nodded again. Definitely, yes. She and the Belgians followed Starman around the bottom of three levels inside the city. Farmers had lived here in circular, double-story, houses with a system of running water through carved channels. The rock had come from a quarry on one side of the mountain, but archaeologists still didn't know how they'd cut the boulders or moved them.

The ruins were so overgrown Ellie's group had to climb over mossy rocks and pull themselves up on vines to reach the middle level where military personnel lived, then the top level where the royal family had built a villa with panoramic views of the Andes. Not a bad penthouse.

Everything about this colossal citadel was fascinating, and Ellie wandered around for most of the afternoon in open-mouthed disbelief. Almost as astonishing—they were the only foreigners here. Kuelap received just fifty tourists a day compared to the 2,000 people who descended on Machu Picchu.

I can't wait to tell Jerry. He's going to flip!

As they relaxed at the highest point, keeping hydrated and admiring the breathtaking setting, Starman provided his interpretation of Kuelap as an important "energy point." He was convinced it was one of five secret locations on the planet— including the Egyptian pyramids, Fatehpur Sikri in India, Angkor Wat in Cambodia, and the Pentagon in the U.S.A.—and buried underneath each of them was…an alien spaceship.

"They will rise up. Yes? Take over the world. Very soon. History always repeats. Yes?"

His theory sounded like a stoner's version of *War of the Worlds*, and Ellie had no doubt Starman would've been right at home on the New York subway. Probably the A line. But she knew better than to disagree with the person they were relying on to get them down safely. So, aliens? Most definitely, yes.

"He was a little nuts," Eva dead-panned over dinner at a sidewalk restaurant.

"A little nuts?" the usually-reserved Dom exclaimed. "He was a loon."

"A bit like you then, babe?" Eva pulled a face, then leaned across the table to kiss him.

"Isn't that one of the reasons we're traveling?" Ellie said once the lovebirds had finished smooching. "To meet new and interesting people? I mean, I think it's not just the places we go, but the people we meet that make it worthwhile."

"Amen to that." Eva raised her glass of water.

"What made you guys start your trip?"

"Dom's a clumsy idiot, that's what. We were rushing to get ready for our retail jobs that we hated and paid us nothing, and he forgot to put the lid on the blender. We both stood there, covered in milk and blueberries—"

"Raspberries."

"—looked at each other and knew. It was time to leave all that shit behind."

"And I wanted to get away from her mother."

"Shut up. You love my mother."

"Her mother wants us to get married and have babies."

"You're half-way there," Ellie pointed out.

"Almost." Eva fed Dom a spoon of *aji de gallina* (shredded chicken in hot cream sauce). "But we did want to meet people from all over the world. Like, if we didn't travel we would never have met you."

"And we would never have met Starman," Dom added. "Maybe we should buy him a shovel so he can start digging for the aliens."

"Yeah, he was a bit weird and all that, babe. But that's why leaving home is so good. You meet people outside your—how do you say?—'closed circle' of family and friends. It helps you understand them. That's what I want our baby to learn too."

It was Dom's turn to lean over the table and kiss Eva.

Ellie's insides warmed. She could sense how in love her Belgian friends were. It wasn't only the way they looked at each other, but the way they looked *after* each other.

This example of love before her eyes was so much more than she'd had with Eduardo. With the benefit of hindsight, he'd been nothing more than sexual desire mixed with passing infatuation. Call it a hard crush. It made Ellie think about the kind of partner she really wanted in her life. And whether she would ever find him.

CHAPTER 43

Túcume, Peru

On the bus back to the Pacific coast, there was no shortage of vendors to keep Ellie and the Belgians fueled with *camotes fritas* (sweet potato chips) and *Inca Kola* (a fluorescent yellow soda that tasted like Hubba Bubba). Hello, sugar rush.

Ellie used the ride to write advice about Kuelap into her *Unique Planet*. She'd grown accustomed to adding to Bella's notes, and although the thought crossed her mind that one day she might have to pass the guidebook onto someone else, for now she was firmly attached to it.

At Túcume, they stopped at the largest complex of pyramids in the world. There were more pyramids here than in Egypt! In the sizzling afternoon sun, Ellie and her friends climbed to a lookout over the sprawling archaeological site dating to 600 AD. Unfortunately, the pyramids had been constructed from mud so were all significantly weathered, the smallest reduced to just mounds of dirt in the desert. Ellie used her imagination to picture the city, once bustling with merchants, tradesmen, and children playing in the streets.

Now it's literally lost to the sands of time.

Nearby stood a modern, concrete, pyramid housing the

museum Jerry had teased would blow her away. The tomb inside contained the skeleton of a king, five-feet two-inches tall and thirty-five years of age at his death 1700 years ago. Buried with him were three wives, a child of ten years old, two llamas, and three male warriors with their feet chopped off.

Someone must've had a foot fetish.

Excavated from the tomb were over 450 artefacts made from gold, silver, copper and precious stones. The necklaces and bracelets laid around the king's sarcophagus rivalled any treasures Ellie had seen in other museums or documentaries. His headdress, a huge semi-circle of gold designed to reflect the sun, left her spellbound. Even more impressive was his gold facemask, spectre, and earspools inlaid with turquoise. For a society that didn't have sophisticated machinery, the quality was astonishing.

How can this civilization have so many similarities to the ancient Egyptians? I mean, they both built pyramids, lusted after treasure, and believed objects buried with them would travel to an afterlife. But it's impossible for the two cultures to have had contact.

The only explanation in the Occam's Razor of Ellie's logical mind was that humans over thousands of miles and thousands of years apart hadn't changed that much.

Surrounded by all these glittering objects, she felt like Howard Carter in 1922 when he shone a light inside Tutankhamun's tomb and exclaimed in response to Lord Carnarvon's question, "Can you see anything?" with, "Yes, wonderful things!"

Hi Jerry,
You were right about the Royal Sipán Museum. MIND. BLOWN. I can barely articulate what I'm feeling. Like, my brain might have imploded and now I'm writing like a teenager lol 😝 *If only more people knew about this place and could see all the incredible things here. Are they the sort of artefacts that'll be in your museum?*

If so, then I must come visit. Can you send me a photo of what it's going to look like? Soooooooooo excited! On an entirely unrelated note (but when did that ever stop me?), what did you think about the food in Peru? I'm loving it and eating everything in sight. Actually, that's no different to usual... Lomo saltado has to be my favorite so far, but tomorrow night we're going to try ceviche and I'm already salivating. You can probably tell I'm pumped about everything right now. All these new places are keeping me happy 😊 *THE WORLD IS AN AMAZING PLACE!*
Ellie.

San Francisco, USA

Jerry completed his domestic duties for the evening with a sigh of resignation. Andrea had cleaned the kitchen, but somehow it always fell to him to put out the trash. As he made his way to the street, it occurred to him that this current activity probably wasn't nearly as thrilling as Ellie's.

He switched off the lights and headed upstairs. With papers spread over every inch of his study, it appeared Jerry had painted himself into a corner. He trod over them, ignoring the implication.

Dear Ellie,
From now on you'll be known as Indiana Ellie! Or perhaps Ellie Croft is more appropriate? Your intrepid adventures would inspire even the most jaded explorers. I'm happy you loved the Royal Sipán museum as much as I did 😊
I've attached a sketch of what our museum will look like. It's called The Pata Museum ('Pata' is the Quechuan word for 'terrace'—you've probably seen a lot of them

*already in Peru). The terrace design was Bella's ingenious
idea. Inside will be filled with Latin American art and
artefacts from the Flores family collection so, yes, you
must come visit when it's finished!*

*Bella often cooked Peruvian food at home so we were
used to a lot of it. My favorite is pollo a la brasa. Flame
grilled chicken marinated in salt, chilli and paprika.
Oh God, my mouth is watering just thinking about
it. Try it with a side of salchipapas and I guarantee
you won't be disappointed* ☺

*Speaking of disappointment, I should probably let
you know it's my birthday next Saturday. I'll be 39,
and despite my best efforts don't seem to be getting any
younger. It's my first birthday without Bella so I'll have
to put on a brave face for the girls.*

Keep exploring,

Jerry.

Trujillo, Peru

Ellie did keep exploring. A minivan four hours through
the desert brought her and the Belgians to the remains of the
Moche civilization at the Pyramid of the Sun and Pyramid of
the Moon. Towering over the sand like ancient megachurches,
the structures dated back 1500 years and were made up of 140
million bricks each.

The better-preserved Pyramid of the Moon contained shrines
to gods long forgotten, and vivid paintings of a jaguar with
ferocious fangs decorated its interiors. How did the paint job
last so long? When modern paints only guaranteed ten years?

One mural stretched thirty-five feet high and seventy feet
across, dwarfing Ellie as she stood in front of it. The painting
depicted the Moche's belief system that the sun and moon

controlled all aspects of life—night, day, weather, harvests, births and deaths. They believed, as did the all-conquering Incas who came a thousand years later, that the sun was the most powerful god of all.

Jerry, I just got back from the Pyramid of the Moon and my head is spinning ☉ I guess I wasn't prepared for the amount of stunning archaeology in Peru. It's like South America's answer to the Mayans. And I haven't even got to Machu Picchu yet!

Do you know what's become clear to me? These different civilizations that lived hundreds, thousands, of years ago—they all thought about the same things we still do today. Why are we on this planet? Is there a God or gods? Is there something after this life?

And it makes perfect sense they worshipped the sun because it gave them everything they needed, like light in the morning, warmth for their bodies, energy to grow crops. Without the sun they wouldn't have existed. Hell, we wouldn't exist! They made meaning out of where they lived and what they had, just like we do. Interesting, right?

Y'know, this may sound crazy, but for the first time in my life I feel like a member of a species that doesn't just live in the present, but goes all the way back to the billions of people who came before me, and the billions more to come after me. I feel connected to it all. Is that weird? I know it sounds weird, but is it actually weird? Maybe I need a pisco sour...

To less mysterious matters, I can definitely see the throughlines (if that's the right word) from ancient Peru to your museum. The design is brilliant, in my humble layperson's opinion, and I'm sure Bella would

appreciate you working so hard to get it finished. I
can't wait to visit one day.
So, yes, I am a total nerd but at least I'm not turning
39 in a few days 😬 *What are your birthday plans,*
old man?

"Who's this guy you keep messaging?"

"Shit!" Ellie almost jumped out of her skin. She flipped over her phone and sat up on the sofa. "You scared me, Eva."

"Sorry. You don't need to stop." Eva dropped onto a cushion in the common room of their hostel.

"I know. I'm not sure why I did that."

"Maybe it's because you like this person…?"

"No, no," Ellie responded hastily. "He's just a friend."

"A *special* friend?"

"Why do you say that?" Ellie felt her cheeks flush.

"Because every time we get WiFi you're emailing someone. And I know it's the same person because you have the same smile every time."

"What smile? No, it's no-one. Really." Ellie tucked her hair behind her ears and took a moment to collect her thoughts. "Well, not no-one. But it's not a thing. Y'know? It's just a friendship. A bit…accidental. His late-wife wrote all the info in the guidebook I've been using."

Ellie handed Eva her *Unique Planet* and she flipped through the pages, glancing at the notes and drawings. "He gave you this before you left home?"

"Not exactly…" Ellie gave an abridged explanation of how she'd come into possession of the guidebook and got in contact with Jerry. It didn't come out as coherent as she hoped.

"Some people might call that fate," Eva said.

Ellie swallowed hard.

One more question, Jerry. Do you believe in fate? I think my mind is too rational to accept something so intangible but I'm curious what you think, as always.
Best,
Indiana Ellie.

Eva's comment still circled around Ellie's head when they went out to dinner. It would be their last meal together so they settled on an upscale seaside restaurant. Easy-listening hits from the '80s like Whitney Houston's *I Wanna Dance With Somebody* were playing. She tried to block out the music, but Eva and Dom serenaded each other.

Instead, Ellie ordered *ceviche* and ascended to gastronomic heaven. Her taste buds danced the *Pachanga* as tart lime and garlic juice flowed across her tongue, tempered by the soft flesh of the corvina fish, then the crunch of peppers and red onion. It wasn't often she licked her knife, but tonight she made an exception.

As her head hit the pillow, Ellie reflected on the back-and-forth emails she and Jerry had been exchanging for the past eight weeks. There was no denying it was unusual, but there was also something comforting about knowing he would always reply. He was, without fail, courteous and respectful, and it felt old-fashioned in that way, like she was a young woman of means on an 18th century Grand Tour of Europe writing letters back home.

And she enjoyed getting to know more about him. They'd never met or even heard each other's voices, but there was an undeniable connection. Where was it all heading? Anywhere? Nowhere? She fell to sleep smiling at the ridiculous thought that one day their messages would be published in a book like Florence Nightingale's *Letters from Egypt*. Now that would be something.

San Francisco, USA

Damn. Almost midnight. Jerry yawned so wide it hurt. He'd phoned Yasmina hours ago to say he wouldn't be home until late, and that she would need to organize dinner and make sure Mia got to bed on time. He hated doing it, but couldn't see any other way—there just weren't enough hours in the day. For the millionth time, he wished Bella were here.

There's no way she'd let me skip dinner with the kids, not even if we were designing the Empire State Building.

Jerry stuffed a stack of papers in his satchel and was about to shut his laptop when he saw Ellie's email. Reading it was the best part of his day.

> *Indiana Ellie,*
> *It's not weird that you feel so connected to everything you're experiencing. It's wonderful. Because understanding another place or time or people helps us to understand ourselves better* 😊
> *When I stood on the Pyramid of the Moon and looked over the ruins, Shelley's 'Ozymandias' jumped into my head. Do you know it? It got me thinking about whether our modern civilization will suffer the same end as all the others that came before it. I guess only time will tell, but I like to be an optimist about these things—as a father I kind of have to be.*
> *As for whether I believe in fate… Well, I think we can only trust what our experience teaches us. For me it's that there are incredible and inexplicable coincidences in life, but we also have free will. So ultimately we have to act to get what we desire. You don't want to let something amazing slip through your fingers and be forever asking 'what if?'*

*For my birthday, I'm hoping fate lets me sleep in for
a few hours* 😌 *Take care,
Jerry.*

As he left the office, Jerry thought about the 21st century pen-pal friendship he and Ellie had developed. They were emailing almost daily now, and he always felt a jolt of anticipation when one of her messages arrived. Like a kid opening a Christmas present. He remained wary of letting grief, loneliness and stress cloud his feelings again, but enjoyed learning more about this intriguing woman. And he wondered where it was all headed, if anywhere.

CHAPTER 44

Lima, Peru

In the capital, Ellie bid a tearful goodbye to Eva and Dom and their unborn baby. The Belgians headed to the airport for their flight home, while Ellie checked into a hostel.

She spent the evening catching up on social media and writing Gabby and other friends she'd been neglecting the past few days. From out here in the real world, though, office politics seemed like an absurd, parallel, universe. She had zero fucks left to give about it. Traveling had led to more than just a change in location. It'd been an awakening.

The next day, Ellie relaxed by playing with the beloved stray cats of Parque Kennedy (hand sanitizer was close at hand) and found another statue of her on-again-off-again lover, Simon Bolivar.

Since their last encounter, Ellie had researched the romantic life of the continent's most revered hero, known as *El Libertador*. After Bolivar's first wife died from yellow fever, he carried on a love affair with women's rights activist Manuela Sáenz. In 1828 she saved him from an assassination attempt and from that point on he called her *La Libertadora del Libertador*—the Liberator of the Liberator.

Why can't I have a love story like that?

"Mr. Bolivar, we meet again. What a splendid coincidence! The pleasure is mine. Yours too? That's grand. What do you think about making things more formal between us? A commitment of sorts, like an engagement?" She took a slurp of tart *maracuyá* juice. "I see…too soon. Well, I'm sure you'll come around. I'm super cute, y'know." If no-one else was going to say it, she sure-as-hell would.

Though surrounded by all the conveniences of modern life in Lima, Ellie was eager to jump ship from the hectic metropolis. She wanted to discover places that didn't have a passing resemblance to New York. The craving for adventure made Ellie wonder if she'd become addicted to the road. And, by extension, if the road would come to own her with its endless freedom and promise of excitement away from the routine of normal life.

21st September – San Francisco, USA

In contrast, Jerry's life was *all* routine. On a typical day he made his daughters breakfast, drove them to school, held meetings, redrafted plans, picked up the kids, cooked them dinner, made sure they did their homework and went to bed on time, slaved away in his study, and only then grabbed a few hours' sleep.

On Saturdays he drove the girls to friends' houses or extra-curricular activities: basketball and track for Yasmina, soccer and debating club for Andrea. Mia wasn't happy to be dragged along, but Jerry usually promised her ice-cream if she cheered for her sisters. Sundays were taken up with seeing his parents and cleaning the house. Andrea's roster system had lightened the load, but he still had to supervise or Yasmina might overload the washing machine and flood the laundry again. As a single parent, there were *no days off.* The only break he got was Sunday mornings before the kids woke up. But this Sunday was different.

God. No. Let me sleep.

Jerry had heard the handle of his bedroom door turn.

Need sleep. More sleep.

The door creaked open. His three daughters attempted to have a hushed conversation about being hushed. Despite his exhaustion, their botched effort at stealth made Jerry smile. Within a few seconds they were upon him, Yasmina and Andrea jumping on the bed like a trampoline and Mia crawling across his face.

"HAPPY BIRTHDAY DAD!"

Jerry laughed as his daughters tickled him mercilessly. "OK, I give up!" They relented and he sat up. "Is it my birthday already?"

"Yes, Dad. You're almost forty," Yasmina said. "We're calling this your 'almost forty' birthday."

"Do I get a say in that? Thirty-nine is a long way from forty, you know."

"Seventeen is longer," Yasmina countered.

"So is twelve," Andrea added.

"And seven is so far from forty I can't even count it," Mia chimed in.

"Thank you, my lovely daughters. You fill me with such happiness on my *thirty-ninth* birthday."

"So...we got you a present." Yasmina handed Jerry an envelope.

"Is that it? It's really small."

"Dad!" his kids cried in unison.

"We thought that you never really get to do what you want," Andrea said. "I mean, you're always looking after us or working, so—"

"It's tickets," Mia blurted out, unable to contain her enthusiasm. Yasmina put a hand over her sister's mouth.

"Well, I love tickets." Jerry tore open the envelope. Inside was a birthday card and four tickets to a Major League Baseball game. "Giants tickets! For…today? This is the best present ever. Thank you." He hugged and kissed each of his daughters. They beamed. "But…you girls hate baseball."

"I think we can deal with it for three hours on our dad's birthday," Yasmina said.

"Minimum three hours, Yas. Let's hope it goes to extra innings."

"Can I get a hot dog?" Mia asked.

"Only if I can too," Jerry replied while reading their card.

> *Dear Dad,*
> *Have a VERY HAPPY 'almost 40' birthday!*
> *We know we don't say it enough, but thanks for everything you do for us. We really appreciate it and promise to be good for you today, even if that doesn't always work out* 😬
> *Although mom couldn't be here to help you celebrate, we know she's looking down and sending you lots of love.*
> *FELIZ CUMPLEAÑOS!*
> *Con amor, Yasmina, Andrea & Mia*
> *xxx ooo*

"That's a lovely message, girls. Very thoughtful. And these tickets are—wait, how did you afford them?"

Andrea and Mia looked sheepish and turned to Yasmina. "Um, we used your credit card."

No clouds in the sky. Bottom of the third. The Giants up 1 to a big fat 0 against the hapless Mets. It couldn't have been more perfect. Jerry carried a tray of hot dogs, fries and sodas down the stadium steps and joined his family in the front row of the balcony. He was decked out in his Giants bomber jacket, and even Yasmina wore a team cap.

"See, isn't this fun?" Jerry said, handing out the food and drinks.

"I haven't had this much fun since Friday's Math class," Yasmina replied.

"I don't mind it." Andrea stuffed a handful of fries in her mouth. "I mean, not much has happened yet, but guy who throws the ball—"

"The pitcher," Jerry corrected.

"Yeah, the pitcher guy with the long hair, he's pretty cute."

"He is *churro*," Yasmina agreed. "The others are a bit *gordo* though. Like that guy standing near the white thing."

"It's called a plate," Jerry corrected again.

"Yeah, he should run a few miles and lose those extra pounds."

"Mia, are you having a good time?" Jerry changed the subject.

Face full of hot dog and cheeks covered in ketchup, she nodded her head.

"Good. Because I'm having a great time. You know I used to come to the baseball with your grandpa every weekend."

"We know, Dad," Yasmina sighed. "We've heard this before."

"Of course, tickets were a lot cheaper back then. Your grandpa used to say that baseball isn't so much a game as a ceremony. The playing of the national anthem, the roar of the crowd before the first pitch, the smell of freshly cut grass." The girls had tuned out of Jerry's lecture and were busy gorging on junk food. "I know you're not listening but—"

The crack of ball meeting bat rang across the stadium.

Jerry and his daughters stood with the crowd, watching the ball sail high over the outfield and into the bleachers. Everyone cheered. 2-0 Giants. It was going to be a great day.

"I almost forgot. We need a photo!"

"Oh Dad, please, no."

"Seriously, Dad?"

"I want a reminder of how much fun we had so you'll come again. Turn around. C'mon Mia." Jerry handed his phone to a bearded man sitting behind them who took a photo of the family with the baseball diamond in the background. Jerry wore a grin like the Giants had won the World Series.

Huacachina, Peru

Ellie sucked in oxygen. It'd been a lung-busting hike to reach the peak of the sand dune. Below, a lagoon glowed like a pool of fire in the sunset. All she could see for miles around the oasis were rippling golden dunes. Shimmering on the horizon, the sun stood out as a giant orange disc.

This place had been an unexpected detour, but not every journey followed a plan. The best ones usually didn't.

In the morning she'd gone on a crazy *Mad Max* buggy ride, leaping over dunes and spinning through the sand. Awesome, except the soupy grains got into…every place they could. In the afternoon she cooled off in the shallow lagoon while students from a nearby school splashed each other. All you really needed to have fun was friends and water.

Now at sunset, Ellie wriggled her butt into the sand and pulled a bottle of pisco from her daypack. Coming here had been Bella's suggestion, and Ellie thought Peru's national drink would be a nice way to honor her. Every time she opened the *Unique Planet*, Bella's words spoke to her—informing, encouraging, inspiring. Bella's indomitable spirit had been preserved in its pages and often Ellie felt they were traveling together, like sisters.

It was easy to understand how Jerry could've fallen in love such an incredible woman. And what loss he and his daughters must feel, especially on his birthday.

How can I cheer him up?

She cracked open the bottle and took a drink. And a few

more. Then started snapping selfies. Duckface. Sparrowface. Frogface. Fishlips. Sexdollface.

OK, stop Ellie. Be present. Enjoy the moment.

Enough sand had been whipped up by the desert winds that the pastel blue sky dissolved into soft pink. One more drink for Bella. One for Ellie. And so on. The radiant sunset continued in peace until night arrived.

Immediately, Ellie felt a chill as the temperature plummeted. She looked at the 300-foot drop to the bottom of the dune.

Oh, hells yeah!

Ellie jumped—running, falling, sliding—until she tumbled head-over-heels down the last thirty feet and landed flat on her face in the sand. She couldn't stop laughing. Pisco was the best.

Jeeeeerrrrryyyyyyy, HAPPY BIRTHDAY to you!!!
I'm singing even thoug you cant hear it 😝 😝 😝 I got your email and it looks like you had great day with your family, fill with lots of loooove. And baseball! Great photo, btw. Your daughters are beautifu and you scrubbed up OK for old man hehehe 😌 See, I say nice things becuase it's your birthday! In case you didnt know, I'm kind of drunk. Only a little. maybe more. Anyway, Ive attach your presentt. I climbed the biggest fricking dune eva to get this pic so you better appreciate it 😳 😁 😂 #emojiqueen
Seriously Jerry, your friendship has mean
a lot to me and if anyone deserve a speccial day, it's youuu. Be good like me, Ellie 😝
PS Go Yankeeeeees

CHAPTER 45

Nazca, Peru

As much fun as it was to eat sand in Huacachina, the real reason Ellie had come through the desert on her way to Machu Picchu was to fulfil a childhood dream.

She'd first read about the Nazca Lines in a *National Geographic* magazine as an eleven year-old. Sitting in the waiting room of a dentist's practice, she'd been captivated by the mystery of how such huge marks had been made on the land. She didn't finish the article before it was her turn to see the dentist but the receptionist let her take it home, and later that night, when she was meant to be sleeping, Ellie spent hours enthralled by the photos of the 700 figures, shapes and lines carved into the desert. Some were more than nine miles long! A list of questions had run through her head then: Who made them? How did they make them? And why?

Now I'll finally be able to get some answers.

Bella had drawn a constellation across the page and recommended a visit to the planetarium with the words: 'We come from stars, and we return to stardust. Learn where you're from and where you're going.'

So Ellie tilted her head back to the curved dome and watched as the projection explained how the Nazca people, living from 1100 BC to 800 AD, had made the lines by pushing the dark layer of topsoil to the side, revealing a lighter layer underneath. These piles of topsoil then acted as wind tunnels that kept the lighter layer clear of debris. From the 1940s they were given a helping hand by German archaeologist Maria Reiche, who dedicated her life to conserving them, eventually going blind from decades under the desert sun.

The presentation explored the most popular theory about the Nazca Lines—that they aligned with planets and stars to function as a map of the sky on earth. Did they know where we came from? Ellie squirmed in her seat. She loved feeling like a kid again, unearthing evidence and solving mysteries.

There were also competing theories. One was that the Nazca people created the lines as offerings to their gods in the hope of more rain. Another was that they were landing strips for spaceships from another world. Where was Starman when you needed him? Either way, they were the remarkable work of countless people over the span of 1000 years.

And tomorrow I'll get to see them.

The six-seater plane hopped down the short strip of tarmac serving as a runway in this apricot desert. Ellie bristled with anticipation as it launched into the air and banked sharply. Being Indiana Ellie required such risks.

"Look to your right." The pilot's voice crackled in her headset. "Down to your right. You can see *la ballena.*"

Ellie pressed her face against the window and caught her first glimpse of a Nazca figure. The whale. Over 150 feet long, the magnificent animal had its mouth open wide about to swallow its prey. Ellie had waited twenty years to be here and her eyes misted. She pulled herself together, striking a balance between taking photos and letting the experience etch into her memory.

Her stomach lurched as the plane banked left and another figure came into view. The monkey. Over 325 feet long, it had an incredible tail that spiraled like a maze.

It was followed by the dog, spider, condor, and gob-smacking long-nosed humming bird.

Oh. My. God.

There were also figures for which there was no explanation, such as the pair of hands with only four fingers extending from the right palm, and the legendary 'astronaut.' Ellie thought it looked more like an alien. But that explanation was just as fantastic as a spaceman existing over 500 years before humans had succeeded in leaving our planet. It was waving at something…up there…

Ellie's eyes grew sore from staring as the plane swooped over the massive geoglyphs, not wanting to blink in case she missed a thing. Scattered between them were hundreds of lines and geometric shapes crisscrossing the landscape like a map.

A map for the gods?

Perhaps a map to the gods?

"Can you hear me, Donna?" Ellie said from her dorm bed. A small reading lamp lit her face.

"I hear you but can't see you. Wait, it's connecting… OK, there you are."

"Hi!"

"Where are you?" Donna walked outside into the backyard.

"Is that Aunty Ellie?" Alex rolled across the grass and into frame.

"It's me, sweetheart. How are you?"

"Good. When are you coming home?"

"Not for a while yet…"

"Ohhhhhh but you need to come home *now*," Alex pleaded. "I want you to play with me."

"And I want to play with you too. But I haven't finished my

trip yet."

"Helllloooooooooo!" Benji's head popped into view from behind the swing set.

"Hi Benji. Are you being good for your mom?"

"Yes."

"Really?" Donna threw him a look.

"Sometimes I am."

In the background, Ellie spotted Donna's husband walking out of the garage. "Roger!"

He stopped and realized his family was on a video call. "Oh, hi Ellie. When are you coming home?"

Ellie took a breath and decided to change tack. "How was Cancún?"

"The resort was beautiful, wasn't it kids?" Donna said.

"The pool was *this* big." Alex opened his arms as wide as he could.

"We had donuts for breakfast," Benji added with a lick of his lips.

"Did you visit Chichen Itza?"

"The resort was all-inclusive so we just stayed there for the week. How about the laser tag, kids?"

While Benji and Alex relived the laser tag game with finger guns and sound effects, Ellie tried to hide her disappointment. Going to Mexico and not visiting Chichen Itza would be like going to New York and skipping the Statue of Liberty. "Hey, today I saw the Nazca Lines."

"What's that?" Alex said.

"I'm glad you asked." Ellie told him what she'd learned at the planetarium and sent a photo of the condor figure to Donna's phone. It had a vast wingspan and elaborate tail-feathers that spread across the ground like a quiver of arrows.

"How big is it?" Alex's face loomed large on Ellie's screen as he looked at the photo.

"That one is over four-hundred feet long."

"Was it made by a giant?"

Ellie laughed. She related to her nephew's wonder for new and extraordinary things. "No sweetheart, they were made by an ancient civilization. Humans who lived a very long time ago."

"I want to go there."

"Mom, I need a cookie," Benji interrupted.

"You can't go," Donna answered her youngest son. "It's not safe. And school is back on Monday."

"Are you excited about starting grade two?" Ellie asked.

"Mom, I want a cookie." Benji stuck a finger in Donna's ear.

She batted it away. "OK, take your brother to the kitchen and I'll be there in a minute."

"Yes!"

"Love you Aunty Ellie," Alex shouted as he chased after Benji.

"Love you too."

Donna shifted forward and lowered her voice. "You're still coming home at the end of this month, right?"

San Francisco, USA

"Follow me." Kyra met Jerry at the elevator with one of her typically blunt greetings. Just once, he would love it if she were waiting with a cream cheese bagel.

"What's going on?" He jogged a few steps to catch up.

"We've got a problem. You're not gonna like it." She led him through the open-plan office space.

"What is it? Tell me." None of his employees were around, which seemed odd, but more concerning was the doom in Kyra's voice.

"You know how we're waiting on that shipment of granite from Peru?"

"Yes."

"It sank."

"What?!"

"I just got word. The boat went belly-up in a storm and sank faster than a sack of shit."

"Jesus Christ!" Jerry threw his hands in the air. "We can't complete the terraces without that granite."

"I have the supplier on the line right now." Kyra sped a step ahead of Jerry and opened the door to his office. He walked inside—

"SURPRISE!"

Jerry's employees cheered and threw streamers across the room.

His distraught face broke into a smile as he realized he'd been tricked.

"I got you good," Kyra declared through a smug grin.

A large rectangular cake had been set on a table in the middle of Jerry's office. The icing read: 'Happy Birthday! (Now finish the museum)'. Hard to disagree with that. He blew out the candles to a round of applause.

"OK, quiet down. I don't often get to say this to you as a group. Thank you for everything you've done this past year. I know how hard you've all worked on our museum. And we will get there. I'm more confident of that now than I was a minute ago when I thought our granite had gone the way of the Bismarck. I also…" Jerry choked on the emotion before swallowing it. "I also want to say thank you for how you've supported me personally. It's been a tough time and I've appreciated your kindness more than words can say. So, please, let's enjoy!"

After ten pounds of cake and a gallon of coffee had been consumed, Jerry was left alone in his office. He flicked a balloon off his desk, opened his laptop and received another surprise. Ellie's drunk 'Happy Birthday' email. He laughed as he read it, imagining her struggling to type after all that pisco. And he howled at the photo she'd attached, trying but failing to make a duckface in the desert.

She's funny. And cute.

It wasn't the first time he'd thought that. Yes, Ellie looked different to Bella, perhaps even the opposite with her white skin, blonde hair and blue eyes—but still undeniably cute.

> *Hi Ellie,*
>
> *Thanks for the birthday message! I love it and will save the photo for any future blackmail opportunities* 😊
> *Your friendship has meant a lot to me too, and there couldn't be a better guardian for Bella's guidebook than you.*
>
> *Are you in Nazca yet? Seeing the Nazca Lines was a childhood dream of mine. I got a bit teary when we flew over the condor because I used to have a picture of it on my wall when I was a kid. It was from a National Geographic magazine, if I remember correctly. So I couldn't believe I was finally there, seeing it with my own eyes. Did you have a maniac pilot as well? Ours banked left and right so many times all the girls threw up. Andrea was the first to go, then it was like a chain reaction with Mia, Yas, and Bella. Thankfully we reached solid ground in time or I would have heaved too! If you're off to Arequipa next, be sure to say hello to Juanita... Safe travels* 😊
> *Jerry.*

CHAPTER 46

Arequipa, Peru

Ellie stepped into the dark room with soft-footed reverence. Her guide, a plump woman with a museum badge on her blouse, flicked a switch by the door. At the far end, a glass box illuminated under a dull light. Inside was one of Peru's—and the world's—most prized archaeological relics.

The hairs on Ellie's neck stood up. Continuing her slow approach, the object in the box came into focus. A girl, literally frozen in time: Juanita, the Incan ice-maiden.

Over 500 years-old, she was positioned with elbows to the floor and knees slightly raised as if trying to push herself out of the icy walls which now trapped her for eternity. She still wore the red and brown robes she'd been buried in. Her teeth and hair had survived, but her skin stretched taut across her face and her eye sockets were eerily hollow. Ellie felt uneasy looking into them and wanted to apologize to Juanita for seeing her this way.

"We need to keep her in this temperature-controlled environment or she will deteriorate," the guide explained.

"Where was she found?" Ellie whispered.

"On Mount Ampato, north-west from here. She had been buried in a ceremonial pit on the summit."

"She was sacrificed?"

The guide nodded. "Inside the pit we found bowls, shells, and gold figurines we believe were offerings to the Incan gods. Juanita was killed by a blow to the head that fractured her skull, causing a fatal hemorrhage."

The instant of Juanita's death on that cold mountaintop hundreds of years ago played through Ellie's mind, sending a shiver down her spine. She fell silent for a moment. "How old was she?"

"Somewhere between eleven and fifteen."

Ellie shook her head in disbelief. "She was just a girl."

"It would have been a great honor for her to die like this. We think she came from a noble family in Cusco. She would have walked almost five-hundred kilometers to Mount Ampato with a priest and soldiers, perhaps given a drug to numb her senses, then killed."

"But why? Why would they sacrifice a girl?"

"For the gods. It's what the Incas believed would help their harvests. We don't do that anymore," the guide added with a wry smile.

Visiting Juanita affected Ellie more than she'd expected. She had a burning desire to share her thoughts with somebody, and the first person that popped into her head was the usual one.

Hi Jerry,
I watched a parade around the main square of Arequipa
this afternoon and it kind of summed up everything I
experienced today, this incredible layering of the Incan
culture and Catholic religion. There were dancers
wearing indigenous costumes and masks, but then
at the center was a group of priests carrying a statue
of some saint. (You can probably tell, I wasn't raised
a Catholic.) I wasn't raised anything, actually. My

parents kind of just left it up to me to figure out in my own time, which was great, but the problem is I'm still trying to figure it out! I'm beginning to wonder if I ever will…

The faith on display here is so different to New York, which isn't exactly the model of religious virtue. People here believe. They really believe something is up there watching them and communicating with them. I understand the temptation. An explanation for everything. A purpose in life. And it's so simple to belong to something bigger than yourself because all it takes is saying 'yes' to the question humans have asked since the beginning of our existence—Is there a higher power?

Juanita believed it so much she gave her life. I keep trying to imagine the courage it would take and I'm pretty sure I could never do that. Be so certain of God's existence. Where other people see evidence, I just see the randomness of nature. Is it possible they're the same thing?

I know I just bombarded you with a whole lotta thoughts again so thanks for reading. What do you believe? Contemplative Ellie.

San Francisco, USA

"How many are broken?" Jerry led Harry and Kevin through the messy construction site, busy with workers and machinery. The skeleton of the third floor was complete and the form of the curved terraces beginning to take shape.

"The whole west side. Ten in all."

"Jesus, Harry. Your guys need to be more careful."

"This was your call, Jerry. I warned you about installing those windows before we'd topped off that side. She's still settling after the rain and this is what you get."

They reached the edge of the museum, where a long row of floor-to-ceiling windows had cracked like hard-boiled eggs.

Jerry pushed his lips together and tried not to curse. "Shit. How long until we can get replacements?"

"At least a week."

"I'd recommend holding off a bit longer," Kevin said. "Maybe to the end of next month. We still have all that cooling equipment to go in above—"

"But we can start the internals in this section? Put up a temporary cover."

"We could…" Kevin hesitated, scratching his neck. "But it's not going to be fully waterproofed."

"I'm talking about the basics. Rough plumbing, electrics."

"Sure…but, again, you're running a risk—"

"I'm trying to find a solution here!" The vein in Jerry's temple throbbed. "We can't afford to fall further behind."

"We know," Harry said. "But do you want to double down?"

Do I have a choice?

Jerry felt his feet sinking deeper into the mud.

"I've been looking for you." Brandon approached across a plank, carrying the clipboard that was always attached to his side like a standard-issue rifle.

"Oh great, my Triad of Doom is complete," Jerry said.

"We need to talk about this letter from Blanch & Radisich."

"Who?"

"The legal firm representing the Flores family. Did you read it? I have a copy—"

"I read it." *Unfortunately.*

"Then you'll know they've been receiving copies of my weekly expenditure reports, and they're concerned. They want a meeting, Jerry."

"Tell me, how is meeting with a bunch of suits going to help get us back on schedule? Do they have any idea what it takes to make all this happen?" Jerry waved his arms over the site. Did anyone?

"You can only avoid them for so long."

"Well, I'll avoid them for as long as possible then." Jerry marched away in the direction of his portable office, the creases on his forehead getting deeper with each step.

Hi Ellie,

Sorry I haven't replied until now. The museum has been consuming every second of my life, waking and sleeping. I haven't glimpsed the light at the end of the tunnel—but it always comes, surely?

For days after visiting Juanita I couldn't stop thinking about her being one of my daughters and it gave me chills, if you'll excuse the terrible pun... Bella was raised Catholic and I'm agnostic, but we decided to expose our girls to different ideas about God, gods, or otherwise, and let them make up their own minds. We knew that would mean challenging questions, like you've faced, but we thought having good values was more important than belonging to a particular religion. So we've taught them to be honest, compassionate, generous, thankful for what they have, and to treat other people—and the planet—with respect. That's more important than what they believe about how it was all created. Anyway, that's my 2 cents!

I hope it helps on your quest for understanding, and I look forward to hearing where your search for meaning takes you next. I think I know where that might be 😉

Jerry.

CHAPTER 47

Cusco, Peru

Ellie's fog of exhaustion from the overnight bus ride, out of the desert and up into the Andes, lifted immediately upon arrival. She recognized this feeling. That special moment when your senses heightened with the anticipation of new experiences.

Like a kid on a treasure hunt, Ellie sought out the wonders of the ancient Incan capital turned modern-day tourist hub. Top of her list was Qorikancha, the Inca's most spectacular temple. Once gilded in gold, the Spanish had stripped the walls and melted all the artefacts to send back to Europe, then built a church on top, destroying generations of culture. Colonialism at its worst.

Climbing hundreds of cobblestone steps, Ellie took in a view over Cusco's terracotta rooftops, folding around the mountains like an orange forest. They were capped with miniature bulls for good luck. She would need some for her next—final—adventure. Especially because she was no longer at sea-level and the altitude at 11,000 feet gave her a nosebleed.

Further along the ridge was the administrative center of the Incan empire, Saqsaywamán (pronounced like 'sexy woman'; much easier to remember it that way). It was here in 1533 that Incan warriors and Spanish conquistadors fought a ferocious battle ultimately leading to the defeat of the indigenous civilization.

Among the ruins, a shepherd tended to his herd of llamas. He was happy to let Ellie snap photos and strokes their soft fleeces. She giggled when one licked her hand, its tongue tickling like wet sandpaper. It was easy to fall in love with the lively atmosphere of Cusco, with food carts offering *anticuchos de pollo* (flame-grilled chicken skewers), colorful markets selling handwoven tapestries, and school students running home for lunch. A living museum.

So Jerry,

Tomorrow it begins…cue dramatic music! My time in Peru has been filled with so many unforgettable experiences that I already feel spoiled, but tomorrow I start my journey to the granddaddy of them all— Machu Picchu.

I don't think I'll be able to sleep a wink tonight. I've got my daypack down to 15 pounds, stocked up on sunscreen, and had my last shower for a while. Nothing else to do except take that first step…

I'll send the obligatory Sun Gate photo when I return to WiFi 😊 Wish me luck,

Ellie.

CHAPTER 48

Inca Trail, Peru

A van dropped Ellie and the other trekkers at Kilometer 82, a marker named for the train line that ran through this point on its way to Aguas Calientes, the small town at the base of Machu Picchu. Except Ellie wouldn't be taking the train. She'd be hiking thirty miles over four days in the footsteps of the ancient Incas.

Bring. It. On.

Ellie had met her group the previous afternoon. They were a potluck mix including a retired Norwegian couple whose affection for each other was as strong as the day they'd wed, a pudgy Japanese-American with a prosthetic leg, and three young New Zealand women already complaining about the lack of cell signal. Ellie managed to keep her mouth shut, for now.

The leader of this troop was Beto, a twenty-eight year-old Peruvian with a broad smile and twinkling eyes. Sunglasses hung permanently around his neck and he wore a bandana that reassured Ellie he was badass enough to help her reach her goal.

"OK, my friends!" Beto gathered the group close by the train track.

Like an eager student, Ellie stood up front, bubbling with so much energy her feet wouldn't stand still. Everyone was decked out in hiking gear and carried small daypacks. The heavy lifting of tents and food would be done by the men standing behind Beto.

"These are our *chaskis*," he explained. "The word was used by the Inca for their couriers. It used to be a full-time job, but today these men are farmers who work as porters after harvest season. They are ready. Are you?"

The group responded with a resounding "Yes!" Ellie shouted the loudest.

Damn straight.

She followed Beto over a suspension bridge spanning a swollen river, her heart pumping with expectation.

This is it.

El Camino Inca.

The Inca Trail.

The reason she'd come all this way. It felt like a pilgrimage. Ellie knew where she was going, but wasn't sure if she would return from Machu Picchu as the same person.

On the other side of the bridge, her boots took their first steps on a dirt path ascending along a narrow ledge. With a determined grin, Ellie set the pace and looked down over a river snaking into a valley.

A horn blew, shattering the quiet. The unmistakable chug of a train got near. The engine charged around the bend, pulling luxury carriages on their morning passage from Cusco. Through the windows, Ellie could see well-heeled tourists eating gourmet pastries and drinking champagne served by immaculate hostesses. But she didn't envy them one bit, because she was living *her dream.*

The undulating trail on the first morning didn't challenge Ellie too much. It gave her the opportunity to chat with Beto and the rest of the group that, in her usual way, she'd started to pass judgement on. The Kiwi trio grated her nerves the most because they wanted to stop every five minutes for a rest. Their expensive hiking poles and drinking pouches didn't seem to be helping them. They were on one of those horrible two week package tours of South America—*SEE 5 COUNTRIES IN 14 DAYS!*—and weren't enjoying any of it. Ellie stifled a groan when after an hour one of the wannabe trekkers exclaimed, "This is the hardest thing I've ever done."

God help them. God help me.

At lunchtime, Beto stopped the group on a grassy outcrop. They devoured sandwiches and fruit with a spectacular view of craggy, snow-capped, mountains stretching into the distance like meringue tops.

"My friends, the path we are taking was built by the Inca civilization who controlled from what we now call Ecuador, all the way down to Chile, and across to Bolivia," Beto explained. "The Inca only ruled for a short time, from the early-1200s to late-1500s, but they had the largest empire in South America before the Spanish arrived. And don't forget that many people in Peru today are descendants of the Inca. For example, I am *mestizo*, part Inca-blood, part Spanish-blood. Most of our *chaskis* are pure Inca. The original language lives on with them because they speak Quechua."

"How does it sound?" Ellie asked, wiping *tamarillo* juice off her chin. "Can you teach us something?"

"You can say *haku haku*."

"*Haku haku*. What does it mean?"

"It means '*Vamos!*' in Spanish. In English, 'Let's go!' Give it a try."

Everyone practiced saying "*Haku haku*" as if they'd just learned a secret password.

"Very good," Beto laughed. "If you ask our *chaskis* I'm sure they'll teach you more. The center of the Inca empire was Cusco.

That was where the royal family lived, and where political and military decisions were made. The Inca were very intelligent. They knew that to control their empire they would need a system of roads for transport and communication. So they constructed *forty-thousand kilometers*, that we know about. There's probably many more. It allowed them to move soldiers, goods and messages quickly through the difficult terrain of the Andes."

"But the Inca never invented the wheel, right?" Ellie had moved onto sweet *guanábana* fruit. "So it's not like a Roman road that was used for carts or chariots."

"You are the curious one, Ellie. It's true, the Inca never developed the wheel even though their technology was very advanced. But look around. A wheel is useless in these mountains. They transported everything on llamas, which can easily walk up-and-down the high…*gradiente*."

"Gradient," Ellie translated. "Angle."

"Yes, the high angle. Even the conquistador Hernando Pizarro said that in Europe there was nothing as impressive as these roads. Luckily, the invaders never found the trail we are on or they would have discovered Machu Picchu and destroyed that too. Any more questions? Ellie?"

"Not now," she smiled.

"OK, my friends." Beto jumped to his feet. *"Haku haku!"*

After a steady climb for the next couple of miles, the group staggered into camp. The super-efficient *chaskis* had already arrived and pitched everyone's tent. For dinner they cooked a tasty *lomo saltado* (marinated beef strips served with onions, tomatoes, fries and rice). Beto had arranged a surprise for dessert—*chicha*. A lady from a nearby village brought everyone a glass of the fermented corn beer, made from juicy kernels four times the size Ellie had ever seen. It had a yummy sour quality that fizzed on her tongue, like alcoholic sherbet. Of course she asked how it was made.

Beto waited until they'd finished before describing the brewing process. "The alcohol is activated by saliva. The locals chew the corn, spit it into a clay pot to ferment, then one week later you drink."

Not so yum after all.

CHAPTER 49

Inca Trail, Peru

A breakfast of banana pancakes and high-octane black coffee provided the energy hit Ellie needed for the climb ahead. The second day of the Inca Trail was reputedly the toughest as it required an ascent to 14,000 feet at Dead Woman's Pass. She hoped it hadn't, in some freakish time-travel way, been named after her. To die on the cusp of achieving your dream, well, that wouldn't be cool.

There weren't any clouds in sight as Ellie led the group in single file out of camp. She'd come to know her companions well. The Norwegian couple were pleasant, but she got on best with William, the widower with a fake leg who pushed through pain on every step. He didn't mind looking like a total dork in his floppy hat and had a wicked sense of humor.

"I'm glad my wife made it to Heaven, but I wish my leg hadn't gone as well," William said after describing how she'd died in a car accident the year before. "Now I feel like I've got one foot in the grave."

As for the N.Z. girls, instead of savoring the experience, they complained about it—the pace, the food, the heat, life. Ellie considered pushing them off the mountain, one by one. Surely she'd get the votes at Tribal Council?

Their dark mood meant they inevitably turned on each other and began cat-fighting for Beto's attention. At a rest stop, when the annoying frizzy-haired one bent over to tie her shoelace, it did answer a question Ellie had never asked: yes, it was possible to hike the Inca Trail in a red G-string.

The fittest of the group because of her previous treks, Ellie's was soon hiking alone under the jungle canopy, on paths winding around ledges, then up into the cloud forest. Every hour or so she came across an enterprising local who'd set up a stall to sell soda and sweets to trekkers at inflated prices. She demolished a Snickers in record time.

It was a punishing climb to Dead Woman's Pass, requiring a break every ten steps. But the reward was worth the effort. The view from the summit as the Andes rolled away in all directions, like waves on a choppy ocean, doubly breathtaking. Ellie propped against a rock to admire the grand, inspirational, beauty that nature provided for free.

I am the luckiest girl alive.

Apart from the vistas, and the chocolate, the feeling of being connected to history was Ellie's favorite part of the trek. She imagined the Incas walking this secret path to Machu Picchu more than 500 years ago—and now here she was on those same stone steps. It was, she decided with a shake of her head and roll of her eyes, Inca-redible!

Darkness hadn't yet lifted when Ellie stumbled out of her tent the next morning. She must've still been tipsy from the pisco and cards session Beto had organized last night. Her favorite *chaski*, a stout farmer named Atuc, stoked the fire and brewed coca leaf tea to offset the effects of altitude sickness. She gladly accepted a mug and cupped it to warm her hands.

Atuc looked to the mountains, rising in silhouette against a majestic purple dawn. "*Pachamama*," he whispered.

"*Pachamama*," Ellie repeated.

They remained in silence, because nothing else needed to be said. The South American equivalent of Mother Earth, Ellie had read that the Incan goddess *Pachamama* sustained all life on the planet. Respect her, and she would provide bountiful harvests. Take too much from her, and she would respond in kind. Love her, and she would bless you with sunrises like this one.

Entirely downhill, Ellie found the third day the most punishing. By the time she reached camp, her knees ached and toes stung from each step's crushing impact. She had to wring blood out of her socks. No grumbling though. She wanted to be here. And the pain made it even more meaningful.

Besides, today had delivered a collection of treats along the trail. From the fortress of Sayaqmarka built on the edge of a vertical cliff, through a tunnel carved by hand in solid rock, past the ceremonial baths of Phuyupatamarka, to the massive terrace complex of Wiñay Wayna constructed at an impossible angle on a mountainside. Ellie couldn't pronounce them, but she loved exploring them.

Beto told her that for every site that'd been excavated, there were probably five more undiscovered. Ellie found that entirely plausible because the jungle didn't discriminate. Unchecked, it would overrun everything, with zero regard for any of humankind's attempts to tame it. *Pachamama* could be ruthless like that.

The ruins Ellie saw today were impressive, but they only served as a tease for what would come tomorrow—the most magnificent of all.

CHAPTER 50

Inca Trail, Peru

Restless, Ellie woke at 3 a.m. She didn't have to be up for another hour, but there was too much adrenaline coursing through her veins. She'd been thinking back to that fateful night after returning from Mount Roraima. Laying on her bunk and looking at the photo of Machu Picchu on the cover of the *Unique Planet*. Finding Bella's message inside, 'Go far and go wild!'

It'd enticed her to make a decision that set her on a different path in life. One that led Ellie here, to this moment. Today she would see the ancient Wonder of the World that sparked her imagination. It was the climax of everything she'd been through on her trip.

Striding through the forest with singular purpose, Ellie's headtorch lit her way in the dark. After a few hours on the heels of Beto, they reached a set of steep stone steps. The final section of the Inca Trail. Her chest swelled with emotion.

I can't believe this is happening.

Beto motioned her ahead as he waited for the others who'd fallen behind. "Enjoy, my friend," he winked.

Ellie bounded up, ignoring the searing pain in her thighs.

She exhaled loudly with each thrust off her knees. Not even a battalion of conquistadors could've stopped her now. Light broke through as she neared the top.

Just a few more steps.

C'mon Ellie.

You can do it.

She climbed over the final stone.

Lifted her head.

Gasped.

In the distance, through the arch of the Sun Gate, lay the sacred citadel of Machu Picchu. Resting on a bed of clouds, it hovered in the sky like a mythical vision. The hundreds of buildings, immaculately preserved, rose from lines of terraces so perfect they looked as if they belonged in a museum diorama.

Ellie let tears run freely down her face. Moving through the Sun Gate, she gazed at the 'Lost City of the Incas' and became enchanted by its spell. She desperately wanted to get down there, to touch it, to convince herself this wasn't a fantasy. To prove that her dream had become reality.

CHAPTER 51

Machu Picchu, Peru

Once the rest of the group had joined Ellie at the Sun Gate, Beto led them down to Machu Picchu. As they drew closer, the sun broke through from the east, heating the air and lifting the clouds. Shafts of light hit the ancient city, and Ellie's excitement increased with each wondrous glimpse.

Soon she was standing on a terrace and beholding the postcard view known around the world, with Machu Picchu in the foreground and Huayna Picchu mountain soaring behind it like a sentry guard. All of Ellie's senses were on fire. She took a deep breath to soak it all in.

Is this real? Am I seeing this? Feeling this?

Beto snapped photos of everyone in various poses for their new Facebook and Instagram profile pics before the crowds arrived. Then he led the group through the sprawling complex, and Ellie got her chance to touch the intricate stonework. She ran her fingers along the barely-visible joins as if stroking a lover, marveling at how the Incas had cut stones so perfectly there were no gaps between them.

Beto explained they'd used the natural form of the mountain to determine the placement of important buildings. "The purpose of Machu Picchu is still being debated by historians, but it's agreed that it was built around 1450 AD for the Inca king Pachacuti. It may have become the new capital after the Spanish captured Cusco, or it could have been the royal family's summer home. But the city was abandoned quickly in 1572. Pots were still on fireplaces and jewelry left behind. Most important, my friends, Machu Picchu was never discovered by the Spanish, which is why it is intact."

A miracle back then.

A gift for us today.

As they explored the ruins, Beto highlighted the finest examples of Incan architecture, including the semi-circular Temple of the Sun and the Royal Tomb with its ceremonial altar. Fresh water still ran in the channels leading to the baths, hundreds of years after being constructed.

From here they walked through the Sacred Plaza to the imposing Temple of the Three Windows that framed the Andes like a painting, and up a staircase to the Intihuatana shrine with its sundial and observatory for studying the stars. The Inca's main god was the sun—*Inti*—because it gave them everything they needed. As Ellie stood at this highest point of Machu Picchu, she closed her eyes and bathed her face in sunlight, appreciating how the star at the center of our solar system also gave her life.

On the other side of the shrine sat the monolithic Sacred Rock and haunting Temple of the Condor, carved in the shape of a condor's outstretched wings. Ellie buzzed as surprises revealed themselves around every corner.

Lastly, the group rested on a wall as Beto told the story of how Machu Picchu was 'found.' In fact, the city had never been lost because local farmers knew of its existence long before foreign explorers arrived. The first archaeologist to have climbed to the city was Hiram Bingham III, a history professor at Yale

University. On 24th July 1911, a farmer named Melchor Arteaga led Bingham up a steep path through thick jungle to the very point at which the group currently sat. Bingham had been astounded at what he saw. An ancient city in a setting unlike any other place in the world. He coined the phrase 'The Lost City of the Incas' when he brought Machu Picchu to the world's attention, and it'd been used incorrectly ever since.

No matter the history, Ellie's soul had found a missing piece. One she'd been searching for her whole life.

Ellie urged her aching legs to climb one last time. High above the ruins she found a quiet spot on a terrace, away from the madding crowd. The entirety of Machu Picchu, cradled on all sides by mountains, now basked in the glow of the sun. Ellie unclipped her daypack and slid to the ground, her pilgrimage complete.

The beauty here…it's unparalleled. No wonder the Incas considered this place sacred. It looks like it was put here by the gods.

Ellie took a long drink of water and thought about how amazing it was that one simple decision to pull up her anchor and let the wind catch her sails, as Donna had inadvertently suggested, led her to this point. To actually achieve her dream of traveling, instead of just fantasizing about it.

That's what dreams are for, right? To provide hope for the future, but also to be fought for. Otherwise they remain unfulfilled—and so do we.

At times on her journey Ellie had questioned her decision, but in this moment she swore that would never happen again. It was time to look forward, not backward. She wouldn't regret leaving her job or apartment or the familiar comforts of home because this, right now, was better than all of that.

Ellie brushed away tears of joy and laughed at herself for

getting so emotional. She finally understood, and cursed herself for not accepting it earlier, that this trip would mark a turning point in her life. There would be before South America, and after South America.

Her life, and herself, would never be the same.

PART III

CHAPTER 52

2nd October – San Francisco, USA

Blah blah blah.

Jerry rapped his shoe on the carpet. Was there anything more soul-destroying than having to justify your creative decisions to a bunch of penny-pinching lawyers? Hell, if the suits in the boardroom of Blanch & Radisich L.L.P. pawned their Armani suits he'd have enough money to finish the damn museum.

Shifting in his chair, Jerry noticed he'd mismatched his socks. Red on one foot, polka dots on the other. He couldn't remember being this jumbled before, but then Bella had organized most things without him realizing.

Usually the socks would've made him laugh, but this meeting had dragged on into eternity and a détente was nowhere in sight. Brandon hadn't helped Jerry's cause to protect the museum from the proposed cuts, but Harry at least tried to mediate with the lawyers hell-bent on ripping the heart out of the project. Having to explain every minor detail made the process infuriating. The arrogant jackasses hadn't even stepped foot on-site.

These issues will never be solved in a boardroom over salmon nigiri and cucumber sandwiches.

"Let's discuss the stonework for the terraces," said a suit with a ludicrous designer goatee. "You've allocated an excessive number of man hours for them relative to the rest of the landscaping."

"Stonemasonry is a highly-skilled trade," Harry replied. "And this is about the most difficult job these guys will do, replicating ancient techniques to make sure the granite fits together without mortar. It's call—"

"So simplify the process. Use concrete, or put on a veneer that costs ten times less."

"Ashlar." Jerry sighed and took off his glasses.

"What?"

"The technique we're using is called ashlar. It's when every face of a stone is cut to fit precisely with the ones adjacent."

"Ashlar," the suit repeated as if it were a foreign language. "But why use it? If you—"

"Because this is The Pata Museum." Jerry's voice jumped an octave. "Pata meaning 'terrace' in Quechua, in case you didn't read the brief. Quechua happens to be the language of the Incan civilization. And guess what? The Incas were master stonemasons who perfected the ashlar technique so their buildings had the most impressive joins in the world. Still are today, five-hundred years after they were built. That's why we're not going to cut costs on the terraces. Because it's the name of the fucking museum!"

The room fell silent. Jerry's anger echoed around it like a canyon.

He stood and packed his papers. "I've been here more than four hours, which counting travel time and the fifteen minutes you kept me waiting as part of your little schoolyard powerplay, is half-a-day I could've been working to get this project back on budget. So, thanks for wasting my time."

This fight isn't over. Not by a long shot.

Carol put a hand on her son's arm. "What are you thinking about?"

"Hmm? Nothing," Jerry replied.

Three generations of his family sat around the dining table at his parent's house. With Halloween approaching, Don entertained his granddaughters with a tall tale about the time he and Carol had become locked in the 'haunted' Winchester Mansion in nearby San Jose.

"You've been staring at the string beans for the past five minutes, and they're not that interesting," Carol said. "I know because I cooked them."

"I'm fine." It sounded unconvincing even to Jerry. "I've heard Dad's story before, and it keeps getting more farfetched." Now they were being chased by pumpkin-headed goblins, which was almost preferable to Jerry's predicament.

"You can't hide anything from me. Cough it up."

"It's just work, Mom. Too much to do and not enough time."

She flattened her lips. "Well, remember everyone needs a break, even my workaholic son. Why don't you and the girls stay over and watch a movie?"

"Maybe." He spun the saltshaker. If it spun fast enough perhaps it would create a black hole he could jump into.

"C'mon, when was the last time you did something fun like that with them?"

"You mean let them stay up late and eat too much popcorn?"

"They're kids. That's what they're supposed to do on a Friday night."

"You never let me do that."

"Because I'm your mother, not your grandmother," Carol smiled and started to clear the dishes. "You need to be present for your children, Jerry. I don't have to tell you how important that is, now more than ever."

Congratulations Ellie,

Your photo from the Sun Gate is incredible! You couldn't have a bigger smile on your dial 😃 *Sunrise at Machu Picchu is a special moment and your elation is well-deserved.*

I've attached a photo of the picnic we had on the terraces. Do you remember I told you they were the inspiration for Bella's design of our museum? Well, she observed how the terraces were designed to follow the natural curve of the mountain, giving them an organic flow. They were also built to capture the sun's heat and maximize water flow, so that's what we're doing too—if I can win my battle with the numbskull lawyers…

Rest up and I look forward to hearing more about your adventures on the trail. How are you going to celebrate?

Jerry.

CHAPTER 53

Cusco, Peru

Blue and pink lights pulsed through the darkness. Ellie blinked a few times to reset her vision. The man sitting next to her at the bar laughed in her face. In focus one second, out of focus the next. Far away one second, close—too close—the next.

What the hell is happening…?

She'd come club-hopping with a group from her hostel to let her hair down and cut loose on the dancefloor after returning from Machu Picchu. But now Ellie felt her body becoming lighter. She looked down at her legs to check they were still there. She could see them, but couldn't feel them. Something wasn't right.

In fact, nothing was right.

Everything was slow. Too slow.

Then fast. Too fast.

Then loud. Then quiet.

Why is my head…throbbing?

Ellie turned to the bartender. He gave her a shit-eating grin. She begged her eyes to search the club for her group, sure they would stand out in this local crowd, but couldn't spot anyone. The man was still laughing in her face. A shiver raced through Ellie like a taser had hit her spine.

I need to go.
Now.

Ellie took her purse from the bar and climbed off the stool. Her legs buckled. Laughing Man seized her by the arm. She pulled away. He tried to grab her again, but Ellie forced through the crowd to the front exit, one thought repeating through her mind.

Get to safety.

The street was a blur of people and rain. Ellie tripped, falling into a puddle. She could hear feet walking by, ignoring her like just another drunk *gringa*. But this was more than just too much alcohol.

Ellie rose to her feet. Took a few steps forward. Lost balance again. She steadied herself against a brick wall as her hair and dress got soaked. Squinting through the haze of her mind, she tried to make out a landmark. A shop, a church, a—

Ahhhhh!

Ellie had no idea who grabbed her from behind. No idea who dragged her into the alley behind an industrial trash bin. No idea who threw her to the ground. Until he knelt over her, gripped her neck, and leaned in to kiss her. Then his familiar smile came into focus—and Ellie's worst fears were confirmed.

She shook her head to avoid Laughing Man's advance. He tightened his hold on her jaw. His mouth was so close she could smell his breath, a putrid mix of cheap beer and stale cigarettes.

One of his fingers slipped across Ellie's lips and she bit down hard. He pulled his hand away—then brought it back, smashing her across the face. He punched her again, striking from the other side.

Ellie shut her eyes as blood poured out her nose and from a cut above her eye. She screamed for help but it came out as a muffled cry, drowned out by a passing truck. He hit her again. Black.

Ellie's eyelids were heavy, but she forced them open. Laughing Man was unbuckling his belt. She must've passed out for only a few seconds. The shock of the attack sparked a self-defense mechanism that cleared her brain long enough to evaluate her options. Though battered, she wasn't going to give up.

Not a fucking chance.

Ellie spotted her purse a few feet away on the wet ground. She tried to stretch for it without him noticing. Just out of reach.

He unzipped his pants.

Different strategy.

Ellie kneed him in the balls.

He reeled back and cursed—"*Hija de puta!*"—then surged forward, hitting her again. The blow was so hard it pushed Ellie closer to her purse.

Small victory.

He pulled down his briefs.

She reached for her purse again. Her fingers dug into the ground.

C'mon...

The man put one hand on Ellie's breasts and the other between her legs.

She squeezed her thighs together. "NO, YOU BASTARD."

He ripped Ellie's panties down to her knees.

She strained to keep her legs closed but he was too strong.

He was almost on top of her.

Ellie pushed his face away with one hand and reached for her purse with the other.

He gripped her flailing hand and pinned it to the ground.

The tips of her fingers touched her purse.

Please...

She made a final, desperate, lunge—grabbing it just as he tried to thrust inside her. She swung her purse around, smashing him across the temple.

He let out a yelp and fell off.

Ellie shuffled backward and fumbled to open it.

He looked up and they locked eyes, his face twisted with rage.

She reached into her purse. Pulled out the pepper spray Donna had made her promise to carry. And as he came at her again, she popped off the lid and sprayed it directly into his face.

TAKE THAT, MOTHERFUCKER!

The man doubled back, shrieking in agony and scratching his eyes.

Ellie scrambled to her feet and ran out of the alley, blood and tears streaming down her face.

CHAPTER 54

Cusco, Peru

"How could I be so stupid?" Ellie sat on a bed in the emergency room of a hospital, holding an icepack over her swollen eye. Barefoot and muddy, an I.V. ran fluid into her arm and a young nurse wiped blood off her forehead. "*Soy estúpida*," Ellie translated her self-condemnation.

"*No eres estúpida*," the nurse replied. "*Muchos hombres son malos. No respectan a las chicas.*"

"*Claro.* No respect. Too many assholes."

"Ms. Bartlett?" A tall doctor came through the curtain drawn around the bed. He had the face of a Peruvian but spoke American English.

"That's me. What's left of me, anyway."

"I'm Dr. Alvarez. Let's have a look at your eye, shall we?" He pulled the icepack away and examined the cut across her brow. "You've had quite a night."

Ellie could only imagine what a mess she looked like. She hadn't dared ask for a mirror.

"We'll get this sewn up in no time," he said with an assurance she appreciated. "Nine or ten stitches then you can go home.

You'll have some nasty bruises for a week, but it should clear up after that."

"No scars?"

"I wouldn't expect so. It's deep but not wide, and I'll fix it up nice and tight."

"Thank you."

Dr. Alvarez prepared a needle and thread. "Do you want to tell me what happened?"

Ellie's fists clenched on reflex and she pulled what was left of her dress around her chest. "I… I'm pretty sure my drink was spiked."

"You're not the first woman to come through here for that reason, and unfortunately you won't be the last. You are one of the lucky ones though."

Ellie was still trying to comprehend how lucky she was. He was so close to… She didn't want to think of the word.

"We can notify the police if you'd like, and you can make a statement."

"Yes. I want that."

He tilted Ellie's head back and prepared to suture her wound. "This will sting a bit. Ready?"

"Do it."

Ellie rested at the hospital until a female police officer arrived. Mustering her best Spanish, she detailed the attack and described her assailant. It wasn't easy when all she could remember clearly was his revolting smirk as he bore down on her. The officer promised to do her best, but Ellie got the impression it was unlikely they'd be able to find him given the number of people moving through Cusco.

By the time daylight spread over the city, Ellie had decided she needed space from the world. After the high of reaching Machu Picchu, she couldn't have imagined a more dreadful turn of events. She put aside thoughts about the state of her budget and hailed a taxi to take her from the hospital to her hostel to pick up her belongings, then to a five-star hotel by a leafy plaza. Here she could have her own room, some long-overdue privacy, and let her physical and emotional wounds heal.

Ellie gave a generous tip to the doorman who carried her backpack upstairs, and locked the door as soon as he'd left. Then triple checked it was locked. She lay on the bed and crumpled into a ball.

CHAPTER 55

Cusco, Peru

Ellie jumped off the bed. Heart pounding out of her ribcage. Drenched in sweat. She looked around and remembered she was in a hotel.

You're safe, Ellie. You're safe.

Lightheaded, she grabbed for the edge of the mattress and wiped the sweat off her face, wincing as salt stung her wounds. After a few minutes of slow breathing, Ellie reached for her phone—6 p.m.

I must've slept all day.

Only now did she check out the room, a converted monastery with high stone walls, and bigger than most of the dorms she'd stayed in. The king-size bed was covered with soft sheets and half-a-dozen pillows, on one side was a bathroom with marble tiles, on the other side a double window with curtains closed. But what drew her focus was a huge mirror on the opposite wall, set in an ornate golden frame.

Ellie raised her sore body and hobbled toward her reflection. The bruised jaw, cut lip, and black, hollow, eyes made her look like a raccoon. If a raccoon were roadkill.

Ellie turned away. She would deal with what happened last

night, but not now. Please, not now. All she wanted was a hot shower to wash away the dirt and blood, and sustenance to heal. She found a room service menu and ordered something that reminded her of home—a good ol' American cheeseburger and fries.

⌒

The sound of birds greeted Ellie early next morning. Their gentle chirps were comforting after a night of intermittent sleep, fighting against the sheets. Rolling gingerly out of bed, she pulled apart the curtains and pushed open the window. Air and light filled the room, warming her body.

In the plaza below, children ran around a fountain, businesspeople ordered tea from a cart, and an elderly couple read the newspaper together on a bench. They sat hip-to-hip, like a pair of swans, holding hands after probably years performing the same ritual.

Ellie turned and shuffled to the mirror. The bruising was worse today. She touched the tender purple and yellow patches under her eyes. They stung like hot wax.

Finding her tablet in her daypack, she retreated to bed. This couldn't be put off any longer. She connected to WiFi and tapped Donna's number, drawing breath while it rang. Thankfully, the call went to voicemail. "Hey sis...um...if you could buzz me back that'd be great... OK, love you. Bye."

Ellie sat in silence. It occurred to her that she did actually want to talk with someone. To get it out of her system and work through the tangle of questions in her head, about how she should've been more careful and if she could've behaved differently. Part of her brain kept blaming herself—and she hated that.

Who can I call?
Who would listen?
Who cares about me?

Opening Facebook, Ellie typed 'Jerry Townsend' into the search box. His profile came up first. She pressed 'Call' before thinking about it too much, fiddling with the volume on her headphones while waiting for it to connect. There were a few seconds of scratchy internet noise.

"Ellie?"

"Jerry? Hi."

"Hi to you too. This is…a surprise."

She heard nerves in his voice. "Yeah. Sorry to call you out of the blue."

"It's fine, I'm just in the office. It's good to finally hear your voice."

"You too."

"Strange."

"Yes."

"But good."

"Yes." Their staccato introductions came to an end and Ellie panicked at the awkward lull in the conversation.

"Are you OK?" Jerry asked.

"Are you busy? Can you talk now?"

"Of course. What's going on? You've got me worried."

"Well…um…I'm kind of embarrassed now that I've called."

"There's no need to be embarrassed."

"No." Ellie heard Jerry sit down, as if he sensed the gravity of what she was about to say. Her breathing sped up.

"Why don't you start by telling me where you are?"

"I'm in Cusco."

"How is it there?"

"Something happened…a couple of nights ago…and I need to talk with someone I trust, Jerry. Even though we've never met I feel like I can tell you anything."

"You can."

Ellie opened her mouth to speak but nothing came out. Her lips trembled and she started to sob.

"Take your time."

"Ugghh, I'm sorry. Just a sec." She reached for a tissue.

"There's no need to apologize," he said.

Ellie took a deep breath and tried again. "Someone tried to rape me…" She erupted in tears as she heard herself speak the words nobody should ever have to say. The emotions she'd been holding inside poured out like a dam had broken.

"Oh, Ellie. I'm sorry. I'm so sorry."

"I just needed to tell someone," she cried.

"I understand."

"I'm not… I don't know what to do…"

"It'll be OK. You'll be OK."

Ellie did her best to recount the events of the weekend. It took a while, and there were still gaps in her memory. Jerry stayed silent until she'd finished. She heard him struggling to maintain his composure.

"Ellie, you've suffered a terrible ordeal. But you know you're not to blame, right? It was entirely that man's fault. His decisions. His actions."

"I know…"

"I don't want you to beat yourself up, because there's nothing you did that caused this to happen. There is nothing you should've done differently. It is not your fault."

Jerry's soothing words resonated in Ellie's ears. If she'd said them, she may not have believed them, but coming from him they sounded entirely reasonable. "Thank you for listening. I don't know why I feel so comfortable talking to you."

"Well, anytime you need to talk you call me, OK? Day or night or middle of the night."

"I will."

"You're strong. You are going to get through this."

Ellie smiled. How did he know how to make her feel better? "Y'know, Jerry, you sound older than I thought."

"I'll try to take that as a compliment," he said.

"I meant in a good way. More…mature."

"I guess being a single dad will do that."

"Yes, it probably will."

"Is there anything I can do for you, Ellie? I don't know what, but if you think of anything—"

"No, nothing. Just listening is enough. I'm pretty exhausted right now so I'm gonna go freshen up."

"Do you mind if I check in with you later? To see how you're holding up?"

"That would be nice."

They said their goodbyes and hung up. Ellie lay on her bed and exhaled. Her eyes tracked the thick oak beams running the length of the ceiling. She resolved to be like them. Stronger than before. Stronger than she'd ever believed. With Jerry's support, it felt possible.

CHAPTER 56

San Francisco, USA

The last page whirred out of the printer and Jerry bundled them together in a folder. He held it in both hands, contemplating whether this was a good idea.

You'd have been able to navigate these lawyers far better than me, Bella. You always had a knack for dealing with people.

And you'd have reminded me that I never did like being told what to do…

He'd stayed late in the office all week attempting to find savings on the museum, his parents tasked with picking up the girls from school, checking they did their homework, and went to bed on time.

When he wasn't thinking about work or family, Jerry was thinking about Ellie. After their first conversation, he'd sat stunned, hands shaking. He was furious someone would hurt her. More than anything, he wanted to send her a hug and tell her everything was going to be all right.

Since then, he'd called every day to see how she was holding up. Thankfully, little by little, she seemed to be improving. She'd even laughed when he told her Mia wanted him to dress up as a pirate for her birthday party next month. He knew how far he would go to protect his daughters, and Ellie's assault made him realize he felt that same instinct for her too.

If I ever got my hands on that bastard…

"You called?" Kyra appeared at the door.

Jerry gave her the folder. "Can you get this couriered to the lawyers by close of business?"

She thumbed through the pages, wrinkling her nose. "Really?"

Jerry eased into his chair and ran his hands through his hair. "Isn't it better to take a shave instead of chopping off a limb?"

"Are you speaking in metaphors again?"

"I was trying not to."

"Do you want to talk about why you do that?"

"Not really."

Kyra continued nosing through the folder. "I'm not sure this is gonna thread the needle."

Jerry let out a running-on-empty chuckle. "What do you think my wife would've done?" He caught the surprise on Kyra's face.

"I think she would've worked the problem, like you've done. Thought about every possibility, like you have. But I also have no doubt she would've been at least twice as efficient."

"Oh, shoot."

"Jerry, it's not my place to say it—"

"When did that ever stop you?"

"I think Bella would be proud of all you've done to get the museum back on track. Not so much the neglecting your family part, but definitely the work part."

"Kyra, you have this unique ability to make someone feel both wonderful and terrible at the same time."

"What can I say? I'm a shrinking violet."

"As gentle as a lamb."

"As smart as a fox!" Kyra sang as she left Jerry's office.

This better work, Bella. Our baby depends on it.

CHAPTER 57

Cusco, Peru

Ellie spent the week recuperating, indulging in the luxury of her hotel. She ordered piles of room service, took frequent bubble baths, and lay in bed for hours watching *telenovelas*. Familiar routines brought comfort, so Ellie updated her trusty TO DO list, dreaming of the day when she would feel up to having a manicure and haircut.

The phone calls from Jerry also lifted her spirits. She felt a burst of expectation when his name popped up on her screen, appreciating not just his time but his willingness to listen to her words—and tears. He'd asked what she was going to do next, but Ellie didn't have an answer. She'd achieved her goal of reaching Machu Picchu, but flying back to the U.S. now seemed like… running away.

Donna had called every day too, and wasn't at all impressed with Ellie's response. Her sister demanded she return immediately—*and never leave home again*. But just the act of talking about her assault had begun the process of recovery, and Ellie decided she wasn't going to let some creep ruin her trip. "If I come back, he's won. And there's no way I'm letting him win."

Besides, Ellie had been gone so long she wasn't sure where home was anymore. Maybe it was time to find a new one?

But where? And with who? With all the absurd situations I get myself into, who would possibly love me?

By the end of the week, her bruises had subsided and Ellie felt safe enough to leave her room. She walked down to the plaza and chose a bench in the shade of a eucalyptus tree to watch the world go by. The elderly couple read the paper together, canoodling as if nothing else mattered. Which, of course, it didn't.

Ellie observed them with a voyeur's eye, like she'd done on the fort wall in Cartagena, and loneliness surfaced again in the chasm of her chest. It dawned on her that she'd fallen into the same pattern she'd been repeating her whole life. This time, traveling had served as the distraction from what was really important. And it hadn't solved her problem. She was still alone. Still empty. Still unhappy. Damn, being human could ache.

Stop it, Ellie.

Stop blaming. Stop criticizing. Stop overthinking.

You'll never be at peace unless you love yourself first.

Isn't that what Bella taught me?

Ellie knew changing her life—starting with her perspective of herself—would take everything she had. But it was necessary.

I need to forgive myself.

Love me, whatever happens, and whatever I do.

CHAPTER 58

Sacred Valley, Peru

Ellie dragged her backpack down the steps of the bus. Sadly, it'd long ago lost its attractive blue sheen. The passengers, mostly farmers returning home from Sunday markets, stared at her as the bus rolled away, probably trying to figure out why a *gringa* would want to get off in the middle of nowhere.

Ellie fixed her ponytail while taking in her surroundings. There was a wooden bridge over a narrow stream, and beyond that two dozen adobe houses huddling in the shadow of the Andes. It wasn't quite Hobbiton, but it was close.

"*Señorita Ellie?*" a voice called from the other side of the bridge.

"*Sí.*" She caught sight of a lanky man waving in welcome. He had a salt-and-pepper beard and wore a shirt and tie, which seemed out of place here. They met halfway across the bridge and shook hands.

"I am Principal Ramirez, but please, call me Hugo." He spoke with an educated British accent.

"Nice to meet you. *Mucho gusto.*"

"Can I help with your bag?"

"It's OK." Ellie slung on her backpack. "I've had a lot of practice."

"I thought we could stop by the school first to show you around."

"Sure thing."

"What made you want to come and help us?" he asked.

Ellie had been thinking about volunteering ever since her encounter with the humble coffee-picking women of Jardín. The last three months had been completely dedicated to herself, but in the aftermath of her assault she wanted to do something for others who, in the lottery of birth and life, were less fortunate. She just wasn't sure *how* to help.

The answer had revealed itself a few days ago while strolling through a market in Cusco. She came across a homeless woman selling handmade pendants in the spiral shape of *Pachamama*, and helping her daughter with schoolwork. The young girl listened to her mom's instructions, then wrote in her notebook, her face concentrating on every pen stroke. Even though mom and daughter owned next-to-nothing, they still carried on that most important family tradition—teaching the next generation.

Ellie bought a pendant from the woman and that afternoon found a not-for-profit which organized English-speaking volunteers to assist Peruvian teachers in their classrooms. There was an opening at an elementary school in the Sacred Valley.

"This is our assembly area." Hugo lifted the latch on a rusty gate and led Ellie across a dirt square where broken buckets served as soccer goals. "Every morning at seven we gather for roll call and to recite the Lord's prayer. We finish at twelve-thirty because most of our students need to work on their family's farms."

He took her inside one of the naked concrete buildings lining the square. It was as cold as an icebox and the chill slithered under Ellie's skin. The walls had been stained brown by leaks and the only decoration was a figure of Jesus hanging above a faded chalkboard. Ellie ran her fingers over the chips in one of the vintage wooden desks.

"What's the name of the teacher I'll be assisting?" she asked.

"I need to talk to you about that." Hugo clicked his tongue ominously. "She dropped by yesterday and handed in her resignation. Most teachers in Peru have second jobs to make ends meet and her other job offered more hours."

Ellie threw him a concerned glance. "Who's the English teacher then?"

Hugo raised his eyebrows.

It took Ellie a few seconds to fully appreciate the horror of what he was suggesting. "Oh... No. That's a terrible idea. You can't throw me in the deep end like that. I mean, I'm not remotely qualified to be a teacher. I was only going to help with classes, that's all."

"Ellie, from the short time we've spent together I have the impression you are intelligent and enthusiastic enough to give it a try. And in case you didn't realize, I have no-one else. So, please, it's only for a month until semester ends."

"But my Spanish... I'm not exactly fluent."

"That's fine. Our kids need most help with pronunciation, so a native English speaker at our school is a godsend. Please."

"I don't think..." Ellie heard her voice fade away as her eyes wandered along the rows of desks. She hadn't signed up for this level of responsibility, but wanted to give back to the continent that'd brought her so much joy. Staying in one place for a while to work through her demons also help appeal.

Could I actually pull this off?

Esmeralda greeted Ellie with a warm embrace. Hugo's curvy, amiable, wife showed her through their modest house near the school. It had a small living space, rudimentary kitchen and two bedrooms, one of which would be Ellie's for the next four weeks. If she lasted that long. On the bed, Hugo had left an English textbook. It looked about twenty years old, but hey, it was a start.

Over a heart-warming *atamalada* (quinoa, yuca and cheese stew) they talked in Spanglish, Hugo explaining that as a college student he'd been awarded a scholarship to complete his degree in Manchester, then taught at an international school in Lima. He and Esmeralda recently settled in the Sacred Valley to help the poorest children of Peru as they believed education was their best pathway out of poverty.

Ellie hoped to contribute to this noble aim, despite a sleepless night thinking about the likelihood of disaster tomorrow. Counting llamas didn't help.

CHAPTER 59

Sacred Valley, Peru

Total bedlam. Hundreds of students ran in all directions around the school square, chasing each other like bumper cars and screaming at the top of their lungs. Ellie did her best to weave through them, ducking as a ball lobbed overhead.

"*Bienvenida*," Hugo welcomed her.

"Is this OK?" Ellie brushed down her winter jacket. "I don't have much else."

"It's fine. Most of our teachers are quite casual." He handed her a sheet of paper. "I wrote your timetable so you know what classes are on today." Then he whistled and clapped his hands, which the other teachers around the yard repeated.

The students quickly lined up in neat rows. Ellie looked over the sea of miniature people dressed in matching blue-and-white uniforms, and stifled a laugh-cry as the reality of what she was about to attempt set in.

What have I got myself into? Again.

Rubbing her hands together as the grade one students poured into the classroom, Ellie lost track somewhere above thirty. They sprinted for the chairs because there weren't enough to go around. Many ended up sharing, and those that missed out sat on the slab-of-ice concrete floor. Ellie studied their grubby faces, ragged hair, and uniforms dotted with holes. Worst of all, these kids were *tiny* for their age.

"My name is Ellie. *Mi nombre es Ellie.*" She spoke slowly and deliberately. "I am your English teacher. *Yo soy su profesora de Ingles. Buenos días.*"

"*Buenos días, Ellie,*" the class replied in unison, with an emphasis on 'Ell-*ie*' that was utterly adorable. Things were going surprisingly well.

In preparation for the lesson, she'd written some English vocab on the blackboard. She planned to practice the words out loud and have the students copy them into their notebooks. But as soon as she turned her back, the trouble began. Girls pulled each other's hair, boys punched each other's arms and threw whatever they could find across the room, including freshly-mined boogers. Some students fell asleep. A few even got up and walked out. Ellie was powerless to control any of it, the fighting and babbling couldn't be stopped no matter how many times she shouted, "*Disculpen, por favor, niños!*"

Ellie decided a better approach may be to ignore the noise. Surely if she just started teaching they'd shut-up? She said each word on the board, then pointed to its corresponding body part. But none of the students joined in. The next class of second graders wasn't any better, and Ellie's heart sunk so low she worried it would drown.

Why won't they listen to me?

A lifebuoy arrived mid-morning in the form of a burly teacher carrying two large buckets, one filled with cups and the other a milky soup. The students stampeded forward, pushing each other out of the way. Ellie saved the smallest from getting crushed and helped everyone receive a cup. She tasted some of the soup from what was left. It was a milk and rice combo, and not too bad. In truth, it was the best thing about her day.

"How did it go?" Hugo popped his head into the classroom.

Ellie stopped sorting the notes she'd intended to teach and burst into tears. "It was terrible."

He pulled up a chair for each of them. "The first day is always the most difficult. For every teacher."

"I totally failed. I'm sorry."

"It's not possible to fail, Ellie. You did your best, and that's all I ask. I know you have high expectations based on your own schooling experience in the United States, but things are different here."

"They didn't learn anything from me. Not a damn thing." She snorted and wiped away more tears.

Hugo put a hand on her shoulder. "They did, even if you don't believe it. And tomorrow they will learn a little more, and a little more the day after that. Trust me, I've been in your position. The students will grow to love you. Please don't give up on them."

CHAPTER 60

Sacred Valley, Peru

A cold shower blasted Ellie awake and gave her fresh determination. These kids were going to learn, goddammit, whether they wanted to or not.

Hugo had given her some tips on discipline, so for the first lesson of the day Ellie directed the grade ones to line up outside the classroom. "*Una línea. Una línea,*" she repeated, recalling his advice not to raise her voice because they would just grow louder in response and she would end up with another headache.

Remarkably, the students did as they were told. She went down the line and counted them in English as they looked up at her with curious eyes. Ellie saw another teacher snickering at her approach, but persevered until every student was silent.

Inside, the students stayed that way for three whole minutes, which was a miracle given yesterday's catastrophe. When they did start chatting, she got all the students to stand, and only when each was silent would she tap them on the shoulder so they could sit. It turned behaving into a game which nobody wanted to lose.

More importantly, it allowed Ellie to do what she'd come here for—teach. Given the level of English was so low, she decided to begin with the basics. Grade ones would learn numbers, grade twos body parts, grade threes animals, and so on up to grade sixes learning simple sentences such as "My name is…" and "I live in…"

By the end of the day, Ellie thought she might enjoy this teaching caper after all.

∼

"How about a drink?" Hugo asked.

"At one o'clock? At school?"

"Esmeralda doesn't like me drinking at home so I have a tipple, as the English say, on Friday afternoons." Hugo set two glasses on Ellie's desk and unscrewed a bottle of Glenfiddich Scotch.

"I'm OK with my water bottle, thank you." Ellie had lost the desire for alcohol after her assault, though she would've liked some way to relax her brain. She'd put every last drop of energy into her classes this week and spent hours preparing lessons, often by candlelight when the electricity went out.

"Do you mind if I have one?" Hugo asked.

"Please, go ahead."

Hugo poured himself a finger. "How was your day?"

"Better. I think the students are finally learning something." Ellie laughed and took a satisfied sip of her water. "I didn't expect to feel this exhausted though. I'm totally spent."

"Teaching will do that to you, so be careful not to get run down. Remember, not every lesson has to be life-changing. Set your students a goal, help them achieve it, then add up all those small steps over time. Small steps, in learning and in life."

"I want to ask you about a student. His name is Mateo, in second grade. I'm no expert, obviously, but I think he's got some sort of learning difficulty."

Hugo nodded. "Mateo Gomez. He's had a rough time. His father left before he was born and as a baby he suffered from malnutrition. I'm sure you noticed how small these kids are. That's why we provide lunch, so they have at least one nutritious meal per day."

"I don't know how to get through to him."

"Unfortunately, with our limited resources, all we can do is support him as best we can. The most important thing is to make sure they enjoy learning. If you do that, you're half-way there. Remember, Ellie, small steps."

"To small steps," she toasted.

Hola Jerry,

I found an internet cafe that's running on dial-up speed, but at least I can let you know I'm alive 😊 Do you remember I told you I was going to be a teacher's assistant? Well guess what, I'm the ACTUAL teacher! Who would've thunk?

I'm teaching English to kids aged 6 to 12, and it's The. Hardest. Thing. I've. Ever. Done. I've come to the nearest town this morning to buy stationary and download teaching materials because we're short on pretty much everything.

How are things there? Did you kill the lawyers yet? Are the girls (mis)behaving? Please send me news, it's been too long and I worry you've been overwhelmed by paperwork and estrogen.

Sorry for the short message but I've gotta catch the only bus back to my village. I'll be online here next Sunday noon Peru time if you want to message then?

Ellie.

San Francisco, USA

Hi Ellie—or should I say, Miss Bartlett?
It's wonderful you're giving back, and I have no doubt
you're doing a fantastic job ☺ I bet all the boys have
a crush on you!
I'll dig out my girls' old English textbooks and see if
there's anything useful I can email across. They're well,
but I've been so busy I feel guilty for neglecting them.
Things need to change, I'm just not sure how I can
make it all work yet...
And if the lawyers don't accept my latest proposal I'm
going to get the construction crew to bury them in
concrete. Sound reasonable?
I'll be online next Sunday, but in the meantime best
of luck in the blackboard jungle.

"Dad?"

Jerry almost fell off his chair. He quickly shut his laptop. "Yas! Why the hell are you sneaking up on me like that?"

"There's not really any other way to come into your study."

"Well, you could knock next time."

"The door was open."

He adjusted his collar for no reason. "What's up?"

"I need to talk to you about something."

Jerry's body stiffened. Yasmina had never come to him like this before. Was she in love with a heroin dealer? Running away to join a guerilla group? Or worse—pregnant? With twins. He tried to shove the most horrible thoughts out of his mind and cleared his throat. "Sure, honey. What is it?"

Yasmina lowered herself into the chair beside Jerry's desk. For a long while she avoided eye contact and no words came out of her mouth.

"Yas, you can talk to me about whatever you want. I'm not your mom, but I'll do my best to listen. Are you in some kind of trouble?"

She shook her head. "No trouble. It's just that… As you know I haven't exactly been on my best behavior this year, but I want to ask—"

"If you want a Mercedes I'm going to have to say no, but if you want a new bike—"

"I want to go on a date," Yasmina blurted out.

Oh. Shit.

"A date?" Jerry almost choked on the word.

"Yes."

"With a boy?"

"Yes."

"But you're still grounded from Alison's party."

"That's why I'm asking you nicely."

Jerry tapped his fingers on his desk. Best to get as much information as possible before saying no. "What's his name?"

"Ed. Edward."

"Last name?"

"Cooper."

"Where do you want to go with this Edward Cooper?"

"Just to, like, dinner and a movie or something."

"Or something?" Jerry repeated, unimpressed.

"No, not 'or something.' Just dinner and a movie."

"Is this boy in your class?"

"No…but he's at my school."

Jerry could see through her vague response like a seasoned cop. "He's a senior."

Yasmina nodded.

"And you think this is a good idea?"

She hesitated. "Yes."

"Why?"

"Well, I got all my homework up to date and I'm helping around the house—"

"And you threw up all over my car."

"Yes, but that was a mistake. Like a one-off thing." She stared at the floor and Jerry sensed she was hoping it would swallow her up.

"Why do you want to go out with this boy?"

"I…I like him. He's funny."

"Funny like me?"

"No. Actually funny."

Jerry grunted in disapproval. "What do you think your mom would say?"

"I think she'd tell me to be careful, but she'd say 'yes' for sure."

Jerry studied Yasmina's pleading puppy eyes, then looked out the window where the sun rose high over the cubbyhouse he'd built for Mia. Why did his girls have to grow up so damn fast?

"Dad? Can you give me an answer?"

"I don't have one yet."

"A hint?"

"You're grounded right now. There's your hint."

CHAPTER 61

Sacred Valley, Peru

Ellie's second week as a teacher began more successfully than the first. The students accepted her line-up ritual, and as behavior improved so did the quality of lessons. She'd thought back to the activities her own teachers had used to make learning fun, such as games, rhymes and songs. The younger students particularly liked "Heads, shoulders, knees and toes, knees and toes..." They practiced it so many times Ellie fell asleep with the maddening tune ringing in her ears.

They also made good use of the paper and pens she'd bought for coloring in pictures of animals, fruit and veggies. Any mention of the word "cow" was inevitably followed by the whole class hollering "Moooooooo!" How could you not love that?

Ellie especially got a kick out of how enthusiastic the girls were for learning, often standing on chairs with their hands up to get her attention. There was Carolina, a bubbly fifth grader who spoke English without any fear, inspiring others to give it a shot. Beatriz had a big heart, always helping others when asked. And Luna, a shy girl whose pullover had been crudely stitched together like a rag doll, didn't say much but beamed when Ellie walked by and patted her on the head.

It wasn't all rainbows and unicorns, however. Ellie kept an eye on Mateo, who struggled with even the most basic tasks. In the U.S.A. he would've had a teaching aide, but here there was nothing. All she could do was encourage him and try to build his confidence. He loved drawing llamas, but would always cover them when she looked his way.

What is he thinking under that mop of black hair?

During break time, Ellie watched kids play in the yard just as they did the world over. The grade six boys were obsessed with soccer and celebrated like crazy when they scored a goal, mimicking their World Cup heroes.

But when one of them pushed a girl off the pitch for attempting to join in, Ellie scolded them and issued a challenge— play against a team of the fairer sex. The boys with their *machismo* scoffed at the idea, but girls flooded the pitch, eager to finally get their turn.

Game. On.

It was physical from the kick-off. Boys bumped girls off the ball, tugged their dresses, and quickly scored a goal. One wannabee-Ronaldo tripped Carolina, sending her sprawling into the dirt. Ellie gave him a verbal red card and he sulked off the pitch.

Once the protests and jeering had stopped, Ellie brought the girls in close for a pep talk. They executed the new strategy to perfection, Ellie kicking the ball to one girl, who passed it to another, and then another, until Carolina received it. She weaved between two boys and took a shot...

Gooooooooaaaaaaallll!!!

The girls cheered and hugged. A chant of *"Niñas, niñas, niñas!"* went up, which brought a grin to Ellie's face. Girl power was alive in rural Peru. Imagine what the future could hold.

San Francisco, USA

Jerry clicked 'refresh' on his Facebook page. Why wasn't Ellie online? With his study door closed to stop Yasmina surprising him again, he took an impatient bite of a sourdough sandwich and clicked refresh again.

Jerry, you around?

I'm here!

*I just saw all the English
material you emailed
Thank you so much
I'll definitely make use of it*

*No problem
How's it all going?*

Good 😄
Check out the pic!

*Hahaha nice photo
It looks like your
students are having fun*

*That's my grade 3s
Any chance to pull silly faces
Cheeky monkeys* 🙈

So you're enjoying it more?

Absolutely! Y'know back home

I was just a faceless employee, a small cog in a
massive profit machine, but here I feel like I'm
making a difference. Maybe only a small one,
but it's something.

I'm happy you're happy 😊

Thanks 😊
I do need help with one
more thing though…

Name it

In 2 weeks we have the final assembly of
semester and I have to prepare my grade 1s
for a performance showcasing what they've
learned. Any ideas?

How about a nursery rhyme?
You could do 'Old MacDonald had
a Farm' but swap in local animals? Bella
used to sing our girls the Spanish version.
I think it was 'Old Pepito had a Farm'

That's awesome!
You're a lifesaver 😊
And how's things with you? Did you get
your work/life balance under control?

Not at all. And we're still waiting
to hear back from the lawyers.
In New York did you ever feel like the world
kept telling you to run faster so you sped up,

but then it told you that's not fast enough
so you sped up more, and then even more?
I don't know I have anything else to give.

I understand exactly how you feel. I wish
there was something I could do to help

There is, actually.
I need some advice because my troublesome
17 year-old has asked if she can go on a date.
As you can imagine I'm about ready
to burn down Rome about it.

Oh Jerry, you poor thing 😔
Number 1, I'd be thankful she told you.
Some teenage girls would make up a story
and say they're going out with friends
(I'm speaking from personal experience here…)
She obviously feels comfortable enough to talk
with you about it. That's a good thing.

Perhaps 😑

Number 2, I'd tell her you want to meet
this boy. Size him up, find out if he's got
a brain and if his intentions are honorable.
She's going to date boys whether you like it
or not, so best to establish a routine where
you meet them beforehand.

No teenage boy has honorable intentions
(now I'm speaking from personal experience)
Even if he does have a brain, he won't be using it.

Oh God, this is becoming too real.
I don't want to meet him.
I want to kill him!

Y'know, he might surprise you.
You might even like him. It might
remind you of meeting Bella's parents
for the first time.

Now that was a nerve-wracking experience.
We flew to Chicago for Thanksgiving and
I must've gone to the restroom 6 times on
the plane. Practically needed an IV drip
when we arrived.

But they loved you, I assume…

I don't know if they loved me,
at least not then, and certainly not
when we told them Bella was pregnant.
But they came around in the end.

Exactly 😉
So take a chill pill and relax,
everything will work itself out.
Didn't you tell me that a while back?

I don't appreciate my own
advice being returned to me…

Well it worked for me
so maybe start practicing
what you're preaching!

You're right, thanks Ellie.
I'm flying solo here and don't
always have answers to this stuff.

Anytime 😊
It's nice that we can help each other
from thousands of miles away.
Same bat time, same bat channel,
next weekend?

You're on 😄

Jerry knocked on Yasmina's door.

"Come in."

He pushed it open and saw his daughter sitting at her desk doing homework. "How's it going?"

"Good. I'm pretty busy though, Dad. Gotta finish this by Monday."

"Well, I want to let you know that I've thought about what you asked."

Yasmina stopped writing and looked up at him.

"You can go on a date with this boy on three conditions."

"Really?!"

"The first is I have to meet him beforehand. The second is no alcohol. And the third is you have to be home by midnight, or you'll turn into a pumpkin."

Yasmina jumped out of her chair and threw her arms around her dad. "Thank you. I'll get him to pick me up, and we'll be home by midnight for sure."

"And no drinking," Jerry said.

"No drinking, and definitely no puking."

CHAPTER 62

Sacred Valley, Peru

There's a Latin proverb that says you will never know yourself better than when you are far from home, in a land that doesn't speak your language, and cut off from all communication. Over the next fortnight, Ellie came to understand it well.

Everyone should try it.

The grade twos learned the colors of the rainbow thanks to the well-known song, and the grade sixes were able to introduce themselves and talk about their families in English. Watching the students improve before her eyes was like a garden blooming—kind of magic.

Meanwhile, the grade ones practiced *Old MacDonald Had a Farm*. They knew the tune in Spanish but with the title *En La Granja de Pepito*. The English lyrics were simple enough to learn, and Ellie substituted South American animals for the North American ones as Jerry suggested, though relied on the students to tell her what they sounded like.

The lessons weren't without their share of hiccups, but the situation forced Ellie to be resilient, and there wasn't enough time to be hard on herself.

Gotta keep moving forward. Small steps, in learning and in life.

On Friday afternoons, she continued to debrief with Hugo while he drank a glass of Scotland's finest, while at home Esmeralda taught her how to cook traditional Peruvian dishes like *tacu tacu* (spicy refried beans with rice).

Best of all, Ellie felt she'd joined a community. She was part of something here, contributing to something bigger than herself for the first time. It didn't just feel good to teach, it felt exhilarating. Helping others helped her heal, and made Ellie think she might finally have found her calling.

San Francisco, USA

Is he kissing her?
Touching her?
Thinking about...?

Half-working, half-watching TV, but unable to concentrate on anything, Jerry perched uneasily on the couch. He checked his watch—11:30 p.m. Shook his wrist. Still 11:30 pm. It sure seemed like the seconds hand was moving slower than usual.

He'd *hated* Yasmina's date. Edward arrived with a cocky smirk and well-rehearsed "Call me Ed" line that made Jerry want to punch him in his blinding-white teeth. Tall and athletic, it was no surprise Yasmina found him attractive, but he also had a darting gaze Jerry didn't trust. Like a cobra calculating its moment to strike. Shithead.

A car door slammed. Jerry jumped up and peeked through the blinds, a cold shower of relief washing over every cell of his tortured soul. Yasmina had returned, early. Her key hit the lock and Jerry dashed back to the couch.

"Oh, hi Yas." He tried to sound casual but failed.

"Hey…" she drawled.

"Everything go OK?" He stood to check on his daughter while she took off her heels in the hall.

"Yeah, it was fine. Just…"

"What, honey?"

"Boring. Dad, he was *so* boring."

Jerry struggled to contain his grin. "I'm sorry to hear that."

"He had nothing to say. *At all.* Like, he knew nothing about current events or politics or history. I mean, he thought Africa was a country, and tried to tell me all Latinos were Mexican. Total bonehead."

Jerry's grin had become a wildfire. He realized, more than ever before, that he and Bella had raised Yasmina right. "Well, it's best to find that out now—"

"I mean, what does he think, I'll just date any cute boy? I've got standards, y'know." She sighed loudly. "So I guess you have nothing to worry about."

"Can I get you anything? Tea? Hot chocolate?" A Mercedes?

"No thanks, Dad, I'm just gonna go to sleep. Good night." Yasmina kissed him on the cheek and headed upstairs.

Jerry waited until she'd reached the landing before punching the air and dancing across the living room.

"Dad?"

He spun around to see Yasmina peering at him from the top of the stairs.

"Oh, hi honey… I thought you'd gone to bed. I was just…"

"Dancing?"

"Dancing? Yes! It's fun. You should try it. But not sexy dancing or anything. Just normal, unsexy, dancing."

"Can you pass my purse? I left it on the side table."

"Sure, honey. Here you go."

"Thanks."

"Good night, Yas." Jerry waited until she'd really gone, then danced some more.

CHAPTER 63

Sacred Valley, Peru

The day had arrived. Ellie dreaded it. She hated goodbyes more than hellos and hoped she wouldn't cry, but packed a bunch of tissues just in case. All the parents had come to watch the final assembly. It progressed without a hitch, with prayers said and the sixth graders leading a rousing rendition of the Peruvian national anthem. Ellie really didn't want to be the one to bring the whole thing crashing down.

Hugo introduced her grade one class over the megaphone and she organized them at the front of the square. The school fell quiet. All Ellie could hear was the wind whistling down from the mountains and the beating of her heart. She touched her *Pachamama* pendant for strength. Her students looked at her anxiously, their limbs trembling with energy.

Be brave, little ones.

She flashed them her biggest smile and counted down with her fingers. "Three, two, one."

> *"Old Pepito had a farm*
> *E-I-E-I-O*

And on his farm he had a llama
E-I-E-I-O
With a mwa mwa here
And a mwa mwa there
Here a mwa, there a mwa
Everywhere a mwa mwa
Old Pepito had a farm
E-I-E-I-O!"

The parents and students laughed along with the animal sounds and movements Ellie had choreographed. Her class felt the approval and grew more animated as they moved through the verses.

"Old Pepito had a farm
E-I-E-I-O
And on his farm he had a cuy
E-I-E-I-O
With a wheek wheek here
And a wheek wheek there
Here a wheek, there a wheek
Everywhere a wheek wheek
Old Pepito had a farm
E-I-E-I-O!"

They finished with a burst of enthusiasm and basked in the applause. Ellie led their proud faces in a bow. Once the clapping had settled, Hugo called Carolina forward.

"Dear Miss Ellie, we want to thank you for be our teacher and help us speak English. We love you and hope you visit soon. Thank you and travel very good."

The school cheered and tears sprang from Ellie's eyes.

Oh damn, these are gonna be hard to stop.

Once the assembly finished and families began drifting home, a young woman with a downturned smile approached Ellie. Holding her hand was Mateo, his eyes on the ground. "*Mateo tiene algo para ti,*" the woman said, then whispered something to her son. He held out a rolled-up sheet of paper.

"For me? *Para mi?*" Ellie crouched to Mateo's eye-level and unfurled the paper. He'd drawn a picture of a llama and glued colorful string on its head like the identifying fabric farmers tied around their herd's ears. Underneath he'd written in messy block letters: THANKYU TEACHR MISS ELEE.

She wiped away more tears. Now it wasn't just her eyes overflowing, it was her heart. "*Muchas gracias, Mateo. Es muy lindo.* This is very beautiful. *Me encanta.* I love it." Ellie opened her arms, and he stepped into her embrace.

Alone in her classroom, Ellie's eyes traced the walls, covered with her students' work. This month-long teaching adventure had been one of the most challenging experiences of her life—but also the most rewarding. She understood now that you could impact the world. All you had to do was try.

"How are you feeling?"

"I don't usually cry this much, Hugo. I think it's the altitude."

"Kids will do that to you. One last tipple?"

"*Sí.*"

He poured a Scotch and raised his glass. "You were fantastic, Ellie. Thank you for staying when others would have given up."

She toasted with her water bottle. "Thank you for the opportunity. I really didn't expect to get this attached to my students."

"Hear what you did there? *My* students. You've become a real teacher."

Ellie laughed. "It's funny how you become so possessive of them."

"It's only natural when you work so closely together. Besides, they love you."

"Even if I only helped them learn a little English, or gave them some confidence, hopefully I've been worthwhile."

"More than worthwhile. You've been a breath of fresh air and I expect our—your—students will be talking about Miss Ellie for a long time to come."

She took a drink and thought for a moment. "Y'know… I believe, and I say this from the bottom of my heart… I believe that I learned more from them than they learned from me."

Hugo smiled. "That's usually how it works."

CHAPTER 64

Halloween, 31st October – San Francisco, USA

"When are you going to grow up?!" Jerry snapped. "You need to be more responsible."

"I am responsible. I just can't remember where I left them." Andrea dashed upstairs to search for her soccer boots.

"Daddy, I want to dress up as Princess Leia tonight," Mia said.

"That's the definition of irresponsible!" Jerry shouted, ignoring his youngest child. His phone rang but he didn't answer it. "You're holding everyone up. Even Yasmina is ready."

"Don't drag me into this." She slouched at the kitchen table, messaging on her phone.

"Daddy, what do you think about Princess Leia?" Mia tried again.

"So the golden child is ready for the first time in her life and the only morning I'm late I get yelled at?" Andrea hurried downstairs, without her boots. "That's the definition of fair."

"Don't talk back to me, young lady."

"I'm not talking back. I'm making a valid point. She never gets in trouble for any of the stupid things she does."

"*Perra.*"

"*Perra también,*" Andrea returned Yasmina's insult.

"You need to stop thinking about your sister and focus on where you left your damn shoes!" Jerry's phone rang again.

"They're boots, not shoes!" Andrea yelled, searching the living room.

"Daddy, what about—"

"Mia, will you just shut up?!"

It was as if all the air got sucked out of the house. The words shot from Jerry's mouth with so much frustration the aftertaste made him sick, and Mia's crumpled face told him everything he needed to know about their impact. She ran down the hallway, tears spilling over her cheeks.

Great. Just great.

Jerry had barely slept a wink. Last night had been a whirlwind of phone calls after receiving a 5 p.m. email from the asshole lawyers. They'd waited until the last moment to screw him, formally cutting off funds to complete the terraces to Bella's design. It wasn't the best state of mind to be in when negotiating with teenagers and children.

"I offered to compromise, but they threw it back in my face," Jerry explained, marching toward the entrance of the museum. Harry and Kyra followed close behind, also wearing hardhats and orange safety vests. "It's a deal-breaker. I'm not willing to accept it."

"Have you got a choice?" Harry said.

"There's always a choice."

"Time's running out, Jerry. According to the lawyers, it's already run out."

"The terraces are going to be done right or I'd rather quit the whole damn thing."

And shove the lawyers' revisions up their pompous asses on the way out.

The external structure of the museum had been topped

out, five levels rising from the ground like a curved pyramid. Enormous glass windows wrapped around the bottom floors and work had commenced on the interior fit-out.

Jerry and his team walked through the front doors and into the massive entrance hall. Two Incan-style floating staircases, still under construction, spiraled up to the east and west wings on the second level. They dodged around scaffolding, building materials and laborers as power tools shrieked into the dusty air. Jerry came to a door with 'FEMALE' scrawled on it in chalk.

He pushed inside. It was immediately clear what'd gone wrong. A row of male urinals had been installed in the women's restroom. "Unbelievable…" Jerry sensed the room spinning. He gripped his hips to stabilize it. "Who did this?"

"An apprentice, working off an old set of plans," Harry explained. "I've already taken care of it."

"Doesn't everyone know we're running a month behind? Son of a bitch!" Jerry kicked a loose brick across the floor and it smashed into the drywall.

"This is minor issue my Q.C. crew picked up the next morning. You have more important things to—"

"It's all important," Jerry barked. "Details, Harry. We need to get the details right. Or it's all for shit."

"I understand, but—"

"Detail is everything. Quality is everything. Finish is everything. It's my reputation on the line."

"A lot of reputations are on the line. As I said, everyone will be on the same page from here on out."

"Do more than get them on the 'same page.' Fix it. And make sure it doesn't happen again." Jerry stormed out of the restroom, kicking up a cloud of dust in his wake.

Above the rim of his glasses, Jerry could see Kyra hovering like a helicopter parent. It only made him more annoyed. They'd returned to the open-plan office to review design changes on a drafting table. Jerry's shoulders hunched over it as if the entire physical weight of the museum were a burden he alone carried.

"These are awful," he said. "A child could've been more creative. Where's Kevin?"

"Do you want to order some lunch?" Kyra asked in an all-too-obvious attempt to defuse his mood.

"Kevin!"

"I'm here, Jerry. What's up?" The civil engineer wore his usual cheery bowtie and suspenders outfit.

"There's only one bench on the south lawn."

Kevin checked the drawings. "Yes, that's right."

"I know it's right. Because I can read a plan. I'm asking *why* you would only put one bench on the south lawn when I'd allotted double that."

"I thought the new brief was to see where we could cut costs—"

"Not on guest amenities!" Jerry thumped the table. "Where the hell are people going to sit? In the trees? Like chimps?"

"Hey, guys." Kyra took a step between them.

"Did you even think about the implications of these changes?"

"I'm sorry. I was just using the updated budget—"

"Well, use your brain next time!" Jerry threw down his pen and strutted toward the model of the Pata Museum holding pride-of-place in the office. "Fuck!" He grabbed its base with both hands and flipped it.

The model crashed to the floor. Wood cracked and broke. Pieces bounced across the carpet. It no longer resembled a building, but a broken monument to a failed idea.

"Jerry!" Kyra shouted. "Your office. Now."

Her demand broke through Jerry's fog of anger. He looked up and saw the shocked expression on Kevin's face. All his employees had stopped what they were doing and stared at him. Jerry suddenly felt like a child couldn't control his temper, followed by a blaze of shame that scorched his face red. He dropped his eyes and paced to his office.

Kyra shadowed him, slamming the door behind them. "You cannot—I repeat, *cannot*—talk to Kevin like that. You humiliated him, in front of everyone. It's completely unacceptable."

Jerry sunk into his chair and disappeared into a grimace.

"You need to get your shit together. What would Bella say if she were here?"

Bella would kill me. Or at the very least refuse to talk to me for a week.

"I've never seen you act like this before," Kyra continued. "But the lawyers screwing us is no excuse."

Jerry rubbed his face and took a long breath to let his emotions dissipate. "You're right."

Kyra pulled up a seat next to him. "Jerry, what's going on inside your head?"

"I don't know… I haven't had much sleep lately."

"Listen, everyone understands what you've been through. They're sympathetic about it, they know the pressure you're under, and they'll always go the extra mile for you. If you didn't have your head up your own ass most of the time you'd see that."

Jerry nodded. "I see it."

"Good. Because they're not sympathetic about you acting like a dick. You need to realize you're doing two jobs now—yours *and* Bella's. And looking after your kids. It's too much."

He finally made eye contact. He could barely keep them open. "I'm not sure what to do."

"Delegating would be a good start. Focus on the big picture. The bull instead of the bullshit. Everyone out there is here to help, and we want to help, but you need to ask. And trust." The phone on Jerry's desk buzzed and Kyra answered it. "Yes. Oh…shit."

CHAPTER 65

San Francisco, USA

Jerry charged through the automatic doors of St Luke's Hospital and into the E.R. waiting room. He scanned the rows of chairs for familiar faces as he headed to reception. "I'm looking for Mia Townsend."

"Relation to patient?" the receptionist asked.

"Father." Since the phone call from Mia's school, nothing else had mattered. All thoughts of budgets and urinals and soccer boots had instantly faded into the background.

"She's in bed six. Through the doors and to the right…"

Jerry left before the receptionist finished speaking. At the end of the corridor he pushed through double doors and into the E.R. Ten beds in various states of use surrounded a central nurses' station.

"Hey, Dad."

Jerry spun around. "Mia! Are you all right?" He rushed to his daughter, who sat up in bed, apparently content. He kissed her and saw her left forearm was in a splint. "What happened?"

"I hurt my arm."

"How are you feeling?" He checked her over to see if anything else was injured.

"I'm OK. They gave me a lollipop."

"Are you in any pain, honey?"

Mia shook her head. "Not anymore."

"Mr. Townsend?" A woman with a white coat, sunny smile and large envelope approached. "I'm Dr. Alice Wong."

"Can you tell me how serious it is?"

"I just received the X-rays so let's have a look." Dr. Wong pulled a sheet of film out of the envelope and clipped it to a light box.

"Is that my arm?" Mia asked.

"Yes, it is. That's what your bone looks like underneath all that skin and muscle," Dr. Wong explained while studying the film.

"Cool."

"Little lady, you have a hairline fracture." Dr. Wong pointed to a break in the bone.

Jerry moved in for a closer look. "A hairline fracture isn't too bad, right?"

"It's pretty common in kids this age with all the running around they do."

"What happened, Mia? How did you hurt yourself?"

"I was playing tag with Chelsea and Tahlia and I tripped on the sandbox."

"Running around," Jerry clarified.

Mia happily sucked on her lollipop.

"She's fractured the radius bone," Dr. Wong continued. "But it's non-displaced, which means none of the bones in the wrist have moved out of position. I recommend a cast for four-to-six weeks. Then we'll take another X-ray and see how it's healed up."

"Can my friends draw on it, Daddy?"

"Is that still allowed?" Jerry looked to Dr. Wong.

"That's allowed. But give it a day or two to make sure it's completely set before letting your friends turn it into a work of art. And you'll have to stop running around for a while."

"That might be difficult." Jerry brushed hair off Mia's face.

"She hasn't got too much swelling, so if you can wait a couple of hours we'll set the cast and send her home tonight. Sound OK, Mia?"

"Sounds great!"

Dr. Wong laughed. "That'll be the painkillers talking."

"She doesn't have to stay in hospital for a few days? To make sure everything's OK?"

"It's a simple fracture, Mr. Townsend. This isn't open heart surgery."

"No, of course not." Jerry relaxed ever-so-slightly.

"Yeah, Dad. And I'm tough."

"I know you are. I'm very proud of you." Her resilience never ceased to amaze him.

"Can we still go trick-or-treating tonight?"

"I'm afraid not, honey." He kissed her head.

"To ensure she remains tough, I'll prescribe some medication to get her through the next couple of days." Dr. Wong scribbled an update on Mia's chart. "And because Halloween is off limits, I might prescribe some ice-cream as well if that's OK with you, Mr. Townsend?"

"I don't think I have a choice."

"Ben & Jerry's Choc-chip Cookie Dough would be nice," Mia said.

"Yes, it would," Jerry sighed.

"Two scoops," she grinned.

CHAPTER 66

Rurrenabaque, Bolivia

The turboprop plane banked to the right. Ellie looked out the window and her entire view became consumed by an ocean of luminescent green stretching as far as she could see and doubtless beyond. The Amazon Rainforest. Her eyes and mouth gaped. She'd wanted—no, needed—to start adventuring again, and hoped an experience in nature would ease the pain of leaving the Sacred Valley and 'her kids.'

Ellie's second grade Geography teacher, Mr. Humpstead, had called the Amazon "the lungs of the earth," and that image stuck with her since then. Flying over the massive sea of jungle, she imagined it heaving up-and-down as it breathed in-and-out, converting carbon dioxide into oxygen to keep everything on our planet alive.

Ellie noticed her own breathing too. Fast, excited, breaths, followed by deep, anxious, ones. It was impossible not to feel insignificant in the face of something so immense.

Why am I always so scared of new things? Do I have a bigger than usual flight response in my D.N.A? Or did I somehow learn to be afraid of everything beyond my current experience?

The answer to those questions hadn't yet revealed themselves. But what Ellie did know, what this trip had taught, was that she had to try new things, no matter how much they scared the shit out of her. Not to try would be the only mistake.

Unless I catch malaria. Because that would suck. Also dengue. Or yellow fever. Or rabies. OK, that last one is unlikely, isn't it?

The Amazon, Bolivia

"*Hola.*"

Ellie turned from the riverbank, where a boat had left her with no instructions except to wait. A young woman emerged from the jungle. With copper skin and shoe-shine black hair, she wore a muddy t-shirt, shorts, flip-flops—and casually carried a machete over her shoulder.

"I didn't hear you coming," Ellie said.

"I am Tacana tribe. We know how to move in silence."

That made sense. But what else moved through the jungle in silence? "I'm Ellie."

The woman looked at her like she was dumb. "I know."

"You are Saywa?"

"Come, it will rain and we need to walk some way."

Ellie threw on her daypack. "Let me guess, about ten minutes?" She'd already figured out indigenous people didn't care for the Western concept of time and ten minutes was the typical answer that could mean two minutes or four hours.

"Ten minutes," Saywa agreed. "More or less."

"Can I ask where you learned English?"

"In school. Where did you learn?"

Ellie liked her already. She'd taken Bella's recommendation of hiring Saywa as a private guide to explore the jungle for a few days, but also requested an additional—*extra special*—activity.

One that, from everything she'd read, might send her soaring over the canopy like a condor. At the very least, it was unlikely she would leave the Amazon as the same person that went in. The thought was exhilarating, yet terrifying.

Saywa twirled her machete like a lightsaber, slashing at vines to reveal a narrow path ahead. Ellie took a lungful of the thick air for courage—and followed her in.

CHAPTER 67

The Amazon, Bolivia

Keeping up with Saywa was a struggle. Ellie couldn't stop looking around, trying to take it all in, tripping more than once. The ground changed from dirt to clay to sponge, and the foliage flaunted every glorious shade of the color wheel. The booming surround sound of insects, birds, and animals intoxicated her.

It's more alive than any place I've ever been.

Saywa held up a hand and motioned for Ellie to crouch. She followed her guide's index finger to the canopy fifteen yards away, where reddish-brown fur stood out against jade leaves.

"Red howler monkeys," Saywa whispered. "One, two, three, and baby on mother's back. You see?"

"I see," Ellie replied, captivated at spotting her first monkeys in the wild.

The baby clung to its mom while the adolescents played, using finger-like claws and curly tails to swing between branches like trapeze artists. Their black faces and bulging eyes resembled humans, and their howls were so loud the sound carried for miles. Then they were gone, dissolving into the shadows.

Ellie finally drew breath. "That was incredible."

"Taste good too," Saywa said.

They pushed deeper into the rainforest, occasionally stopping when Saywa pointed out medicinal plants discovered by her ancestors and still used today.

In a valley they came across a five-foot high termite mound being attacked by an army of black bullet ants. The war was epic, tens-of-thousands of insects working in perfect unison. Saywa explained that although humans saw beauty here, life in the Amazon was in fact a desperate, never-ending, fight for survival. Animals fed on animals, insects on insects, birds on both. Even trees consumed other trees, strangling them in a slow death lasting centuries. Life always meant something else's death.

Ellie felt a sting and slapped her neck. She looked at the red and black remains of a mosquito smeared across her palm. She was part of the cycle too. But also armed with malaria tablets, so take that blood suckers.

Saywa whistled her over to see the Amazon's most infamous animal. Its body was four inches long, with legs adding another six inches to its span. A deep shade of purple, almost black, and covered with spiky fur, the female tarantula crawled through the leaves outside its burrow.

"Gorgeous," Ellie said, dropping to her haunches to get a photo.

The spider bared its fangs—a deadly beast that didn't just eat its prey, but its male mate as well. Now there was an idea.

Something touched Ellie's ear. She screamed and jumped a foot, almost falling prey to the tarantula. Saywa held up a twig and laughed.

We obviously have a very different definition of funny.

With every step, the jungle became more dense. In the afternoon, they rested by a watering hole where hundreds of bright blue morpho butterflies gathered. *Mariposa*—butterfly— was Ellie's favorite word in Spanish. Actually, it sounded equally delightful in both languages. She felt like a princess in a fairytale as they flitted their wings around her head and landed on her outstretched arms.

Do they call themselves 'pretty little things?' Or maybe they exist without worrying about labeling everything like we do? If I only lived for a hundred days, I wouldn't worry about it either.

Wouldn't it be wonderful to just exist? To never think about the past or future? Just be. Now.

"Your turn." Saywa handed Ellie her machete.

"But…I've never used one before."

"What could go wrong?" her guide said with a toothy grin. Saywa gave Ellie a quick lesson in how to wield the sharp blade down and on an angle, then let her lead the way.

At first Ellie enjoyed the power, but after chopping vines for ten minutes her arms burned as if she'd been lifting weights. Jerry probably wouldn't be calling her 'Indiana Ellie' now. They mercifully emerged into a clearing of soft, fluorescent, grass.

"In rain season this area is flood, but now is best time to see birds," Saywa explained.

They lay down in the *Jurassic Park* setting and were blessed to spot kingfishers and a pair of macaws, mated for life. On a nearby trunk, a woodpecker tapped relentlessly like a toy whose batteries never ran out. On the branch opposite, a potoo camouflaged itself so well that only when it opened its huge yellow eyes could Ellie notice it.

The colors were eye-popping: the aqua wings of the quetzals, the orange crest of the cock-of-the-rock, and bright yellow weaver birds flying out of their upside-down nests. There was so much chatter among the birds, Ellie imagined it was like an air traffic control tower with flight paths and landing spots being communicated.

"Saywa, what's for dinner?" she asked.

"I don't know."

"What do you mean?"
"We need to catch it."
"Um…catch what?"

By dusk they were sitting on a riverbank, each holding a fishing line. Saywa had scooped some bugs from a decaying log to use for bait. They'd only been here five minutes, but Ellie was already impatient with their lack of progress. "Does it always take this long?"

"Sometimes yes. Sometimes no."

Saywa's straightforward manner was endearing. In a world full of bullshit, she was consistently to the point. It didn't help conversation though, and the quiet amplified Ellie's rumbling gut. She felt a tug on her line. "Oh, I think I've got something."

"Pull up. Fast."

Ellie whipped up her line. A fish flew out of the water and landed with a splat on the rock between them. It flopped around a few times before Saywa put it out of its misery with the tip of her machete.

Ellie's excitement at catching her prize vanished. She'd been complicit in killing a living animal. She consoled her conscience by picking up the piranha, studying its sharp teeth, and telling herself that it would've eaten her too if it had the chance.

Curiosity got the better of Ellie and she put a finger inside the piranha's jaw to touch its gigantic chompers—

"Oww!" The fish clamped on Ellie's finger. She whacked it against the rock until it let go. Then grabbed the machete and stabbed the piranha again, making sure it was really dead this time. "Little shit. I'm gonna eat you now."

Saywa howled with laughter.

Together they made a fire while Saywa ribbed Ellie about her fishing skills. There wasn't much meat on each piranha, but the white flesh was tasty. As they gobbled dinner, Saywa described how her tribe had lived here for thousands of years and had no desire to leave the rainforest, the only way of life they'd ever known.

Ellie's stomach tightened in anticipation of reaching their remote village for her *extra special* activity. It could turn out to be the most spiritual—or foolish—decision of her life.

After stripping the fish to their bones, Saywa and Ellie put on headtorches for a night walk. A second shift had taken over from the daytime Amazon crew, and this one was even more fantastic. There were wolf spiders spinning elaborate webs, stick insects so well disguised only Saywa's trained eye could spot them, black scorpions, poison dart frogs, and red assassin bugs. Above, vampire bats swirled in the moonlight.

The dark moss of the rainforest hid a centipede a foot long, and a cockroach twice as big as Ellie's hand crawled across a branch like a commando. She was both disgusted and impressed. After all, cockroaches were fricking ugly but had been around for 300 million years before humans, and would probably be around for 300 million years after humans. So, yeah, they had us bested on that front.

Before coming here, Ellie would've sprinted from these creepy-crawlies. But in their habitat, they were a wonder to behold.

"Get back," Saywa said.

Ellie had never heard her guide so alarmed. "What is it?"

Saywa kept moving backward, arms out to protect Ellie. She scanned a swamp with her headtorch.

Ellie looked around nervously but couldn't see a thing.

"There!"

Ellie's eyes traced Saywa's beam. She caught a glimpse of a creature rolling through the water. The unmistakable green and black patterned skin of an anaconda. "Holy shit. It's huge."

"Fifteen, sixteen feet."

It surfaced again, closer this time.

"We go now." Saywa pulled Ellie away from the swamp.
"It can move fast?"
"Yes. When I was a girl, one took my friend."
"I'm sorry."
"It's what they do."

Cocooned in a hammock, Ellie buzzed from the variety of life she'd encountered today. Like SCUBA diving had made her less afraid of the ocean, the Amazon taught her to love the jungle. Even the unidentified creature rustling in the grass beneath her butt was exciting. It stopped for a few seconds, then continued on its merry way.

The symphony of nature filled every space in the pitch black around her hanging island. Without being able to see where the sounds were coming from, they became so loud, so dense, she could *feel* them. They were on her, in her, and Ellie became part of these lungs of the earth.

CHAPTER 68

The Amazon, Bolivia

Rain continued to fall on the canopy, which covered the jungle floor like a leaky umbrella. Ellie had been trudging for hours along this not-so-well-worn path, following the fading impression of Saywa's footprints in the undergrowth.

She was relieved when they came to a small village snuggled among kapok trees. It looked about as removed from civilization as a person could get, ten or twelve bamboo huts with no sign of electricity or running water. At the far end, Ellie noticed a circular hut with a roof but no walls. There was a burnt-out fireplace at its center.

"Your ceremony is there," Saywa said.

"You'll come with me?"

"Yes."

Ellie had only agreed to the ceremony if Saywa joined her. She needed to be with someone she trusted. "What does it feel like?"

"Everyone is different. Best you find yourself."

Does she mean 'find yourself' or 'find out for yourself'?

"First we rest. Come."

As Ellie and Saywa walked through the village, round faces

appeared in doorways, naked children jostling for a glimpse of the wet stranger. Ellie smiled and the children giggled back. Their eyes were innocent, like they hadn't been tainted by the problems of the outside world.

"This is my house. I was born here and I will die here," Saywa said before ushering Ellie inside.

An old lady tended to a hearth that puffed wispy smoke up to the roof. Saywa spoke a few words in a language Ellie didn't recognize, and the lady tipped her head in welcome.

"Sit. My grandmother make *guayusa*. Like English tea but not really. Remember, no eat before ceremony. Only drink."

Ellie took off her jacket and kneeled by the fire. She embraced the warm cup Saywa's grandmother offered her, and for a few minutes forgot her anxiety about tonight.

After napping the afternoon away in a corner of the hut, Ellie stirred when Saywa shook her awake. There was no-one else around. Maybe a faint sound of drums, but it was hard to tell. She grabbed her waterbottle and followed her guide out the doorway.

In the ceremonial hut, a fire raged. Sitting cross-legged in front of it, bare-chested and with a headdress of bright feathers, was a wiry old man—the shaman Ellie had traveled all this way to meet. So far she'd overcome all her physical fears about what lay in the jungle, but tonight she would confront her emotional fears through the sacred medicine known as *ayahuasca*. Made from a vine growing deep in the Amazon, tribal healers boiled it down to a drinkable form to release its hallucinogenic properties. Apparently the effect was…life changing.

Or something.

Ellie had never been 'into' drugs. Sure, there'd been the occasional puff on a joint in college, but it never did anything so amazing to make her repeat the experience. But *ayahuasca* was different. It wasn't a Western party drug. It was a revelatory medicine.

Will it take me on a voyage outside my body?

Uncover secrets about my inner self?

Reveal mysteries about how the universe came to be?

Approaching the hut, all Ellie could hear was the battering ram of her heart against her ribs. The shaman mixed something in a small bowl and didn't look up until Ellie and Saywa sat on the other side of the fire. His eyes bore through the flames and into Ellie's mind.

It felt like he saw everything in her life as if it were a movie playing in super-fast rewind from this instant, back through her assault in Cusco, her life in New York, childhood with her parents, to the moment of her birth. Ellie held his gaze as long as possible before averting her eyes.

How did he do that?

Could he tell she was troubled? That she'd come here for a reason—to understand herself better, to make sense of her life, and how she fit into this world? Would she finally understand *her truth*? Ellie had a hunch he already knew the answers to these questions.

The shaman motioned for her to stand. She did. He motioned for her to remove her shoes, top, and pants. Saywa gave Ellie a reassuring nod. He motioned for her to remove her bra and panties. Ellie hesitated again. The shaman placed a gentle hand on her shoulder. Her thumping heart cooled. They locked eyes and Ellie's fear evaporated. There was no danger here. She slipped off her underwear and threw them on the bamboo mat with her clothes.

The shaman took a brush of leaves and dipped them into a pot bubbling over the fire. He rubbed the hot, khaki-colored, mixture down Ellie's arms, back and legs. It tickled, but she tried not to flinch.

Then he stood facing Ellie with palms upturned, closed his eyes and began to chant in his native tongue. Ellie supposed he was invoking ancient spirits or cleansing her in some way for the journey to come. Then again, he may have just been singing his favorite song.

Saywa joined in and Ellie followed her lead, upturning her palms and shutting her eyes. After a moment, she sensed smoke being blown across her limbs in a warm massage. Then a flare of intense heat. She snapped her eyes open.

The shaman was a few paces away, blowing over a stick of fire that ignited into a ball of flame. Ellie held her ground as another fireball charged through the air, vaporizing just before it hit her skin. But instead of escalating her fear, it made her feel stronger, as if the weak parts of her were being burned off at the edges, and only the tough core remained.

The shaman nodded, and Ellie did the same in return. There was no need for words because the message was clear—she was ready.

Ellie put her clothes back on and sat next to him on the mat. He swirled the *ayahuasca* lovingly, like it was more precious than gold. He let it settle, drank half in one gulp, then passed the bowl to Ellie. The liquid had a rich brown hue, like a broth, but there wasn't much of it.

How can such a small dose possibly be effective?

Saywa gestured for her to drink. Ellie tilted the bowl to her lips and downed it all in one hit. It tasted like dishwater. She gagged but forced herself to hold it down.

Zilch. Zip. Nada. For fifteen minutes, Ellie wondered whether the *ayahuasca* was having any effect at all. She snuck a peek at the shaman and saw him in the same position, eyes lightly closed. The only movement came from the shadows of the flames as they flickered across his face like a zoetrope.

Oh...

Ellie felt a pang of nausea. She shooed the sensation away, but it spread from her stomach to her head like a fast-moving virus.

Oh, shit...

Soon she was sure she'd never felt this nauseous before. No matter if Ellie opened or shut her eyes, there was no avoiding it. Like being on a looping roller coaster in a raging ocean while her brain spun inside her skull.

Please.

No.

Stop.

Ellie crawled to the edge of the hut and bent over the circle of rocks acting as a loose boundary to the jungle. Then it came. A surge of vomit so strong it almost knocked her forward into her own sick.

Saywa held Ellie's hair back as she gripped the rocks and spewed again. This wasn't the normal 'I drank too much' or 'I have food poisoning' vomit. This stuff was coming from the very pit of her gut. Ellie chanced opening her eyes and saw an orange fluid, flecked with black, shoot out of her mouth. She'd never thrown up from this place before. This hard before. Again it came. And again.

Jesus...

Ellie eventually fell back on her rump. Head pounding, throat stinging, diaphragm aching, she prayed to every god she'd heard of for it to be over. There couldn't possibly be anything left in her stomach or intestines or wherever the hell else this stuff had come from.

Oh no.

She was wrong. Again it came. And again.

She screamed as she vomited, a primal scream from the depth of her being that sent wildlife scurrying. Ellie had read that everyone who took *ayahuasca* puked, but this was something else. *This was a purge.* She screamed again as the last of whatever was deep down inside exited her body.

Ellie collapsed on her side, gasping for air. She clumsily wiped away the sick trickling down her chin and Saywa passed her waterbottle. Rinsing her mouth and spitting bitterly into the jungle, Ellie tried to comprehend what'd just happened. Something had changed... She no longer felt nauseous. In fact, she'd never felt this *good* before. Within the space of a few minutes Ellie had gone from feeling the worst of her entire life, to feeling the best!

Saywa took Ellie's hand and led her back to the fire. She lay down on the mat and shut her eyes again. "Oh... My... God..." All the colors of life's palette gushed toward her in a beam of refracted light. It was the most dazzling display she'd ever seen. Every single ray vivid, streaming past her face and curving around her body with an intensity that took her breath away.

Ellie flashed her eyes open to check reality still existed.

The shaman stood over her, chanting what she somehow knew was a prayer to the animal spirits of the Amazon. It was the most mesmerizing song she'd ever heard. She turned her head to the side and the fire was the most intense fire she'd ever seen, the dirt was the softest dirt she'd ever touched. And the jungle, how fucking beautiful it looked in the moonlight!

Ellie could see *everything* in a detail she'd never known before. Hear *everything.* Feel *everything.* The super-charged power of her senses was astonishing, as if they'd been turned up from 100 to 1,000,000. Her brain was suddenly able to dissect the sounds radiating from the jungle and jump from cackling monkeys in a distant tree to the tiniest insect singing for a mate.

She returned her laser focus to the shaman. He'd started to move around the hut, chanting and shaking a branch, gaining volume and speed into a hypnotic dance. The rhythm was soothing and Ellie let her eyelids droop like unfurling curtains.

But instead of closing a window, they opened her mind…

Instantly, Ellie was transported from her body. Into the night sky. She looked down on herself lying by the fire. So peaceful. Beyond the river weaving through this part of the jungle, a sparkle of light caught her eye.

Soon it was a storm of glittering crystals of all shapes and sizes, dropping from the heavens to surround her rising consciousness. Ellie could see thousands of them all at once in stunning high-def. She'd never observed anything with such clarity, every piece in perfect focus no matter how near or far it was. And in this instant she realized her mind was infinitely more powerful than she'd ever thought possible. Than she'd ever let herself believe.

The crystals glided around Ellie like a collection of Christmas ornaments, spinning and reflecting each other's light. Beams of gold bounced between them as if she were in the middle of a connect-the-dots game. Then she understood what was happening—they were all connected. Not just the shards in her field of vision, but *everything in the world.*

With a flick of her mind, the crystals melted away and Ellie soared high above the Amazon. She watched as thousands, then millions, then billions of gold threads of connection ran through the rainforest, from the tallest trees to the sloths sleeping in them to the snakes slithering around them to the ants marching along their mossy beds.

How could I not have realized this before? It's so obvious. It's connected.

It's all connected.

We're all connected.

Sweeping across the tree-tops, Ellie noticed a condor flying beside her, the sound of its feathers the same as the shaman's shaking branch. She marveled at the beast's magnificent ten-foot wingspan. It's noble black face. Ellie felt utterly protected for the first time since her parents had died.

It is always there.
It has always been there.
Looking after me.
I am not alone.

Ellie sailed up and beyond. The black of the rainforest gave way to the yellow lights of cities. Hovering in space, she looked down on earth spinning silently in nothingness. Behind our home, the blazing sun gave life to everything on it.

Ellie turned and raced away from the pale blue dot, gaining speed as she zoomed past the moon and Mars and Jupiter and Pluto—then it was all gone.

She'd left our solar system. Entered deep space. Spiral galaxies of the most brilliant colors spun past her like carnival rides. Stars going supernova exploded as if she was attending the greatest fireworks show ever staged. Frozen comets rocketed by with ice trails like a bride's wedding gown. Black holes sucked light down the curve of their rims with immeasurable force. Two planets collided in the distance, creating a vast asteroid field rushing through space.

It took a while to figure out she wasn't just traveling through space, but through time as well. The farther Ellie traveled away from earth, the further back in time she went.

Planets became less frequent, stars less bright. She passed the last galaxy in view and there was only darkness now. Nothing but black all around. Ellie slowed, floating like a jellyfish.

Is this the center of the universe?
Is this when the universe began?

She felt a gentle breeze caress her skin and tickle her hair. It was so tender, like her mother's breath.

Ellie followed its source and spotted a figure ahead. She approached cautiously, appreciating its jaw-dropping size. The figure was the shape of a woman, with a white robe and blue hood, but instead of a face there was a pool of radiant light. Her arms and legs were also rays of light so intense they blurred Ellie's vision. She was the most beautiful thing Ellie had ever seen.

Are you…Pachamama?

The figure slowly pulled back her robe to reveal a glowing stomach. From her womb a ball of dazzling white energy burst forth, born into space.

It fell away into the darkness and Ellie watched it tumble… and tumble…then explode in a stunning flash of light. Now Ellie understood what she was witnessing.

The birth of the universe.

Energy shot out in all directions, creating stars and planets and galaxies at a rate so fast it defied human comprehension. The cosmos populated through time, evolving and reproducing as life spread with it.

Ellie turned to the figure as it watched its own creation blossom around her like a field of sunflowers. Ellie could almost detect a smile and, for the first time in a long time—she felt love.

Pure, untainted, absolute *love.*

A love so strong it couldn't be denied by anyone or anything. This being, this mother, loved her, little her, despite her flaws. It loved her just as much as it loved everything else it'd created in the entire universe.

And Ellie loved it back.

She felt a touch on her forehead. Opening her eyes, Ellie returned to earth and the present, just in time to see dawn spread through the Amazon. Saywa knelt next to her and smiled. Now they both shared a knowledge most people would never experience. Through tears of joy, Ellie smiled too.

CHAPTER 69

San Francisco, USA

The tantalizing sound of a beer cracking open. Jerry took a sip, dropped onto the couch, and flicked through TV channels. But between screaming cable news hosts and reality shows about cake decorating, nothing held his interest. It'd been a long day. Make that a long week.

He'd mostly worked from home to look after Mia until her arm was strong enough to return to school. His youngest daughter put on an Oscar-worthy performance, wrapping him so tightly around her pinky that he estimated they went through a gallon of ice-cream and Jell-O.

But Jerry's time away from the office had done wonders for his stress levels and gave him much-needed perspective on what was important. Kyra was right, he had to find a better balance or there would be nothing left to balance. So when he returned to work, Jerry coordinated with her to delegate more tasks and apologized to Kevin for his outburst. His employees surprised him by restoring the broken model of the museum to its original state. It almost gave him hope.

Jerry's phone rang and his mood leaped. "Hi, Ellie!"

"Hey, Jerry. How are you?"

"Not bad." He scratched his two-day beard and gave thanks they weren't on a video call. "I assume this means you're back in civilization?"

"Yep, I'm in La Paz. Calling from the balcony of my hostel. It's above a night market and there's lots of families out eating street food."

"I remember it well. Our kids stuffed themselves on *picarones*," Jerry said, referring to the moreish deep-fried donut balls smothered in sticky sweet syrup.

"Oh God, they're to die for. I need some now."

"Can you let me know how your Amazon adventure was before running off and making yourself sick?"

"Sure," Ellie laughed. "It was amazing. Incredible. I'm still buzzing." She described her time in the rainforest, eagerly recalling all the animals, fishing for piranhas, and escaping from an anaconda. "I also asked Saywa to add something to my trip. An *ayahuasca* ceremony."

Jerry sat forward. "Geez, Ellie. That's brave. But aren't you too old to be taking drugs?"

"Very funny."

"Did you enter the fourth dimension?"

"Maybe."

"Are you still there?"

"I'm not going to tell you about it if you keep this up."

"OK, OK. I'm actually very interested. Did you see…or feel anything?"

"It was out of this world. I mean, I was out of this world. I saw things I never thought possible, that I never believed before. I'm still processing it all."

"How did it change what you believe?"

"I've told you before that I consider myself non-religious. I've got a pretty logical mind and spiritual ideas never appealed to me. But *ayahuasca* helped me understand there's something bigger at work than just ourselves. Not in a traditional God-like sense, but in a connected energy-like sense. Maybe it sounds crazy, but I truly feel I have a capacity for love I didn't think possible before. That I've never explored."

"That sounds like an important revelation."

"It is. All of it. Let's just say that I'm having trouble reconciling what I experienced with what I thought was true. So…I've got a lot to think about."

"Well, it's good to have our ideas challenged. At the very least it makes you think about whether you want to hold onto them, or replace them with something more useful for a new stage of your life." Jerry took a sip of beer, happy the conversation was going well.

"Can you stop making so much sense, please? Anyway, I want to know what you've been doing while I've been off chasing comets and all that."

"Unfortunately, I've been firmly entrenched in the real world. Mia broke her arm—"

"Oh gosh. Is she OK?"

"She's fine now. Just a playground accident, and after the pain passed she couldn't wait to return to school and be the center of attention with her cast. Within a day it was completely colored in so she started calling it her 'tattoo.'"

"Did you say, 'and that's the only tattoo you're ever gonna get.'"

"Something like that. Though Bella had a tattoo so they're used to seeing them."

"What did she have?"

"The Tree of Life, on her shoulder blade. I think shoulders are sexy regardless, but add a tattoo to them and…wow!" He laughed and Ellie joined in.

"I think I've found out more about you than I need to know, Jerry."

"Likewise, Ellie." There was a pause, but it felt comfortable, like old friends chatting.

"You know, I want to apologize," she said.

"Why's that?"

"You've always been there for me on my travels, but when you have an emergency I'm in the middle of the jungle on a wild trip."

"There's no need to apologize, Ellie. You needed to go. And you sound much better for it."

"I am, thank you. But I want you to know…I'm here for you too if you need it."

"That's very kind. Just talking with you again has lifted my spirits."

"Mine too. Can you tell me what's going on with the museum?"

"It's fine. Bubbling along."

"Hmmm… From the tone of your voice it's clearly not 'fine.'"

Jerry grinned. She knew him too well. "I was skipping over the gory details."

"You listen to me vent a lot, so let me hear you out this time."

He drew breath and updated Ellie on the progress of the build, including the email from the lawyers dictating revisions he hated. "I'm sick about it. My vision for the museum—Bella's too—is being ruined by a bunch of paper-pushing bean-counters, and there's nothing I can do."

"I don't mean to be too forward, Jerry—"

"But you will." He knew her well too.

"Yes, I will. From everything you've told me about Bella, there's no way she would've accepted what the lawyers are saying. She would've fought tooth and nail to realize her vision, and never taken 'no' for an answer."

"She did have a way of getting people to do what she wanted. They usually came away wanting the same thing too."

"Then I'm sure you can find a way. Hey, ages ago you told

me that the museum was being financed by the Flores family."

"Yes, Nancy Flores. Widow of Juan Carlos Flores, the Peruvian mining tycoon."

"So why not talk to her directly? Bypass the lawyers."

Jerry paced into the kitchen and opened another beer. "I don't think that's possible. We met during the design phase, but once she signed off on the plans everything has been handled at arm's length. I haven't spoken with her in almost a year."

"But she loved the design or else she wouldn't have signed off on it, right?"

"Correct."

"So if the lawyers are trying to replace it with something second-rate just to make a spreadsheet add up, wouldn't she want to know about it?"

"That follows."

"So there is something more you can do."

"You are a very persuasive woman."

Ellie laughed. "I just think life is too short not to go out and get what you want. And a few nights ago I was flying through space on my way to watch the birth of the universe, so that'll give you some perspective."

"I imagine it would."

Perhaps there was reason for hope after all.

CHAPTER 70

San Francisco, USA

Jerry lengthened his stride as he approached the 1880s Victorian mansion in the upmarket Pacific Heights neighborhood. He'd been here once before and appreciated the architecture of the restored four-story home with its bay windows and round towers. Tapered gables formed a crown suitable for the most expensive street in the city.

He'd decided to wear a tie, which he straightened while climbing steps to the ornate iron door. It served its purpose, which was to awe visitors before they'd even entered. Jerry knocked the heavy handle.

There was enough of a wait to think about all the ways this unannounced visit could go wrong. He might get the door slammed in his face. At the very worst, he might get kicked off the museum. But Ellie was right—it was time for a Hail Mary pass.

The door unlocked and slowly swung open. Inside stood a pocket-sized woman in her seventies, white hair in a bun and wearing a necklace of giant pearls. A frown spread across her forehead. "Mr. Townsend? This is a surprise."

"Good morning, Mrs. Flores."

She spoke deliberately. "It's unusual for me to have a guest who isn't coordinated through one of my assistants."

"Yes...and I apologize for that," Jerry said. "I did try to make an appointment but was told I should speak with your lawyers instead."

"That would be best." She began to close the door.

"Wait, please, Mrs. Flores. I understand the process but, to be honest, I've had more than enough of your lawyers over the past couple of months."

She looked at him before surrendering a half-smile and waving him inside. "Me too."

"Thank you," Jerry exhaled.

Nancy Flores glided with a ballet dancer's posture toward the rear of the mansion. Jerry followed along the high-ceiling hallway, peering at rooms filled with rare Latin American artefacts and paintings. They entered a sunroom with sweeping views over the Presidio National Park.

"Please, have a seat." She motioned for him to sit in one of two antique velvet chairs on either side of a teak coffee table. Looming large on the wall was an oversized painting of her late husband, Juan Carlos. "I was just about to have some tea. Would you like some?"

"Thank you."

Mrs. Flores poured Jerry and herself a cup from a silver pot. "Milk?"

"Yes."

She added a healthy dash to both. "Sugar?"

"Just one." The clipped conversation felt awkward, but Jerry didn't want to play his hand just yet.

"My doctor tells me not to, but today I'm going to have two," she declared with a hint of mischief. "Now tell me, how are your children?"

"They're good. Well, Mia fractured her arm but she's on the mend. Kids bounce back quickly."

"They do. How are they coping without their mother?"

"As good as could be expected. I received your card when Bella passed away. It was very kind."

"Your wife designed a wonderful museum for me. She was a very talented woman." Mrs. Flores took a sip of tea and focused her piercing eyes on him. "Now, what can I do for you on this Sunday morning, Mr. Townsend? I presume this isn't a social visit."

"No, it isn't." Jerry placed his cup and saucer on the table. "As you know, your lawyers are concerned—as am I—about the delays we've had due to bad weather and some of the more difficult aspects of the build."

"Those delays have led to increased costs."

"Yes. Some of which rest squarely on my shoulders." Jerry met her eyes.

"Go on."

"Well, they responded with a list of items to be amended or cut entirely from the museum, including the stonework for the terraces."

"You're not comfortable with that."

Jerry shifted forward. "Not at all. And I don't think you should be either, with all due respect. I believe in my heart, and I know Bella believed it too, that we're creating something special here. The Pata Museum was never meant to be another prefabbed concrete block. The design has to reflect the Latin art and culture inside, in particular the collection you're contributing, or else it'll just be another building indistinct from all the others we pass by every day without giving a second thought. It has to be a monument."

Jerry took a breath. Mrs. Flores remained silent so he continued. "Something that adds to the skyline of San Francisco, draws people in to experience it, and also leaves a legacy. Or else I wonder what the hell we're doing, if you'll excuse my language. So I've come here today, not to beg for more money, but to offer a solution." Here we go. "I would like you to consider my company forfeiting its fee for work on the museum, in return for reinstating the cuts your lawyers have imposed."

Mrs. Flores studied Jerry for a long moment before putting down her tea.

He felt sweat soak his shirt while trying to guess what she was thinking, and if he still had a job.

"I know your standards are exacting, Mr. Townsend."

"They are."

"It's one of the reasons I hired you. And I know you are a passionate person."

"I am."

"It's important to have passion. My husband was passionate about just three things in his life." She glanced at his portrait, where he'd been immortalized in front of the red and white Peruvian flag. "His business, which afforded us all this preposterous extravagance, his love for me—and to be frank, I was never sure which came first—and his heritage. He wanted to ensure that Latin culture was preserved not only in private collections like our own, but through public galleries and museums. He wanted his culture to be understood, respected, and not considered any less worthy than the so-called 'high cultures' of Europe. The museum is a tribute to this idea. So there is nothing I consider more important at this late stage of my life than fulfilling his vision. You feel the same way about fulfilling Bella's."

"I do."

"Mr. Townsend, I appreciate the offer to forfeit your fee. In fact, I appreciate the gesture more than the offer because although I'm paying your firm a significant amount of money, it is ultimately less than the cost of what you are asking to accomplish."

"We can meet the deficit half-way at least," Jerry suggested, trying not to sound too desperate.

Mrs. Flores raised her hand. "If you would let me finish. I respect that you came here today, bypassing my wall of assistants and, to be candid, my family. It has reminded me that the museum means as much to you as it does to me. And all this lawyer talk has just been muddying my husband's—and your wife's—vision. But as long as I am walking on God's green earth, I will not allow that to happen." She struggled to contain the emotion in her voice and cleared her throat. "So let me ask you a question, Mr. Townsend. Do you remember the significance of our scheduled opening on February 8th?"

"It's the anniversary of your husband's passing," Jerry replied.

"And are you confident that if you have the extra funds to complete the museum to its original specifications, we can still open on time?"

Ellie, I'm walking to my car but couldn't wait to tell you the news. Your idea worked! Mrs. Flores is going to give us the money to finish the museum as intended. I'm so happy I could cry. Thank you for helping me see this was the best way forward ☺ And now that you've had a hand in it, you really must come visit when it's done! I hope your bus ride goes smoothly, Jerry.

CHAPTER 71

La Paz, Bolivia

Ellie squirmed on the row of plastic chairs, trying not to think about the stabbing pains in her stomach or how much this grubby place made her skin crawl. She cast her eyes around. All the shops had shut, the yells of ticket touts had faded, and it was eerily quiet after midnight in the long-distance bus terminal. Lurking in pockets of darkness where fluorescent globes had blown were pimps, prostitutes, hustlers, drug dealers and addicts. Outside of prison, you couldn't have found a more suspect collection of characters.

Ellie winced as her stomach cramped again. Almost certainly toxic bacteria from the *sandwich de chola* (roasted pork and pickled vegetables sandwich) she'd eaten for dinner, and it didn't seem like it was going to end well.

She went back to reading her *Unique Planet*. Bella had convinced her to visit a legendary train graveyard on the edge of the world's biggest salt flat, Salar de Uyuni, by sketching an old locomotive and series of footsteps leading away to the horizon. Next to the drawing she'd written: 'We travel to find ourselves, only to learn we are creating ourselves with each step.' Bella wasn't wrong, but at the moment all Ellie could create were gurgling sounds in her belly.

A bus eventually rolled into the terminal at 2 a.m. Its banged-up chassis wasn't the hotel-on-wheels Ellie had fantasized about. If Peruvian buses were the equivalent of Business Class on Emirates Airlines, Bolivian buses were an animal cage on a cargo plane out of the Congo.

Another downside of being back on the road was the road. Bouncing, bumping and twisting, the rolling death machine took a perilous route through the mountains. Ellie's insides churned like a butter machine. The foul smell wafting from the rear toilet didn't help.

She fought an unspoken battle over the armrest with a space invader, but gave up to focus on not letting her butt explode. To make matters worse, the driver had switched the air-con to Arctic Blast and the cold made Ellie need to use the toilet even more. She shuffled down the aisle, only to find the lock on the door was broken.

How the hell is this going to work?

Using the light from her phone, she peered inside and saw a seat spattered with pee.

Oh God. Deep breath.

Ellie clambered into the small space. She pulled down her pants and attempted to balance above the filthy seat—daypack in her lap, one hand against the wall, and the other holding the door shut. The challenge of being a woman in a world designed by males. There really should be a law that men had to sit down too.

The bus lurched back-and-forth across the road, and Ellie's hips swung like a pendulum. Unfortunately, not everything made it into the bowl.

Uyuni, Bolivia

Ellie limped off the bus after eighteen hours of torture. Arriving in one of the highest towns in the world, she needed to grab hold of a pole and catch her breath after only a few steps. The altitude had also taken an axe to her skull.

After migraine pills and a hot shower at her hostel, Ellie was desperate for sleep. But her dreams of a restful night were rudely interrupted by other travelers in her dorm. Along with the usual combination of farting, burping, snoring, masturbating and rustling of plastic bags, added into the soundtrack tonight was a woman sleeptalking gibberish and a group of drunk Irishmen banging into everything on their way to bed at 4 a.m.

Ellie lay on her back, staring at the stained mattress above, and contemplated the glamorous life of a backpacker. Something bit her foot.

I could really use my hand sanitizer right now.

CHAPTER 72

Uyuni, Bolivia

Hey Jerry,
I'm so happy to hear the news about your museum. It's
wonderful you'll get to finish it as Bella planned. See,
I'm very helpful and you should listen to me more often
☺ And I will definitely come visit. Just not right now
because my belly is running circles around itself. I'm
stuck in an endless loop between bed and bathroom.
It's like Groundhog Day without the groundhog. I don't
even know if that makes sense. Where's Bill Murray
when you need him? Anyway, I'm going to spend a few
days letting nature run its course. I'm sure you wanted
that update on my bodily functions… How's things
with the girls? Mia's birthday is coming up?
Sick Ellie.

She pressed send and wiped sleep from her eyes. It was
morning in the dorm, it stunk of drunk people, and she was
grumpy as hell.

"Mornin', mate." A bearded face appeared, hanging upside-
down from the bunk above.

"Hi," she replied reluctantly.

"I'm Shane," he said in a thick Australian accent.

"Ellie."

"Righto. Where you from?"

"New York." She faked a smile to be nice, but instantly regretted it.

"The Big Apple! Fuck me, I heard shit's fair dinkum there."

Ellie didn't understand the comment so couldn't respond.

"I'm from 'Straya."

It took her a moment to realize he meant 'Australia.'

"Perth, out west. You can pro'ly tell from me accent. You been?"

"Not yet." And getting less likely by the second.

"You gotta come," Shane insisted. "No apeshit stuff like 'ere but a whole lotta drinkin', if you know what I mean."

Ellie didn't, so closed her eyes. This guy was far too cheery for her current state of mind.

"Watcha doin' today?"

"Resting." Ellie turned away, hoping Shane would shut up so she could concentrate on not letting her bowels detonate again.

His head dropped down on the other side of the bunk. "I've just come from La Paz," he said, oblivious to Ellie's disinterest. "Ripper bars there, I tell ya. I was with these fellas from…ah fuck I forgot where, somewhere in Europe like Japan or some shit, and we were partyin' like nobody's business. Lines of coke from here to Woop Woop. Anyway, I 'erd about this place called Sa-lar d-e U-yu-ni." He pronounced every syllable, but got all the inflections wrong. "You know it?"

"No," Ellie lied.

"It's meant to be real flat. So much salt and…shit. I'm roundin' up some guys to share a 4WD. You wanna come?"

"I'm headed in the other direction," Ellie lied again. No way she was gonna get stuck in a car for four days with this backpacking man-child. It would end in murder.

"How about a ciggie?" Shane lit up a cigarette and offered it to her.

"Can you not smoke inside," she growled. Murder might happen sooner than expected.

"Oh, yeah. Sometimes I forget, y'know. Gotta have me mornin' hit or things don't feel right up 'ere." He tapped his head before taking a final drag and exhaling smoke all around her bed.

For crying out loud!

Ellie coughed and gagged, the stale smell bringing back memories of her assault. She pushed out of bed and made a hasty getaway from the dorm.

On the outskirts of town, the train graveyard Bella had suggested visiting was filled with rusted engines and derelict carriages abandoned from old mines in the region. The post-apocalyptic scene was a photographer's delight, but all Ellie could manage to do was buy a plain bread roll to soothe her gut and find a bench to people watch.

Nearby was a bronze statue of her unconsummated love, Simon Bolivar. His arms were outstretched to represent the unity of the country bearing his name, but he once again refused to meet Ellie's eyes. She realized this was probably the last time they would see each other. Next week she would be in Chile, which had been liberated by another South American hero, José de San Martín.

"Oh Mr. Bolivar, it's been fine and dandy, us dating and all, but it's time for me to leave. For us to go our separate ways. We've tried this relationship thing for four months, but you won't commit. Isn't that always the way? I will remember you as a classy guy, Mr. Bolivar. In the league of Mr. Darcy, for sure. You even have the whole 'cat got your tongue' thing he suffered from when talking to an adorable girl like me. It's OK though,

I've got someone who talks to me all the time…"

Ellie stopped her train of talk in its tracks. How strange that thinking of Bolivar led to thinking of Darcy led to thinking of Jerry.

"I've been calling for three days," Donna said.

"I'm sorry. I got side-tracked." Ellie sat on the toilet in her hostel.

"Too side-tracked to let your sister know you're not dead? Benji, come here!" Donna yelled across the clothing racks in a department store.

"What are you doing?"

"I need a new dress for Roger's Christmas party. It's at the Four Seasons this year."

"Need or want?"

"Same thing. Boys, say hi to Aunty Ellie."

Benji and Alex filled her screen with crazy faces and growled at the camera. "How are my favorite nephews?"

"I got a gold star for my writing," Alex said.

"Oh that's excellent, sweetheart. Are you keeping up with your reading too?"

Alex nodded. "Mommy said I can get a toy because I was so good."

"Hey, me too!" Benji turned the phone upside-down.

Donna grabbed it back off him. "OK, you two go over to the toy section. But don't leave my sight. Jesus, sometimes I wish they would leave my sight. Where are you?"

"In the restroom. But I'm feeling better now."

"Better from what?"

"Food poisoning."

"Shit, Ellie. I keep telling you to be careful but you don't listen. Did you eat street food again?"

"Calm down, Donna. You ended up in hospital after eating a hot dog from Times Square, remember?"

"That could've been anything."

"In fact, didn't the doctor order a colonoscopy but you refused?"

"Well, he was a sleazy prick and I wasn't going to let him look up my ass. Stop changing the subject. How are you going to stay out of trouble?"

"I thought I might go see a soccer game tonight."

"Perfect." Donna rolled her eyes. "They're not crazy about soccer down there, are they?"

"Should be a riot."

CHAPTER 73

San Francisco, USA

"Sorry I'm late." Jerry set his hardhat on the table in the portable office. "I had to help Andrea carry her science project into class, and naturally my child decides to build the most elaborate one."

Harry, Brandon, Kevin and Kyra, whose outfits never failed to look out of place on a construction site, were already present for the meeting. Through the window behind them, workers and heavy machinery moved busily around the museum.

"What did she make?" Kevin asked.

"A magnetic levitation train."

"You may have yourself a future engineer there."

"It moved along the track and stopped at a station. Kids these days."

"My son built his own rocket once," Harry said. "Set off a grass fire, but still one of the proudest days of my life."

"If you've all finished bragging about your snotty-nosed offspring," Kyra interrupted. "We have work to do."

"Yes, we do." Jerry took a seat. "Let's get to it."

Kyra passed everyone a copy of a bound document. "This

is the schedule for the next twelve weeks until Opening Day. Final revision. Right, Jerry?"

"Right."

"*Right,* Jerry?" she pressed.

"If it isn't, I won't be the person you're asking."

Kyra addressed the rest of the team. "I need you all to check it over, line-by-line, and let me know if you anticipate any issues."

Brandon, Harry and Kevin reviewed the pages. It didn't take long for the sighs and exclamations to begin.

"Jesus, guys. I know you're my Triad of Doom, but can't you be happy for once? Mrs. Flores gave us what we need."

"More money, yes, but not more time." Harry shook his head. "There's a lot of things that have to go right for this to work."

"And it will," Jerry said, attempting to pass his renewed optimism onto his colleagues.

"You've scheduled a six-day work week." Brandon pursed his lips.

"That's what it's going to take to get this thing finished, considering the Christmas and New Year's shutdown. We're close, gentlemen."

"If just one thing goes wrong. One delay—"

"We can't afford for anything else to go wrong. Not for a single day. Not for a single hour." Jerry looked each of them in the eyes. "So, are you in or out?"

Hi Ellie,

You poor thing! Food poisoning is horrible. I hope you're feeling better, and don't forget to stay hydrated 😊
Next weekend is Mia's birthday and I've bought her some adventure books, a Lego set, and Beanie Boo doll. At least I think it's called Beanie Boo. It's hard to keep up with what's popular these days. Is Tickle

Me Elmo still a thing?
As for the museum, I'm feeling really positive about it
again. I can finally see the finish line so it's full steam
ahead until we make it—or drag ourselves across.
Take care and please call when you're feeling up to it,
Jerry.
PS Groundhog Day is one of my favorite movies too 😊

Salar de Uyuni, Bolivia

Loaded with backpacks and supplies, the 4WD blasted across the salt flat. Ellie sat up front next to a stout Bolivian named Fredo, doubling as driver and guide. From behind sunglasses to protect her eyes from the blinding glare, she marveled at the otherworldly landscape. Everything was as white and smooth as a bleached tablecloth, with no end in sight. Her gut felt healthy again and Operation Escape Annoying Backpackers had been successful.

You gotta love the smell of freedom in the morning!

Fredo explained that the flat was the remnant of a prehistoric lake. Long evaporated, the salt that remained was perfectly level, and often used by daredevils to break land-speed records in jet-powered cars. It was also the ideal spot to stage perspective photos. He swerved the 4WD to a stop.

Ellie jumped out and onto the sparkling ground, each step crunching like cereal. Though the sun shone bright and there wasn't a cloud to be found, it was freezing at 12,000 feet above sea-level. She scooped a handful of salt into her glove and licked it.

Yep, definitely salty.

Fredo lay on the ground with Ellie's phone and directed her into different poses to create perspective tricks. Placing a Coca-Cola in front of the lens and positioning Ellie a few yards behind

gave the illusion she was a tiny figurine standing on a gigantic can. Her favorite photo was a kung-fu jump that looked like she'd soared clear over the 4WD as if it were a Matchbox toy.
Jackie Chan, eat your heart out.

Ellie got woken by Fredo at 5 a.m. They'd slept in Hotel del Sal, constructed entirely from blocks of salt—walls, roof, bed. No exactly comfortable, but the novelty was fun. She pulled on her coat and beanie, and followed Fredo outside.

More bitter than a Pennsylvanian winter, the cold felt like breathing daggers of ice. Ellie climbed onto the hood of the 4WD with Fredo. He poured them both a steaming tea, which they drank while watching the flaming ball of the sun peek over the horizon in a glorious salutation. The black sky caught fire and melted into shades of plum, strawberry, and lemon, like an animated Monet painting. There'd been rain overnight that pooled on the flat, creating a perfect symmetrical reflection of it all. Ellie was again awed by nature. How could you not be?

She'd never prayed before, but this feeling of wonder led her to say the only thing you should probably ever say to a god. "Thank you, *Pachamama.* Thank you for life. Thank you for everything."

The most spectacular sunrise of her life allowed Ellie to take the most beautiful photo of her trip. She just wished she had someone special to share it with. Because the loneliness ached more than the cold.

The next three days were a rip-roaring off-road adventure. Ellie and Fredo headed south through an active volcano zone, where the rugged earth had been carved from eons of lava, water and wind.
Thank you.

At a geyser field, steam and boiling mud vented from holes in the ground like primordial fountains.

Thank you.

Colorful lagoons framed their path. Laguna Blanca turned white from borax, Laguna Verde tinted green from copper, and Laguna Colorada stained red from algae. It'd stained the flamingos too.

Thank you.

They descended onto plains populated by grazing llamas. Ellie loved how they looked as if Mother Nature had blended a goat, sheep, and horse. She loved how they chewed grass with a bottom jaw that sprung out so far it could've been broken. And she loved how they strutted around like models on a catwalk.

Thank you. Thank you. Thank you.

CHAPTER 74

San Francisco, USA

The squeals of a dozen children splashing in the pool rang into the hot afternoon. Carol and Don's backyard had been decorated in a pirate theme in honor of the birthday girl turning eight today. Andrea served snacks to parents chatting in the shade, while Yasmina made sure Mia and her friends went down the slide safely. Mia's cast, protected by plastic wrap, didn't slow her down at all.

Meanwhile, Jerry kept watch over the kids riding inflatable animals. Decked out as a pirate captain, he had to admit he enjoyed playing the role. He'd already supervised buccaneer versions of classic games, such as pin the tail on the Kraken, pass the cannon ball, and musical sinking ships. There'd also been a treasure hunt, of course.

If only you were here to see this, Bella. Our little girl is growing up. Soon there'll be no more children's parties, no more talk of pirates or fairies or magic.

I hope you're happy with how I'm raising our daughters, baby. God knows I don't always get it right, particularly lately, but I'm trying my best. I need you to know that I'm trying my best for our girls.

"Here you go," Carol said, passing him an iced-tea.

"Thanks, Mom. And thanks again for letting Mia have her party here."

She put an arm around him. "We're glad we could help out. Having all the kids around makes your father and I feel young again."

"That's good, because they make me feel old."

"I thought I saw a few gray hairs, but didn't want to say anything."

"Really?" He pulled his hat lower.

"Oh Jerry, relax. Shall I bring the cake out now?"

"Yo-ho me hearties!" he shouted in his best pirate voice. "Avast for cake. Last one out'll be goin' to Davy Jones' Locker. Arrrrrrrrrr!"

Mia and her friends screamed and scrambled out of the pool, assembling around a table on the lawn. Don filmed Carol carrying the homemade cake down the steps while Jerry led a boisterous rendition of 'Happy Birthday.'

Mia's eyes goggled when her grandma placed the cake in front of her. It was a pirate ship decorated with the Jolly Roger 'skull and crossbones' flag. Her grin was as wide as her ears, and it reminded Jerry of Bella's smile. Because it was Bella's smile.

"Make a wish, then blow out the candles," he said.

Mia blew them all out in one go, with a little help from her grandma.

"OK, who wants cake?"

"Me, me, me!" shrieked the kids, hands shooting into the air.

"Your mother put spinach in the hamburgers. Can you believe it? I swear she does it to irritate me." By early evening all the children and parents had gone, leaving Don and Jerry to clean up the backyard.

"I thought the hamburgers were a hit. The kids loved 'em."

"Because they don't know any better. They'll eat anything with ketchup on it."

"So will you, Dad."

"You know, I don't mind the spinach. It's the treachery of it that bothers me."

"Treachery? Are we still playing pirates?" Jerry laughed. "And don't think I didn't see you take the last s'more."

Don shrugged. "It would've been a shame to waste it. Your mother does make the best s'mores west of the Mississippi."

They continued to collect paper cups, plates and streamers, putting them in a recycling bag.

"Dad, do you remember we spoke a couple of months back? In your garage?"

"It's not a garage. It's an automotive workshop."

"For an automobile you don't drive. Anyway, I told you about this woman I was emailing."

"I remember."

"Well, we're still emailing. Actually, we're not just emailing, we're texting, and...y'know, talking."

"How's that going?"

"Good. Really good. We help each other out. Support each other when things get tough."

"Grab that one, would you?" Don pointed to a plate that'd blown into the flowerbed.

"And we've sort of come to lean on each other."

"What's her name?"

"Ellie Bartlett." Jerry had never said her full name out loud before. He liked how it rolled off his tongue, like a ball spinning effortlessly in water.

"What's going to happen?"

"What do you mean?"

"With this Ellie woman. What's going to happen? Will you just talk? Or meet up?"

"Meet up?" Jerry straightened his back. Of course he and Ellie had messaged about her coming to visit the museum one day, but weren't those just polite words? Now that someone else had suggested it out loud, the idea seemed…ridiculous. And frightening.

How could it even happen? She's there and I'm here. She's traveling and I've got a family. It would be like crossing the Rubicon.

"Jerry. Can you get those inflatables out of the pool?"

"Hmm? Oh, yeah."

"Don't worry about the woman. If you're meant to meet, it'll be when the time's right. You can cross that river when you come to it," Don said as if he'd read his son's mind. He walked around the side of the house with the recycling bag, leaving Jerry alone in the twilight to contemplate the ludicrousness of using historical metaphors to make life decisions.

Then again, Julius Caesar did cross the Rubicon.

CHAPTER 75

San Pedro de Atacama, Chile

"Welcome to Tranquility Base, you sexy minx," a lady's voice called out.

Ellie searched the darkness to see where it came from. She'd walked into an airy courtyard, filled with hammocks, crystals and candles. The hostel, built from mud brick like everything else in town, had warped walls and a sticky clay floor. Following her nose, Ellie poked her head around the door to the kitchen.

Inside, a plump lady stirred a huge pot of pasta. Her thin lips spread into a smile and she loped forward, grappling Ellie in an unexpected bear hug. When she finally let go, Ellie got a better view of the lady's blue eyes, piercing out of a tanned face creased with wrinkles. A mane of silver hair cascaded over her shoulders like a waterfall of wisdom, and she clearly wasn't wearing a bra to support those incredible drooping breasts.

"Ah…do you know where I can check in?" Ellie said.

"Gorgeous Robbie with the cute tushy ain't here at the moment. He's prob'ly off shaggin' that pretty Chilean tail with the bee-sting boobs." The lady sported a Yorkshire accent, requiring a lot of concentration to interpret. "Take any bed. We're all family here."

"OK…" Ellie sputtered, unsure about being adopted into a family that could turn out to be a Jonestown cult and end with her drinking cyanide in the Guyanese jungle.

"Relax missy. We're just friendly, is all. It's got somethin' to do with the stars blessin' us with their brilliance ev'ry night. And the E.T.s with their anal probes."

Ellie's eyes widened in horror.

"But don't worry, they only visit on weekends." The lady winked and broke the tension.

"That's good to hear. I'm Ellie, by the way."

"I'm Meredith, but you can call me Merry. It means happy. You'll be happy here too."

"I'll just find a bed then?"

"Okeydokey. Once you're settled, come 'n have tea with us before we go stargazin'. I've cooked up a big pot of veggie pasta for ev'ryone."

"Thanks, but I'm really tired so might just hit the hay."

"Me cutie-pie blondie-baby, you're thinner than a pole on a diet. And it's a free meal! What backpacker in their right mind would pass up a freebie? See you in a jiff." Merry turned back to her cooking.

Ellie smiled at the force of nature she'd just encountered. Sometimes you meet a person you know will be with you forever.

"That's Saturn?" Ellie said.

"*Oui*," Pierre replied in nasally French. "Because of the angle of the earth, we are fortunate to observe its rings tonight."

Ellie pressed her eye to the telescope's ocular lens. The brown rubber ball of Saturn loomed large, with blue and white ice rings circling it like a belt. "Wow. I never thought I'd see another planet so clearly with my own eyes. Can I visit?"

"At this stage of our orbit, Saturn is 0.00015 light years away."

"Y'know, I never really understood the light year thing."

"It's simple, *fille*. Light is the fastest object in the universe, traveling at 300,000 kilometers per second. A light year is therefore the distance light travels in one earth year, which is 9.5 trillion kilometers. That would make Saturn about 1.2 billion kilometers from us."

"A fricking long way then."

"*Oui.*"

If you wanted to observe the heavens, the Atacama Desert was *the best* place on earth to do it. All the major space agencies were here, including a joint facility between the U.S.A. and E.U. operating seventy-three enormous radio telescopes seeking answers about the birth of the universe.

Maybe they'd be interested in my ayahuasca experience?

Out in the middle of the desert, miles from any light pollution, Ellie and a half-dozen travelers had gathered for a smaller scale stargazing session. They were wrapped in jackets and scarves to fend off the freezing night. Pierre, a Professor of Astronomy whose wild hair pointed to the stars he studied, had set up two telescopes in the sand, one the size of a basketball and one long like a baseball bat. Ellie reluctantly pulled herself away to let others look through.

"Take a swig. It'll warm you up," Merry said. She'd appropriated the bottle of rum doing the rounds.

Ellie took a drink and felt the heat spread through her chest. She passed the bottle back to Merry and joined her laying on a blanket. Ellie's field of vision instantly filled with tens-of-thousands of glittering stars. Our Milky Way galaxy stretched above in an elliptical shape, as if an artist had kicked over cans of paint and sent vivid colors gushing across a black canvas. The planet Venus and star Sirius stood out as yellow and blue flares, surrounded by the violets, scarlets and pearls of the Magellanic galaxies and interstellar gas clouds.

Unbelievable.

If you couldn't see it, you wouldn't believe this existed.

But how can we possibly comprehend something so vast? Something with hundreds of billions of stars and planets? Something still expanding?

Ellie's mind drifted back to her bedroom as a kid, the ceiling decorated with glow-in-the-dark space stickers. Now she felt like that girl again, giddy with excitement at seeing the cosmos and all its wonders, breathtakingly laid out before her.

And we can only see a tiny part of it. Imagine how far it goes!

"What I wouldn't give to have the Frenchman's telescope between me legs," Merry dead-panned.

Ellie burst out laughing. "If I didn't know you better already, I'd think you were kidding."

"A regular dose of lovin' is the best reason to be on our planet, young Ellie. If not for a bit of cock-a-doodle-do, how would I keep me-self sane on this crazy ball of rock?" Merry nodded at Pierre, peering into one of his telescopes. "Look at how he bends over with those baguettes for arse cheeks. I'd like to spread some butta' on 'em and give 'em a bite. I'd take him somewhere light years from here."

"Enough with the astronomical metaphors!"

"I'm just gettin' started, baby. I want to lick his shuttle. Nibble on his satellites. Let him give me a meteor shower, then travel all the way to Uranus."

"Please, I'm blushing."

"You're a right prude, aren't you? Odd for someone so young."

"I'm not a prude," Ellie said. "I'm just…cautious. Y'know, slow and steady wins the race and all that."

"Don't be cautious for too long or you'll miss the last seat on the rocket ship."

She's not wrong. And every day there are less and less tickets available.

A blazing yellow line flashed across the sky.

"Shooting star!" Ellie exclaimed. "Did you see it?"

"I saw it, kiddo. Only it's not a shooting star, it's a meteor burning up in earth's atmosphere."

"Did the Professor teach you that?"

Merry chuckled. "This week we've been learnin' the constellations. See those three stars in a row? That's Orion's Belt. And over there, below the hazy patch, that's the Southern Cross. We don't get that in the norf'n hemisphere. And did you know the Milky Way is merging with the Andromeda galaxy?"

"Merging? I'm not sure I like the sound of that."

"Don't worry, it won't happen for another six billion years. Of course our sun is gonna die out in five billion years, so that'll put a damp'ner on things."

"You're filling me with such positive thoughts."

"Us Brits are optimists at heart."

"It does make me think about my place in it all," Ellie said. "I mean, to be blunt—what the fuck are we doing on this planet?"

"Ah, the eternal question. More rum?"

Ellie took a drink before continuing. "I wonder if we're here for any special purpose? Or is it just random? Everyone has been looking up at the heavens for the last 200,000 years humans have been around, but we still don't know *why* we're here. It's almost…beyond not just science to figure it out, but beyond our understanding. It makes my head hurt."

"If you knew why we're here, would it change what you're doing?" Merry asked.

Ellie thought for a moment. It was a good question. "I don't know."

"If you knew what it all meant, would it change how you lived your life?"

"I'm not sure. Maybe not."

"So there's your answer. Knowin' why all this was created doesn't change your situation, any more than knowin' the sun will rise tomorra' and there ain't a damn thing you can do about it. So it doesn't matter that we don't know, and never will know. It means the real reason we're here is entirely up to you. You decide, Ellie. *You make the meaning.*"

Ellie considered Merry's words for a long while. Despite the rum, they made sense. Perfect sense.

"It took me too long to figure that out," Merry eventually went on. "More years than you've been alive. But once I accepted it, I was liberated. Free to do whatever I wanted. No more thinkin' about it, wonderin' what other people thought, havin' them tell me what to believe. The meaning was mine—all mine."

"Are you talking about God?" Ellie felt Merry clasp her hand. It was doughy and warm.

"If that's what you want to believe, go for it. Or gods. Or no God. Whatever makes you happy, whatever gets you through the night. There's no single spiritual truth for everyone, and any charlatan preachin' that is sellin' horseshit. All that matters is what you want to believe at any point in time. Under this sky, right now, whatever you believe is the truth for you. *It's your choice.*"

Ellie's heart surged. Maybe some questions couldn't be answered—and didn't need to be. Maybe she could choose her own meaning in life, free from anyone else's beliefs or expectations or demands. That would be true freedom.

Another meteor streaked across the sky and Ellie made a wish. *After all, if I believe in wishes, then it will come true.*

CHAPTER 76

San Pedro de Atacama, Chile

Ellie had tossed and turned all night. Merry's advice to make her own meaning in life had her brain doing cartwheels. Stretching awake in the courtyard and admiring the tangerine dawn of the desert, she spied a figure leaving the laundry room. Buckling his belt as he slunk to the front door, his wild hair gave him away.

So Merry did put the Frenchman's telescope between her legs after all…

Her new B.F.F. overshared details of the *liaison* when she emerged to cook breakfast for everyone a short while later. But Merry hadn't been too impressed with the Professor's sexual prowess.

"He was more dwarf planet than supernova, if you get me drift, Ellie baby. They talk a big game, our Frenchie cousins, but more oft'n than not don't live up to the puff. He's from the norf', so that prob'ly had somethin' to do with it. I once had an affair with a fisherman from Marseilles. That week was hotter than a Mediterranean summer and it took 'nother week before I could walk proper again without lookin' like I had a stick up me arse."

Ellie choked on her coffee. She watched Merry flit around the kitchen in her kaftan and marveled at her 'anything goes' nature. It was just as appealing as her scrambled eggs, fried sausage and Yorkshire pud. The hot food in her belly and Merry's welcoming spirit felt like being back in her mom's kitchen.

"Hi Jerry, how's things?"

"Great. And great to hear your voice again, Ellie."

She liked how he said her name. There was a melody to it that gave her goosebumps. "Are you busy?"

"I was about to make lunch, so your timing is impeccable."

Ellie sunk into a hammock in a shady corner of the courtyard. "How's the museum coming?"

"Good, thanks. Touch wood."

"Any chance you can send another photo through? I'd love to see its progress."

"Sure, but don't you also owe me a photo from Uyuni?"

Ellie narrated her four-day trip through the salt flats in enthusiastic detail. She also told Jerry about the most spectacular sunrise *ever*, but left out the part about not having anyone special to share it with. That feeling had dissipated for now. "If I never have to go up to that altitude again I'll be happy though. I'm more of a sea-level kind a gal."

"Where are you now? It sounds like you're calling from another planet."

"Believe it or not, I'm on earth. In San Pedro de Atacama, trying to figure out the meaning of life and all that. Got any tips?"

"Well, for me the meaning of life is my family. If you have children they become your reason for existing, so it stops you having to think about it much more after that."

"Are you saying I should have kids?"

"I'd never presume to do that," Jerry said. "If I know anything about you, Ellie, it's that you'll do what *you* want to do. And probably the opposite of what other people tell you to do…"

"Am I that predictable?" she sighed and laughed.

"Not at all. Have you ever considered it, though? Having a kid? Or three?"

"I guess I have, like everyone at some point, but I never really met anyone I wanted to have a baby with. And, y'know, spend the rest of my life with…" Ellie trailed off and there was an awkward silence.

"Are you there?"

"Yeah. Sorry, you got me thinking."

"You think a lot."

"Too much."

"You know, I didn't get a chance to decide whether to have kids, at least not our first one. Bella fell pregnant despite our best precautions so I lucked into being a dad at a young age. If I'd planned it I would have waited another ten years, but then missed out on so much."

"I'm starting to feel I've missed out."

"Oh no, I don't mean to make you feel that way—"

"It's OK. I like it when you tell me about Bella and your family. It gives me…hope."

"I like telling you about them too."

Another silence fell between them. Ellie wanted to say how much she enjoyed talking to Jerry about *everything*, but wasn't sure how it would be received.

"So, where are you off to next?" He rescued the conversation again.

"Probably Argentina."

"Wine country or Patagonia?"

"Do I have to choose?"

"Well, if you're taking a plane over the Andes, be careful.

Remember the one with the rugby team that crashed and they ate each other? You don't want to turn into a cannibal."

"Thanks for the warning, Jerry."

"You know I like to be helpful, Ellie."

Yep, she really did like the way he said her name.

CHAPTER 77

San Pedro de Atacama, Chile

Ellie rode beside Merry as they galloped out of town. Her friend's gray hair billowed like a flag in the wind. They'd rented horses to shake off the million-degree temperatures and catch sunset at the Valley of the Moon. Though it'd been years since Ellie had ridden, Merry's zeal boosted her confidence.

She heard a commotion and looked behind. A group of local men raced past on their horses, hooting, waving cowboy hats and showing off. Ellie ignored them. They wouldn't understand how uncomfortable it was riding while having your period.

Anything you can do, I can do bleeding.

The view made any pain worth it. Crimson and alabaster cliffs rolled into the distance, with freakish rock formations dotting the Martian landscape. The sky had been scorched orange as if alien invaders rained hellfire upon the earth.

Ellie and Merry tied their horses to a lifeless tree and chose a boulder on the edge of the valley. Merry pulled a couple of beers and *empanadas* from her slouch bag.

"Wow, I've never seen them so big," Ellie said.

"That is what all the boys say about me titties. These are Chilean *empanadas*. Not to be confused with lesser versions made by their neighbors."

Ellie had long ago fallen in love with *empanadas*. Juicy beef, onions, olives and spices wrapped in thick golden pastry, they were the original take-out meal before McDonalds 'invented' it. These baked Chilean *empanadas* were the size of a novel and required both hands to hold. Ellie chomped into the crust and moaned. She went in for a second bite before finishing the first. "Merry, do you mind me asking how old you are?"

"Sixty-seven, and damn proud of every year. I bloody survived. From a coal miner's daughter to the first person in me family to graduate university to becomin' a registered nurse to marryin' an abusive twat and raisin' two kids. Now I'm sittin' here at the Valley of the fuckin' Moon. It's been a crackin' ride."

"How long have you been traveling?"

"Dunno. I don't have a house so traveling is not somethin' I do on holidays, it's me life. The whole world is me home."

Interesting... A modern-day nomad, without the digital crap.

"How do you fund it?" Ellie took another orgasm-inducing bite.

"I couchsurf or help out at hostels, so accommodation is free. I hitchhike most places, so don't pay for transport. I eat cheaply, like *empanadas*. Tell me these aren't better than your aver'ge British sarnie or whatever deep-fried shite passes for food in your country." Merry let out an ear-splitting burp, spooking the horses.

Ellie grunted in agreement. "You don't want to return to the U.K. then?"

"I go back every two or three years, or the kids come visit me. But they've got their own lives now. And there's more of the world I want to see before this ol' body gives out."

It was hard to tell if Merry was running away from something or on the road toward something. Or maybe she was in a limbo of her own making that she enjoyed too much to put down roots anywhere.

An attractive proposition.

"How 'bout you? The backpackin' life treatin' you well?"

"Best decision I ever made, without a doubt. I mean, look at this…" Ellie wiped a pastry flake off her cheek and gestured at the valley below. "I just wish I'd done it five, ten, years ago."

"You're doing it now, that's all that matters. Most people never do it. And besides, you weren't ready before."

That's…true.

It was freakish how Merry could read her like a book. And how she trusted the universe, whereas Ellie questioned every part of it. Which was the right way of living? A better question—who was happier?

"How is it you seem to have everything, y'know, together?" Ellie asked.

"Darlin', are you jokin'? I don't have it together. No-one does. You need to stop faffin' about tryin' to have it together and just get on with livin'. Once you accept that life isn't perfect—and *never* will be—you'll be free to enjoy life as it is, with all its fuckin' ridiculous twists and turns. Remember, we don't have nearly as many days as we'd like. And it can all be over in an instant."

"You're starting to sound like my personal guru."

Merry shook her head but smiled tenderly. "I'm not your guru. You're the one takin' risks and teachin' yourself. That's the only way it can be in the end. No, dear Ellie—you are your own guru."

CHAPTER 78

San Francisco, USA

The first Saturday of December was always Christmas Tree Day in the Townsend-Vasquez household. Jerry drove Mia to choose a fir from a farm east of the Bay, leaving Andrea to dig through the garage for decorations and Yasmina to whip up a batch of eggnog to keep them warm. Bella used to handle this part of the family ritual. The secret was what she'd called "the Holy Trinity plus one"—fresh nutmeg, cinnamon, cloves, and seeds from a Guatemalan vanilla pod.

Jerry carried the tree inside and fixed it upright in the living room. Was this one heavier than usual? Or was he getting older?

As a family, they hung tinsel and ornaments on its branches. Some held special meaning, like the ceramic llamas with their names Bella had commissioned for their last Christmas together. After stringing fairy lights around the room, Jerry and the girls collapsed on the couch.

"Ahh…just like your mom used to make it," Jerry said, tasting the eggnog.

Yasmina beamed. "Next time I should put some brandy in it."

"Maybe not."

"Dad, what am I getting for Christmas?" Mia had an eggnog moustache.

"Well, have you been behaving?"

"Yes."

"Are you sure?"

"Dad, I have!"

"OK. Why don't you each tell me one thing you want."

"You mean you haven't started shopping yet?" Yasmina topped up everyone's glass.

"There's plenty of time."

"But we want lots of presents."

"Yeah, like lots," Mia nodded vigorously.

"Let's remember that some children don't get any presents. Right, Andrea?" Jerry thought his sensible middle child would support him.

"You should buy presents for everyone then."

"With what billion dollars? I'm getting ambushed here. One request each, girls. Hit me."

"*Quiero un unicornio*," Mia said.

"A unicorn? I'm not sure that's possible, honey."

"Yasmina said if you really loved me you'd find one."

"Your sister says a lot of things. Andrea?"

"How about a library?"

"I'll never say no to buying books, but perhaps we can build this library one at a time. Yas?"

"Well, I thought you could get me a flight to Europe after I graduate."

"Did you?" Jerry raised an eyebrow.

"But I'll settle for Cabo."

"OK girls, I'll tell you what I'll do. Because you've all been so magnanimous—if you don't know what it means, look it up—I'm going to sing my favorite Christmas song."

"Oh Dad, no!" the girls cried.

Despite their protests, Yasmina, Andrea and Mia joined Jerry for a chorus of the Mariah Carey song, '*All I Want For Christmas Is You!*' As he sang, Jerry wondered how his daughters would cope on their first Christmas without their mom. Would his love be enough for them?

San Pedro de Atacama, Chile

"I haven't smoked since my sophomore year," Ellie said as she clumsily handled the joint.

Merry didn't respond. Like a pro, she'd taken a long drag and closed her eyes to drift away. They sat on crates at a bonfire in the desert. A few locals were nearby, sharing beers and laughs.

Ellie took a quick puff. It was pleasant enough, like freshly-cut hay laced with lemon. She tried again, and the high crept through her brain like the Pink Panther. Her limbs began to float. The fire flamed in slow-motion. Smoke tiptoed up to the starry sky. "Merry?"

"Yes, baby?"

"Holy cow."

"I'll second that."

"Can you see the spaceship?"

"That'd be the dope talkin', Ellie."

"I'm serious. I think it's…yep, it's the International…Space…Station."

Merry let out a whoop. "You spot any U.F.O.s?"

"Not yet. But I'm gonna keep looking."

"If you do, I wouldn't mind being official translator for the great people o' Yorkshire."

Ellie handed the joint back to her friend. "Y'know, I've been thinking about what you said the other night. You never told me what meaning you chose in life."

Merry grinned and took another drag, her eyes lighting up like fireflies. "I did tell you."

Ellie thought hard, unsure whether things were becoming more clear or more hazy. "Is it the same meaning I saw sneaking out of your room the other morning?"

"What other meaning is there? For me, that's why we're on this planet. Love is what it's all about. Makin' love, givin' love, feelin' love, in every way. Right now I'm lovin' cocks."

Ellie laughed so hard she fell off her crate. She lay in the sand, staring up at the heavens. "Oh Merry, how much longer will you stay here?"

"Only a few more days. Any longer and I'll end up a hostel rat like Robbie with the cute tushy."

"Wanna travel together?"

"There's no-one I'd rather travel with, me gorgeous minx."

"I swear I just saw a U.F.O."

"Let's hitch a ride."

CHAPTER 79

San Pedro de Atacama, Chile

"Are we really going to hitchhike?" Ellie needed to verbalize the idea. It didn't help. She stood with Merry on a desolate highway leading out of San Pedro, searching for a ride to Chile's coastal wine-growing region.

"It's only a short trip."

"It's seven-hundred miles!"

"Ellie, when I turned nineteen me boyfriend and me bummed all the way 'cross Europe, from Calais to Istanbul and back again. I did return with a differ'nt boyfriend, but that's another story."

After their pot smoking in the desert, Ellie had told Merry about her assault in Cusco and how getting in a car with a stranger was a scary proposition. But Merry promised to keep her safe, pulling a flick knife from her pocket and popping the blade. "Don't worry, I always carry insurance. I'll cut off every man's fucking balls before I let anyone touch you."

I actually believe she would do that.

The tarmac wobbled with heat and Ellie sucked on her waterbottle. "I'm just wondering about the logic of standing around for much longer in the driest desert in the world."

"This one'll stop. Trust me." Merry stuck her thumb out as

far as it'd go. A pickup slowed and she threw Ellie a playful 'told you so' glance. They tossed their packs in the tray and climbed into the cabin.

The chubby driver introduced himself as Jorge, but something about the way it came out of his crooked mouth didn't ring true. Ellie was also suspicious of his handlebar moustache, cowboy boots and Stetson hat. He wouldn't have looked out of place in a Wild West stagecoach posse.

While Merry dozed on her shoulder, Ellie chatted with 'Jorge' in an effort to humanize herself and make him less likely to chop her body into pieces and dump them in a shallow grave in the desert. She made a point of telling him about her boyfriend, Chad, currently serving in the U.S. Marines. Special Ops, no less.

After an hour on the highway, the pickup approached a checkpoint. Heavily-armed police shepherded passengers off a bus and a sniffer dog searched the luggage compartment.

Ellie nudged Merry awake. "You don't have anything we need to worry about, right?"

"Nope. Just a couple of joints."

"What?!"

"Don't fret," Merry yawned. "I stuffed 'em down me undies and no copper's gonna wanna check me old clacker."

Ellie wasn't sure whether to laugh or cry or kill her friend. Maybe Chad would mount a mission and rescue her from the prison firing squad with seconds to spare.

Merry went back to sleep as Jorge slowed the pickup. A policeman peered through the windscreen. Ellie smiled as genuinely as possible given execution was imminent. He waved them through, and Jorge grinned at Ellie. Not in a good way.

A few miles later, Jorge pulled into a gas station for "*cigarillos*," though more likely was buying rope. Ellie took her chance to inspect the cabin. If she found even a nail file, she'd already decided to stab him in the eye next time he so much as looked in her direction. She tried the latch on the glove compartment. Locked.

Who locks their glove compartment?

She tried again.

This is ridiculous.

Ellie pushed her foot against the dash for leverage—

SNAP!

The cover broke off and her arm recoiled, hitting Merry in the head.

"Ouch!" Her friend woke instantly.

Ellie peered inside the compartment. "Is that a...gun?"

"Go," Merry yelled, pushing Ellie out the door. They tumbled onto the concrete and ducked behind the pickup. "Where is he?"

Ellie peeped over the bonnet. "At the cashier."

"Bugger."

A semi roared to life at the other side of the station. Ellie looked at Merry. They both grabbed their backpacks—and ran.

CHAPTER 80

Somewhere in Chile

Rain pelted the minivan. It was the third, and hopefully last, vehicle change of Hitchhiking Hell. They'd chosen this option more carefully than the first, so Ellie and Merry sat crammed in the back with an extended family dressed to the nines for a *Quinceañera* celebration.

"So what's his name?" Merry asked.

"Who's that?"

"The chap you're thinking about." Her friend had a twinkle in her eye.

Ellie glared back. How could she know that?

"Dear Ellie, your face is more open than a 24-hour coffee shop. I've given you plenty of time to think about tellin' me, but now I'm just too bloody curious. And this driver is a maniac so I'd like to know before we crash."

Ellie chewed her lip and realized, remarkably, that she hadn't spoken to anyone about Jerry except for a few passing comments to traveling companions. She hadn't even told Donna. That'd be a fun conversation.

"There is this guy. But I don't know him very well. Actually, that's not true—I know him very well. It's just that we've never met, so it might all be, like, an obsession in my head."

"Obsession can be fun as long as it's not the bunny-boilin' type."

"I don't think it is…"

"What's his name?"

"Jerry."

"That's unfortunate. What else?"

"He has three kids."

"A D.I.L.F. Sexy."

"It kind of complicates things."

"Ellie, *you* complicate things. What are you lookin' for, a fairy tale? I'll let you in on a secret—they don't exist. *Sleeping Beauty* was a lie!"

Ellie laughed. It was true, she did want a fairy tale. She always had. But she was beginning to understand that love was the fairy tale, and everything else just noise.

If I have love, maybe that's all I need.

"What is it about him?" Merry asked.

"He's really caring. And supportive. He encourages me a lot to, y'know, get outside my comfort zone. He's smart, hardworking, funny. Sensitive too. Loves his kids. His wife died a year ago, so he's been through a lot but come out strong."

"Do you believe he has a good heart?"

"I do," Ellie nodded. "But the whole thing is…stupid. I mean, I'm backpacking through South America but can't stop thinking about a guy who's a million miles away."

"It's called being human, kiddo. To want someone, and to want them to want you in return. That's the core of our D.N.A. Why are you so reluctant to take a chance?"

She traced the rain streaking down the window with her finger. "Why is anyone? Fear, I guess. I don't want to repeat my mistakes. It's amazing how you think you've learned something, but then you go and make exactly the same mistake again. Is that being human too? Or is that just being a dumb human?" The last thing she wanted was another calamity like Eduardo.

"Stop it, Ellie. You're beatin' yourself up like a prize fighter. You can't let the past get in the way of livin' your future. I've made more mistakes than I could possibly fuckin' count, but time really does heal everything. The only things I regret are those chances I didn't take. Those times I stood in the proverbial yellow wood with two roads divergin' and decided not to take the road less traveled."

"It's not easy for me."

"It's not meant to be. But you've come so far already. Tell me—if Jerry lived an hour away would you jump in a car and go visit?"

"Yes." Ellie's answer shot out of her mouth quicker than she could catch it.

"Then eight or twelve or even sixteen hours away is just time, and not much at that."

"Are you saying I should get on a plane and fly to San Francisco?"

"Why not? If that's what you want."

"What if I'm not sure what I want?"

Merry took Ellie's hand. She had a habit of doing that when Ellie needed it most. "If this guy makes you happy, if he makes you laugh, if you like his attention, if he has a generous nature, then what else do you need? Take a chance. Tell him how you feel. If you don't, he'll never know, and you'll never know if it's gonna work out. And you'll regret if for the rest of your life."

"But what if—"

"No buts!" Merry raised a finger. "I understand you don't want any more heartache, Ellie baby. You've closed yourself off for so long because you feel it more than most. But everybody gets hurt. It's the price we pay for love."

Rain thumped against the roof, filling the van with a hypnotic rhythm.

"Why didn't you say something earlier? If you knew I was thinking about it?" Ellie asked.

"I wanted to give you time to open up."

"And I didn't."

"It's not too late," Merry winked.

Ellie managed a faint smile before turning back to the window. Trails of raindrops ran along the glass, shimmering like sequins on a dress. One she'd really like to wear on a date with Jerry.

CHAPTER 81

La Serena, Chile

Ellie and Merry's raspberry-red pushbikes zigzagged like bees down the dirt road. No matter how hard they tried, they couldn't head in a straight line. The problem was that the Bike & Wine tour included, well, wine, and they'd been meandering from vineyard to vineyard 'tasting' (official term, but let's get real) all afternoon.

Did we have nine glasses or ten? I liked the sweet white. Twelve glasses? I liked the dry red. Where are we? It's getting dark. Or is that my sunglasses? Am I wearing sunglasses?

Oh, look, a butterfly. Hey, Merry. Look, mariposa! Did I say that in my head or out loud? Where are we? I really love wine. I think it's my favorite thing. That and sleep. And Jerry. Yikes, that's a big rock—

Ellie listened to the wheels spinning on her bike. It sounded so serene, like birds twittering. They eventually slowed and she opened her eyes. Excellent, not dead. Just lying in the grass on the side of the road. She must've hit that big rock and vaulted over the handlebars in a crowd-pleasing gymnastic dismount. 11/10 from the judges, for sure.

Humans really are at an odd point in our evolutionary journey.
Ellie wasn't badly hurt but Merry insisted on flagging down a
farmer who took pity and drove them and their bikes into town.
Over dinner, they solved the world's problems and ordered more
wine because, what were they going to do, not taste it all? Ellie
gorged on Patagonian toothfish (known by its more attractive
name, Chilean seabass), and a *digestif* or three of pisco. Hey, if
you're gonna go, go big.

Merry held Ellie upright. After a few attempts, she got the
key in the lock of their couchsurfing house.

"Y'know, I can walk myself," Ellie said.

"I have no doubt, kiddo."

"I have a certain talent when it comes to walking."

"And ridin' a bicycle too."

"You're right." It took Ellie a moment to process Merry's
tone. "Are you dissing my riding?"

"Not at all." She lay Ellie on the sofa in the living room. "I'd
never do that."

"Hey, Merry." Ellie grabbed her friend's arm and stared into
her eyes as if it the fate of the free world depended on what she
was going to say next. "Thank you."

"Anytime, baby. Now I have to go piss."

"Yes. That would be good." Ellie's head flopped back and the
room twisted on a mind-bending angle. "What's happening...?
I gotta get outta..." She fumbled her phone out of her pocket
and stubbed her toe on a table before lurching outside into the
garden.

Lit with fairy lights and incense sticks, it seemed like a dream.
Ellie dropped into a hammock. It was a miracle she didn't flip
out. "*Rock-a-bye baby...in the tree-tops...* Hehehe I'm funny."

She struggled to untangle her headphones, freeing just enough cord to fit one in each ear, then tapped her phone—hard. Objects were closer than they appeared, or whatever that line was…

San Francisco, USA

Jerry rolled over in bed. He switched on the lamp and checked his watch—2 a.m. Who the heck would be calling at this hour? He looked at his phone. "Ellie?"

"Jerry!"

He sat up and rubbed his face. "Are you OK?"

"Oh I'm good. So good…"

There was a lag in the connection, but then again it might've been in his head. Jerry looked closely at his screen. "Are you drunk?"

"Not drunk, *per se*. A little tipsy, maybe…" Ellie giggled.

"Well…it's good to finally see you in person. I mean, on video."

"Finally! Crazy, right?"

"You look happy."

"You look tired. You should get some sleep."

Jerry laughed and patted down his hair. "I'll try to. Have you been drinking Chilean wine?"

"I think so. It could've been Italian wine. But I guess I'm in Chile so it makes sense the wine is from…"

"Chile?" Jerry found all this hilarious. "What have you been doing to end up at this point?"

"I've been riding a bike, Jerry. And I was *damn* good at it."

"I'm sure you were. Did you manage to travel in a straight line?"

"Um, the wineries weren't like, in a row, so it was kinda difficult and I had to…" Ellie did a weaving motion with her hands. "…be all James Bond and shit."

"I'm sure you were all James Bond and shit."

Ellie's eyes rolled closed, then snapped open. "Hey Jerry, enough about me. How are *you*?"

"I'm fine. The kids are getting excited about Christmas."

"Christmas…amazing…so much…*feeling*. Oh, thanks for sending the photo of your moo-seum. It's almost done!"

"Almost."

"I liked it, a lot. But you know what I liked even more?"

"Surprise me."

"When you dressed up…as a pirate."

Jerry belly laughed. "Well, I didn't expect anyone to say that, but…thank you. I think."

"Pirates are *hot!* Your costume was very…*sexy*."

"OK Ellie, now I'm worried about you."

"Oh, you're very kind, Jerry. But there's nothing to worry about. With all my mad bi-cyc-ling and drink-ing skills…and the fact that I really, really, like you…"

There was no sound except for Ellie breathing and Jerry holding his breath. Then she shut her eyes…and passed out.

Jerry looked at Ellie's face, the camera pointed up her nose as she snorted into sleep, and he smiled. "I really like you too."

CHAPTER 82

La Serena, Chile

The divine smell of bacon prodded Ellie from sleep. She lifted her eyelids and realized she was cradling her phone like a lover. Snippets of last night flickered back. It took a few before they formed enough of a picture to cause panic.

"Oh God, Ellie." She sat up in the hammock. Scrambled to check her call history. Buried her face in her hands. "When are you going to grow up?"

> *Hi Jerry*
> *So yeah this is humiliating*
> *I'm so sorry about last night*

> *Don't worry about it* 😉

> *I'm an idiot*
> *Did I wake you?*

> *It's no problem*
> *It was very funny*
> *You were having a good time*

Too much of a good time…
What did I say exactly?

Nothing much
Just telling me how you're
a secret agent

I said that?
Total moron!

It was nice to see you
for the first time
Even if it was drunk you

Anything else I should know about?
Something that might cause me to
hide in bed for the next week?

Besides cataloguing all
your sexual experiences?

WHAT???

Names, dates, places

OH SHIT
🧕

Ellie, I'm joking

Not funny!

Hahaha

I'm enjoying this

I bet you are…

We should video chat again 😁

I'll take a breathalyzer first.
Sorry again…
😥

Ellie curled into a ball in the hammock. She couldn't shake the feeling that she'd said more last night than Jerry was letting on.

Would it be so bad if I told him I liked him? Or did I tell him and he rejected me? And now he's just being a gentleman about it but really it's totally awkward?

Arrggghhhh!

San Francisco, USA

"It's weird how you do that," Jerry said.

Kyra had been leaning against the door to his office for five minutes. "Do what?"

"Look at me when I'm working. Invade my privacy. Any activity that involves you staring at me without announcing you're here." He stood and shuffled a stack of papers together.

"You weren't working."

"Are you keeping a minute-by-minute account of my day?"

"You do realize you've been dating this girl for months and don't even know it."

Jerry froze for a second, then went back to organizing his papers. "What do you mean?"

"This girl you keep messaging."

"What girl? There is no girl." He moved to his drafting table to avoid Kyra, but realized it was empty so turned back around.

"Jerry, how long have I worked for you?"

"Too long."

"Long enough to know you. So, what's her name?"

"Her name is…Ellie, not that it's any of your business. And we are *not* dating."

"Really."

"That's right. *Not dating.*"

"Do you message her every day?"

"Sometimes."

"Speak with her a couple of times a week?"

He could see where this was going. "Once or twice."

"Think about her when you're not in contact?"

Jerry hesitated and they both caught it. He slid past Kyra into the open-plan office. "I have a meeting. And why are we even talking about this? I don't want to have this discussion with you."

She trailed on his heels. "You need to talk about it with someone, so I'm doing you a favor as usual."

"I wish you would ask before doing me favors."

"You should tell her how you feel."

"I don't know how I feel."

"You're lying."

"I'm not lying to you, Kyra."

"You're not lying to *me*, Jerry. You're lying to yourself."

"I'm confused."

"Of course you're confused."

"I don't like it when you psychoanalyze me."

"I'm psychoanalyzing your half of the species. Try not to take it personally. Though taking things personally is something your half of the species does particularly well."

"Oh God, Kyra, enough. Please. You're…hurting my brain."

"OK. You're only confused because you won't accept that you're already dating this Ellie girl. As your employee, your friend, your conscience—tell her what you feel."

Jerry put a hand on the door to the meeting room. "So you're saying I should be honest?"

"Well not too honest because that would be stupid." Kyra walked away, leaving Jerry even more perplexed about what to do.

Despite the unusual situation, he felt happier than he had in a long time. Ellie said that she liked him. *Really liked him.* Yes, his emotions were all over the place, and perhaps she was just drunk, but the thought that it might be true filled him with so much…strength. There was nothing he couldn't accomplish.

CHAPTER 83

Valparaíso, Chile

Three days later, Ellie was still thinking about what she might've said to Jerry. Truth be told, she was thinking about Jerry all the time. She'd even added STOP THINKING ABOUT JERRY to her TO DO list, but it had the opposite effect.

Her feelings were only boosted by Merry dragging her empty heart and anguished mind to Isla Negra. Nestled between tall pine trees, the great Chilean poet Pablo Neruda's home had been converted into a museum for his beloved collection of marine paraphernalia.

There were rooms filled with sextants once used for navigating the high seas and mermaid figureheads that'd sailed the world on the bows of brave ships. Visible through every window, the Pacific Ocean raged like the storm of emotions Ellie was experiencing.

On a driftwood desk in Neruda's study lay the original handwritten version of one of his most famous poems, *Here I Love You.*

Here I love you and the horizon hides you in vain.
I love you still among these cold things.

Sometimes my kisses go on those heavy vessels
that cross the sea toward no arrival.
I see myself forgotten like those old anchors.
The piers sadden when the afternoon moors there.
My life grows tired, hungry to no purpose.
I love what I do not have. You are so far.

Ellie could feel the passion in his words, and assumed Neruda was a hopeless romantic like her.

Merry, on the other hand, had no such troubles. After making their way through the colorful murals and bohemian bars of Valpo, Merry had already hooked up with three men. She ultimately decided to stay with a musician-artist-philosopher-stoner forty years her junior who harbored a Mrs. Robinson fantasy. Lucky guy!

⌒⌇

Ellie took off her backpack and rested it against the stone seawall. She sat next to Merry and let her legs dangle over the water. Her friend tore chunks of bread and threw them to pigeons flying past.

"Will I see you again?" Ellie asked.

"I hope so, baby. Somewhere, sometime. I can't wait to see how much you change."

"I'm going to miss you, Merry."

"And me you. But you need to keep goin' on *your* journey. You can't follo' an old bat like me around forever!" She let out one of her crazy cackle laughs, scaring the birds.

Ellie checked the time on her phone. "My bus is leaving soon."

"I have something for you." Merry held out her flick knife. "Be prepared, not afraid. And don't hesitate to castrate any motherfucker who dares hurt you."

"Thank you."

"Promise me you'll take care of yourself, kiddo," Merry said, clutching Ellie in a bear hug.

"I will. Thank you for everything."

"It was all bollocks," Merry laughed. "Just do what makes you happy, Ellie, every single day of your life. Because if you're not happy—"

"Then what the fuck am I doing on the planet?"

"Exactly." They both wiped away tears. "OK, no more life lessons. Go grab it by the balls."

Absolutely.

Ellie slung on her backpack and walked along the seafront, past a bustling fish market where anglers yelled out prices for today's catch. She turned and saw Merry still sitting on the seawall, throwing bread to the pigeons.

San Francisco, USA

A towering Christmas tree lit up Union Square, the star on top shining like a beacon against the wintry night. Jerry pulled up the collar on his coat as he walked past buskers playing carols and families ice-skating in that Bay Area holiday tradition.

Inside Macy's, he stopped to study the department store directory. He had no idea where to start. Bella had always bought the Christmas presents, and she wouldn't even let Jerry wrap them because apparently it wasn't high on his skillset. He couldn't argue with that.

"Can I help you, Sir?" asked a female staff member wearing foam antlers.

Jerry crossed his arms. "I'm not sure."

"Are you buying a gift for someone special?"

"For my daughters, yes."

"Did you ask them what they wanted?"

"I tried, but I don't think you stock mythical creatures or all-expenses paid trips to Paris."

"I'm afraid not. Can I ask what they like to do?"

"Well, Mia's very active, Andrea reads at every opportunity, and Yasmina…she's on her phone a lot."

"Then I'd recommend visiting the book department on level three, children's play section on level four, and electronics on level six."

"Sounds like a plan. Thanks for your help."

"My pleasure, Sir. Can I suggest one more thing?"

"Sure."

"Don't stress too much. Your kids will love you no matter what you get them."

Jerry hoped that was true, but didn't want to risk it. He spent the next three hours wandering through the store, surrounded by shoppers who seemed to have a much better idea what they were doing. Traveling up-and-down so many escalators, he eventually got lost.

With only a handful of gifts under his arm and about to call it a night, Jerry browsed the book department. A cover drew his eye: *Sumptuous Street Foods of South America*. He flicked through the photos, fondly remembering the conversations he and Ellie had shared about all the exotic food on their travels.

This would make a great present. If only Ellie were here for Christmas.

PART IV

CHAPTER 84

7th December – Pucón, Chile

Ellie jolted awake. She'd felt a rumble. Her first thought was it might be her belly about to let loose. Through the darkness of the dorm, she saw someone sit up. More rumbling.

What's going on?

She put a hand on the bed frame. It vibrated. Lockers started banging against the wall. A chunk of plaster fell from the ceiling.

"Earthquake!" one of the backpackers shouted.

Ellie scrambled out of bed and shook the others. "Wake up!"

The owner of the hostel, Diego, threw open the door and waved a torch around the room. "Everybody out. *Ahora!*"

The walls swayed and floor shook. Ellie lost her footing in the hallway. Fell to her knees. Diego grabbed her arm and pulled her up. Together they pushed through the front door as the ceiling collapsed behind them.

That was close…

Ellie had arrived in the pleasant lakeside town yesterday. The object of her visit, Villarrica volcano, hovered over the landscape, smoke billowing out of its perfect cone-shaped crater. She'd planned to climb it because seismologists judged there to be little chance of eruption.

I guess they were wrong.

Ellie and Diego ran into the main street, joining scores of others fleeing their houses. Cries rang out, car alarms repeated out-of-sync, and police sirens shrieked into action.

In the distance, Villarrica had roared to life. A mile-high torrent of gas and ash ejected from its crater and raced into the night. Boiling magma shot over its lip, dissolving its icy slopes.

Another quake rocked the ground. Everyone dropped to their haunches. It was like trying to balance on a trampoline.

"Are you OK?" Diego asked.

"I think so." Ellie looked at the hostel. All the windows had shattered and a fracture ran across the brickwork like a seismogram. "You?"

BOOM!

An ear-shattering crack thundered out of the volcano and echoed over the town.

"*Ella despierta,*" he said. "She woke up."

Over the next few hours, Ellie and other backpackers assisted as best they could, searching the streets and calling out for survivors. Some buildings were crumpled heaps, others engulfed in flames. Diego coordinated a chain of people to remove bricks from a collapsed apartment block where a voice had been heard. Under the rubble, a rescue dog located a boy and firefighters carried him to safety. There were cheers—and tears—of relief.

But then the cries for help stopped.

Ellie sat alone on the sidewalk, trying to comprehend what'd happened. She ran her hands through her hair and realized it was caked in ash. She sniffed her t-shirt. It smelled like a chimney.

Villarrica boomed and shots its guts into the sky again.

Nature can be so beautiful, yet so violent. Us humans are nothing compared to its power.

Diego jogged by and Ellie scrambled to catch up. "What've you heard?"

"It's bad. The whole coast has been hit, from Osorno up to Valparaíso."

Valpo? Oh no. Merry.

"The police said all foreigners must go to the stadium for evacuation. You should take your bag and leave."

"Is there anything else we can do?"

Diego shook his head. "It's up to the rescue teams now."

"What about you?"

"This is my home. I have to stay." An aftershock rolled through the street and they crouched to the ground. "Thank you for your help, Ellie, but you must go. Now."

CHAPTER 85

"Benji, Alex. Get your backsides down here!" Donna poured sugary cereal into two bowls.

The boys sprinted into the kitchen, shoving each other out the way. Benji won and started eating before taking a seat.

"Mom, he pushed me down the stairs again," Alex said.

"I told you not to do that. Do you want to get spanked?"

"He was in my way," Benji spluttered through a mouthful of milk.

"He's four years younger than you. How would you like it if I pushed you down the stairs?"

"That's child abuse."

"Exactly." Donna gave up talking to her children and switched on the TV. It was tuned to CNN but the volume was muted.

"I need some help." Roger came into the kitchen, fighting his tie.

"I can't believe you still don't know how to do this." Donna made a perfect knot and pulled it tight around his neck.

Roger pecked her cheek. "Have to run. Early meeting. Bye kids."

"Bye Dad," Benji and Alex replied with zero enthusiasm.

"Who wants toast?" Donna asked. But she didn't hear their answer. Her focus had been drawn to the TV where images of collapsed buildings, crushed cars and lifeless bodies filled the screen. The chyron announced: *HUNDREDS DEAD IN CHILE EARTHQUAKE.* She felt the blood drain from her face. "Benji, turn it up."

"But you said we can't watch TV in the morn—"

"Do it!"

A journalist reported live from the disaster zone, emergency vehicles rushing past her into a haze of smoke. "*The devastating earthquake that hit central Chile at 1 a.m. this morning measured 8.4 on the Richter scale. That's the strongest on record here for twenty years. So far authorities have confirmed 116 people have lost their lives, but with roads damaged and communications down, the death toll is expected to rise...*"

"Mom," Alex's voice trembled. "Where's Aunty Ellie?"

CHAPTER 86

San Francisco, USA

"Good morning. Have a coffee." Kyra banged a mug on Jerry's desk.

"Thanks. But aren't I paying you too much to make me coffee?"

"I figured you needed a pick-me-up."

"Why's that?"

Kyra threw him a sideways look. "Haven't you seen the news?"

"Not yet. I had to take Mia to get her cast removed. She wants to turn it into a worm farm, of all things." Jerry slurped a taste. "Hmm, not bad. What's the news?"

"Your friend, Ellie… She's in Chile at the moment?"

"Yeah. Why?"

"Have you heard from her?"

"I've been on hold for an hour!" Jerry shouted into the phone while refreshing the news feed on his laptop. "Listen…as I told the person who transferred me, and the person before that, I want to know if my friend has contacted the Embassy. Her name is Ellie Bartlett. I don't know her middle name." He sighed. "No, I'm not a relative. No, I don't know her address. She lived in New York. Of course I tried contacting her. She hasn't been online.

I said I'm not a relative." Jerry gripped the receiver so hard his knuckles turned white. "Well, is there anything you can do for me? No? Then thanks for nothing!" He slammed it down.

Jerry called Ellie for what felt like the hundredth time that morning.

Answer. Answer. Please answer.

The call timed out.

CHAPTER 87

Pucón, Chile

Ellie leaned against her backpack on the pitch of a minor-league soccer stadium, surrounded by other travelers and locals waiting to escape the horror of last night's quake. In the face of repeated tremors, few could muster a smile.

There were glimmers of hope though—a bloody-faced father joyfully reuniting with his wife and newborn brought tears to Ellie's exhausted eyes.

So that's what it's like to have a family and want to protect them. Is that what I want? Am I ready for it? What is life without it?

She urgently wanted to contact Donna and all her friends to let them know she was safe. And Jerry. Especially Jerry.

A convoy of buses pulled up outside the stadium. The mass of evacuees rose slowly to their feet. Too shattered to push or argue, they formed orderly lines with mothers, children and the elderly given priority. Most of the buses were going north to the capital, but Ellie missed out on those so sat squashed in the aisle of a bus headed south. She didn't really care where it went—as long as it was away from this cursed place.

It took ten agonizing hours to travel 200 miles. Broken roads and bridges meant countless detours, and when Ellie finally got off in a town unaffected by the quake, it was twilight. She went in search of a room, but every bed had already been spoken for by others fleeing the chaos.

A hotel receptionist gave Ellie a WiFi password and she sat on the curb outside to connect. It started to rain. Across the road, two men carried a sofa into a house, supervised by an elderly lady who Ellie hoped might give shelter to a distraught *gringa*. Her phone buzzed with dozens of messages. Jerry had sent many of them, warming her insides in spite of the wet.

Not a peep from Merry though. An alarm rang in Ellie's head, but she told herself it was because the internet was still down in Valpo. That must be it.

She sent her friend a quick message, checked in safe on social media, then phoned Donna. They cried together as Ellie told her sister everything she'd witnessed last night. Donna had long given up trying to convince her to come home, but now even Ellie wasn't sure what her next move would be. Where *could* she go?

San Francisco, USA

Jerry took off his V.R. headset. His afternoon had been spent trying to finalize placement of lights inside the museum, but it was a jigsaw without end and he hadn't made much progress. Feeling sick about what might've happened to Ellie didn't help.

What if she's hurt?
Knocked unconscious?
Trapped in a building?
What if she's…?

He couldn't finish the thought.

"You're still here," Kyra said.

"Yes," Jerry exhaled. "What are you wearing?"

She was decked out in a flashy exercise get-up. "I just did Zumba."

"Is that still a thing?"

"It's a great work-out. I met my new boyfriend there."

"You're not dating the insurance salesman anymore?"

"Oh Jerry, that was like five boyfriends ago."

"I can't keep up with your love life."

"That's what he said."

Jerry laughed for the first time today. He could always count on Kyra for that.

"Any word?" she asked.

He shook his head.

"I'm sure she's fine. From what you've told me, she's a tough cookie."

Jerry's phone rang and he snatched it from the table. "Ellie?"

"Hi Jerry, it's me."

"Oh thank God." He gave Kyra a thumbs-up. She smiled and left him alone. "Are you OK?"

"I can't hear you very well."

"I said, *are you OK?*"

"I'm not sure if you can hear me, Jerry, but I'm safe. A bit rattled, but otherwise fine."

"You're not hurt?"

"Not really." Ellie started to sob.

"Are you there?"

"Yeah," her voice cracked. "I...I saw some horrible things last night."

"I'm sorry. I wish I could be there for you."

Ellie snorted away her tears. "But I'm OK, y'know, no broken bones or anything."

"I was worried about you. I called the State Department, the Embassy, all the news outlets."

"Thank you, Jerry. That's very sweet."

"I was going to send up a smoke signal next." This got a laugh out of her. "I'm happy you're safe, Ellie. I'd like to give you a big hug."

"I'd like that too," she said.

Jerry listened to the comforting sound of Ellie breathing, then the line went dead.

CHAPTER 88

Bariloche, Argentina

The chocolate capital of Argentina couldn't have been further removed from the destruction of central Chile. It was as if a small slice of Switzerland had been transplanted from Europe, with rolling green hills and charming chalets. There were even Saint Bernards playing on the slopes.

Ellie had slept on the kind lady's sofa, got fed a hot breakfast which brought some strength back, and caught a ferry across the Andean lakes. Now she set herself up in the TV room of a hostel to access the internet and watch CNN *Español*. The news wasn't good. The toll had risen to over 1,000 dead, with hundreds more missing.

And she still hadn't heard from Merry. The uneasy feeling in her stomach screwed tighter throughout the day. She was about to close her phone when a notification dinged on her Facebook—*Meredith Greenwood, R.I.P.*

Ellie stiffened, then her heart crashed through her chest.

Dear Family and Friends,
It is with great sadness that we tell you our beloved
mother, Meredith Katherine Greenwood, passed away

yesterday in Valparaiso, Chile.
We had been unable to contact her since the earthquake hit, but a representative from the British Embassy has confirmed she was killed in a building collapse. If there is any consolation, it appears she passed away in her sleep.
We will advise of further information as it comes to hand, including funeral arrangements in the U.K. Please keep 'Merry' in your thoughts and prayers.
Much love,
Darren & Elisabeth.

Ellie dropped her phone. Keeled onto her knees. Screamed. Just three days ago they'd hugged and Merry flashed her eye-twinkling grin.
And now she's gone?
NO.
IT'S NOT POSSIBLE.
How can someone so full of life be taken away?
It can't be real. It can't be…
Please tell me it's not…
The tears flowed so fast there was no way to stop them. She didn't want to. Ellie cried and cried, until there was nothing left. Merry was dead.

CHAPTER 89

Perito Moreno, Argentina

Ellie had lost track of how many hours she'd been sitting on the viewing platform. The face of the glacier spread more than three miles wide and towered 250 feet above the lake. One of the last remnants of the Ice Age, this colossal frozen river had forged a path through the Patagonian Andes over 10,000 years. On its sparkling surface, waves of ice appeared suspended in time, but actually crept forward a few feet every day.

CRACK!

An enormous chunk sheared off the glacier's face and crashed into the water. It tumbled angrily before stabilizing, then floated away from its parent like a child going off into the world alone.

Hi Jerry,

I'm sorry I didn't call today. I got your message but didn't want to bother you because I'd just be a blubbering mess and I've done that to you too many times already. I'm still trying to comprehend that Merry is gone. I feel… helpless is probably the right word. There's absolutely nothing I can do. And it hurts so much. But this isn't anything you don't already know, Jerry. You've been

through it much worse. It fucking sucks, doesn't it?
To get away from my grief I visited the Perito Moreno
glacier and did some ice hiking. I wasn't very good
with the crampons or axe, but it was mesmerizing
inside the ice tunnels. Merry always reminded me to
enjoy life, and I believe she was with me every step of
the way today.
Anyway, I just wanted to let you know where my head
is at. Thanks for all your support these last few days.
Even though you're far away, you're closer to me than
anyone. Yours,
Ellie.

San Francisco, USA

Dear Ellie,
I imagine you are still in shock, and that's only natural.
You and Merry had so many wonderful adventures
together, and I remember you telling me how much
you learned from her. Those memories will be with
you forever.
The only advice I can give you is to feel the grief. Don't
hide from it. Let it run its course. Then, at some point
in the future, you have to continue living your life. Yes,
it will be without the person you loved, and that will
seem impossible at times, but you will get through it.
There are going to be a lot of emotions here today as well.
It's Bella's birthday and I've got a surprise planned for
the girls to help with their grieving. Honoring Bella,
and Merry, is the best way to keep their spirits alive.
Take care and talk soon,
Jerry.

"Breakfast!" Jerry called from the bottom of the stairs, but there was no response. "I made pancakes!"

"Don't lie to us, Daddy." Mia appeared at the top of the stairs in her PJs, looking unimpressed with Jerry's claim and the hour of the morning.

"I swear it's true. Buttermilk pancakes with maple syrup, all the way from Canada. But if you don't want any, that's fine. It means more for me." Jerry turned away, and the familiar pitter-patter of little feet running down the stairs brought a smile to his face.

Mia bounded into the kitchen after him. Her eyes lit up when she saw the steaming stack on the table. "It's true. Pancakes!"

"Come and get 'em while they're hot," Jerry shouted to his other daughters.

Mia grabbed the top pancake, juggling it between her fingers.

"Careful honey. What would you like with it? Strawberries, blueberries—"

"Maple syrup."

"I thought so." Jerry drizzled a generous dose over her pancake while Yasmina and Andrea scampered downstairs in their dressing gowns. Without a word, they piled food onto their plates and began eating.

"Well, I'm glad everyone is in a talkative mood this morning." Jerry poured each of them a glass of freshly-squeezed OJ. "Does anybody want to say anything? I could sing a song. Or act out a scene."

"Please don't," Yasmina mumbled.

"Dad, no," Andrea pleaded.

"How about some Shakespeare? *A Midsummer Night's Dream?* *'Love looks not with the eyes, but with the mind, and therefore is winged Cupid painted blind—'*"

"You know what day it is?" Yasmina interrupted. "You haven't forgotten?"

Jerry switched off the stove and joined his family at the table. "Of course I know, honey."

"Then why are you so happy? Why are you pretending everything is normal?"

"You're right, Yas, it's not a normal day. It's your mom's birthday. And I miss her every single second, just like you do. But I thought instead of us being sad, we could do something fun to remind us how lucky we were to have had her in our lives, even if it wasn't for nearly long enough."

Mia stopped eating. "What about school?"

"School is obviously important, honey, but this morning I emailed Principal Mercer to let her know none of you would be coming in. Today is all about celebrating your mom. So, what'll it be?"

Yasmina and Andrea threw suggestions around the table, including a drive through Big Sur to the McWay Waterfall and a picnic in Golden Gate Park, where Bella had often taken them during school vacations.

"We could go sailing," Mia said amidst the noise. "Mom loved that."

Jerry looked at Yasmina and Andrea, who both nodded.

"OK girls, let's hit the Bay."

The mainsail unfurled, then snapped out as it captured the wind. Standing feet astride the helm, Jerry surveyed the way forward through his sunglasses. To port was the U.S.S. Pampanito, a World War 2 submarine converted into a museum, to starboard was the infamous Alcatraz Island. Ahead, the hulking Golden Gate Bridge rose above the ocean, glowing orange like a blacksmith's forge.

The last time he'd rented this thirty-foot sailboat was earlier this year, to scatter Bella's ashes with the girls. Today, Yasmina and Andrea perched near the bow as the vessel glided through

San Francisco Bay, dangling their legs off the side and laughing as water tickled their feet. Mia sat next to Jerry, wearing the life jacket he'd strapped around her body.

She looks just like her mom. Wind in her hair, smile on her face, not a care in the world.

They sailed past Fisherman's Wharf and Jerry spun the wheel, tacking the boat toward Alcatraz. Once the home of ruthless Chicago mobster Al Capone, imprisoned for tax evasion of all things, the prison was now occupied by tourists instead of inmates.

"Honey, come here a minute." Mia scooted closer and Jerry maneuvered her between himself and the wheel. "Put your left hand here. Good. And your right hand here. Got it? Now make sure you keep it straight." Jerry lifted his hands slightly off the helm. "OK, you're steering now. You're the captain."

Mia looked up at Jerry and flashed a huge grin.

"Keep your eyes forward, honey," he said, stabilizing the wheel.

"Oops. Sorry, *papi*."

He lifted his hands again and let her steer the boat, just like Bella used to do.

Jerry's route took them north around Alcatraz, then west to the quaint village of Sausalito. They moored and hiked the nature trail to Slackers Hill, enjoying stunning views of the Pacific Ocean and a rarely-seen side of the Golden Gate Bridge with the San Francisco skyline rising behind it.

Jerry had brought Bella here on their first date, almost twenty years ago, and he still remembered the kiss they shared. She tasted sweet—which could've had something to do with the Skittles they shared on the way up—and he was hooked. He told his daughters the story, showing them where their mom had stood on the cliff.

"What was she wearing?" Yasmina asked.

"Blue jeans and a white t-shirt with little flowers embroidered at the bottom. It was simple, but your mom could make anything look good. Her hair was down to her waist back then, longer than yours, Yas, and the breeze blew it all around her face."

"How did she stand?"

"How?"

"Yeah, like what position?"

"With one hand on her hip and the other at the front. Exactly like you are now."

"Was she happy?"

"I hope so, honey. I tried my best. I do know you girls made her happy. Every day."

The family huddled together in the wind, admiring the view.

"Y'know, Dad, we think you're doing a pretty awesome job raising us," Andrea said out-of-the-blue. "You don't do everything right, but we know you love us."

Jerry struggled to hold back tears while hugging his daughters. "Thank you. It's nice to hear that."

"Look!" Mia screamed.

In the shadow of the Golden Gate Bridge, a lone creature extended its head out of the water and exhaled through its blowhole.

"A whale," Jerry said. "Humpback."

The girls stared at the ocean with wide-eyed expectation, waiting for its return.

"There!" Yasmina pointed as its massive tail skimmed the surface.

Another moment of quiet.

Then the whale breached its enormous body out of the ocean, twisted in the air, and landed with a magnificent splash.

As crazy as it might've sounded to say out loud, Jerry imagined it was Bella, come to say hello to her family.

CHAPTER 90

Torres del Paine National Park, Chile

Patagonia. Just the word evoked images of silver mountains, jagged peaks and virgin snow. As it turned out, everything Ellie had imagined about Patagonia was true. Except now she was here, she could *feel* it too.

Two days ago she'd arrived deep in southern Chile, checked into the aptly-named Hostel of Last Hope in the isolated town of Puerto Natales, and set about hiring equipment for a trek. In addition to a tent, gas stove, sleeping bag and mat, she also stocked up on food. Hiking at least ten miles every day for eight days meant having enough energy would be essential.

If I die, I sure-as-hell don't want to die hungry.

Packing only what was necessary, including her jacket, thermals, beanie and gloves, Ellie stored the rest at the hostel. She made a final call to Jerry to let him know she was going off-grid to work through the gremlins in her head, and he wished her well in finding the peace she so desperately sought.

The only thing left to do was pick up a map at the rangers' station, fling on her backpack, and hike across the windswept plain toward the soaring alps that loomed over her like a Goliath to her David. The casual way she did it, almost without thinking, surprised her at first, but then Ellie remembered this was the fifth multi-day trek of her trip.

Not for a second before leaving New York would she have believed she could attempt the famed 'O' trek to Torres del Paine—colossal granite towers named after the word for 'blue' in the indigenous language.

And Ellie was going to do it alone. No guide. No group. No porters. No-one except herself and the wilderness. Nerves were high, naturally, but each step gave her confidence. It was time to apply everything she'd learned.

I'm gonna slay this Goliath.

Ellie headed along a narrow path that ran parallel to a frozen river. The majestic snow-capped peaks were never out of view. Although her backpack was heavy, her body surged with so much adrenaline she didn't feel the weight. Besides, Ellie loved how everything she needed to survive was contained in just this one bag. All the other things she used to think were essential had just been superfluous crap tying her down.

It's funny how I consider myself a big-city girl, but the times on my trip when I've been most content are when I'm out in nature, in the mountains and ocean and jungle and desert. There's nothing in a city that can come close to this beauty, this feeling, that Pachamama has given us—for free!

Ellie knew by now that if anywhere was going to be her church or mosque or temple, it was here in the natural environment where she could appreciate the limitless splendor of the universe.

After eight hours of hiking, including several photo stops, Ellie reached the first campsite. She chatted to a couple of other trekkers about the trail ahead, then chose a space between the trees to set up her tent while there was still light.

After cooking a dinner of rice and beans, followed by an entirely necessary bar of chocolate, she went to bed early. It was only going to get more difficult from here on out.

CHAPTER 91

Torres del Paine National Park, Chile

Ellie arched her back and filled her lungs with pristine alpine air. Just the act of breathing here was invigorating. She made oatmeal to warm her insides, added honey to sweeten, and was gone from camp before anyone else had risen.

Today would take her twelve miles around the back of the mountain range, the rocky path flanked with green shrubs and purple orchids pollinated by bumblebees. Packs of wild horses galloped in nearby fields. Even the cloud formations were striking, like icebergs in the sky painted by a master who'd been practicing for billions of years.

The solitude gave Ellie an opportunity to reflect on how much she'd changed. Yes, on the outside she was more lean and sinewy, with thighs to make a gym-junkie proud. But it was on the inside where there'd been lasting transformation.

Ellie recalled the question that'd run through her head before she left home, about whether the happiness she sought would come from within or outside herself. As her mind's eye traced back through the places she'd been over the past five months, including all the ecstasy and agony, Ellie realized her happiness had been a mix of both internal and external forces.

The one element which had really mattered, though, were the *decisions* she'd made. They helped her take risks to embark on new adventures like this one, picked her up off the mat when she got knocked down, and let her experience the full range of human emotions.

Decisions are what give us real power.

And it was goddamn time to make a decision about Jerry.

In the long shadows of afternoon, Ellie stopped at a lagoon. Bordered by pebbles, the stillness of its milky-white surface was mesmerizing. She pulled off her boots and waded into the icy water to soothe her swollen feet. It folded through her toes, making her gasp. But she didn't want to leave. Because it was life. And it was exhilarating.

～

Over the next week, Ellie continued her Zen trek through Patagonia. The focus needed for the placement of each footstep led to a state of mindfulness you could never achieve in a hectic city. In nature, with no distractions, you had to be present or you'd slide off the fricking mountain.

As she gained altitude and moved into the glacier zone, the landscape changed from grass and forests to boulder fields and ice sheets. Though her feet hurt, her backpack cut into her shoulders, and the terrain was uncompromising—one afternoon she was almost blown off a ridge by gale-force winds—Ellie relished every minute. Because after each challenge the reward was breathtaking views of bright blue glacial lakes and shiny white peaks.

With every notch of the rising sun, the towering summits tossed avalanches off their slopes like shedding old skin. Ellie watched the ice fall, then heard its roar a few seconds later, rolling down the mountain in a terrifying tsunami. But she didn't just see and hear these wonders—she *felt* them. She was part of nature, and it filled her with humility.

Resting every couple of hours, Ellie drank the pure water running in streams and refueled with fruit and granola bars. Eating had the added benefit of lightening her pack. The breaks also gave her a chance to think about Jerry.

I'm so tired of being lonely. I want someone to share my life with. To talk and laugh and cry with. To touch and hold at night. Someone to care about, and who'll care for me in return.

An idea had slowly been forming in Ellie's head. At first she dismissed it as silly, ridiculous, totally foolish, yet couldn't shake it. Maybe that's what makes it a good idea?

CHAPTER 92

San Francisco, USA

"We're going to get rain, Kyra!" Jerry exclaimed, looking up at the black clouds through the windshield of his SUV.

"And this makes you happy?" She tapped the car's touchscreen to bring up a weather radar.

"Yes. Don't you know what it means?"

"Not really. And please keep your eyes on the road."

Drops of water fell on the windshield. "Look! It'll be an incredible show."

Kevin leaned forward from the back seat. "Tell me again why you want rain when we're still behind schedule?"

The heavens had well and truly opened by the time Jerry's SUV reached the construction site. The exterior of the Pata Museum was nearly complete, with glass curtain walls installed on every level and significant progress made on the terraces that stepped up out of the dirt like a curved pyramid.

Kyra and Kevin jumped out of the car and ran to a shelter where a group of workers sought refuge from the downpour.

Jerry didn't join them. Instead, he walked straight into the deluge. Within a few seconds he was soaked—and loving it. "Come on," he implored, gazing up at the museum.

"What the hell are you doing?" Harry shouted from the doorway of his portable office.

"Just wait," Jerry called back, splashing through the mud.

The rain fell even harder, a torrential storm across the city. His shirt stuck to his back and his hair flattened across his head. A bolt of lightning cracked through the sky and thunder clapped over the site. Everyone flinched, except Jerry.

"Come on, baby."

Then it happened. The vertical channels of exposed drainage running along the sides of each terrace filled with enough rain that they funneled rivers of water down from one level to the next. It looked just like Bella had planned—a series of spectacular waterfalls representing those in the Amazon jungle.

"Yes!" Jerry threw his hands into the air. "We did it, baby! Oh Bella, we did it. You did it."

⌒

The party had been going for hours. Drinks were followed by dinner and Jerry's customary speech, followed by dancing and more drinks. Now, close to midnight, only a few energetic feet remained on the dancefloor.

"I haven't talked to you all night," Jerry said.

"And it's been a relief, let me tell you," Kyra replied.

He took a seat beside her in a corner of the Italian restaurant. It was reassuring to know that even at this late stage of the evening, his trusted assistant hadn't lost her bite. They were surrounded by empty wine glasses and half-eaten gingerbread men. Jerry always hosted a Christmas party to thank his employees for their work, and these last twelve months had been more unrelenting than usual.

"Are you enjoying yourself?" he asked.

"So so," Kyra threw back a mouthful of wine. "As much as I can while being subjected to the fashion choices of architects all night. I mean, check out Taya's dress. That thing would've been rejected by Goodwill. Frank's shirt was purchased on imacheapdick.com, and Shonda's being Shonda again. Damn girl's stockings belong in the Chernobyl dead zone."

"Oh Kyra," Jerry stifled a laugh. "You're even more abrasive when you drink."

"I know." She finished off her glass. "But, hey, I can choose a venue."

"A good choice. I knew I could leave it in your capable hands."

"You know what else you could leave in my capable hands?"

"A Christmas bonus?"

"With lots of zeros."

"Well, you'll have to wait until Monday like everyone else. I do have something for you now, though, if you're interested."

Kyra's face lit up, then fell in suspicion. "Is it a pink slip? Are you firing me?! Jesus—"

"It's not a pink slip. Even if I wanted to fire you, I don't think you'd let me." Jerry pulled an envelope out of his jacket.

"True." Kyra snatched it and tore it open. She took a moment to read the card inside. "It says a plane ticket."

"Yes."

"To where?"

"Wherever you want."

"In the world?"

"You can read, right?"

"Oh my God!" Kyra screamed. She launched herself at Jerry and wrapped her arms around him. "How could you do this? Why did you do this?" She wiped away tears, smudging her make-up.

"I know how hard you've worked since Bella passed, so consider this a big 'thank you' from someone who appreciates you more than I've let on. Fly somewhere exotic, have a fantastic vacation, then come back and tell us all about it."

"I don't know how to thank you, Jerry."

"You go have the time of your life, that's how."

Kyra blew her nose into a napkin. "I hate you for making me cry like this."

"I know," he smiled.

CHAPTER 93

Torres del Paine National Park, Chile

Everything hurt. Even her fingernails. Especially her toenails. Ellie unclipped her backpack and propped it against a tree. On this penultimate day of her trek, she'd finally made it around the front side of the mountain range. The 'O' was almost complete.

She eased her aching body onto a rock warmed by the sun and marveled at the range of colors. The soil under her feet was burnt orange, the bushes olive green, and the lake royal blue. Its surface reflected the surrounding peaks in a flawless optical illusion. With an eagle circling above to keep her company, Ellie was sure the world couldn't possibly get any more beautiful.

Merry would've loved this place. Oh Merry… You would've sat here and drank your rum and laughed about how no-one realizes happiness is free. We just have to get off our arses to find it.

A lump grew in Ellie's throat and tears streamed down her cheeks. Her mind drifted back to the bonfire in the desert and what Merry had told her about why humans exist—*to love, in all its forms.* Ellie knew it was true. Nothing else could bring her contentment. But knowing it was one thing. She still had to practice it.

Or else what the fuck am I doing on the planet?

Not being able to talk with Jerry for the past week had been painful. And the pain hadn't dissipated over time—it had gotten worse.

There'd been months of emails, messages, phone calls and video chats, but more than all of that Jerry had always been in her mind. She knew what she felt. *She loved him.* Even though it seemed irrational given they'd never met, Ellie was mature enough, and scarred enough, to know the difference between love and infatuation.

"I love you, Jerry Townsend," Ellie whispered, drawing an infinity sign in the dirt with a stick. She liked how it sounded. "I love you, Jerry Townsend," she said a bit louder. It sounded even better.

Ellie stood and cupped her hands around her mouth. "I love you, Jerry Townsend!" Her voice rolled across the lake and sprang back at her from all directions. "I love you. I love you. I love you Jerry Townsend!"

She laughed at her exuberance. "OK Ellie, now you've accepted it, what are you going to do about it?"

Fate, or a higher power, or perhaps just sheer coincidence, had put Bella's guidebook in her hands, but now it was up to her to *make a decision.* One that could change the course of her life. Ellie understood the plan she'd been hatching would take a risk. One that may hurt, more than she'd ever been hurt before. But it would be worth it.

It's time to open my heart again.

Ellie wasn't sure how long she'd been sitting on the rock, but there was a half-day of hiking ahead. She willed her body upright and swung on her backpack. "Argghhh!" The momentum carried her sideways and her ankle twisted awkwardly.

She toppled off the trail.

Slid down an embankment.

Grabbed hold of a root to stop from falling off the mountain. It held firm.

Using all the strength left in her arms, she pulled herself back up and caught her breath in the dirt.

"Ellie, you clumsy idiot!" She touched her ankle. Winced. Pounded her fist into the ground. She knew her limits were being tested, as they'd been a thousand times before and would be a thousand times again.

Ellie looked back the way she'd come. She could walk down to last night's campsite and catch a ferry to Puerto Natales, or she could soldier on up the mountain. It took a fraction of a second to dismiss the first option. There'd be no quitting. She'd crawl the rest of the way if she had to. The biggest reward was yet to come.

The sky was black when Ellie hobbled into the final campsite. A branch took the pressure off her ankle, but progress had been slow. With only the light from her headtorch, Ellie set up her tent and cooked her last packet of noodles while thinking about pepperoni pizza with extra cheese. And buffalo wings. And a Coke. Upsized.

She woke at 3 a.m. to begin the ascent to the crowning glory of her solo quest. The first sliver of light had just spread across Patagonia when Ellie arrived, ankle throbbing, at Torres del Paine. The Towers of Blue.

In her gender role-breaking 1878 expedition here, British explorer Lady Florence Dixie had described the three mammoth granite obelisks as 'Cleopatra's Needles.' Their tapered peaks cut so high into the sky that they created their own weather patterns, clouds swirling around them like fog in a freezer of popsicles.

When the sun hit the tips of the towers, then spread down their icy torsos, they magically changed color before Ellie's eyes. From blue to orange, red to pink, and back again, as if looking through a kaleidoscope. She forgot all her pain.

Her brain scrolled through all the things she wanted to do after returning to civilization: take a hot shower, eat a nice meal, call Jerry. Not necessarily in that order. She suddenly realized that she hadn't added any of these to her TO DO list. In fact, she'd completely forgotten about her list. Maybe it was time to ditch it for good?

Not the hand sanitizer though. I'm not ready to give that up yet...

As Ellie headed back across the windswept plain and away from the mountains, she reflected on her accomplishment. She'd hiked eighty miles and climbed from sea-level to 3,000 feet and back again, three times. She'd been challenged, but pushed through, conquered her fears, and accepted—once and for all, *hells yes*—there was nothing she couldn't do if she just put enough grit into it.

Her feet ached, her ankle stung, and her shoulders were raw, but she'd never felt more alive.

CHAPTER 94

San Francisco, USA

Pots and pans cluttered the kitchen as Jerry and his daughters prepared for tomorrow's Christmas lunch. Yasmina helped Mia chop veggies and taught her how to say them in Spanish, while Andrea made *chicha morada* (a tangy purple corn drink boiled with pineapple, cinnamon and cloves).

"You need to put some sugar in it," Yasmina said, looking over her shoulder.

"I don't think so."

"That's what Mom used to do." Yasmina dipped a spoon into the *chicha*. "Yep, it needs a pinch." She threw in some brown sugar from a line of condiment jars and tasted it again. "Perfect." Then she turned her attention to Jerry's effort at a spice rub for the turkey. "Dad, what are you doing?"

"Well, the recipe said oregano but I don't want to follow the recipe."

"And what happens *every time* you don't follow the recipe."

"I know, but—"

"Dad," Andrea and Mia yelled.

"No 'buts.'" Yasmina bumped him out of the way. "*No queremos morir de hambre.*"

The girls giggled while Jerry slowly translated the words in his head: 'We don't want to starve to death.' Fair point.

He gladly stepped back and watched Yasmina take responsibility for all the dishes Bella loved to make. She added oregano, cumin and paprika to the spice rub, then supervised cooking desserts, including *tres leches* (sponge cake soaked in three types of milk) and *pecan pie* with organic Peruvian chocolate. Not only was Yasmina growing up to look like her mom, she was acting like her too.

"What can I do to help?" Jerry asked.

"Nada!" his daughters replied.

At least he'd get to eat it.

Ushuaia, Argentina

Ellie threw her hands in the air for a photo-op at the 'End of the World' sign in front of the Beagle Channel. As the crow flies it was 6,615 miles from New York to this point, the most southern inhabited piece of land on our planet. As far away from home as she'd ever been. Of course Ellie's zigzagging journey through South America had taken an incalculable number of miles on buses, boats, trucks, trains, planes and a variety of other unroadworthy vehicles, including the backs of a few hapless animals.

She returned the photo favor for Clara, a gap-year backpacker with doe eyes and a Californian drawl who'd recently started her trip. The wind blustering up from Antarctica nearly blew them off their feet.

Two ships were anchored in the nearby port, a research vessel and cruise liner, though neither Ellie nor Clara had the US$10,000 to buy a berth heading to the great white continent. The thought of paying such a vast sum for a ten-day boat ride seemed ludicrous. Ellie could travel for a year on that!

Anyway, the plan which had formed in the clutches of her tenacious mind would, if it panned out, surpass any polar experience.

He just has to say 'yes.'

Ellie had met Clara after her marathon trek, and together they hitched a nighttime ride in a semi through Tierra del Fuego, the Land of Fire, named by Portuguese explorer Ferdinand Magellan who in 1520 observed fires along the shore lit by the native people. There was nothing fiery about shivering in the frigid cabin of the truck for twelve hours, but Ellie needed to keep moving. Tomorrow would be Christmas Day and soon it would be New Year's Eve and she had a goal about where to spend the final night of the most momentous year of her life.

He just has to say 'yes.'

At their hostel in Ushuaia, Ellie, Clara and other travelers pitched in to make a Christmas Eve feast, the tradition in this part of the world. An *asado* had been set up out back to grill a humongous slab of Argentine beef, and everyone got into the festive spirit by drinking *ananá fizz* (a cider mixed with pineapple juice). It almost felt like a normal Christmas, except it was stinking hot in the southern hemisphere. There'd be no snow angels this year.

Ellie used a break in the party to head upstairs to her dorm. She popped a pimple, fixed her hair, and checked nothing was stuck between her teeth. She'd been thinking about this moment all day. In truth, she'd been thinking about it for a week since the idea materialized while hiking the back side of Torres del Paine. She was about to find out if it her instincts were correct.

Ellie took a long, deep, breath and thought about the times on her trip when she'd been most nervous. Standing on the edge of Mount Roraima, diving with sharks in the Galápagos, taking *ayahuasca* in the Amazon, jumping off a bridge in Baños.

All you need is one second of courage. Just one second. The rest will take care of itself.

Jerry's advice applied now more than ever because Ellie's adventure had revealed a truth. She didn't want to be alone anymore. She wanted to share not just this trip with someone, but this life. The Great Wall she'd built around herself had to come down.

He just has to say 'yes.'

CHAPTER 95

San Francisco, USA

Jerry looked at his phone. He'd been waiting for this video call. He put the last strip of tape on a present he was wrapping on the bedroom floor and jumped up to check himself in the mirror. He ran his hands through his hair a few times, made sure nothing was stuck between his teeth, then answered it. "Hi Ellie."

"Merry Christmas Eve," she chimed from her bunk.

"Merry Christmas Eve to you too. I saw the photos from your trek. It looked incredible."

"Thanks. The scenery was fantastic, and I really needed the quiet-time."

Jerry sat on his bed. "You figured some things out?"

"I did." Ellie opened her mouth to say something more, then closed it, leading to an uneasy pause.

"Where are you headed next then?" Jerry asked to fill the void.

"I've got a flight up to Buenos Aires in a couple of days."

Another pause, even more uncomfortable.

"If I recall correctly our last video chat didn't go so well," Jerry laughed.

"Don't worry, I haven't drunk too much this time," Ellie said. "So…what are you up to?"

"We just finished prepping Christmas lunch. Well, the girls did most of it and have gone to buy ice-cream while I wrap the last of the presents. I'm not doing such a great job of that either."

"You can talk then?"

He detected a quiver in her voice. "Of course. What's up?"

"I have a question to ask."

"Shoot. Anything."

"It's a bit awkward. And I'm not sure what your response is going to be." Ellie looked away from her phone, then back at Jerry, who smiled half out of concern and half out of encouragement. "So I was wondering—"

Connection Lost.

Ushuaia, Argentina

Ellie's screen went blank. "You're kidding me!" She tapped Jerry's number and he answered it within a ring. "Great timing, as usual."

"You were about to say?" he asked.

"Yeah, I was slowly getting to my question… Um, after B.A. I've decided to head to Rio de Janeiro for New Year's Eve."

"Wow, Ellie. That's going to be one helluva party. The fireworks are meant to be the best in the world."

"I hope so…"

All you need is one second of courage.

Just one second.

The rest will take care of itself.

"So I was wondering if you would, y'know…like to come?"

Silence. Of such emptiness Ellie felt as if the world had stopped spinning on its axis and collapsed in on itself. She couldn't quite believe she'd asked the question, and the shocked expression on Jerry's face told her he couldn't quite comprehend it.

"Come where?" he asked.

"To Rio. For New Year's Eve. With me." With each passing second, she wanted to die a little more.

Jerry finally spoke, the words tumbling out of his mouth. "It's very kind of you to ask... But I'm not ready to do anything, like that. I lost Bella a year ago, and I've got my kids to think about. And my business. And my parents..."

"I understand," Ellie nodded, trying to hide her crushing disappointment with a poorly-designed smile. "It was a long shot but I thought I'd ask—no, I needed to ask. If my trip has taught me anything it's that if your heart is telling you to do something then you have to do it, no matter how silly it might make you look. That's why I asked. Because I want to see you, Jerry."

"Thank you, Ellie. That's...a lovely thing to say. Listen, my girls are about to come home so I should go. Have a Merry Christmas."

"You too," Ellie said.

But Jerry had already hung up.

San Francisco, USA

After checking his daughters had fallen asleep, Jerry carried a stack of presents downstairs. The lights on the tree gave the living room a homely glow and made him feel content for the first time since Ellie's call that afternoon.

He hadn't been able to stop thinking about her proposal. It was so out of left field. Or was it? Hadn't all their exchanges been leading to this? He knew what his heart was telling him, but his life was more complicated than that. Wasn't it?

Jerry picked up a photo from the mantelpiece. Bella was looking straight at the camera and radiating that infectious smile Jerry had fallen in love with all those years ago. He touched her face. Tears filled his eyes.

"Baby, did you arrange this connection between Ellie and me?

So I wouldn't be alone for the rest of my life?" He broke down and wiped his nose with the back of his hand. "Please send me a sign, because I have no idea what to do. I need help, Bella. I really need your help."

CHAPTER 96

Christmas Day – San Francisco, USA

Mia jumped on Jerry. He rolled her up in the bedsheet and tickled her until she screamed. He let her rest a moment, then tickled her again. Their Christmas morning tradition.

"What time is it?" Andrea mumbled from the doorway. Yasmina also arrived in a dressing gown, rubbing sleep from her face.

"Present time!" Jerry leaped out of bed and planted a wet kiss on both their cheeks.

"Oh Dad, gross."

"Who wants to open the first one?" He bounded down the stairs.

"Me," Mia squealed, pushing between her sisters and chasing him to the living room.

There was nothing better than seeing his girls' faces as they tore the paper off their presents. Mia got roller blades with unicorn horns, Andrea a 3D puzzle and collection of detective novels, and Yasmina tickets to see a band she was obsessed with. Jerry also gave her a blank cookbook so she could record her mom's recipes. There were too many presents, but Jerry couldn't help himself. It was their first Christmas without Bella and he wanted his family to be happy.

"OK Dad, time for yours," Yasmina said.

"You didn't have to get me anything. You girls are my gift."

"That's sweet and all, but everybody wants a present."

"Yeah, you're right. Give it to me!"

Yasmina handed the present to Jerry and he slowly peeled off the wrapping, building the suspense.

"Dad, hurry up." Mia bounced up-and-down.

Inside was a book titled *Our Family's Huge, Crazy & Amazing South American Adventure.* The cover had a photo of the Townsend-Vasquez clan on the never-ending white of the Bolivian salt flats.

Jerry flipped through the pages one-by-one. There were photos he hadn't seen since their trip: Bella eating a mango on the streets of Cartagena, the girls posing with a fat Botero statue in Medellín, and ice hiking on the Perito Moreno Glacier. Then there were photos he'd never seen before: tongue-out selfies from Yasmina's phone, and a picture of him and Bella holding hands at Machu Picchu.

"Well? Do you like it?" Andrea asked.

Jerry couldn't stop his tears from flowing. "Your mom used to make these photo books."

"She never got to make one for South America," Yasmina said. "So we thought it'd be good to, y'know, continue the tradition."

"It's wonderful, girls. I will cherish it." He hugged his daughters. "OK, now let's not forget the lesson your mom wanted us to remember after we opened our presents."

"Not everyone has as much as we do." Mia stuck out her bottom lip.

"That's right. So I have one last thing for you all, except it's not for you." Jerry handed each of them an envelope.

Mia tore hers open and held up a card. "I got a chicken."

"This is a goat," Andrea said.

"Mine's a cow," Yasmina added.

"I bought these animals in your names for a family in Peru who needs them much more than we do. They'll be able to harvest eggs, and have fresh milk too."

"That's awesome," Andrea said. "Thanks, Dad."

Mia scrunched up her face. "So I don't really get a chicken?"

Christmas Day – Ushuaia, Argentina

Ellie woke feeling marginally better, if only because she had no more tears left to shed. She washed her face to remove the lines of salt crusted on her cheeks, then tiptoed downstairs past backpackers passed out in the lounge.

The party last night had gone long, but after her call with Jerry, celebrating had been the last thing on Ellie's mind. All she wanted to do was crawl into a ball. The man she loved had rejected her. There was no avoiding that.

Clara had found her, provided a shoulder to bawl on for a while, then dragged her down to dinner. But Ellie couldn't stomach any food. And watching everyone else partner up for the evening only distressed her more. After Clara found a pretty Argentine girl to flirt with, Ellie fled to bed and hid under her pillow, begging for the darkness to swallow her up. It was Christmas, for Pete's sake, and she'd never been this miserable.

Ellie sat on a pile of bricks in the backyard of the hostel, mug of coffee in one hand, phone in the other.

"Merry Christmas!" Donna, Benji and Alex shouted from their living room, surrounded by piles of wrapping paper and shiny new toys.

"Merry Christmas to you too," Ellie replied. "It looks like you're having a good morning."

"I got Captain America." Alex lifted the toy for her to see.

"Look at my Nerf gun." Benji shot a string of darts across the room while making a machine gun sound.

"Oh, that looks like…fun. And the necklace, Donna?"

"From Roger."

"Very thoughtful."

"I had to tell him what to buy. Even then the idiot got the wrong one."

"Hey, Aunty Ellie." Benji pulled an angry face. "Where's my present from you?"

Ellie yawned, giving her time to catch herself from saying he was a spoiled brat. "I couldn't buy you one this year because I'm not there."

He pointed the barrel of the Nerf gun directly at her. "You can send it to me."

"Benjamin Wallace!" Donna scolded. "She's half-a-world away and doesn't have time to worry about getting you anything. Be grateful for what you have or I'll take it all back."

Benji commando-rolled behind the couch and out of frame.

"What did you get for Christmas, Aunty Ellie?" Alex chirped.

"My present is that I get to talk to you. And you know what? It's the best present I've ever had."

"I love you."

"I love you too, sweetheart."

"Are you coming home now?"

"Soon."

"When?"

Ellie rubbed her forehead. She really should've finished her caffeine hit before dialing into this interrogation.

"OK boys, let me talk to Aunty Ellie. Go play outside with your new toys and don't break them." Benji and Alex ran off through the kitchen. Donna followed to check on pots bubbling on the stove. "Is everything OK?"

Ellie sat up in an attempt to look more alive. "Yeah. Why?"

"It's our first Christmas apart in a long time. I want to make sure you're not lonely."

"I'm fine."

"What is it?"

"Nothing. Everything's fine."

"Don't you fib to me, Eleanor Rose Bartlett."

Ellie shut her eyes. The last thing she needed this morning was a fricking lecture, but after so long, coming clean to her sister about Jerry was inevitable. Oh, screw it. Moment of truth. "There is this guy. Or 'was' this guy is more accurate."

Donna slammed the oven door. "I knew it! Tell me everything."

"There's nothing to say because it's not happening. So I'm upset about it, is all." Ellie understated her devastation, hoping Donna would leave it be.

"Where'd you meet?"

"Um… We never… We haven't met."

"I don't understand."

"He's… We've just been talking on the phone, and stuff."

"Don't be so cryptic with me, Ellie. How do you know him?" Donna's stare drilled out of her screen.

Ellie steeled herself and recounted the entire story from when she'd found the *Unique Planet*. The initial emails with Jerry, reminiscing about Bella, had forged a bond that led to messages, phone calls and video calls about their lives, and then the invite to spend N.Y.E. with her in Rio.

Donna listened with an open mouth, occasionally shaking her head, like one of those clown games at a carnival. "Only my sister could get herself involved in such a fucked-up situation. You couldn't just find another Latin lover? You have to fall for a guy who's on the other side of the world? With dead wife issues? Jesus, don't tell me you're in love with a man you've never even met."

Ellie threw a stone against the brick wall. It bounced back and hit her foot. "You told me to be more open with my emotions. I asked him to come to Rio to find out exactly what was going on."

"You mean to find out he's a serial killer!" Donna crashed a pile of plates on the bench.

"He's not a serial killer. If he is, it's the most elaborate, long-distance, stalking I've ever heard of. He probably thinks I'm stalking him. Jerry is a good, decent, family man. He has three daughters."

"Oh great, an excellent prospect! So this is why you didn't tell me before. As usual you wanted to keep living in your little fantasy world and not have reality intrude on it."

"It doesn't matter anyway," Ellie cried. "He said 'no.' OK? He said 'no.'"

"Good. Because it was never going to work. You know, this completes the circle of crazy that started when you quit your job. In fact, it's not just crazy anymore—it's *stupid*." Donna spat the last word.

Ellie glared at her screen. If not even her own sister could understand what she'd been through on her trip, who would?

CHAPTER 97

San Francisco, USA

Jerry pushed out his chair. There'd been far too much food, and tasting every dessert probably wasn't the best idea. He and Don washed dishes while Carol and the girls played with their presents in the living room. Mia was enthralled with a bracelet-making contraption she'd received from her grandparents.

"What's on your mind?" Don said.

"Never eating again." Jerry handed his dad another bowl to dry.

"I can tell when your head is spinning like a cat stuck in a washing machine."

Jerry turned off the tap. "You remember I told you about Ellie? The woman I've been talking with? Well, she called yesterday and invited me to spend New Year's Eve with her."

"OK."

"In Brazil."

"Oh…" Don whistled. "What did you say?"

Jerry shook his head.

"You don't want to go?"

"I'm not sure. I mean, yes, I want to go but… I don't want to get hurt, Dad. And I especially don't want to hurt the girls.

I'm afraid they wouldn't understand."

"Yasmina will understand. She's older than you think."

"She's older than I'd like her to be."

"And Andrea has a level head on her shoulders. Like her grandfather."

"A bit too level."

"The girls will be fine, Jerry. The older two may push back at first because that's what teenagers do, but they'll understand. And Mia will accept it because she just wants her dad to be happy. They love you. Trust them."

"Maybe you're right." Jerry grabbed a cloth and wiped the bench.

"How do you feel about Ellie?"

"She's smart. And funny. Really funny. Independent, compassionate, honest. She has a good heart. But also vulnerable. I know she wants a connection with someone as much as I do."

"Those are great qualities, but you didn't answer my question. How do you *feel* about her?"

Jerry stopped pretending to clean. "I...I really like her, Dad. I look forward to her messages. I get worried when I don't hear from her. We haven't met, but it's like I've known her for years. I also know there's so much more to find out. So I feel something. I just don't know if it's right."

"If it's right?" Don repeated. "Are you waiting for permission from someone?"

Jerry smacked his lips. Perhaps his father had a point.

"The permission is she invited you. That's the only sign you need."

"I fell in love once, and Bella died. I don't want that pain again. I couldn't bare it."

"I understand, but you can't live in the past. You need to have new experiences and make new memories. Not to replace the old ones, but to add to the tapestry of your life. Bella will still be a part of you, but she wouldn't want you to grow old alone. She loved you too much for that."

Jerry smiled. She did love him that much.

"We all need love, son, but it never comes without risk. You need to be willing to get hurt again. So, is a chance at love worth a trip to Brazil?"

CHAPTER 98

Buenos Aires, Argentina

The couple moved in head-spinning tandem, twirling across the road while somehow keeping perfect posture. Their feet kicked between each other's legs with absolute precision to prevent serious injury.

Ellie had joined an audience on the sidewalk, charmed by the professional street dancers who looked like they'd stepped out of a 1930s Ginger Rogers and Fred Astaire movie. His hair was slicked back like asphalt, hers pulled firm in a bun. His expression was resolute, hers fierce as if going into battle. The *tango* was slow then fast, controlled then passionate. Ellie got dizzy watching the couple whirl around until the woman plunged dramatically into the man's arms. Everyone burst into applause.

The couple broke apart and stalked the audience. The man stopped in front of Ellie and held out his hand. Maybe he'd sensed her sadness. She shook her head, but his unyielding gaze told her there was no way out.

Ellie placed her hand in his and he pulled her into the middle of the crowd. He straightened her back, locked her arms, then led her on a spinning *tango* that left her breathless. Her feet were moving, but it felt like flying. And yet, despite the thrill, all Ellie could think about was she wanted to be dancing with Jerry.

The home of *tango* wasn't a city you should experience alone. Wide, tree-lined, boulevards and grand, neoclassical, buildings like the Teatro Colón evoked feelings of romance, passion—and longing.

To soothe her broken heart, Ellie hunkered in the corner of a cafe to gorge on *alfajores*. The Argentine capital was known for this moreish treat made by sandwiching two butter cookies around *dulce de leche*, a sweet caramel sauce A.K.A. Nectar of the Gods. Each bite dulled the pain of Jerry's rejection just a little.

She'd already decided to head to Rio without him. Before this trip, she wasn't sure she would've had the strength to carry on, but now—well, she respected herself too much to abandon her goal.

Ellie opened her guidebook to a page memorializing Evita Perón, South America's most legendary female figure. As a girl, Ellie had listened to Andrew Lloyd Webber's musical and been captivated by her story. Born in 1919 as an illegitimate child to a poor family, Evita grew up to become First Lady of Argentina. A feminist and social justice activist long before it was fashionable, she fought for higher wages, distributed food to the needy, and established a network of women's shelters. She also led the suffrage movement that won the right for women to vote. Sadly, she died from cancer in 1952 at the age of just thirty-three.

Around the text, Bella had written lyrics from the musical and a note that brought Ellie some solace: 'Life may be short, but have faith in its cycles. Dark is always followed by dawn. You will see light again.'

Ellie couldn't help but see the parallel between Bella and Evita's early deaths, and wondered whether Bella had felt her own life coming to an end when she wrote it. How could she be so hopeful?

Ellie connected her phone to WiFi for the first time all day. There were a series of missed video calls. From Jerry, surprisingly. She took a breath and hit redial.

He answered immediately. "Hi Ellie, I've been trying to reach you. Are you all right?"

"I've been better, actually."

"You've got a crumb there," Jerry pointed at her cheek.

Ellie brushed it off. "Did you want to chat about something?"

"Well, our last conversation ended abruptly and I want to apologize for that."

"OK... Thank you."

Jerry shifted in his chair. "And I was wondering if your offer still stands?"

So wishes on stars do come true after all.

CHAPTER 99

San Francisco, USA

Jerry poked his head into Mia's bedroom. They'd spent the day after Christmas at the park, where she got countless scrapes from testing her new rollerblades. She'd also exhausted herself and passed out early.

He knocked on Yasmina's door next. His eldest daughter and Andrea were on the bed listening to music together—a holiday miracle. "Girls, can I talk to you a minute?"

"We're kinda busy," Yasmina said.

"I can see that. But it's important." He'd put this off too long already. Given time zones and flight schedules, it was now or never. Jerry pulled Yasmina's desk chair over to her bed and she switched off the music. He could feel blood pumping through his neck as his eyes roved between them. They stared back like he'd gone mad.

"What is it, Dad?" Andrea said. "You're scaring us."

"I'm sorry. The thing is… OK, you know how much I loved your mom, right?"

"Yeah."

"She will always be in my heart. In yours too. And I love you girls more than anything in the whole world."

"Can you get to the point?" Yasmina said. "I'm on a group chat."

"A friend has invited me to go to Rio de Janeiro and spend New Year's Eve with them," Jerry blurted out. "With her."

The girls considered his words in silence.

"Her?" Andrea clarified.

"Is this the woman you've been messaging?" Yasmina tilted her head.

Jerry's jaw dropped. "How do you…?"

"Because we're not dumb, Dad," she continued. "You can't stop checking your phone. Like, all the time."

"Even more than Yas," Andrea added.

"Yeah, even more than me. It's like you're a teenager."

Jerry's face spread into a guilty grin. "You're right, it is the woman I've been messaging. But before I book anything, I need to know you're OK with it."

"You mean you haven't booked your ticket yet?!" Yasmina yelled.

"I wanted to speak with you first."

"Dad, book it already. Girls don't wait around forever, y'know. And it's Rio."

Jerry chuckled at her enthusiasm. "Andrea?"

His middle daughter picked at a cuticle. "Is it…a date?"

"I'm not sure. I think so. We like talking, we like each other, but I honestly don't know what it is yet. It may be nothing or it may be something."

Andrea looked up. "I think you should go for it, Dad. It'll be good for you."

Jerry breathed a sigh of relief. "I need you both to understand that this woman—Ellie is her name—she's not replacing your mom. No-one can do that."

"We get it." Yasmina said. "We're not going to be the stereotypical teenagers on this one. You need to be happy, and we don't want you to be old and lonely and even more grumpy than you are now."

They all cracked up.

"Honey, I'll never be alone. I have you girls."

"You're gonna owe us though."

"Yeah, I figured."

"What are you going to tell Mia?" Andrea asked.

"Tell me what?" a voice squeaked from the hallway. Mia came out of the shadows, her blanket trailing her like a princess' gown.

"Honey, you're meant to be asleep." Jerry lifted her onto his knee. "I'm thinking about going to see a friend in a country called Brazil."

She rubbed her eyes. "Is it far?"

"It's near Argentina, where we were last year. Do you remember?"

"That's far."

"When I'm there… Do you remember the guidebook that mom used during our trip? The one where she was always writing things to help other people? Well, a lady found it and started using it. She emailed me, and I emailed her back, and now we might meet up. Does that sound OK?"

"Are you coming back?"

"Of course! I'll only be gone for a week."

"Who will look after me?"

"Your grandma and grandpa will come and stay."

"It's not exactly going to be a raging New Year's Eve for us then, is it?" Yasmina sighed.

"Not this time."

"When are you leaving?" Andrea said.

"I'll have to take a couple of flights. The first one leaves in a few days so I'll need to get everything packed and—"

"Dad," Yasmina put her hand on his. "We've seen you pack. You're gonna need some help."

CHAPTER 100

New Year's Eve – Atlanta, USA

"Excuse me!" Jerry ran through the terminal, dodging between passengers moving at a snail's pace. Didn't they understand he had a plane to catch? "Watch out!" He sprinted along a travelator, pivoted around the corner to his boarding gate and—

DELAYED.

You have to be joking.

Last night he'd taken the red-eye out of S.F.O., and this 5:45 a.m. connecting flight in Atlanta direct to Rio was his one chance to make it to Ellie on time. If it didn't depart as scheduled, there'd be no romantic New Year's Eve rendezvous.

Jerry skirted around the feet of passengers seated at the gate and breathlessly greeted an attendant behind the desk. "My flight is meant to leave in ten minutes."

"We're sorry, Sir, but there's a snowstorm in New York and the plane has been delayed out of La Guardia."

Jerry's muscles clenched. "What time will it get here?"

"We're doing everything possible, Sir. Please have a seat and as soon as we know more we'll provide an update. Thank you for your patience."

Patience?!

For the next three hours, Jerry stalked the terminal like a lion caught in a cage. He browsed expensive watch shops and bought an overpriced aftershave, but after drinking his third coffee and checking the Departures screen a dozen times, he was ready to jump out of his skin. The idea of meeting Ellie was turning into a disaster.

New Year's Eve – Buenos Aires, Argentina

For once, Ellie was happy about standing in an airport line. Though security was as tedious as watching clothes dry, every step got her closer to her objective. She located the gate and logged onto free WiFi. Waiting for it to connect, she tried to contain her excitement about what might happen tonight.

Will we just talk? Kiss? Something else…?

It took a few seconds to internalize Jerry's message about his plane being delayed. Ellie's mood cratered reading it, just as his probably had writing it. Maybe her plan, so well thought-out, was doomed from the start.

CHAPTER 101

Atlanta, USA

Jerry almost slid out of his chair. The announcement over the p.a. system was what he'd been praying to hear for the last four hours. He jumped up and checked a screen— BOARDING.

About damn time. He grabbed his jacket and hurried to join the hastily formed queue. While the attendant scanned boarding passes, Jerry calculated their likely time of arrival.

It's now 10:05 a.m. By the time we get off the ground it'll be 10:40 a.m., more likely 10:45 a.m. The flight is scheduled to take ten hours, but the captain will try and make up time, so we could arrive at 8 p.m. Atlanta time, which would be…9 p.m. Rio time.

Immigration shouldn't take more than an hour, allow another hour for a taxi to the hotel and quick shower, which will put me on Copacabana Beach at 11 p.m. That's if nothing else goes wrong…

Jerry wiped his brow. It was going to be close.

Rio de Janeiro, Brazil

In contrast to Jerry's travel glitches, Ellie's plane landed on schedule. She'd tried not to spend the flight stressing about if he would make it, and her mood improved when she got his message that take-off was imminent. Maybe the gods were in their favor after all…

While waiting for her backpack to come around the carousel, Ellie tried to figure out what time he might arrive. Even if he landed at 9 p.m., there was only a slight chance he would get to their meeting point before midnight. For it to work, everything had to go *just right.*

But nothing on her trip—or in her life—had ever gone *just right.*

CHAPTER 102

Somewhere over the Caribbean

The cabin lights had been dimmed as the A340 cruised at 40,000 feet on its voyage south to Brazil. Most of the passengers were sleeping, but not Jerry. Jammed into a window seat, he studied his screen. The jet icon was moving at an excruciatingly slow speed across the map. Why hadn't the captain sped up?!

He blew on it a few times to see if that would help before realizing ordering another red wine probably wasn't a good idea. He took the safety card from the seat pocket and started reading it. If anything could send him to sleep, it was that.

Rio, Brazil

Ellie's stomach did flips in anticipation of finally meeting the man she loved. She commandeered one of the hostel bathrooms to prepare for whatever might happen in the night ahead. She knew what she *wanted* to happen, but her anxiety threatened to overwhelm any desire.

What if we don't get along? What if we aren't attracted to each other? What if he sees a pimple on my forehead and decides he's not interested?

Stop it, Ellie, he's not that shallow.

What if I see a pimple on his forehead and decide I'm not interested?

Ellie calmed her racing mind with music. George Michael's *Careless Whisper* did the trick while she undressed. She stared at her naked body in the mirror. It'd changed so much since leaving New York that it was hard to believe she was looking at the same person. Her face was noticeably thinner, and she'd lost so much weight off her hips that the bones stuck out like tiny antlers. Her breasts were smaller, not that they were ever big, and her arms had become wiry, but strong. She flexed her calves, sculpted from all that hiking, and—booyah, her butt was tighter too. Undeniably *peachy*.

Most of all, she loved how her eyes had more spark. More life.

Before leaving B.A., Ellie had taken care of the major aesthetic tasks: getting her hair cut, nails done, and buying a dress for tonight. Holding the ivory number up against her body, it was super cute, making her look like a 1970s Flower Power girl about to run through a field of daisies. She hadn't worried about looking good for anyone, including herself, for so long that it felt nice to do it again. First, though, her legs needed shaving. That beauty procedure she hadn't missed.

It better be worth the pain.

CHAPTER 103

In the air over Rio, Brazil

Jesus…

Jerry peered out the window as they cruised over the iconic Rio skyline. The mountains running down the city's spine were floodlit like a runway and the colossal statue of Christ the Redeemer, bathed in brilliant white, kept a watchful eye over the City of God.

The plane banked over the crescent-moon of Copacabana Beach, where the party was already in full swing. Jumbotrons, disco lights and lasers danced across the Atlantic Ocean. Jerry imagined Ellie below, heading to Forte de Copacabana where they'd agreed to meet. Damn, he wanted to jump out of the plane right now and parachute down to join her.

He checked his watch—9:05 p.m.

Ipanema

Ellie stepped out of her hostel and into pandemonium. Thousands of partygoers moved in every direction like ants who'd lost their way. In the heat and humidity, men were mostly shirtless and women wore only bikinis or sarongs. Everyone was liquored-up from the hawkers selling cheap beer and *cachaça*, the popular Brazilian alcohol mixed with sugar and lime to make *caipirinhas*. *Samba* music, the legendary sound of Rio, erupted from boomboxes locals carried on their shoulders like it was the '80s.

Ellie eased into the fray and began making her way toward Forte de Copacabana—and hopefully the best night of her life.

Rio International Airport

Jerry stood first. The seatbelt light was still on, but who the hell cared? Before landing he'd retrieved his jacket from the overhead locker, and now as the plane jerked to a stop he leaped over the passengers in his row and rushed down the aisle.

"Sit down, Sir!" a flight attendant yelled, but not even an armed Air Marshal could've stopped him.

Jerry made it to the front of the plane just as the door swung open. He didn't miss a step, jogging along the jet bridge and out of the gate. Moving as quickly as possible through the terminal without drawing the eye of heavily-armed security personnel, he arrived at immigration in record time.

"Oh, shit." Jerry's face fell.

The hall was packed with passengers like a fleet of A380s had landed. The next forty-seven minutes and twenty-three seconds were the cruelest form of suffering. Jerry dealt with it by looking at the time, watching a fly hit its head repeatedly on the ceiling, and convincing himself all the other queues were moving faster than the one he'd chosen. Someone seriously needed to rethink this ridiculous process.

Finally, a disinterested hand waved Jerry forward. The immigration officer, with a military buzz-cut and attitude to match, snatched his passport and examined it like he were a criminal.

Could you just hurry up?

Jerry felt sweat bead on his forehead and tried to brush it away without the officer noticing. A drop landed on the counter between them. They both looked at it. Jerry wiped it off and shrugged. "Hot. Very hot in here."

The officer stamped his passport and handed it back.

Hallelujah!

Golden ticket in hand, Jerry high-tailed it in the direction of baggage claim. By some stroke of good fortune, his suitcase was already circling the carousel and he didn't even have to break stride as he lifted it off and continued to customs.

The bored guard gestured for him to use the 'Nothing To Declare' exit, and Jerry began to think things were looking up. He hailed a cab, bundled his case into the backseat, and handed the driver his hotel's address.

"How long will it take?" Jerry asked as they pulled away from the curb.

"*O que?*" the driver replied in Portuguese.

"How long to my hotel?" He tapped his watch.

"*Uma hora.*" The driver held up one finger then pointed to the traffic ahead, clogging the highway into central Rio. "*Muito tráfego.*"

Jerry checked the time—10:20 p.m. He sank into the seat, unable to do anything again except wait.

Forte de Copacabana

He's going to make it.

Ellie touched her *Pachamama* necklace, hoping it would bring her luck. She'd been standing in this same spot for an hour. The ticketed event at the early-20th century fort situated on a narrow peninsular jutting out between Ipanema and Copacabana was reportedly *the best* place to view fireworks. The money shot.

From her vantage point on the roof, Ellie could see all the way along Copacabana Beach. Starting with the rusted cannons protruding out of the fort, to the cable cars running up Sugarloaf Mountain three miles in the distance. In between, *more than two million* revelers covered the wide stretch of sand, dancing, drinking, and running into the shallows to cool off. Above it all, Christ the Redeemer stood with arms outstretched, like a DJ in control of his club. This simmering mass of humanity had assembled to join the biggest party in the world and witness the greatest pyrotechnics show on earth.

He has to make it.

CHAPTER 104

Botafogo

The taxi hadn't budged for three minutes and Jerry was beginning to think it never would. Through the windscreen he could see only gridlock, hundreds of cars and people surging toward Copacabana. To be this close yet completely immobile was like being trapped in freshly poured concrete. He looked at his watch—11:15 p.m.

If we don't move soon, I won't make it.

Jerry opened the door and craned his neck to see the way ahead. Hopeless. He could be stuck at this intersection all night and well into next morning. He pulled out his phone and opened Google Maps. Just over a mile to his hotel.

My only chance is by foot.

He gave the driver a generous tip, grabbed his case—and ran.

Forte de Copacabana

The knots in Ellie's stomach had become unbearable. She'd already downed one extra-strong *caipirinha*, but it didn't put a dent in her nerves. A countdown clock on one of the jumbotrons ticked over to 11:30 p.m. and a cheer went up from the crowded beach, spreading through the steamy night.

Ellie looked through the partygoers at the fort for the hundredth time. No sign of Jerry. She tried to console herself with the idea that if he came late that would be OK, but surrounded by couples celebrating New Year's Eve together, the reality was that she didn't want to be alone at midnight. Not again.

He'll be here.

As sure as I know I love him, he will come.

Avenida Atlântica

Jerry ran out of the lobby of his hotel and onto the boulevard winding around Copacabana Beach. In record time, he'd brushed his teeth, thrown water on his face to look alive, and changed his shirt. Now—11:45 p.m.

Less than half-a-mile away, the bulky Forte de Copacabana projected out into the ocean. On any other night he might've been able to make it, but with a crowd this thick…it'd be all but impossible.

I have to try. Even if I'm five minutes late, I have to try!

He pushed into the throng.

CHAPTER 105

Forte de Copacabana

With each second that ticked down to midnight, Ellie's heart fell deeper into what felt like the bottomless cavern of her chest. She stood on her toes, searching for him again. Still nothing. Absolutely nothing.

Jerry, where are you?!

The jumbotron flashed 11:58 p.m.

Jerry showed his ticket at the fort entrance. Security patted him down and he ducked between partygoers. A loudspeaker announced midnight was just one minute away.

Where are you, Ellie?!

He reached the stairs to the roof and dashed up two-at-a-time. If his heart thumped any harder it would've burst out of his ribcage. Using his height, Jerry scanned the roof. Still no Ellie. No-one even resembl—

He froze.

To his left, not ten yards away, a petite blonde woman stood with her back to him. The breeze played with her ivory dress while she looked out over the ocean.

"Ellie?"

She recognized that voice. Tried to contain the emotions gushing up inside her like a geyser. Turned around.

"Jerry."

Ellie studied him a moment, connecting with his eyes and embracing his smile. Then he strode forward and drew her into an unexpected kiss. Ellie's senses exploded as their lips met. And as their tongues touched for the first time, months of expectation erupted into fire that coursed through her veins and produced a high so potent it lifted her off her feet.

Ellie heard the crowd around them applaud. She opened her eyes and realized it was for their kiss.

"I hope that was OK?" Jerry said.

"Yep," she replied, beaming from head-to-toe.

The jumbotrons on the beach began the countdown to midnight, which millions of voices echoed with deafening enthusiasm.

10

9

8 "How was your flight?"

7

6 "Could've been smoother."

5

4 "I'm glad you came."

3

2 "I'm glad I'm here."

1

Jerry took Ellie's hand and together they watched the fireworks explode over Copacabana Beach. First came the whistles as the rockets launched into the sky from barges, then the booms as they detonated in spectacular displays of color and light. There were fireworks in the shape of red hearts, spheres filled with glittering blue stars, and bursts of dazzling white which dropped like horsetails into the night.

His eyes flitted between the pyrotechnics in the sky, the party on the beach, and Ellie's face. He couldn't stop smiling. Inside, his mind was somersaulting.

She's really cute.
Shorter than I thought.
I hope she likes me.
My hand's getting sore.
Can I kiss her again?
I wonder if we'll have sex tonight.

Ellie smiled back at Jerry, unable to hide her excitement. Together they gasped as fireworks shaped like giant blue, green and yellow chrysanthemums—the national colors of Brazil—detonated across the ocean, leaving a trail of flames in their wake. There was no-one else she wanted to be here with.

He's really handsome.
Fricking tall.
I wonder if he likes me.
My hand's getting sore.
When the hell are we going to kiss again?
We better have sex tonight.

The fireworks reached their crescendo, the whole sky exploding. Ellie wrapped her arms around Jerry's neck and kissed him again. "Happy New Year."

"Happy New Year to you too," he replied.

The smoke cleared, everyone cheered, and music began thumping again.

"So," he raised his eyebrows. "What now?"

CHAPTER 106

Avenida Atlântica

Jerry and Ellie strolled along the boulevard, and he could sense a crackling tension in the tropical air between them. They sipped *caipirinhas* while the residents of Rio partied all around. Drum troupes bashed out beats, performers in feathered costumes danced along the street, and bonfires raged on the sand.

"It's hard to believe I'm here," he said. "It feels like a dream."

"I have that feeling every time I arrive in a new place. So... welcome to my dream."

"Are they always this surreal?"

"Usually," Ellie smiled, her cheeks flushed.

Jerry took a tense sip. "Just so you know, this...us...it's strange for me."

"Me too." She nudged him playfully.

"So where are you staying?"

"In some sketchy hostel. About thirty minutes' walk from here."

"In a dorm?"

Ellie nodded. "It's all I can afford, and the prices are absurdly inflated anyway. What did you find at the last minute?"

"Well, I got lucky when someone cancelled at the Copacabana Palace Hotel."

"*The* Copacabana Palace Hotel?" She stopped walking. "Where all the rich and famous people go?"

"That's the one," Jerry laughed. "It's just up here."

"Marilyn Monroe stayed there. Brigitte Bardot. Princess Diana."

"And now me. It's a bit of a step down for them, I'll admit."

"Wow, it must be super expensive."

"Yeah, I might have splurged a little..." Jerry couldn't hide his lopsided grin. "But there wasn't anything else available on the beach, so I figured why the heck not?"

They walked in silence for a while. He couldn't decide whether Ellie was thinking the same thing.

"Jerry, do you want me to—"

"Yes."

Copacabana Palace Hotel

Ellie slipped out of her dress and hung it over a chair. The light in the bedroom was off, but moonlight bounced in from the ocean and through the balcony windows. The moment was more magical than she could've imagined.

Is this really happening?

She took a condom from her purse and turned around. Jerry had pulled off his shoes and stood nervously in front of the king-size bed. Ellie approached him with confidence.

Yep, this is happening.

One tantalizing button at a time, she undid Jerry's shirt, firing her desire with every touch of his skin. She slid it off and ran her hands over his shoulders. Smooth and broad. A tremor ran down his arms and Ellie looked into his eyes for a sign she should stop. He nodded for her to continue.

Ellie unbuckled Jerry's belt and pulled down the zipper on his pants, dropping them to the floor. She felt him. He was already hard, and Ellie wondered if they would fit together. She tore open the condom and slid it gently over him. She met his gaze and he smiled.

This is right.

With firm hands, Jerry grabbed Ellie's butt and lifted her up. They kissed passionately. Inside her, a blaze roared. He swung her around to the bed and lay her down. Maneuvered on top and kissed her again, moving down her neck to her breasts. Bold in his actions now. Ellie liked that.

She arched her back and unclasped her bra. He slid it off and tossed it away. Teased her nipples with his tongue. They were so hard Ellie thought they would explode. He sucked them and she exhaled a moan to let him know he was heading in the right direction.

Jerry moved past her belly-button to her thighs. Kissing them tenderly. Caressing her panties. They were already soaked through. She lifted her hips and Jerry pulled them off. He licked her, and her pelvis bucked. He licked her again, and she gave into her desires, moaning over and over, enjoying every moment of this ecstasy.

Jerry climbed on top and they locked eyes. Ellie's hunger was so strong, nothing could stop them joining. She slowly let him enter. They both drew breath at the sensation. She felt his heat inside her body. It took a moment for them to fit together, given he was six-foot-four and she was five-foot-eight, but she gradually shaped around him.

"Are you OK?" he whispered.

"Yes…"

The sex was slow at first, like gentle waves flowing back and forth, before they found their rhythm. As she learned more about Jerry's body, and desires, they sped up until they were moving in synch like a piston engine.

Jerry thrusted into Ellie's hips. Her nipples rubbed against him. She wrapped her arms around his neck, clutching his back. Ellie loved how Jerry panted with each push, the smell of his hair, and how his sweat tasted like honey.

She moved and felt pleasure without shame. A pleasure so intense she didn't want it to end. Her entire body was on fire. Every touch, every sound. Passion, unbridled. Ellie was sure sex had *never* been this good.

They rolled over and Ellie sat on top of him. She rocked her hips back and forth. Leaned forward to kiss him. Her hair fell across Jerry's face, each strand striking him like electricity. He gripped her hips and moved deeper into her, gasping for air.

Ellie bit her lip, closed her eyes, and threw her head to the ceiling as they climaxed.

She lay snug next to Jerry in the darkness, toying with the hair on his chest. His arm cradled her close. After so much anticipation, the release of tension had brought her serenity.

"Jerry…it's an unusual name. Where does it come from?" Ellie asked.

"That's an embarrasing story. I'm not sure you want to hear it."

"Try me."

"Do you know that song from the '70s, *Joy to the World*?"

"You're the bullfrog!"

"Unfortunately."

Ellie erupted into a belly laugh. "Oh, yeah, that's embarrassing."

"What can I say? My parents were hippies."

"It's hilarious, Jeremiah Townsend." She pecked him on the cheek, then placed her head on his chest and listened to the soothing beat of his heart.

"You're an extraordinary woman," he said after a while.

"How so? I mean, I know it, but I'd like to hear it from you."

"Well, because most people only dream about all the things you've done. You came down here, a female traveling solo in a *machismo* culture. It takes a lot of courage."

"It didn't always go my way."

"But you never quit and ran home. You stuck it out. And then you invited me to Rio and seduced me against my better judgement."

"Oh, so you didn't want to be seduced?"

"Maybe," he grinned.

How easy was it to love that grin? "I think you're pretty amazing too. Raising three girls on your own after everything you've been through. Not many men could deal with that."

"I just do what I have to. And you learn to cope." He shifted so they lay facing each other. "Tell me, what did you learn on your trip?"

"Most people just ask what place I liked best."

"That would be too easy."

Ellie twisted her lip. "I learned that I need to be more thankful for what I have. Definitely more tolerant of other people. And also that if I challenge myself I can do things I never thought possible, like learning another language, trekking up mountains, sleeping in dorms…"

"How's that dorm thing going for you, by the way?"

"Let's just say I'm enjoying your hospitality." Ellie cast her eyes around the luxurious bedroom. "But the most important thing I learned is that you should do whatever makes you happy, every day of your life."

"Great advice. So would it make you happy to…?"

"Can you? I mean, let's face it, you're not twenty-one anymore."

"We can only try," Jerry laughed. He rolled on top and kissed her again.

"For the record," Ellie whispered. "Let's keep trying."

CHAPTER 107

New Year's Day – Rio, Brazil

The sun rose high in the sky, but Jerry still slept, half-wrapped in the messy sheets of last night's marathon. He heard the door shut and stirred. Ellie came over to the bed with a tray of fresh fruit, pastries and coffee. She looked even more beautiful today.

"Good afternoon, sleepy-head. I took the liberty of ordering room service. On your tab, of course."

"That's the best idea I've heard all day." Jerry sat up and reached for his watch, but Ellie put out a hand to stop him.

"Time isn't important right now. Be Latin for a bit, will you?" She poured them both a cup of coffee. "To us."

"To us," Jerry toasted. "I think we did all right last night."

"More than all right," Ellie laughed. "But if we keep up this pace we're gonna need more condoms."

"I have some. I had hours to kill in the airport and nothing to do except think about making love to you."

"So who seduced who then?"

"Good question."

Ellie stuffed a croissant in her mouth and patted him on the knee. "First, I have to call my sister. She's sent ten messages and threatened to call the Embassy in the last one. She thinks you're a serial killer."

"Sorry to disappoint. I better call my kids too, though I'm pretty sure they're enjoying life without me."

Ellie took her phone and headed onto the balcony.

"You're alive," Donna said flatly, stacking the dishwasher with champagne glasses.

"Alive and well. Happy New Year!"

"You want to tell me about it?"

"Not really."

"How was the sex?"

"No comment," Ellie stifled a laugh.

"That good, huh. So you're OK?"

Ellie looked through the window at Jerry, hair a mess and goofy grin on his face. "That would be an understatement."

"What did the girls get up to?" Jerry asked.

"They ate pizza and sang karaoke," Carol said. "Andrea and Mia were asleep by ten so Yasmina and I watched a movie. It was a fun girls' night."

"I appreciate you looking after them, Mom."

"Don't mention it. Wait, here they come."

"Hi Dad!" his daughters sang.

"How are you all?"

"There were fireworks on TV from...where was it? Ri-o-de-Jan-eir-o," Mia said. "Did you see them?"

"I did, honey." Jerry looked through the window at Ellie, bathed in sunshine on the balcony. "It was incredible."

After brunch, Jerry showered while Ellie collected her backpack from her hostel. He buttoned up a fresh shirt and watched her unpack in the walk-in robe, visibly excited about being able to hang up her clothes.

"It's nice to have a home," Ellie explained. "Even a temporary one."

"Can I ask you something?" Jerry said. "Do you mind if I see Bella's guidebook? Your guidebook."

"Of course." She dug the *Unique Planet* out of her daypack and passed it to him. "I'm afraid it's a little the worse for wear."

"That's OK. I just want to… I'm not sure what I want to do, just hold it." Jerry sat in an armchair and thumbed through the pages. Bella's sketches and handwriting jumped out at him, bringing back memories—wonderful and painful—from their trip. He ran his fingers over words she had written next to a passage about the life of Evita: 'Dark is always followed by dawn. You will see light again.' She was right, as always.

He flipped the page and noticed a different handwriting. "You've added to it."

Ellie turned to him. "I hope that's OK. I figured it's the least I could do, to continue what Bella started."

Jerry smiled. Could Ellie be any more perfect?

CHAPTER 108

Rio, Brazil

Over the next three days, Ellie spent every possible moment by Jerry's side. They walked hand-in-hand past the Art Deco buildings hugging Copacabana Beach, climbed the colorful Lapa Steps where Snoop Dogg filmed *Beautiful,* and took a tramrail up to the city's most cinematic statement, Christ the Redeemer.

From the base of the 124-foot high statue of Jesus, they had a panoramic view of Rio, including the historic Maracanã Stadium where World Cups and Olympics had taken center stage. Ellie asked someone to snap a photo of her and Jerry—their first photo together. They made a cute couple, obviously.

She also organized a guide to take them into the Rocinha *favela.* Exploring the alleyways that crisscrossed like spaghetti between the cramped houses, Ellie enjoyed being able to include Jerry in one of her off-the-tourist-trail adventures. He was fascinated and couldn't stop asking questions about the haphazard constructions. Painted in vivid colors and built on the cliffs of the mountains dividing Rio's social classes, the poorest residents of the City of God had the million-dollar views!

An afternoon on the golden sand of Ipanema Beach was exactly what they needed to chillax after sightseeing. Here, Brazil's rich and beautiful came to parade for each other's viewing pleasure. Ellie and Jerry watched glistening men and G-stringed women emerge from under sun umbrellas to splash in the shallows and play *futevôlei*, an athletic mix of football and volleyball.

Ellie loved that Jerry was more interested in her body than anyone else's. She appreciated his too, tall and strong, with love handles so adorable they begged to be squeezed.

"You have beautiful shoulders," Jerry said, rubbing sunscreen on Ellie's back.

"You told me about your shoulder fetish before. I'm glad it's still alive and kicking."

"Only for special people."

Ellie held back tears of joy. After traveling alone for so long, it felt wonderful to have a connection with someone she cared about deeply, and who looked at her with the same longing. So they peppered their outside adventures with frequent inside activities, including an unforgettable oral lovemaking session in the shower. Best of all time, for sure.

One evening, Ellie and Jerry caught a cable car up Sugarloaf Mountain, named because its rounded vertical edges resembled a loaf of bread. It made Ellie hungry. They watched sunset over the Atlantic Ocean and stayed into the evening to see Rio's lights flicker on.

"This is quite a view," she exhaled.

"Ellie, I need to say something."

"OK…"

Jerry faced her. "I need you to know that a part of me will always love Bella. We were together for twenty years, she gave me my daughters, and she will forever be a part of my family."

"I don't want you to forget her, Jerry. She was your first love, and will always be the mother of your girls. I know the place she has in your heart and your family."

"Thank you. For understanding."

"Maybe we should thank Bella for bringing us together."

"Do you believe that?"

Ellie looked over the sparkling city. "The logical part of my brain says 'no.' But my trip has shown me that life is often strange and mysterious. I mean, the string of coincidences is long. I had my iPad stolen so needed a map, then I found Bella's guidebook because it miraculously made its way to Caracas thanks to…God knows who or what or how, I happened to open it one night and see Bella's message, then I decided to email her."

"And I decided to reply."

"Exactly. And my message could just as easily have ended up in your junk mail, never to be seen."

"And we wouldn't be here together, five months later. It's a one in a million."

"A billion."

"So do you think it's all just a coincidence? Or something more?"

"Jerry, you once told me that fate, or life, or the universe, or whatever you want to call it—maybe just sheer coincidence—presents us with opportunities, but it's up to us to take hold of them. We'll never know for sure whether fate exists, but we have to make a decision, take a chance, or we'll never get what we want. I mean, look at us, we're living proof that it's worth the risk, right?"

He kissed her and held it. "Ellie, sometimes you make too much sense."

"It's tough being this smart. A real burden."

They giggled like teenagers.

Meanwhile, the marmosets had come out to play. Ellie marvelled at the tiny monkeys, less than eight inches high, chasing each other through the trees. The wind picked up, scattering them into the shadows again.

"Do you remember when you called me after your winery tour?" Jerry said.

"How could I forget? One of the most embarrassing nights of my life."

"You were pretty drunk."

"Pretty drunk or pretty and drunk?"

"Both," he laughed.

"I got the feeling I said more than you let on. Do I get to know how I humiliated myself?"

"You didn't humiliate yourself, Ellie. You said that you liked me."

"And did you respond?"

"Well, you passed out before I could."

She folded her arms. "Thanks for reminding me."

"But after you passed out, I said that I liked you too."

Ellie stared into Jerry's eyes, searching for an answer to the question she desperately wanted to ask. Her heart pounded so hard her whole body shook. "I don't just like you, Jerry. I love you."

The second it took for him to respond seemed like an eternity.

"I love you too, Ellie. With all my heart."

Filled with the incomparable euphoria of loving someone and being loved in return, Ellie held Jerry tight. Her head cradled into his chest, and the rest of the world disappeared. She *thought* she'd been in love before, but this was like turning those feelings up to infinity. Then doubling it. And doubling it again. Ellie never wanted to leave his arms.

CHAPTER 109

Iguazu Falls, Brazil & Argentina

"This was quite a spontaneous idea coming from the Queen of Planning." Jerry walked behind Ellie on a wooden pathway through the jungle. Even with his long legs, he struggled to keep up.

"You'll be surprised to hear I've stopped writing my lists."

"How's that going?"

Ellie just smiled back. It'd been her suggestion to get out of the city, hopping a short flight to the border with Argentina to see one of the greatest wonders of the natural world. Jerry didn't need any convincing.

His first glimpse came when they emerged from the jungle trail. Before them lay a sweeping view of the 275 separate waterfalls making up Iguazu Falls. Over 50,000 cubic feet of water flowed over the cliffs every second, giving the impression of a massive, animated, curtain. There was so much spray no less than three rainbows arced above, overdosing the sky with color.

Jerry helped Ellie onto a raised walkway spanning the river that fed the falls. Every step of their shoes reverberated on the rusted metal. Below, torrents of water raged. Then he couldn't hear their footsteps anymore. The only sound was the roar of

Garganta del Diablo—The Devil's Throat. Up ahead, the end of the walkway hung precariously over the largest waterfall, the point at which thousands of gallons of water plummeted over the edge and smashed onto the rocks below.

Jerry and Ellie slowed as they approached the threshold. A storm of wind lashed against them, pushing their bodies back. Spray flew up from the waterfall's face and soaked their clothes. He gripped the railing and pulled Ellie to the extreme end of the walkway, deep inside the Devil's Throat.

"Oh my God!" Ellie shouted. The water was so loud Jerry had to read her lips.

"It's unbelievable!" He held her hand in the middle of this super-natural force.

Iguazu Falls had meant to be the next stop on his family's itinerary, before Bella fell ill and they'd returned home early. He felt a wrench of sadness that she'd never had the chance to witness this sight. She would've loved it.

Now though, in some inexplicable way, Bella had brought him here—and presented him with a new love.

Rio, Brazil

Ellie didn't want to say it, and suspected Jerry had been avoiding it all week too. But the time had come to accept that today would be their last together. They ate breakfast on the balcony overlooking Copacabana Beach, then fell back into bed to satisfy their other appetites. Now she lay facing him for perhaps the final time.

"I don't want this to be a love affair that just peters out to nothing," Jerry said, tucking a loose strand of hair behind Ellie's ear. "Or worse, ends in an argument and we never talk again."

"Me neither."

"But how does this work? You and me? I've turned it over

again and again in my head, and I still don't have an answer."

"I've thought about a lot it too." Ellie stroked the stubble on his chin.

"I can't leave my kids. Or my business."

"I know. And I need to decide what to do next with my life."

"What are you thinking?"

"Teaching, or something like it. Getting out of the bubble of the U.S.A. has shown me I'm more than just a citizen of my own country, I'm a citizen of the world. And helping people less fortunate is what really makes me feel fulfilled. I want to leave the world in a better state than before I arrived, and sitting behind a desk on the twelfth story of an office building isn't going to do that."

"There's a lot of not-for-profits in San Francisco. The weather is better than New York, and there's less rats too."

"You're working hard to convince me, aren't you?" she smiled.

Jerry sat up and took both her hands. "Ellie, I've only loved two women in my life. And I'll be damned if I'm going to lose another one."

Butterflies flapped around her stomach, hitting her insides. She sat up beside him. "Y'know, I had an epiphany way back when in Colombia. I'd been on the road for three or four weeks and already experienced the revolving door of backpacking friends. Our paths would meet, run parallel for a few days, or even just a few hours, then we'd go our separate ways again. It helped me understand that everyone is on their own journey, on billions of different paths. So when I visualize it like that, I know in my heart, my very soul, that I want my path to run parallel with your path for more than just a week in Rio. I want it for the rest of my life, Jerry. Because I love you. Because that's what life is about. That's why we're on the planet. Everything else is just noise."

Tears fell out of Jerry's eyes, and Ellie's answered in kind.

"So although I'm not yet sure *how* we make it work, I know the *why*—because for us, for our love, we have to try."

"So fly back with me tonight," he said.

"I'd be lying if I said I hadn't thought about it."

"Then come. And we'll figure out the rest when you're there."

Ellie squeezed Jerry's fingers. "I want to. You know I do. But…" She took a breath. "First I need to finish my journey. I promised myself that. There's still a few places I have to go. Things to see and learn."

He smiled. "I should've known you would say that."

"Are you disappointed?"

"It's one of the reasons I fell in love with you."

Ellie and Jerry made an odd pair as they walked out of the elevator and through the lobby of the Copacabana Palace Hotel. He wore a shirt and pants and carried a suitcase, she had on a singlet and shorts and backpack. Ellie took a last look around at the marble and polished brass extravagance.

On the steps outside, they bid farewell with a kiss and hug Ellie didn't want to break. "Message me when you get home," she said.

"Message me when you get to wherever it is you're going," Jerry replied. "I love you."

"I love you too."

A horn beeped and Ellie wrenched herself away, climbing into the first of two taxis that'd arrived to collect them. Together the cabs swept along the horseshoe driveway toward Avenida Atlântica. Then Ellie's turned left and Jerry's turned right, heading in opposite directions to different destinations. When would she see him again?

CHAPTER 110

Jericoacoara, Brazil

For the next month, Ellie returned to dorm life. To say it was challenging after the 6-star luxury of Jerry's hotel would be putting it mildly.

In Belo Horizonte she visited the work of legendary Brazilian architect Oscar Niemeyer, including the modernist Church of Saint Francis of Assisi. Niemeyer was one of Jerry's favorite designers and his pioneering use of free-flowing curves had been incorporated into the Pata Museum. She snapped lots of pics to send, including some silly selfies.

A flight up to Salvador on the central coast introduced Ellie to an entirely different culture. Afro-Brazilians, descendants of slaves, filled the streets with booming percussion and gravity-defying *capoeira* dancing. In a *candomblé* temple, Ellie observed the unique blend of West African, Roman Catholic, and indigenous religions as local women invoked spirits to enter a trance, swaying until the early hours of the morning. Just like love made you feel.

Yet there was a gap in Ellie's heart. The notorious 'loneliness of the solo traveler' had hit her hard and she yearned for Jerry to share these experiences.

Dearest Jerry,
The internet is terrible so fingers crossed this email gets through. It's a miracle there's internet at all in Jericoacoara because there's no roads in or out. Getting here took an hour in a buggy through the desert. It's awesome though, nothing to do but relax and swim in the lagoons between the dunes. That rhymes, ha!
You won't be surprised to hear that I've continued my food and drink tour of northern Brazil. And may have put on a few pounds... Last night I tried moqueca, a delicious fish stew with tomatoes, coriander and cassava. I'm missing you like mad and wishing you could do all these things with me. And more ☺
Now I'm going to climb the biggest dune and watch sunset over the Atlantic. Apparently there's a guy at the top who makes caipirinhas. I'll have one for you! I hope you are well and everything's on schedule for the opening. Lots of love and hugs and kisses,
Ellie.
PS It's weird to be in Jeri without Jerry. Yes, I'm sooooooo funny...

San Francisco, USA

The weeks after Jerry came home were the busiest on the Pata Museum since breaking ground. With the external structure finished, the crane had been dismantled and work ramped-up on landscaping the terraces to his exacting standards. Inside the fit-out of exhibition spaces continued as the first priceless artefacts were moved into the ground floor of the West Wing, housing mummies from the Chinchorro civilization of Chile.

We'll be ready for opening day, come hell or high water.

With workers rotating through a six-day schedule, Jerry stayed on-site to ensure everything ran smoothly. Or as smoothly as possible given the absurdly complex logistics. By his side every step of the way, Kyra liaised with contractors with her usual bravado, and grilled him about what'd happened in Rio.

"But she stayed in your room?" she said.

"I told you I'm not talking about it, Kyra."

"So you at least kissed? At a minimum."

He couldn't stop a grin spreading from ear-to-ear. Every. Single. Time.

The only breaks Jerry allowed himself were to make it home for dinner with his daughters. They'd also quizzed him about Ellie. He enjoyed telling them about her travels and emphasized how courageous she was to do it alone. As much as he wanted to protect his girls *forever*, he hoped they'd be inspired to one day embark on their own adventure. Bella would've wanted that for them too.

Every time his phone rang, Jerry prayed it was Ellie calling to say she was safe and loved him. Her voice on the other end of a bad line filled him with the strength to get through the long hours. Without it...well, he couldn't imagine life without it.

On the plane back to San Francisco, Jerry's brain had done loops thinking about what might happen next. He still didn't know Ellie's plans after Brazil—because she didn't know them either. It burned a hole in his heart.

My dear Ellie,
Jeri sounds wonderful! There's nothing quite like finding a unique place. Or person. I wish I could be in that lagoon with you, though I expect we'd do more than just relax. I have a few things in mind ☺
It's hard to believe, but the museum is opening in just

one week. OMG, as my kids would say! I can't wait for you to see it. The invitations have gone out, and the Governor is coming, so it'll be 18-hour days to make sure we're finished. You may have put on some pounds, but I've aged 10 years…

Please try not to fall down another sand dune, and call me when you can. Safe travels and much love,

Jerry.

CHAPTER 111

Belem, Brazil

Arriving at the docks before dawn, Ellie found the wooden boat squeezed between a row of rusty cargo ships. Her ticket allowed just enough space on the middle deck to tie up the hammock she'd bought from a market.

Unfortunately, Ellie's knot skills weren't exactly Popeye-level and her first attempt at fixing it to the rafters failed. The chain-smoking captain took pity and showed her how to secure it so she wouldn't crash to the floor in the middle of the night.

The other passengers eyed Ellie like a novelty but offered friendly nods. She was the only non-indigenous person taking the week-long passage to their traditional lands in the middle of the Amazon Rainforest. The final leg of her epic adventure.

Each morning Ellie climbed to the top deck to watch sunrise, drink sweet tea, and eat the dry cake that passed for breakfast. For dinner, the kitchen cooked simple meals like chicken and rice which were tasty but not hygienic.

Then again, not much was on the boat. The toilets, if they could be called that, were just a hole in the deck. And showers were a bucket dipped into the Amazon's muddy waters. One morning, Ellie unwittingly poured a frog over her head.

But she'd been hardened by her travels, and not much phased her anymore. It was easy to be proud of how far she'd grown out of her O.C.D. life. Stepping outside your box will inevitably do that to you.

Ellie passed hours rocking in her hammock, reading a book and watching the jungle float by. Yellow-headed caracaras flew out of the canopy and troops of squirrel monkeys swung through the trees on their noodle arms. All around rang the thriving, unceasing, symphony of the rainforest she'd come to love.

Eventually, she would slip into a *siesta*. It gave her time to think. About what to do next, and Jerry of course. She was relieved they felt the same way and had fulfilled their urges in Rio. Her gamble had paid off, for the first time. But Ellie also knew that before this boat reached its destination, she needed to make another decision that would shape the rest of her life.

On the final afternoon they stopped at a small village to drop off supplies. Ellie watched a group of children swimming in the tributary, a creature bobbing between their brown limbs. She moved to the stern for a better look.

A pink dolphin!

Though it had a melon-shaped head and mermaid tail, its smiling snout made it look like a human. Other snouts broke the surface. The pod had come to play.

Ellie stripped to her underwear and dove off the boat. Soon she was surrounded by the famous pink dolphins of the Amazon, nudging her with their flippers and swimming between her legs. A life highlight on a journey overflowing with life highlights.

Imagine if she'd just stayed home.

San Francisco, USA

The past two see-sawing years had led to this moment. The ceiling lights were off and the most valuable gold artefacts li up in their display cases. Like a cathedral at midnight, all Jerry could hear was the sound of his footsteps on the polished floors as he walked alone through the Pata Museum.

He checked everything was ready for tomorrow's opening: patches of painting finished, signposts erected, and glass streak-free. It had to be perfect.

Heading along the hallway from the East Wing, which housed zoomorphic figurines from the Mayan civilization of Mexico, Jerry reached the vast entrance hall. At its center stood a fourteen-foot high stone totem from the Tiwanaku culture of Bolivia, welcoming visitors to the museum.

Rising beside it were the two floating staircases which spiraled up as if by magic and split in opposite directions at the second level. Inspired by staircases built by the Incas, these had caused an engineering migraine to design to modern specifications. But they were Bella's idea, so Jerry insisted they get it right.

"She would've loved 'em." Harry came through the front doors.

"I hope so."

"It's a damn work of art, Jerry."

They admired the product of their hard labor.

"I'm sorry I was such a pain in the ass," Jerry said.

"No, you're not."

He laughed. "No, I'm not. We all good out there?"

"The marquee is up, ready for the big-wigs. There's only one thing left to do."

"What's that?"

"Grab a beer."

"Absolutely." Jerry slapped Harry on the back and they headed outside.

CHAPTER 112

8th February – San Francisco, USA

"On this, the anniversary of my husband's passing, I would like to thank everyone who labored so tirelessly to bring his dream to fruition." Mrs. Flores stood at a lectern on the front steps of the museum. The sun gleamed off every surface and a nervous breeze ruffled columns of balloons.

It doesn't seem real.

Jerry sat under a large marquee with his parents and daughters, who'd convinced him they needed new dresses for the occasion. Harry, Kyra, Brandon, Kevin and Jerry's other team members were sprinkled throughout the V.I.P. crowd.

"To promote Latin American culture through a dedicated museum on the West Coast is a great step forward in helping us understand each other," Mrs. Flores continued. "Although we may come from different places and speak different languages, we share a mutual history—human history—that we can all learn from. In fact, I am told school groups will be visiting the museum from next week."

Everyone applauded, though Jerry was slow to react. When would this out-of-body experience end?

"Finally, I would like to express my utmost appreciation to

Mr. Townsend, who has been the engine of this project from conception to birth. Mr. Townsend and his wife, Bella, designed every detail of the magnificent building behind me, and for that I will be eternally grateful. I am sure Bella is looking down—and very proud."

Carol squeezed her son's hand. Jerry tried not to let his emotions spill out.

"Without further ado, I declare the Pata Museum of San Francisco—open!" The crowd cheered as Mrs. Flores cut the red ribbon hanging across the entrance.

In the few seconds it took the ribbon to fall to the ground, Jerry felt time slow to a crawl. He exhaled and closed his eyes. His job was done.

Oh Bella, I wish you could see it.

Don and Carol walked through sliding doors, from the interior of the museum outside onto the top terrace. Jerry and his daughters were close behind, Mia in her dad's arms.

Stepped below them were the four other terrace levels, covered in grass and dotted with sculptures. The master stonework Jerry had fought so hard to protect wrapped around the terraces like a tight-fitting belt, each stone cut and placed with expert precision. At the base of the museum, V.I.P.s mingled while sipping champagne and surrounded by gardens sprouting orchids, heliconias and bromeliads native to South America.

Jerry put Mia down and she cartwheeled across the grass. He looked at all the different elements and couldn't help but puff out his chest. A bird flew overhead and perched in a newly-planted tree. The museum was coming alive.

"It's damn impressive," Don said, joining Carol on one of the benches.

"Thanks, Dad."

"I think Mom would've loved it," Andrea added.

"I hope so, honey." Jerry put an arm around her. "This place is part of you too." His phone beeped and he checked it. "Hey kids, I've got a surprise for you."

"I love surprises!" Mia ran up to him. "What is it?"

"C'mon, let's go look."

The girls followed Jerry to a set of stone steps at the end of the terrace. Climbing the last few was Danielle, the ranger from the San Francisco Zoo who'd taken Jerry and Yasmina into the penguin clinic. She led up two adult llamas and a baby that looked as fluffy as a new-born chick.

Mia squealed. "Can I touch it?"

"You sure can," Danielle said. "They like it when you stroke their neck."

"This is awesome." Yasmina took a selfie.

"Real llamas, Dad?" Andrea said.

"They'll cut the grass, just like at Machu Picchu."

"And keep it fertilized," Danielle added.

"What are their names?"

"This is Sebastián, and this is Valentina. But we haven't named the baby girl yet. Your dad thought you might want to do that."

"Seriously?" Mia jumped up-and-down.

"Make sure you choose a good one," Jerry said.

Yasmina pulled Andrea and Mia into a huddle. They chatted briefly before nodding in agreement. "We want to call her Bella," she announced.

Jerry smiled and pulled his children into a hug.

CHAPTER 113

Manaus, Brazil

Ellie packed her backpack for the last time. It was dirty and scuffed from being thrown around planes, buses, boats, hostel floors and everything in between, yet despite its appearance the material seemed to have grown stronger. Like a thick skin.

Although she'd become a packing expert, this time there was an empty feeling about the process. Her South American odyssey had come to an end. Ellie zipped it up, fastened the lock, and stood it next to her bunk.

She sat cross-legged on the bed and picked up her *Unique Planet*. Flipping through its pages, memories flooded her head. From her first hostel experience in Caracas, when she wasn't sure whether she would survive the night—or the bathroom, to her emotional trek up Mount Roraima with Javier, Hannah and Eric, to conquering her mortal fear of heights. It felt like a lifetime ago.

One page reminded her of the coffee plantation in Jardín, where the women shared their food and drink when they had nothing compared to Ellie's blessed upbringing. The lottery of birth and life. Then she'd joined the Top Secret mission with Donté into Pablo Escobar's bombed-out mansion. Put that on a list of things that couldn't be experienced through a screen.

There were difficult memories too, like the betrayal by Eduardo in the Galápagos. But Ellie preferred to focus on all the creatures she'd shared the ocean with—turtles, rays, sea-lions and the incomparable hammerhead sharks.

Next came her Indiana Ellie exploration of Peru with the pregnant Belgians, Eva and Dom. She wondered how they were dealing with the upcoming birth of their baby. From the dreamlike oasis of Huacachina to reaching Machu Picchu, there were a million reminders of her bond to nature and humanity

I left to see the world, and in return the world helped me see.

Other pages brought back intimate moments, such as the homeless girl who inspired Ellie to volunteer in the Sacred Valley She sighed at how much she missed her students, and hoped they were growing up happy and practicing their English. Teaching helping other people, had given her a sense of meaning in life she'd never felt before.

More memories rushed forward. Hiking into the Amazon Rainforest with Saywa and participating in an *ayahuasca* ceremony that showed her the birth of the universe. And the power of her own mind.

Just as fascinating as the places, were the colorful character Ellie had met along the way. People like Alfonse, the hippie guide at Kuelap with his madcap conspiracy theories, and William the one-legged widower, walking the Inca Trail for his late-wife

Then in the desert of northern Chile she'd met Merry. Dea Merry. The gregarious woman from Yorkshire showed Ellie how to live life—by grabbing it by the balls and swinging it above your head.

It'd been Merry who urged her to take a chance on love. To take a chance with Jerry. How could she ever thank her for that Ellie and Merry's rollicking good time was followed by the tragic earthquake, and Ellie's escape from civilization to the tranquility of hiking solo through Patagonia.

The cycle of life continued to turn, and heartbreak gave way to elation when Jerry said 'yes' and joined her for New Year's Eve in Rio. Love, that most necessary thing, had arrived to wrap its arms around her.

What would my parents think of everything I've done? I want to tell you all about it, Mom and Dad. I miss you so much.

There was no doubt Ellie had lived more during this wild adventure than her whole life. Why were other people so afraid to do the same? Work until you're sixty-five and then—if still breathing—go see the world? Screw that. The system was upside down.

Now, as she flicked back through the pages of her *Unique Planet*, she could see how everything on her trip connected. How one decision led to another, how one experience led to another, how one action built her confidence to try something new, how everything she'd done led her to this point.

Ellie's heart swelled at the accomplishment of achieving her dream, and the way she'd grown through all her challenges. The love and belief in herself to fight for what she wanted was alone worth it. She was Ellie Bartlett 2.0, with knowledge and wisdom and maturity beyond what she could possibly have gained if she hadn't smashed out of her comfort zone. Life could be so fucking amazing when you didn't give up.

Ellie flipped to the inside cover. Beneath the heading THIS BOOK BELONGS TO, and under Bella's name and note, she wrote:

Ellie Bartlett
elliebtraveling@gmail.com
Fellow explorer, enjoy your adventures in life and love.
Let the wind catch your sails—and be bold!

Backpack on her shoulders and daypack across her front, Ellie left the dorm and walked into the common area of the hostel. She approached a shelf marked BOOK EXCHANGE and placed her guidebook on top. Her hand lingered on it for a moment…then she let go.

Somewhere over the USA

"Cabin crew, prepare for landing," the captain buzzed over the plane's p.a. system.

Ellie pulled out her plastic earphones, wrapped them in a ball and tucked them into the seat pocket. Then she squeezed out the last of her hand sanitizer, wondering if it was a sign not to buy any more.

Pressing her face to the window, Ellie looked at the country of her birth spreading out below. She hadn't seen it in six months, and the thought of stepping back onto its soil brought a wistful smile to her face.

Home.

The thought was so appealing. But where was home now? For the short term at least, here. She'd decided that much. But in the long term, Ellie wasn't sure where she would plant roots and make a new life. Maybe she'd be a nomad, traveling the world, continually searching for her next great adventure. She'd always wanted to visit the pyramids of Egypt, and track the wild gorillas of Uganda…

There were so many questions, yet unanswered. And for the first time in her life, she liked it.

Ellie stood behind the automatic doors leading from baggage claim to the terminal. This was it.

Home.

She took a deep breath and strode toward the doors. They

plit open and she walked the length of the barrier separating
newly-arrived passengers from their families and friends. She
scanned the crowd, looking for a familiar face. There he was.

Jerry.

He held Mia's hand and on either side of him stood Yasmina
and Andrea. The three girls stared curiously at Ellie, as if she
were familiar but not yet known.

Ellie's face blossomed into a smile and her eyes filled with tears.

Mia ran forward and handed her a paper flower. "I made
this for you."

"Thank you, it's beautiful. You must be Mia."

"And I'm Yasmina. Dad didn't want us to come but we'd
heard so much about you that we insisted."

"Hi, I'm Andrea."

"It's nice to meet you all. I've heard a lot about you too."

Ellie and the girls turned to Jerry, who'd remained silent,
struggling to contain his emotions.

"Well, Dad. Aren't you going to say something?"

"Welcome home, Ellie."

ACKNOWLEDGMENTS

I am indebted to all the people who helped guide this novel to publication.

A huge thank you to those who read early drafts and gave feedback for improvement: Sally Levy, Golda Schoenbaum, Susan Anderson, Paul Moder, Shyra Khosla, and Prerana Sinha.

A special thank you to author Alli Sinclair for reviewing my manuscript and providing ongoing career advice. It has been invaluable in my development as a writer.

I was inspired to write the story of Ellie Bartlett's journey through South America because of the many incredible women I met on my own travels, including: Liesbeth Affourtit, Rieko Aiba, Alejandra Arango, Ana Aguirre, Diana Arcentales, Mia Azani, Christina Bassel, Quena Batres, Jess Bonner, Luana Botelho, Milena Borges, Ashley Cabrera, Giulietta Caruso, Francis Carvajal, Geraldine Cordova, Emma Croft, Lauren Croft, Kathryn Eastwood, Lisanne van den Engel, Mayra Enriquez, Hayley Follett, Selena Gillian-Mulder, Yariley Hernandez, Eva Hobin, Cathy Huiza, Fida Ib, Naomi Jallais, Ellie Johnston, Adhele Jimenez, Shyra Khosla, Nimarta Khuman, Nary Khun, Evelyne le Grelle, Ivette van der Lee, Lucila Longo, Pearl Loo, Brody Lys-Mathews, Bhavya Mandanna, Maria Muñiz, Glenda

Myles, Lotem Nesher, Hadas Nir, Angélica Otoni, Simas Phly, Elizabeth Pucius, Aviv Reichkind, Fiorella Ricciardi, Miranda Riou-Green, Jayde Roberts, Vanessa Romo, Dileswari Sahu, Heather Seltzer, Ana Sgarbi, Silvina Sgarbi, Lucia Souto, Nora Toumi, Tania Vasquez, Priya Verma, Jasmin Waida, and Irene Yugai. Their courage, passion, kindness and humor encouraged me to break out of my comfort zone and grow as a person.

I would also like to acknowledge my family and friends whose unwavering support made this novel possible, including: Madeleine Allnutt, Michael Allnutt, Michael Atkinson, Ashley Bear, Chris Bardsley, Barbara Brown, Ron Brown, Kirsty Campbell, Andrew Carr, Jason Chen, T.M. Clark, Kimberley Crowley, Lesley Cunningham, Gil Davidson, John De Carro, Natasha De Carro, Simon De Carro, Winsome De Carro, John Deane, Margaret Deane, Lucy Gregg, Nicole Grinberg, Denise Gurrieri, John Gurrieri, Lauren Gurrieri, Mike Gurrieri, Michael Hanrahan, David Henshall, Liza Henshall, Jenny Orford Hill, Nathan Hill, Sarah Hill, Yasmin Jarkan, Irene Krause, Sally Levy, Ruby Levy-Murray, Alison Lim, Jeremy Livingston, Naoko Sasaki Livingston, Paul Moder, Neil Morley, Jeremy Mulholland, Linda Mulholland, Peter Mulholland, Nerida Murray, Stephen Murray, Zac Murray, Raelene Park, Steven Phillips, Melinda Schambre, Golda Schoenbaum, Prerana Sinha, Heather Thake, Megan Worley Trantino, Vito Trantino, Candy Wilson, Marc Wilson, and Shannon Young.

Finally, I would like to express deep gratitude to my parents, Wayne Levy and Marilyn Levy, for instilling in me a love of travel, history and books. This novel wouldn't have happened if they didn't drag me to the far corners of our planet in search of adventure and knowledge.

Printed in Great Britain
by Amazon